Edited by Laura Jorstad and Rebecca Brewer

Cover Art & Design by Kate O'Hara
Interior Design by Kevin Miller
Published by Nikota Publishing House Incorporated
Distributed by Riyria Enterprises

ISBN: 978-1-966662-07-5

THE ETHER WITCH

VOLUME 2: CONFRONTING THE CRAFTY CONCUBINE

by

Delemhach

DEDICATION

To my siblings—including my siblings in-law. Thank you for getting excited for my work, and for supplying me with the family dynamics that offer me a reference for bringing these characters to life.

CHAPTER 1

FAMILIAR FEELINGS

"Tam, we need to leave. Now. Lord Kim's carriage is about half a day away on foot, but when these soldiers don't return to report to their superiors, we're in trouble." Eli rose and clasped her hands in front of her skirts.

The men she spoke of were littered around them on the forest floor. The imperial soldiers had been trying to apprehend Tam and his son, Luca, as they escaped the Zinferan city of Junya. This was because Tam had killed a number of Zinferan soldiers as well as a witch belonging to the Giong Coven when they were attacked by the docks more than a week ago. The confrontation and their desperate flight through the city gates had left Tam's magic spent. So when he and Luca were cornered by more soldiers, he had doubted he could fight them all.

Eli had come to their rescue. Not that Tam had known the giant black cat that had defeated the soldiers had been Eli. It hadn't been until she had shifted back into her human form that he'd realized it was her. His assistant, and the woman he was in love with. Tam had never seen anyone, witch or ancient beast, change their forms before. To make matters even stranger, the jolt of awareness and powerful knowing he'd gotten when he'd laid eyes on Eli's cat form had revealed to him that she was his familiar. The rush of shock continued to roar in Tam's ears. "Eli. Are you… Are you aware that you are my—"

Her eyes widened before she stalked toward Tam, then hurriedly stepped past him.

Tam almost bolted after her to continue his line of questioning, but first he turned to double-check that Luca was safe behind him.

"D-Dad, where did the big cat go?"

"I can't answer that right now." Tam gently cupped Luca's cheek and redirected his gaze to him when the seven-year-old's eyes started to wander over to the bodies littering the ground. "Don't look at them. Look at me. Come on, I'll give you a piggyback ride. Climb on." Crouching, Tam managed to angle his back away from the carnage, which offered a clear sight of the hilly terrain with its sparse vegetation, as well as Eli's retreating figure.

Once he felt Luca's slim arms wrap around his neck, Tam slipped his arms under his son's knees and stood, then darted after Eli, with the delightful result of Luca giving a surprised giggle.

Despite the alarming discovery he had just made, Tam spared a smile when he heard his son laugh—it meant he probably hadn't seen much during the attack. That or he was in shock.

Tam shoved that issue aside to be dealt with once they made it back to the carriage.

"Eli… What was that?" the future duke panted upon reaching his assistant's side.

Eli kept her eyes fixed ahead of herself, her arms barely swinging as she moved through the brush with an impressive amount of grace given that she was in a long gray maid's skirt. Her hair was also displaying its ability to flip up in places Tam knew Eli wasn't fond of. While her hair was still short, it had grown significantly since they'd come to Zinfera. She often tried to sweep what she could of her black locks behind her ear and out of her eyes, but was usually unsuccessful. She had been given an orange ribbon by Lord Kim, the Zinferan nobleman helping them flee Junya, but still the flyaways of her hair persisted.

"That was my magic. Did Luca see anything?" Eli replied shortly.

"A little… Dad told me to look away. So I just saw the big cat," Luca answered for himself while issuing a yawn.

Daylight had only just begun to lighten the world around them, which was helpful to Tam as he navigated over roots and rocks, but also created a new question. "Are you able to see in the dark?" he wondered aloud carefully. He was hoping that the less direct question would warrant a response from Eli.

"What went wrong with your magic?" she countered instead.

Tam slid a firm glance in her direction that was meant to communicate that sooner or later they *were* going to be having the discussion. Still, he didn't want to start a fight when they had to travel expediently with no privacy from Luca, so Tam conceded and left the matter alone for the time being.

Instead Tam said, "I need more time to rest and recover my magic thanks to the last few days. It takes time to train up magical endurance, and some witches need more time to get accustomed to their ability and learn it. How long were we in the void for?"

"Only the night. If you weren't back by mid-morning, Lord Kim would've continued without us, and I'd have waited until Jeong joined me."

Tam nodded to himself. "At least it wasn't longer."

Eli said nothing.

"Were there any other problems with you and Lord Kim leaving the city?"

"No. After the soldiers went through Lord Kim's things, they let us leave."

Tam eyed his assistant's profile. She wore a stony mask and held her back impeccably straight.

Knowing that there was nothing else to say until they had a chance for more privacy, Tam turned over the discovery that his ornery assistant also happened to be his familiar.

Had there been signs?

Had he simply been obtuse and missed all the hints that could've revealed this mind-blowing truth sooner?

He thought back to when they'd first met. He'd instantly felt as if he'd met her before. She had felt so familiar to him. However when she had revealed that she was the niece of Lord Oscar Harris, a close family friend of his parents, he had assumed it was because of that relation.

Then, there had been all the times she had been remarkably light on her feet. She moved so nimbly that Tam struggled to hear her approaching. Even their rapport had been completely comfortable almost instantly. Tam had noticed how she was more open with him than anyone else, and she had even said herself how much better she felt at his side.

Uneasiness brewed in Tam's gut as he started to suspect what Eli might be thinking in that moment. Had she begun to like Tam in a more romantic nature of her own volition? Or was it because she was his familiar?

He swallowed with difficulty. How in the world was it possible?

Technically, if she was a witch, wouldn't she be able to have an animal familiar of her own? Or maybe she wasn't a witch at all. Was she technically a new kind of familiar or beast? What if she was a variant of an ancient beast?

Tam drowned in such thoughts as they made their way through the brush the rest of the morning. The heat of the day rose rapidly in the maturing summer, making the shade of the trees a lovely reprieve from the sun, until at last Eli turned and started moving toward the road.

While Eli's sense of direction amazed Tam, he also couldn't help but wonder how she knew exactly where to go. Was it an animalistic instinct?

"Do you have a cat's sense of smell?" he blurted before he could help himself.

Eli's head snapped around, her eyes wide and her mouth pursing as though she were angry with him.

Luckily, Tam was spared from whatever reaction was on its way out of her when a familiar voice called out.

"Ah! Lord Tam! Thank you kindly for joining us again!" Lord Kim stood beside his carriage which was pulled off to the side of the road. Beside the vehicle, the lone footman he had brought with him for his journey was boiling a pot of water over a small flame he had built.

Tam bowed his head in acknowledgment and lowered himself to let Luca off his back. The boy's movements were clumsy and heavy, and Tam could see the exhaustion in his face.

"Luca, I'll get you set up to sleep in the carriage. I'll wake you up when we have lunch ready," he informed his son gently yet firmly.

Luca couldn't object as his mouth stretched into another big yawn while he rubbed his eyes. His father's hand pressed gently into his shoulder and redirected him to the carriage.

Eli wordlessly turned to the vehicle, opened the door, and climbed in to set down a pillow. She then pulled out Luca's coat, which had been stuffed between the bench and the cushion. Once Luca lay down, his eyes already fluttering, Eli tucked his coat over his small body.

Tam watched from the door of the carriage that could comfortably sit six adults on its two benches, his right arm braced against the frame, his left resting on the open windowsill of the door, while Eli gently brushed back a lock of Luca's hair. When she eventually risked a look back at him, it was only a momentary one before she glanced away and exited the other side of the carriage.

Frowning, Tam closed the door quietly then rounded the back of the vehicle. Eli stood beside Lord Kim and kept her attention fixed on the pot of boiling water.

"Eli, a word?"

Lord Kim, who was standing to Tam's left and Eli's right, regarded first the future duke, then Eli. "Everything alright?"

"I think so, but I'd like to speak to my assistant privately."

Lord Kim raised a curious eyebrow, then nodded toward the trees away from the dirt road. "Do so over there just in case you need to get out of sight or we need to move."

Tam nodded his approval, and when he looked at Eli he saw her hands fidgeting with her skirts.

Despite obviously not wanting to have a private conversation, she still made her way over to Tam, and they ventured into the woods until they were out of earshot.

Eli still refused to meet Tam's eyes, and her expression remained blank.

"What's wrong?" Tam asked softly. "Are you alright?"

The gentleness of his tone succeeded in making Eli's eyes snap up to him. At first it looked like she was about to start shouting at him, but after a moment of battling against whatever her instinctive reaction might be, she allowed her shoulders to relax.

"I don't like it," she began awkwardly.

"Being my familiar?"

"Yes. It now feels like I'm enslaved to you."

Tam recoiled. "Gods no. You most definitely are not."

"I have to come whenever you call, and I will forever be connected to you," Eli argued, her throat audibly thickening as she once again moved her eyes from him.

Tam saw the fear and pain that shook her, and his gut dropped. "Ignore me then. You think Kraken does everything my dad wants him to?"

Eli swallowed and didn't respond, but he could sense that she wasn't in any way convinced.

"Did you know before today?" Tam asked quietly.

Eli shook her head. "When we met, I thought you felt safe. And I found it easy to be around you. Like I'd known you for years already. But… I had no idea."

"Is it only the panther you can transform into, or is it other animals? What did the Giong Coven think of your abilities?"

At first, Eli recoiled from the inquiries, but Tam could see her mind starting to sink a little more easily into the logical questions as opposed to the emotional ones.

"I have never tried to transform into anything else. Though I did wonder why I was experiencing a growth spurt shortly after we met. I had assumed I was fully grown, but I'm now twice the size I used to be when I transform. As for the coven, they simply dubbed me a mutated witch and said it was straightforward. I could turn into an animal."

"Are you able to talk to other animals?" Tam wondered next.

"I haven't really tried before, but I don't believe so."

Tam pondered this in silence for a minute before adding, "When my father and his familiar first bonded, they couldn't communicate—not until their relationship deepened. Given that you are a witch—human—maybe that is something that happens as you and I become closer."

"Possibly." Eli gave a slight shrug.

"What would you like to do about this?" Slipping his hands into his pockets, Tam dipped his knees, bringing his face closer to Eli's level, prompting her to once again look at him. He made sure that she could see the sincerity and concern in his expression. He truly did need her to communicate with him. Otherwise his worries for her would consume him.

"I don't know!" Eli burst out in frustration. "What if I don't want it to change anything—can we do that? Can I just not be your familiar?"

Tam nodded instantly. "Okay."

Eli balked, then continued. "What if I don't ever want to use my magic again?"

"Do you really think that *I*, of *all* people, am going to argue with you on that point?" Tam asked wryly.

For a moment, it looked like Eli was fighting off a smile. "I don't want you to tell anyone about my magic, or that I… I could *possibly* be your familiar."

"You were my familiar," Tam corrected. "But you quit. Which is fine. Having you as my assistant and significant other sounds like more than enough. And I don't think other people need to know about your abilities, either."

Tam watched Eli's posture relax, even if there was still a wary air about her.

"What if I want to stop being anything to you—assistant or… or someone you're in a relationship with—and I want to instead go off on my own?"

This question made Tam hesitate. Fear and sadness started to dig through his chest. "What right would I have to stop you if that is what you really wanted?"

A shuddering breath of relief left Eli's body.

As much as Tam hoped this wasn't what she wanted to do, he held himself back. He knew exercising her freedom and choice over her life was of the utmost importance to Eli—even if it was physically painful for him in the present.

"I'm still angry you went to meet with my brother without telling me," Eli blurted suddenly.

Tam stood straight once more, making Eli tilt her chin up to stare at him more directly. "It was from one noble to another. I had no intention of meddling in your business; I just thought he should know about his assistant undermining him."

Eli reached up and touched her forehead wearily. "Just promise me you won't do something like that again without telling me?"

"Are you asking me as my assistant or my romantic partner?"

Pink flushed into Eli's cheeks, and she barely resisted fidgeting. "The latter."

"The latter? Which was the latter?" Tam wondered teasingly, his eyes rolling to the sky as he secretly relished the fact that Eli didn't seem to be ending their relationship.

She scowled up at him. "You know what I mean."

"I'm afraid I haven't a clue. I think I need you to put it simply for me." Tam grinned mischievously and leaned closer.

Eli continued to glare until she shocked Tam by lifting herself up on her toes to press a quick kiss on his mouth.

The rush of tingling and the wonderful warmth that spread through Tam turned him into a dazed fool.

Eli turned with a bashful smile and scurried back toward the carriage, leaving him behind to gather his wits.

Eventually, Tam's mind whirred back to life. It had been the first time that Eli had initiated something more physical with him, and potent happiness filled him as he turned and made his way back to the camp, a little swagger in his step.

So what if she didn't want to be his familiar?

He already had everything he needed anyway.

CHAPTER 2
QUICK-FIRE QUESTIONING

"But why?"

"Because we have to figure out a way to get home safely to Daxaria."

"But why?"

"Because we keep getting attacked."

"Why do we keep getting attacked?"

"It's complicated."

"Why is it—"

"Luca." Lord Kim interrupted the back-and-forth between father and son, his right fingertips pressing into his temple. "Perhaps you should try to get a bit more sleep, hm? Soon you will have to leave the carriage with your father and Her Highness, and it will be some time before you are able to sleep comfortably again."

"I'm not tired," Luca returned stiffly, then looked back at Tam who was stifling a yawn of his own.

Eli reached over and gently tidied an errant lock of hair behind Luca's ear.

The move drew a sharp look from Lord Kim, but he didn't comment on it. Tam gave Eli an appreciative smile then settled back into the carriage, arms folded.

"Again, thank you, Lord Kim. I know you said that you and Eli have a deal already worked out in exchange for your help, but if there is anything I can do, I'm more than happy to."

Lord Kim raised an eyebrow, his attention sliding to Eli. She stared back coolly but said nothing.

"What Her Highness has promised in return is more than enough. Will you gather any more evidence of the palace trying to control the rumors about the dragon?"

"If we can, but surviving and not being discovered takes priority," Tam responded wearily. He didn't like that Eli had promised Lord Kim something in exchange for his help without his knowledge, but there was no point in arguing about it now.

Lord Kim leaned forward. "I must confess, I did not expect you to travel so close to Zinfera's capital city, Gondol, Your Highness."

"Concubine Soo Hebin won't expect me to take a route that wastes so much time."

"Soo Hebin is a bad person, right?" Luca interjected.

"Yes, she is," Lord Kim confirmed hastily. "Though she is also powerful and frightening, and she dislikes Her Highness Elisara here very much."

Luca turned to Eli with a frown. "Why doesn't she like you?"

"She's worried I will take away the power she has," Eli replied calmly.

"Do you want to take away her power?" the child asked.

"No, I do not."

"Then why does she still not like you?" Luca looked around at everyone in the carriage, openly wondering if they were as befuddled as he was.

"Because she doesn't think I'm telling the truth that I don't want her power."

Once he'd considered this answer for a while, Luca's mouth twisted and he slowly nodded. "That's annoying."

Surprised at the response, Eli cracked a smile. "Very much so."

"Why doesn't she believe you?" Luca plundered on.

Lord Kim was starting to get a glazed look in his eyes, and Tam forced back a grin. He was willing to bet that the elder Zinferan noble had forgotten the way children could be, what with his own daughters fully grown and married off.

"She doesn't believe me because a lot of people *do* lie. Especially when they want something."

"Why would they lie about what they want? Isn't it easiest to tell people what you want?"

"It is, but there are all kinds of reasons not to tell someone what you want. For instance, you might want something you know a person is not going to give you. Or you might worry that if you point out what you want, other people will want it as well, which means more competition."

"I must say, it is both refreshing and concerning that a child of his age has no duplicity in him," Lord Kim chuckled to himself.

"What does duplicity mean?" Luca adjusted his attention to Lord Kim, who looked at Tam with a silent plea screaming from his eyes.

Tam was already turning toward his son. "Duplicity means to hide something. To be sneaky and clever about it."

"People said I was sneaky all the time when I lived with my mother…" Luca trailed off, his chin lowering as though shameful memories were replaying in his mind.

"Why did they say that?" Eli pressed gently.

"I don't know. I never did anything or said anything bad, they just said I was creepy."

Tam noted the way Luca was starting to fidget, and the way he visibly struggled to swallow.

Resting his hand atop his son's head, he ruffled the black hair that was like his own and said, "People said that about me all the time. Don't worry. You aren't creepy, Luca. You're just like me."

Luca turned and stared up at his father, appreciation and happiness brightening his face.

With the promise of peace being restored to the carriage, Lord Kim settled back, his eyes starting to close.

"Dad, are you going to have another baby?"

Lord Kim's eyes flew open, and he looked at Eli in frantic alarm.

"Erm. I don't… know?" Tam looked at Eli with a wince, but she gave him a wide-eyed glance then hastily darted her eyes in Lord Kim's general direction. "I haven't really thought about it," Tam concluded while clearing his throat uncomfortably.

"Oh. Well… I think it's okay if you do. Because then I'd have a brother or sister that looks like me, and then maybe more people won't think I'm creepy."

Tam smiled at his son while giving a nervous laugh. "That is… I don't… Oh look, *trees!*" He gestured out the window desperately.

Sadly, Luca was already latched onto this idea and so he stared at the carriage roof quite seriously while turning over the possibility of a new family member. "I heard some kids don't like their siblings, but I think it'd be fun as long as they're nice. I think girls might be nicer, so a sister could be good. Dad, do you have a sister?"

Lord Kim looked questioningly at Tam, and the future duke could tell it was because he wondered how Luca couldn't know that Tam's twin sister just happened to be the queen of Daxaria.

In a way, this change of topic was good. It helped distract Tam from the uncomfortable nature of the original conversation. "I do, yes."

"Do you like having a sister?"

"Most of the time."

"Is she nice?"

"Sometimes."

"Did you play together growing up?"

"All the time."

"Hm." Luca paused his rapid-fire questioning as he processed this information. "Does she look like you?"

Tam chuckled. "Not really. We're both tall, and she has slanted eyes like I do, but she has red hair and golden eyes."

"*Golden eyes?*" Luca perked up. "Like they say the queen does?"

Tam opened his mouth, then closed it again. He guessed Rosaline Evans, Luca's biological mother, hadn't explained much about him and his family. What did a seven-year-old who lived in a tavern care about the monarchy?

"Luca… my sister *is* the queen."

Luca's eyebrows shot upward—making him look incredibly like his father—then they crashed straight into a frown. "You're teasing me, aren't you?"

"Not at all. Katarina's last name, before she married His Majesty Eric Reyes, was Ashowan," Tam assured.

Luca looked at Lord Kim, who nodded in confirmation.

Then Luca turned to Eli, who did the same, though everyone was smiling at the hilarity of the situation.

After investigating whether the adults in the carriage were having a bit of fun at his expense, Luca turned with yet another question for Tam. "Do I have to call her Aunt Queen?"

Tam snorted, and then succumbed to complete hysterics, followed shortly by Eli. Eventually even Lord Kim was chuckling along.

"You made it up, didn't you!" Luca accused. Unfortunately for him, no one could placate him. They just continued to laugh at the image of Tam's illegitimate son strolling up to the Daxarian queen—who was known for being outrageous and blunt—and calling her Aunt Queen.

Three days following their escape from Junya, it was time to say farewell to the prudish Lord Kim. The nobleman would continue on the main road toward Gondol, while they would be forced to travel off the roads to avoid the imperial soldiers looking for Eli and Tam.

At present, the largest threat was the royal concubine who wished her son to be the next emperor. However, there also happened to be an assistant working for Eli's birth family in Zinfera who was after her, because her brother wished to pass the title and wealth of her family to whatever son she bore.

They stopped at an inn far enough away from Junya that no one would be on the lookout for them. Of course, Luca's presence helped, too, as it wasn't well known that they were traveling as a family yet. At least they hoped it wasn't…

Oh, and the daughter of the Gods, the first witch, Aradia, was interested in them because of the rumors that her brother, the devil, was alive and prowling through Zinfera.

The cause of those rumors was Tam himself. Not only did he supposedly bear an uncanny resemblance to the devil, but his magic emitted wisps of black and silver. And it just so happened that the devil was known to wield a fearful darkness that filled everyone around him with terror unlike anything they'd ever felt before.

The devil was known to reincarnate as a newborn babe from piles of ashes upon his death—ash piles that were the remains of his previous self. In his past lives, however, the devil had arranged it so that the ancient beasts that served him would save some of the ash piles and move parts various parts of it to safe locations. Then when their master died, he could be reborn in *any* of the places the ash remains were, making the devil hard to track.

And because the devil had last been slain by the Troivackian queen seven years ago, Tam *also* worried that his surprise illegitimate son could be the devil—the same devil who would've reincarnated from an ash pile as a newborn.

But Luca had always felt like exactly what he was.

A child.

Innocent, without any guile. Furthermore, a letter from Tam's former paramour confirming he was Luca's father also made it difficult to think that he could be the devil.

All of this meant…

Ever since Tam had left Daxaria, he had found himself lying awake at night for more than one reason.

That didn't even include the problem that Eli was technically a high-ranking member of the royal family, and he had fallen in love with her while she worked as his assistant—and surprisingly, she seemed to like him well enough that they had begun some sort of relationship.

Only *now* everything had an extra layer of complication, as it turned out her own magical power allowed her to turn into a large cat.

A cat that wound up being Tam's very own familiar.

"What are you thinking about?" Eli's voice interrupted Tam's thoughts.

"I'm thinking I should start drinking more seriously."

His assistant frowned in concern as the footman handed Tam a large gray sack loaded with supplies.

"Developing a drinking habit now of all times?" Eli asked quite seriously.

"It sounds like a lovely alternative to having a breakdown."

"Developing a bad drinking habit *is* a breakdown."

“Mm,” Tam murmured thoughtfully while gently ushering Luca toward the inn. He gave a final farewell wave to Lord Kim as the carriage had finished changing over its horses and was set to resume traveling.

“There is such a thing as a high-functioning alcoholic, you know,” Tam pointed out helpfully.

Eli stared up at him flatly.

Luca interrupted while tilting his head back to stare at his father in the dim light, “Back in Daxaria, Mum used to say alcoholics with jobs were good for business and bad for lovers.”

“There is some wisdom to that,” Tam agreed.

“I don’t think we should continue educating Luca on the pros and cons of alcoholism,” Eli interjected sharply.

Tam grinned at her. “Alright, alright. I’ll stop. Luca, never become an alcoholic, okay?”

Rolling her eyes, Eli reached for the door handle of the inn. The building was a perfect square that sat between a road that went straight, and one that branched off to the right. There was even a third option that veered left.

When Tam opened the door to the inn, the mouthwatering aroma of sizzling marinated beef wafted out. Well aware that they wouldn’t be eating anything so tasty for a long while after that night, Eli, Tam, and Luca exchanged excited looks. They were going to stuff themselves silly and have absolutely no regrets.

CHAPTER 3

A TURBULENT TRANSFORMATION

Stretching in a most luxurious fashion, and groaning with the pleasure of the movement, Eli smiled as she allowed her body to become limp against the starched sheets.

Tam was beside her, and as a result, she had once again experienced a good night's rest after their forced separation while hiding in Lord Kim's keep back in the city of Junya.

A quiet grumble on the other side of the room broadened the smile on Eli's face as she heard Luca struggle to wake up.

Somehow, being on the run from the royal concubine, the coven, and even the daughter of the Gods had failed to dampen Eli's mood.

Why was this?

Her eyes cracked open against the pale light of the day. It was a muted light, which meant there was a chance that rain was on its way. Staring out the window, Eli listened to the leaves rustling in the wind and pondered the shift from her usual tense mood.

The truth was that with her magic revealed, and their successful escape from Junya, Eli felt… free.

At last, completely and truly free.

Tam had seen her in her magical form and given her the choice to make her own life, even when it would have been easy for him to force her into servitude.

As much as she logically knew it was not in Tamlin Ashowan's nature to take advantage of another person, particularly one close to him, Eli's past wounds pertaining to betrayal ran deep. But as was his way, Tam had responded perfectly.

Besides, wasn't being a familiar to a witch a two-way relationship? She would have an intimate knowledge of Tam's true nature. That explained how she had instantly felt like she'd understood him when they'd first met, and how easily she could focus on him and his life. How when he had used his magic to defeat their assailants the night at the dock, she had felt more alive—excited, even. At the time, Jeong had reasoned that it was because they were starting to feel hopeful that the legendary power of the Ashowan family was coming through, but Eli had a deeper sense that this was only the beginning of Tam's power growth, and she was looking forward to seeing what he could do.

Maybe this was why for the first time in Eli's life, despite being hunted by every powerful sort imaginable, she felt safe. At last, she had someone behind her who let her make her own choices.

And she chose to be with Tam.

Trying out a relationship with him, and having more power over her own self and life than she'd ever had before…

It was addictive.

Sitting up, Eli found her reflection smiling back at herself thanks to the floor-length mirror a few feet from the foot of the bed she and Tam slept in.

Her smile disappeared when she saw the state of her hair. "Godsdamnit." With its increasing length, her hair was prone to sticking stubbornly upward and sideways from her scalp in the mornings.

"If I weren't trying to make it obvious that I'm a woman, I'd just cut these ruddy hair bits off," Eli grumbled to herself. She slipped out of bed and over to the washbasin to give her face a good scrubbing.

Today they'd start on the walking portion of their journey, making their way toward Gondol.

Dread simmered in her belly, but Eli pushed it aside the best she could. She wanted her good mood to last as long as possible.

After dabbing her face dry and making a couple of halfhearted attempts to wet down the hairs that were devoid of gravity, Eli stared at her reflection in the mirror. She had never given much thought to whether or not she was pretty. She had always assumed she wasn't, given that everyone had been convinced for years that she was a man.

And yet Tam had said she was pretty and identified her as a woman instantly.

She tilted her head.

Her jaw was narrow and her cheekbones were high, giving her a proud look. Her eyes were dark and her skin pale thanks to her Daxarian mother.

"I guess I'm not atrocious to look at," she muttered to herself. She stepped back to stare at her body.

"Average." She shrugged while pretending not to feel uncomfortable. She still wasn't used to no longer binding her breasts, and what with no longer trying to avoid putting on weight, well… the results spoke for themselves. Her hips were wider, and she had finally taken on a distinctly female shape.

She wasn't any raving beauty, but she was passable.

Then a new curiosity crept up.

Glancing at Luca's sleeping form, and then over her shoulder toward Tam, she turned to grab a folding screen that rested against the wall. They had used it the previous night while they all took baths.

Setting it back a safe distance, Eli shook out her arms, cracked her neck, and allowed her power to flow.

It was a strange feeling. Kind of like being turned inside out without any pain. She also found it a bit off-putting once complete as she was significantly fuzzier and acquired more muscle.

Opening her eyes, Eli peered up to see her new reflection. She had to admit, she was a majestic yet menacing-looking beast. Her fangs were long and sharp, her paws massive. A long ropy tail swished gracefully through the air.

In this form, all her senses were heightened, and she felt powerful; like she could defeat anyone or anything. Though that hubris had been proven wrong before. Despite having learned this hard lesson in the past, with her sudden growth spurt, Eli was feeling her old sense of indomitability start to return.

Then something else caught her attention. Squinting her golden eyes, Eli noticed that two nubs had appeared on her back. They looked black and fleshy…

What in the world are those? Tumors?

Eli wiggled her shoulders a little to see them in a better light.

And one… unfurled.

A limp, fleshy little bit of skin waved about in the air and it almost looked like—

IS THAT A WING?

She leapt back in shock, only, she was a lot bigger than usual and as a result crashed into the screen, knocking it over, which only made her flail about in a panic.

She looked round and saw Tam sitting up in bed, staring at her wide-eyed.

She froze.

Until a shrill shriek from beside her snapped her head around to view Luca scrambling back against the wall in terror.

Eli immediately shifted back to her human form, thinking this might calm him down.

It. Did. Not.

"IT'S INSIDE ELI!" The cry rang throughout the inn, and so their inconspicuous presence became, well, conspicuous.

"Everything is alright. You know how children are," Tam explained after his initial exuberant apology to the innkeeper—an older man who had been polite the day before, but who presently revealed that he was *not* a morning person. "My son just had a nightmare."

Tam smiled awkwardly, while behind him Eli patted Luca's head and murmured soothing words.

The innkeeper only grunted about keeping quiet until a reasonable hour. He turned with his lantern in hand to amble back down the hallway toward the stairs.

One or two other guests had poked their heads outside to see what the commotion was about, but Tam made sure he was still standing farther back in the room during the exchange and was quick about closing the door once the innkeeper left.

Turning to Eli and his son with his hands finding his hips, Tam sighed. "Luca, are you all right?"

"I-It's such a *big* cat. Eli, you're not big! H-How can you be so huge?" Luca mumbled.

Eli handed him a handkerchief to blow his nose. "I don't know," she admitted weakly, shooting Tam a quick look of guilt.

He gave her a shrug as if to say, *It's fine; it is what it is.*

"Come on, you two, we need to get ready to leave. Jeong will be with us soon!" Tam tried to say brightly, hoping to improve his son's shaky mood.

"W-Why can't Bong come with us, too?" Luca wondered before noisily blowing his nose.

"He has to go give an incredibly important message to his family, but we'll see him again one day." Tam tugged off his sleep shirt and moved over to the sack filled with their things to pull out a fresh tunic. But he stopped moving as he realized both Eli and Luca had gone very still. "What?"

Eli blushed, cleared her throat, and averted her eyes, while Luca continued staring with keen interest.

"Dad, will I get muscles one day?"

Tam snorted awkwardly. "Um… maybe? If you train?"

"I wanna train."

Tam coughed. "Er. Sure. We can… we can definitely look into that once we are back in Daxaria."

"Where did you get the scar on your belly?" the boy asked next.

Tam glanced down. He had forgotten about the pirate wound that was still bright pink as it continued to heal. "I, uh, slipped."

"Daaad?"

"Yes?"

"That looks like it hurt."

"It did. Yes." Glancing at Eli, Tam felt his eyebrows rise at the scarlet hue on her face. Her eyes were most definitely not staring at his. "Anything *you'd* like to comment on?"

Eli shook her head, the color in her face deepening to a near purple. As flattered as Tam knew he should be from getting such a reaction from his usually composed assistant and romantic partner, he had to silently confess he was feeling a bit self conscious.

"Right," Tam said. "I think I'll just pop behind this screen to finish getting dressed."

"Eli?" Tam heard his son address his assistant as he busied himself getting changed as quickly as possible behind the screen, hoping he would feel significantly less embarrassed.

"Hm?"

"Do all men have hair on their chests?"

"Yes. Unless they shave or wax it."

"Oh. Do they have to brush it?"

Tam heard a garbled noise that was most definitely Eli struggling not to laugh. "No. No, they don't have to brush it."

"That's good. I hate having to brush just the hair on my head."

"Mm."

Tam stepped out from behind the screen wearing his usual outfit of a white tunic, a black Zinferan-style vest that buttoned on the diagonal, and black pants. It was strange wearing clothes that actually fit him correctly. Eli had seen to updating his wardrobe in Zinfera, and she had had the clothes tailored exactly. It was not the way Tam had dressed in Daxaria.

"Luca?" Tam asked while rolling up his sleeves. "What do you think about me growing a beard?"

The boy smiled while Eli leaned back, looking dubious.

"That'd be great!" Luca cheered excitedly.

"Men and facial hair," Eli said with a sigh.

Tam grinned at her.

"Eli?" Luca turned to the princess suddenly.

"Yes?"

"Why were you jumping around when you were the big cat? Did something scare you?"

The sudden shift in discussion visibly caught Eli off guard, and it took a breath of time for her to answer. "Oh, I… In that form, I'm still growing I guess, and I was… startled."

Tam's head tilted. She had mentioned that she seemed to be growing ever since they had met, which made sense—a familiar's potential increased once they found their witch. Still, there was a shiftiness in Eli that told Tam there was another reason she had woken them all so abruptly that morning.

"Was everything alright?" Tam watched Eli carefully.

Her ability to transform into a large cat was still a fresh topic. He was already surprised that she had transformed at all that morning, and that she seemed fine with Luca asking her about it. Overall, she seemed a lot more relaxed, which was nice, but still felt odd for Eli.

"Well, I think…" Eli trailed off; she was visibly struggling to find the words.

She was spared from answering by a knock on the door. "Joe! It's Jeong!" The familiar voice of Jeong Ryu called out Tam's alias.

Tam opened the door to reveal the beaming Zinferan. He wore a plain peasant shirt and brown pants—a sharp contrast with his normally very colorful attire. However, the expression on his round face was entirely typical: unbridled happiness and friendliness

"Good morning! Are we ready to head out?"

Tam nodded and moved back so that Jeong could enter, then closed the door behind him. Luca launched himself off the bed and threw his arms around Jeong excitedly.

Jeong chortled and lowered his sack to the ground. "What a fantastic way to start my morning!"

Tam smiled back at his son's exuberant greeting.

"I'll finish getting dressed myself and then we'll be ready to go," Eli announced while pushing herself off the bed.

Tam nodded and gestured politely toward the screen.

"Eli?"

Everyone looked down at Luca.

"When you're a cat, do you think I could… I could try riding on your back?"

Startled, Jeong looked up at Eli—unaware of what the child was talking about—while she became flustered all over again.

Tam rubbed the back of his neck and casually moved over to tap his son's shoulder. "Right. So there's a very important thing I forgot to tell you earlier, Luca. That's my fault. The fact that Eli can turn into a giant cat? That's a secret."

Luca blinked up at his father.

Jeong's jaw dropped.

After several moments of silence passed, Luca leaned around his father to stare at Eli while slowly shaking his head. "Eli? I think our family has too many secrets."

Tam snorted before he could stop himself. Even Eli couldn't help but give a weak smile at the sweet mention that he considered her family.

"I know."

"Do you have any other secrets?" Luca asked, sounding hilariously exasperated.

"Yes."

Luca sighed, sounding far too much like an adult at that moment. "I still like you, but you're really confusing. Dad, even you have too many. It's getting ridiculous."

Eli bobbed her head in acknowledgment of Luca's opinion before ducking behind the screen.

Tam looked at Jeong, who met his eyes and in a low voice whispered, "I have to admit, I agree with Luca on this matter."

Tam clapped a hand on the man's shoulder, at a loss as to how to defend himself and Eli. Instead he said, "How about we go see about finding some coffee?"

And so the two men and Luca left the room, focusing intently on how this was most likely their last chance to get a decent cup of coffee for a very long, long time.

CHAPTER 4

ENCROACHING ELEMENTS

The door slammed open.

A golden aura sparkling with red flooded into the room, its source stalking furiously toward the long table of the castle council room, where seven people sat waiting.

"What in the absolute *hell* is happening in Zinfera?" Katarina Reyes shouted, her eyes glinting as she stared at each waiting face.

There was her husband, Eric Reyes; his assistant, Morgan Linsey; her parents, Fin and Annika Ashowan; the former king, Norman Reyes; the former king's assistant, Mr. Howard; and the Coven of Wittica leader, Louise Riddel.

"We're trying to figure that out," Eric informed his wife grimly. "How's Antony?"

At the mention of their eldest son, the Daxarian queen's mood did not improve. "He's still struggling to control his magic—he almost roasted his teacher this morning."

Louise Riddel leaned forward. "It is confirmed, then? His Highness is a mutated witch?"

Kat's eyes narrowed on the coven leader. The two were barely on cordial terms on a good day. "Yes. He's a weather witch according to his teacher. Can call a bloody storm or clear the skies. He's going to be wildly popular with the farmers, that's for damn sure."

The queen plunked herself down gracelessly in the seat on the right side of her husband, her hand casually resting on her sword hilt. "Now, what is happening with Tam? Captain Taylor said it had something to do with imperial soldiers getting mobilized?"

Eric's eyes briefly darted to Fin before he responded. "Kat, do you remember when Tam said he would send his first letter?"

The queen paused as she cast her memory back; her aura started to dwindle. "It should've been a fortnight ago."

"No. Longer. A month," Fin interjected somberly.

"And the sailors tasked with delivering Lord Tam had… alarming things to report," Annika added. "They came back terrified of him and kept saying he was the devil. Apparently they were besieged by pirates at one point on their journey. During the confrontation, they said his eyes filled with blackness, and he had shadows all around him."

Kat's eyes rounded in alarm. "What?"

"What is even more concerning, is that they said there is a boy with him. A young boy, around the age of seven, whom he insisted stay by his side and who looks remarkably like him."

"Holy shit." Kat looked at Eric, who nodded. "It sounds like the devil found Tam and is taking over his mind. Is that even possible?"

"You and His Majesty have the most experience with the son of the Gods," Louise Riddel interrupted. "You tell us."

Kat leaned back in her seat, once again falling into pensive quiet.

Eric responded for the both of them. "I don't think it is possible. During our encounters with the devil, he simply made us all terrified beyond reason. Maybe he's making people frightened of Tam and forcing Tam to do as he says."

Kat tilted her head back and forth. "That sounds close to what I thought."

"There's more," Louise Riddel pressed sternly. "The Coven of Giong has reported the death of one of their witches, along with a number of Concubine Soo Hebin's men-at-arms, when they went to investigate a group of people attempting to leave Zinfera by the cover of night."

The room fell into a deathly quiet.

"Whoever committed these murders escaped, and Her Highness, Soo Hebin, has men scouring Junya trying to find them."

"I don't like this," Eric said slowly. "We still don't know where the first witch is, the devil is allegedly with Tam, and I don't trust Concubine Soo Hebin at all. Something is very, *very* wrong."

"Da, what about the guides that were supposed to be with Tam? They should have reported to Lord Ryu, too. Has there been any word?" Kat questioned, her anxiety rising.

Fin hesitated, then said, "Nothing yet."

Kat's eyebrows twitched. That was a lie. Why had her father just lied?

"What do we do now?" the former king of Daxaria, Norman Reyes, asked calmly.

"Someone needs to go over there and find Tam and figure this out, and it has to be someone with power. So I'll go," Kat announced firmly.

"Kat," Eric started, already wincing at the expected reaction.

"Your identity will be too obvious," Annika informed her daughter softly. "And it will be the same with your father. Red hair in Zinfera? The second you stepped off a ship, every eye would be on you."

"So I shave my head! I've always wanted to try it!" Kat announced flippantly with a mischievous glint in her eyes.

"Please no," Eric sounded on the verge of begging.

"Oh, now we get final say on each other's chosen hair length? Why the bloody hell do you have long hair again? And trim your beard!" Kat snapped before looking to her mother. "Who the hell else can we trust to go?"

"Your Majesty, the coven is able to send assistance to Lord Tamlin," Louise Riddel suggested.

Kat's eye twitched again, and Eric gingerly reached over to brush her hand as a gentle reminder to not curse at the woman *too* much.

"Oh? You're absolutely confident the coven can handle the devil? Who are you thinking of sending?" The acid in Kat's words made the coven leader's lips purse.

"It would of course need to be discussed among the other coven elders to discern—"

"And how long would that take?" Kat interrupted sharply. "The way I hear it, people are dying, my brother is missing, and the children of the Gods are on the loose. How long do you think it'll be until the first witch hears about the devil being spotted? We don't have an abundance of time."

"But we can't charge in recklessly, either." Annika Ashowan's eyes rested heavily on her daughter until the queen looked back at her.

Kat straightened and let out a very loud breath through her nose.

Mr. Howard leaned forward to speak. "Your Majesty, we did just receive word this morning that Leader Gregory Faucher has sent Sir Hugo Cas and Mr. Kraft to investigate the state of the Zinferan court and the Coven of Giong."

"Sir Cas has blond hair and he gets to go—wait. Why can't I just go and not worry about who the hell recognizes me? I'm going because concerning things are happening with the coven!" Kat perked up.

"Sir Hugo Cas is going as an escort to Mr. Kraft, a member of the Coven of Aguas from Troivack. Given that you are no longer technically a member of the Coven of Wittica since you took the Daxarian crown, Your Majesty, that cannot be the reason for your visit."

"Rumors of the devil damn well could be, though," Kat growled in warning at the coven leader.

"I agree with Kat."

Every head snapped over to look at the house witch, Finlay Ashowan. "As much as I want to go and find my son, I think leaving Daxaria unguarded right now when we have no idea where the first witch is would be foolish. My apologies, coven leader, I know this falls under my duties as the diplomat for the coven, and given that this is my son involved in the matter it would be ideal if I were the one going to Zinfera. However, if I need any kind of power to help him, that might lead to more tensions and issues with Zinfera—I would have to declare Zinfera part of the home in some manner. I think Kat accompanying whoever the Coven of Wittica selects as their representative is the best way of figuring out what is happening, and Kat knows what to expect when it comes to facing the children of the Gods."

Louise Riddel did not look at all pleased by this suggestion, but the fact that she was unable to find a good reason to refute it made Kat's lips start to quirk upward.

"Who else should go with Her Majesty?" Morgan, the king's assistant, interrupted in a business-like tone.

"I'll go with Kat and make sure she doesn't accidentally start a war," Eric declared with a sigh.

"Eric—"

"Your Majesty—"

Both the former king and the coven leader spoke at the same time, though after a brief bow to Norman from the coven leader, he continued.

"Eric, you two were just recently crowned. It is a bad idea for *both* of you to leave the kingdom at a time like this. Not to mention, as wonderful as their grandparents are—myself included, of course—I do worry about your sons being left alone. Particularly now during a dangerous time," Norman cautioned.

"I don't—"

"I'll go," Annika volunteered, cutting off the king.

Eric cast her a firm glance.

"I think that would make the most sense. Your grace has a marvelous sense of tact and…" Louise Riddel trailed off when Kat's glittering stare turned to her. "Her Grace also knows Lord Tamlin well, and has always contributed a very calming presence whenever she has been included in our meetings," the coven leader finished stiffly.

"I want someone else as well. Someone else we can trust to go with them," Eric insisted. Everyone could see the king's mood had blackened when he was prevented from joining his wife.

"I have an idea," Norman started carefully. "But I will leave it for everyone here to discuss."

The group waited to hear who he had in mind, though—judging from his hesitancy—no one was sure if it would be a good idea or not.

"Here."

Tam drank from the cup, then shot his assistant a narrow-eyed look.

Eli turned her attention back to innocently drying off the breakfast dishes.

Swallowing the contents of his cup, Tam set it down on the table and folded his arms. "You aren't going to win the argument this way."

"We have to ration what we have left of supplies, and your lordship has a high standard. We have to make adjustments."

"*Do we now?*"

Luca was sitting beside his father, working on writing out a math problem Eli had set for him, and leaned over to look in his father's cup.

"What's wrong, Dad?"

"Eli here thinks she can convert me to a morning tea drinker."

Jeong, who had just finished piling dirt over the remains of their fire, looked up in alarm. "Goddess, Eli. There are some things you do not try to change in a person!"

"I've been drinking coffee since I was thirteen years old. You can't change me now." Tam rose to his feet.

"Coffee stunts your growth," Luca put in helpfully, then visibly second-guessed himself as he stared up to his father's great height. "Could I start drinking coffee now?" he asked Jeong, who grinned down at him in response.

Eli set down one of their tin bowls briskly. "We have been walking through the wilds of Zinfera for two weeks, and we won't be anywhere near a town for another two days! You have next to no coffee left!"

"We have enough for two days!" Tam argued.

Eli crossed her arms and lifted her chin imperially. "You enjoy tea the other times of the day. I don't understand why you struggle to adapt to enjoying it in the morning."

"It isn't strong enough to wake me up in the morning. Besides, do I seem like I have an overabundance of energy?"

Eli arched an eyebrow. "Black tea is just as strong."

"Like hell it is," Tam scoffed.

"Coffee drinkers are all so aggressive," Eli declared with a disapproving sigh.

"At least we aren't pretentious about it, and we don't try to convert others to the beverage—I said it!" Tam cut himself off to make sure she knew he was not going to back down when he saw Eli's jaw drop in shock and fury.

"Every coffee drinker tries to convert others!" Eli shouted.

"Have I tried to convert you?" Tam ducked his head closer to her, his eyes wild, but a barely restrained smile in the right corner of his mouth hinted that he was rather enjoying this little fight of theirs.

"Just kiss already." Luca gave a sigh of undisguised disgust.

Jeong let out a booming laugh and finished packing away the last of their things.

During the two-week journey hiking through the Zinferan forest known as the Kaphe Forest, the nature of Tam and Eli's relationship had become increasingly obvious to both Jeong and Luca, and while nothing had explicitly been said, there were a great number of assumptions made.

Eli didn't even blush at Luca's interruption, as it had become so commonplace for little comments and moments of teasing to take place. Nor did she look away from her employer in shyness as much as before.

Instead, doubling down on her resolve, she peered up at Tam and said, "Coffee makes your breath smell rancid. I couldn't stand kissing you in the morning after you drink that stuff anyway."

While it was the new norm for Luca and Jeong to tease Eli, it was a different thing altogether for *her* to acknowledge the relationship.

In a fit of disgruntled surprise, Tam grabbed her and hoisted her up, making her let out a squeak and forcing her arms around his neck to steady herself.

"Is that so?" he asked while Luca mimed puking on the ground behind him.

Jeong ushered the boy to stand up so that he could break down the small stools to add to Tam's pack.

Eli stared down as haughtily as she could at Tam, though she had once again discovered how to blush.

"Put me down; we need to start walking."

"Mm. Well. I haven't had any coffee this morning because my helpful *assistant—*" Tam pretended to drop Eli, making her grip him even more firmly, her eyes wide in surprise. "—made me tea. So. how is my breath? Still too gross for you to kiss me?"

"You… are… *incorrigible*!" Eli ground out around her embarrassment.

Tam—after stealing a quick look around her to make sure neither Luca or Jeong was watching—kissed her very quickly before setting her down on the ground and walking confidently over to where his pack lay.

"Dad, that was gross," Luca said flatly. Apparently despite Tam's best efforts his son had figured out what was happening.

Tam grinned. "One day you'll understand."

Luca shuddered then plundered on ahead of all of them, leaving Tam to smile after him while pulling his own pack on his shoulders.

He was enjoying getting to see Luca act more comfortable and confident around him as they settled into their routine of traveling. Yes, the boy was starting to develop more attitude, but Tam took it as a good sign that he was feeling secure around them.

Looking toward Jeong, Tam's smile grew as he discovered the man was still giggling to himself.

"Guess the cat's out of the bag," Tam surmised with a sigh.

"I think there is already a very large cat out of the bag stalking behind us," Jeong joked. "You two can hang back and hold hands. I'll quiz Luca on his homework for a league before you can take over."

Tam nodded appreciatively, then loitered until Eli caught up to him. Once the two had fallen into step, he took Jeong's advice and reached over and grasped her hand.

"It'll be hard to climb the terrain like this," Eli pointed out practically.

"Just for a little while. This way you can help support me in case I'm too tired from a lack of coffee."

Eli scowled, but Tam could tell it was a façade in the name of her competitive nature not wanting to back down. He had to admit, he never thought hiding from a coven and the imperial army could be such a lovely time. He almost wished their long journey was a little longer.

Oh well, at least I'll have another few weeks of traveling with them. That's still a while yet.

Unfortunately for Tam, his blissful reprieve from stress was coming to an end far sooner than he hoped. Soon he would be longing for the simple days of hiking and flirting followed by nights of teaching and stories with his son.

CHAPTER 5
PARENTING PAINS

"How many times was that?"

"Twenty-three."

"It's an improvement!"

Tamlin Ashowan nodded silently at Eli's praise, his eyes closed as he rubbed them wearily.

Jeong and Eli stood a short way back, observing Tam disappearing and reappearing throughout the forest surrounding them while Luca waited even farther away at the camp. He was still within sight, and the lad had to work on his reading abilities with the few books they had.

After taking a moment to rest, Tam gradually straightened.

Ever since he had recovered some of his stamina, he'd been practicing traveling through his void, then gradually increasing how often he could do so without bringing himself to the point of fainting.

In the beginning he had only been able to step in and out around ten times, and Tam quickly learned what exactly was the most draining part of using his abilities: the entry and exit. He was all right once he was in the void, but the process by which he left and then reentered the world took a lot of effort.

He also discovered that the greater the distance he traveled, the more tiring it was. In addition, he either had to have been to the location before, or had to see where he was going.

At one point, he had reappeared at one of the camps they'd stayed at the night before, but when he returned to the current one, unconsciousness instantly took him over, and he stayed asleep until late the next morning.

"Alright! Eli, you're up." Tam pushed himself to a stand, though his left knee buckled for a minute, making both Eli and Jeong reach for him out of concern.

He held up a hand, signifying he was fine, then gave a playful half grin at Eli.

"Don't you want to rest?" she asked while ignoring the mischievous look on his face.

"You're not getting out of this that easily. We haven't checked since almost a week ago," Tam reminded her while adding a little more emphasis to his authoritative tone.

This made Eli scowl openly at him. "I doubt they've grown!"

"Only one way to find out," Tam said with a shrug before slipping his hands into his pockets.

Jeong raised his eyebrows at Eli expectantly.

After a moment of quiet stubbornness, she moved a short way off from the two men. Then with a tilt of her head and a crack of her neck, the massive black cat surged forward.

While they had successfully kept the fact that Eli was technically Tam's familiar a secret, Tam had to admit, it was hard to not react when she transformed.

When she switched from human to familiar, he felt like he'd suddenly gained a whole other person that was weirdly a part of himself. He could sense where she was and roughly how she was feeling. While he liked to think he was always aware of Eli because of his romantic interest in her, in her familiar form, it was a different matter entirely.

Tam gaped at her now, slowly drawing himself back to the matter at hand.

Eli *had* grown bigger; she was nearing the size of a pony.

As Tam and Jeong moved up to her shoulders, Tam had to remind himself not to casually pet her again. He had done that once, and when she transformed back she had been wildly indignant.

Leaning closer, Tam and Jeong inspected the fleshy wings on her back, and the two shared a look.

"They are absolutely bigger. Just like the rest of you," Tam called out to Eli.

"Mrr?" She turned her great head in his direction, her golden eyes wide.

Tam showed her by the serious look on his face that he was in no way jesting. "I'm going to run my hand down one so you can feel how big, alright?"

Tam hadn't even known it was possible for a catlike animal to scowl until that moment. Seeing her reaction, he squared himself to her. "Do you not want to have a sense how big those things are?"

"Hrrrg." Eli dropped her head begrudgingly, and Tam took that as consent. He removed his hand from his pocket and brushed down the part of the wing that looked like it was growing a bone or cartilage. It felt similar to the pads of Eli's feet, which he had once been granted permission to prod.

A low grumble emanated from Eli when Tam finally worked his way to the tip of the wing.

"I would say these are about three feet long now," Jeong said, nodding to himself without disguising the awe he was clearly feeling. "It definitely looks like whatever species of beast you are in this form is supposed to fly. Though I wonder why you are only experiencing the growth now. It makes no sense." The Zinferan man tilted his head thoughtfully.

Tam cleared his throat while Eli padded forward to give herself more space from the two men before she shifted back to her human form, clothes intact as they always were despite her transformations. "Let's head back. I'm already feeling drained, and tomorrow is when we get to a town. It'll be better if I'm rested in case something happens."

Eli lifted her hand and carefully swept the front of her hair out of her eyes as they moved to return to the camp without comment.

Jeong set off walking at a far swifter place, leaving Eli and Tam behind to talk on their own. It was something he was doing more and more often, and it was earning all kinds of favorable feelings from Tam.

"Any new theories or developments about your power?" Tam asked quietly while watching Eli's profile.

"Not really. I've never understood how hard it was to restrain magic. When you initially described your issues, I just assumed it was either because your magic was more powerful, or because you simply had poor control."

Tam arched an eyebrow.

Eli ignored him. "I'm doubting that I'm a witch. Both my mother and father were quite adamant that neither of them had witches in the family. And though I've heard that sometimes the magic is so weak it is undetected, there were other things. You know that every witch has a unique symbol that marks a place or person their magic touched?"

"Yes?" Tam nodded. The symbols could only really be seen in most cases by a revealing spell that a member of the coven performed. It was the one bit of magic that could be taught, and only selected coven members knew how to wield it.

"I never had a symbol."

Tam straightened and blinked at this. "Huh."

"What does yours look like?" Eli asked interestedly.

Tam moved his hands through the air haltingly. "Lots of whirls and flowing… Flowing lines… I can try to draw it for you?"

"I take it you are not artistically inclined?"

He blew out a long breath. "Luca is already a lot better than I am at that kind of thing."

Eli smiled and looked at the ground as they slowed their pace even more. "Here I was beginning to worry you didn't have enough flaws."

Snorting, Tam looked at Eli more directly, his face practically aching from the smile he wore. "The socially awkward man who had to be reminded by a child to compliment you? I don't have enough flaws?"

"Well, you're the ideal employer."

"Very romantic," Tam teased, making Eli laugh.

"You're respectful and attractive. You're intelligent, you read a lot, and you aren't the worst at brewing tea."

"I'm glad you've forgiven my coffee habit."

"I'll break you one day," Eli added quite seriously.

The intensity in her eyes had Tam faltering in his steps before he gave a tentative chortle. "I'm terrible at idle conversation with strangers; I have an illegitimate son; I'm not artistically inclined—"

"Tam?" Eli cut him off abruptly. Her hands had started to fidget nervously.

Tam had noticed that she fidgeted less when she had been wearing skirts, but since they were traveling and she was once again wearing pants, the habit had become far more pronounced.

"Yes?"

"What should I—we—What should I call what we are?"

Tam blinked, dumbfounded. "Er. It's up to you how fast you'd like us to go."

"So if I wanted us to get married right away, you would?" Eli challenged next, sounding far more like herself once the skepticism entered her tone.

"I mean… Back before I left Daxaria, my da made a point of having me promise him I wouldn't get married without him or my mother there, but if you wanted to when we got back—"

"You already think we'll get married soon?" Eli burst out.

Tam leaned back. "Did you think we were having a fling?"

"No, I-I guess I did know that you were serious about where it'd end up. It just… It feels big. And that's my fault. I asked. I asked and I'm the one who wanted to go slow. You've always been clear about where you're feelings are. I guess I'm—"

"Eli? Eli, Eli." Tam reached over and grasped her upper arms, cutting off her spiraling tangent. "We are going to move at whatever pace you want."

"I just don't know what to call you! That's all! I suppose we're technically courting, but then would people say you're my intended? Gods, that sounds awful, though. And strange. And—"

Tam quieted Eli by pulling her into himself, wrapping his arms around her, and slowly rocking her side-to-side. "What do you want to call me?" He could feel her rapid heartbeat with her chest pressed against him, which temporarily gave him very improper thoughts that he had to battle back to stay focused on the moment.

"I don't know… You're not my friend. But I don't know that I want to agree to marrying you. I hate when people say that they have a lover."

"Then make up a new word."

"No one will know what it means, though."

"Who are you talking to about me that doesn't know our situation?" Tam wondered with a laugh.

"Well, eventually I will!"

Letting out a breath, Tam plucked up Eli's left hand and tapped the gold band she still wore on her ring finger. "How about while you're here in Zinfera, I'm still your husband, and when we're on our way back to Daxaria, we revisit this."

Eli stared up at him, her expression unreadable. "That's stupid."

"Yeah, but it isn't making you as uncomfortable as calling me *lover* or *intended* or *betrothed*."

"Ugh!" Eli cringed away from Tam—or rather she tried to. He gripped her harder and lowered his face to hers, making her laugh and blush.

Cupping her face, Tam proceeded to kiss Eli soundly. She stopped squirming and leaned back into him.

The kiss turned deeper, and Tam discovered that by the time he felt Eli's tongue over his bottom lip, he didn't have any thoughts to spare.

Time blurred away, and at one point or another, Tam found the bark of a tree underneath his hand, Eli pinned beneath him, which was when he started feeling encumbered by clothes…

"Dad?"

In that moment, Luca's small voice was the equivalent to a bucket of icy water getting dumped on both Tam and Eli as they sprang apart. Tam's breath was a little uneven, and, without seeing himself, knew his hair—which moments ago had Eli's hands running through it—was looking incredibly unkempt.

"Ah, yes? Yes, Luca? Everything alright?" Tam cleared his throat and rubbed the back of his neck while Eli wiped at her mouth with the back of her wrist and then rubbed her palms on her black pant legs awkwardly.

Luca stared up at them skeptically.

First he looked at Eli, then his father. "Am I going to get a little brother or sister soon?"

Tam choked then proceeded to cough, as Eli groaned and covered her face. "Luca that… This isn't how… Why do you ask?" Tam placed his hands on his hips and tried to school his expression.

Luca was looking even more dubious when he turned his attention to Eli. "You and Eli are together now. And… And you share a bed at night. I know babies can be born even when people aren't married. Like me."

"Right. Uh. Right. So that isn't… That isn't exactly how—"

"Even if they don't look like me, a brother would be nice. Sisters could be good, but if it is a sister, I think she'll need more sisters. If there are a few of them, they can play together, which would be good, because I don't think I'll want to play with babies, and if it's just one sister she might be lonely. I mean I was lonely, but—"

"I think I'll go help Jeong with laying out the bedrolls," Eli announced haltingly.

"Coward," Tam whispered.

She didn't bother arguing, just continued heading toward Jeong, who was lighting the campfire.

Tam knelt down in front of his son and rested an arm over his bent knee. He cast a mischievous glance at Eli's back before saying, "We aren't having any babies right now, and won't for a while. Though when we do, I'm sure you'll have a *lot* of siblings. Six. Maybe seven, who knows!"

The speed with which Eli rounded back and stalked over to Tam, her eyes wild, almost had him laughing, but he kept his face serious.

Which was perfect because Luca's wide-eyed response was, "Whoa. That would be *a lot* of babies. Do you know when they're getting here?"

"*If* there are babies, there will be *one! Only one!*" Eli nearly shouted.

"Luca is worried they would be lonely because he'll be so much older," Tam pointed out perfectly reasonably. "Besides, just imagine, with nine children, my nephews might actually get tired out."

"*Nine?*" Eli squawked, her expression mortified.

Luca on the other hand seemed to catch on to what his father was doing. "What if we had five boys and five girls? Then I could be the captain of their teams!"

"What teams?" Tam asked good-naturedly while behind Luca, Eli was growing apoplectic.

"Snowball fights? Tag? Hide and seek?"

"Hm, you know, what if you ran multiple games at once? Maybe we should just say *twelve* siblings and—"

Eli exploded, her hands beating the air adamantly punctuating each word. "*Stop raising the number!*" Then, when she finally noticed Tam's barely suppressed grin and the way Luca was already giggling, she dropped her hands.

"Luca, you might stay an only child." Turning on her heel, Eli stomped back to the camp without allowing either Tam or Luca to goad her into another reaction.

Ruffling Luca's hair, Tam decided he probably should take this opportunity to explain a few facts of life to his son. So he did.

Luckily, Luca was a smart child and grasped the basic understanding of how babies were made, the importance of asking consent, and that neither the man nor the woman controlled what gender baby they had. Though the poor boy was more than a little horrified when he learned about a woman's monthly courses.

By the end of the explanation, Luca looked like he was about to go cross-eyed, and with nighttime falling around them, Tam was feeling a whole new level of exhaustion.

The father and son picked their way back to the tents, though during that time, Luca figured out some new questions to ask.

"So it's impossible that you and Eli could be having a baby right now?"

"Yes."

"Oh. Just so you know, I'm okay if I stay an only child," Luca added conversationally.

Stifling a snort, Tam slid a curious glance at his son, right as the first fireflies started to flicker in the greenery around them. The summer heat had continued climbing during their journey, giving the insects more foliage to hide in.

"I thought you said you were lonely growing up?" Tam felt a familiar pang of guilt over that fact.

"I was, but now I have you, Dad. And I already have to share you now with Eli." There was a faint glum note in Luca's voice that prompted Tam to frown and face his son directly.

"Luca, am I not spending enough time with you? If so, I'm sorry."

"I shouldn't complain! *I'm* sorry!" Luca burst out quickly, his face tensed in panic.

Tam's eyes widened in surprise, and then he recalled that Luca's birth mother, Rosaline Evans, had probably scolded the boy if he tried to ask for more time with her while she worked.

"Luca, it's okay to tell me if you aren't happy about something. We can try to find a way to fix it together. Even if I can't do anything about whatever it is, it's important that you can still talk to me, alright?"

Luca's chastened expression shifted to one of uncertainty.

"How about tomorrow morning, just you and I walk together? Then when Eli and Jeong go to the village, instead of schoolwork, you and I play games. Would you like that?"

Luca nodded instantly, his smile bright enough that Tam could see it clearly in the night right before his son threw his arms around his waist and hugged him.

Tam embraced him back, smiling down at the top of Luca's head.

He felt guilty that he hadn't been noticing Luca feeling left out, and started mentally planning ways to avoid it occurring again in the future.

When the hug eventually ended, Luca peeked up at his father with bright eyes. "Dad, I-I'm okay if I'm an only child or, or if there is a baby, or even multiple other babies. So do you… do you want me to start sleeping in Jeong's tent?"

Mortification and appreciation for his son's consideration filled Tam.

The embarrassment outweighed the other emotion, sadly, but after an uncomfortable moment, Tam managed, "That's okay, Luca. I think it'll be a while before you have a sibling."

Silently Tam confessed to himself, *Though given my family's history and fertility, it will be entirely thanks to Eli and her wonderful boundaries.*

CHAPTER 6

THE FORLORN FUGITIVES

Slipping her pack on her shoulders, Eli stifled a yawn.

They had gotten up outrageously early to reach the town in good time, and while it had been brutal—particularly as her calf muscles still screamed at her for all the walking they had endured over rough terrain—it was a very good thing. By the time she and Jeong set foot in the town called Dahg, the stores were only just opening.

It was the ideal time to make purchases while remaining unnoticed.

The first shop they visited was the tea merchant, who did in fact have a couple bags of ground coffee to sell them. Though Eli tried to talk Jeong out of purchasing both bags, the Zinferan held his ground for both his own and Tam's sakes.

After that, they visited the bakery for some traveler's bread. Standing in front of a butcher's shop, Eli had removed her pack to fill it up—their next stop was going to be a local herbalist who allegedly also sold salt—when the first two imperial soldiers meandered by.

Jeong tensed as he stood in front of Eli, blocking her from view. Luckily there was a barrel of fish that Eli could casually crouch behind as she finished loading her bag. If they got caught and taken to the coven or palace, Eli knew it wasn't likely she'd see Tam again, and they may just choose to kill Jeong.

"Do you want to risk getting the salt?" Jeong asked quietly.

The imperial guards didn't pay him much mind. They looked barely awake as they moved, their shoulders slumped, their spears being used more as walking sticks than weapons.

"If we get a bag of salt, we can make it all the way to Noksa if we portion properly," Eli murmured.

"Then you get back to Tam and Luca, and I'll go. I'm the least suspicious of any of us," Jeong responded, moving his lips as little as possible.

"Alright. Where are the soldiers right now?"

"They are almost at the end of the road, and… they've just turned left. Leave down by that alley to the right, circle around on the far side, and head back north. I'll try to get back to you all as soon as possible."

Eli nodded, pulled the thread to her bag tight, and then smoothly rose and ducked down the nearest alleyway.

She had just reached the back corner of the butcher shop and was going to peek around to see if there were any other patrols when she spotted something in the corner of her eye that stopped her dead in her tracks.

There, on the wall, was a poster.

With her face on it.

Her heart plummeting to her stomach, Eli's eyes swept across the page.

MISSING

PRINCESS ELISARA TAEJO

REWARD

FOR RETURNING HER HIGHNESS

TO THE PALACE:

$25,000 GOLD

Cold sweat prickled along Eli's back.

The picture showed her with short hair, which was damn close to how she presently looked.

How the hell do they know what I look like now? Soo Hebin hasn't seen me in years!

Eli didn't have a chance to figure this out as from behind her, a shout echoed.

"HEY! YOU THERE! COME IDENTIFY YOURSELF!"

Her heart surged into her throat and she jolted into motion.

The voice had come from back near the main road, and so she rounded the corner of the butcher's hastily, not thinking to check around the corner… Which resulted with her crashing into an imperial soldier who had a partner.

Wiry arms wrapped around Eli, pinning her in place.

"Sir, you need to—"

Eli was grateful that she had worn pants to town. It meant that even with her longer hair, at a glimpse she was still thought to be male.

Using this moment of confusion, she kneed the groin of the soldier with his arms around her. When his comrade tried to grab her, she bent herself over and rammed her shoulder into his middle, tackling him.

She could hear soldiers running down the alley behind her.

She needed to get into the trees as quickly as possible so she could transform into the beast and outrun them. Or hide.

Barely scrambling to her feet before the other soldiers descended on her, Eli bolted. Panic and adrenaline propelled her forward, her strength surging.

She knew it wasn't enough, though; she could hear two men closing in too quickly. She was weighed down and awkward with her pack, and her muscles were already fatigued.

She was at a severe disadvantage.

"Damnit." Swinging the pack from her shoulders, Eli tossed it to the right side, lunged to her left to barely avoid getting speared by the soldier who had gotten nearest to her, then leapt backward just in time for the spear from the second soldier, aimed at her middle, to miss.

She couldn't wait any longer.

The beast exploded out of her.

The soldiers gave shouts of shock and terror.

Not wasting an instant of their surprise, Eli leapt over the men as they cowered, her new size making it an easy feat. She grabbed her pack in her jaws and galloped into the woods, a growl rumbling in the back of her throat. The forest blurred around her and yet her eyes, nose, and ears guided her easily through the trees, over hills and rocks.

She ran west for a while to prevent the soldiers from discovering Tam and Luca. When she was certain she couldn't hear anyone after her for at least a league, she resumed moving northeast. To make it even more difficult on anyone tracking her, she made a point of taking massive pounces and splashing in any river she came across on the way back to the camp.

The smells of the forest were intoxicating, and a thrill started to course through her in a way she had never experienced before. Then again, she had never run free in this form before.

By the time Eli could hear Tam and Luca's voices, she slowed so that she had time to drop her pack, change back into herself, pick the pack back up, and run the rest of the way. Her legs resumed their protests against the physical exertion.

When she approached Tam, she saw that he had smothered and buried their fire, and was ready to resume traveling with Luca at his side. Upon noticing her approach, Luca waved cheerily, while Tam's eyes took in her harried state, already donning a tense expression.

"I had to… transform… back in the town. There were soldiers… and there's… a poster with my face on it offering… a reward if I can be delivered to the palace," Eli gasped.

Ironically it was the last quarter mile running as a human that had winded her the most.

Tam nodded. "I know. Jeong isn't back yet. We'll wait a short while, but let's at least start moving away from the camp."

"What do you mean you know? How could—" Eli stopped talking, her eyes rounding.

Familiars and witches could share images, particularly when there was a stressful or dangerous situation. Clenching her teeth, she battled back another wave of dread and anger. Apparently it didn't matter if she rejected being Tam's familiar, and he agreed to not have that kind of connection. It seemed that their relationship was fixed.

But this was not the time to spiral over the matter. Right now, what was most important was finding Jeong and deciding what to do from here.

Her heart still pounding in her chest, Eli kept training her ears to listen for sounds of anyone pursuing them from the west, but she heard nothing.

They waited while gradually drifting eastward away from the campsite. Any snapping of twigs or rustling of the underbrush had Tam and Eli's heads turning every which way to ensure no one was sneaking up on them. Luca merely held Tam's hand and kept his eyes on the south, as though willing Jeong to appear.

At long last, the Zinferan did come into view, and relief instantly filled Eli. Her biggest worry had been that because of her transformation and flight, anyone who didn't live in the town would've been apprehended.

As soon as Jeong was close enough to speak, Eli noted the heavy perspiration along his brow.

The Zinferan had gone through a drastic change since their journey began. His wide, protruding middle had shrunk during the two weeks of walking, and his rounded cheeks had thinned. That said, he was still prone to softness.

"There is a search party looking for Eli. They think she's either an ancient beast or the devil in a new unnatural form," Jeong explained without even managing a greeting. "What happened?"

"I got cornered while leaving," Eli returned shortly. "We need to get moving. I went west for a while before coming back here, but if they have horses to follow us, we're in trouble."

Jeong paused to take a deep drink from his waterskin, then said, "I was lucky. They believed me when I told them I was running an errand for a merchant who was traveling nearby but didn't want to get off the main road. When I was leaving, I overheard that the imperial army set up checkpoints along all roads to Gondol, and they have regular patrols between all of them—including in the woods and fields."

"Damn," Tam cursed, his brows furrowing. "Thank the Gods you were able to learn that."

Jeong nodded seriously in agreement.

"We'll have to switch to plan B," Eli informed them all as they started to move even more quickly.

"What's your—"

"The imperial soldiers will be even more present in Bani," Jeong interjected, cutting off Tam.

"We'll aim for Eusa. It's a small town that the larger city of Bani hasn't absorbed yet, and it has its own harbor. We'll have to sail around Zinfera's east side to get to the fishing town on the opposite side of Gondol."

"Hang on. We're going to take an even longer route?" Tam frowned.

Luca moaned at the mention of their travel plans extending.

"Yes. The imperial soldiers are not an infinite resource. If Soo Hebin has a ring around Gondol, and most likely a large number of men still in Junya, that means she's spread thin everywhere else. Eusa is so far away, and seemingly inconsequential; it's unlikely she'll send any more than a handful of men."

"What about the other concubines? What if some of them are persuaded to lend their family reservoirs of fighters?" Tam speculated next.

"Soo Hebin is the most powerful of the concubines. However, given the number of children she has taken from the other concubines, she has lost a lot of leverage, and some may be wanting revenge," Eli explained.

"What about the coven? They are hiding the first witch, and the first witch is allied with the concubine," the future duke pressed.

"Other than her connections, the first witch herself is powerless, yes?" Eli ventured thoughtfully.

"She is unless she gets her hands Chronos or the dagger. Besides, if the coven is now adding people to search for us like they did back in Junya—"

Eli cast a sharp look at Tam. "Do you have a better plan?"

The future duke let out a very long breath, his eyes staring blindly ahead of himself as they walked.

"Luca, are you alright?" It was Jeong who asked the question as he glanced over to his companions and noticed the young boy clutching his head.

"I have a bad headache," Luca replied faintly.

Alarmed, Tam stopped walking and immediately pulled out his waterskin. "Drink some water. We were playing a lot, and you weren't drinking enough."

Luca obeyed and took a long, deep draught, but everyone could see by the way he was squinting against the light of the day that he was in pain.

Lifting his hand up, Tam pressed his palm to Luca's forehead. "Godsdamnit. He's burning up."

"How did that come on so quickly?" Eli dropped to a crouch, her face taut with concern as Luca closed his eyes with a wince. "Does anything else feel wrong, Luca?"

"I'm tired." Luca swayed on his feet after answering.

"When did you start not feeling well?" Tam persisted, making his voice gentle despite the panic he was visibly seized with. If they needed a doctor, they were in a world of trouble.

"Just. while we were waiting for... For Jeong."

"Okay." Tam took back the waterskin, keeping his eyes on his son's pale face. "Luca, I'm going to carry you on my back."

"I can take some of the items from your pack to make it a bit lighter," Jeong offered.

Eli shook her head.

"No. Luca, you will ride me while I'm a big cat, alright? Just like you wanted to try when we first started walking!"

Tam's eyes snapped to her. "Are you sure you can handle it?"

Eli nodded. "I can carry my pack in my mouth. I'm a lot stronger than either of you in that form."

Tam looked at Jeong, who nodded. "Alright."

Standing back, Eli shook out her arms, dropped her pack, and, for the second time that day, shifted into a beast.

Which wound up revealing how serious Luca's condition was, as he barely managed to crack open an eye to look at her.

Tam carefully lifted Luca onto Eli's back.

"Ready?" Jeong asked with forced jubilance, as though trying to lighten everyone's grim moods.

Luca managed to wrap his arms partially around Eli's thick neck then nod.

"I guess we'll head to Eusa. We don't have any other choice. It's the closest and safest option given Luca's state," Tam said, though the idea still made him visibly uneasy.

"Dad?" Luca asked with a faint croak as they once again began to move.

Eli's ears perked up at the sound of his voice, already worried about how weak his grasp was around her neck.

"Yeah?"

"What happens to Eli's clothes when she transforms?"

Eli snorted, which instantly drew Tam's gaze to her as hearing a giant cat snort was not something one heard every day. She didn't react to his look. The truth was that she didn't know the answer, either. Her clothes seemed to just get absorbed in her being, then later reappear. The exception was her pack.

"Not sure. I guess we'll ask her when we make our next stop."

Eli heard the laughter in Tam's voice, and even caught Jeong grinning. Well, at least Luca was not sick enough to stop asking interesting questions, which had to mean he'd be okay. But she knew that she might be just leaning into hopeful optimism more out of desperation than sincerely believing everything would be alright.

CHAPTER 7
POWER PLAYS

In Concubine Soo Hebin's palace, there were three gardens.

While all of them were spectacular, maintained immaculately, and often a source of envy for the other concubines, one of the three was more hidden than its sisters.

This particular garden lay on the west side of Soo Hebin's palace, and while it was still well cared for, it tended to embrace overgrown beauty more than the others.

Lattice walls with climbing star jasmine vines created various secluded seating areas. Some of these areas had small round tables with wooden chairs. Others had large marble daises with tall vases filled with fresh flowers every day. Others had fountains, and some had statues.

As whimsical and delightful as the garden was, its beauty was more or less a secret. One couldn't be dazzled by it upon stepping outside. Rather, the first sight of the garden was a tall row of leafy hedges—unlike the other two gardens that sprawled out before anyone who stepped out the double doors.

Soo Hebin respected that her secret garden was the best area for her to meet with officials, lords, and other people under her employ whom she didn't necessarily want anyone to know about. Still, it irked her a little not to be able to show it off to others.

At least, that was what Aradia, the first witch, daughter of the Gods, surmised as she sat in a corner far away from the remote wing of the palace that Soo Hebin had stashed her in.

It was a beautiful, sunny day. The wind rustled the leaves, it was neither too hot nor too cold, and Aradia was reading a very interesting missive from the Coven of Giong's leader.

"There was a symbol of a witch left at the crime scene by the docks. A symbol that there is no record of. Wasn't that princess that Soo Hebin disliked odd for not having a symbol? Isn't it possible that she developed one?" Aradia asked aloud while lowering the missive and lifting her icy eyes to Ansar.

Acadia's faithful servant still knelt on the gravel in front of her. "You would know best."

"Hm." Aradia set the page beside herself on the wooden bench she was seated on. "Sit over there, Ansar. I want to speak my mind to you before Her Highness seeks me out."

There was a subtle twitch in Ansar's mouth before he raised his warm gaze to Aradia, then sat in the chair she had gestured to with her chin.

"My brother is here in Zinfera. I feel it. And that incident at the docks tells me he has another witch helping him. The assistant that sent a missive to Soo Hebin… Yun Shik? He said there was a dark, mysterious man married to Elisara, and that they had a son."

Ansar's eyebrow arched. "Which is the devil? The man or the child?"

Aradia shook her head slowly, her eyes drifting downward. "I don't know. What was reported to the coven and to the emperor from the Troivackian court was that the devil had been reduced to ash and disappeared, which leads me to at first think it is the child. However…" The first witch paused while settling back comfortably in her seat and crossing her legs. "They could have lied. Maybe they said he died and kept him as a prisoner for information. I couldn't see what happened when he was allegedly killed in Troivack."

"What makes you think it's a lie?" Ansar leaned forward interestedly.

"The descriptions of the shadows. If he's a child, he can't use his abilities yet. He probably can't even re—"

"Your Holiness?" The distant call came from the very concubine Aradia had been hoping to avoid.

Aradia rolled her eyes, shared a telling look with Ansar, and responded, alerting the concubine to her location.

A few short minutes later Soo Hebin appeared, dressed as extravagantly as possible in a long white dress patterned with gold leaves. A black skirt underneath added volume, while the sleeves were cut wide so that the concubine could slip her hands in them as she strolled gracefully. Her hair was piled high and adorned with an assortment of gold pins studded with rubies and diamonds.

In contrast, Aradia was clad all in black. The loose pants she had acquired, the long silk coat, and even her corset were black, and unlike the concubine, she didn't wear a speck of jewelry.

The concubine regarded Aradia's unconventional appearance and relaxed posture with only the barest of eyebrow raises before lowering herself into a chair. "I have news," she announced coolly.

Aradia knew the concubine hated not having anyone around to prostrate themselves for her; it was amusing. It was at times like this that she had a vague inkling of missing her brother. As much as Aradia defended humanity, even she wasn't blind to some of the worst characters. They used to laugh together at some of humanity's awful antics.

"Princess Elisara was spotted in a town north of Bani. She escaped using her magic and headed west. They tracked her for two days but couldn't tell where in the Kaphe Forest she wound up going. She may have rerouted to go to Haeson, or simply found another long route to Bani. She most likely thinks she can go to her former family for assistance," Soo Hebin explained with a light twitching around the corners of her eyes.

Aradia almost smiled.

She hadn't been told the full details about the adopted princess, but something about her certainly made the concubine nervous. It was intriguing.

"She was alone. So her husband and child either fled somewhere else or were waiting for her in the forest."

Aradia considered this. "The edge of the Kaphe Forest north of Bani is more or less in the middle of Zinfera. Your princess is leaving herself a great many options and forcing you to spread your resources thinly." The first witch didn't hide her high appraisal of Elisara.

The more she irritated the concubine, the more the woman was prone to letting things slip.

Sure enough, upon hearing Aradia's complimentary tone for the princess that Soo Hebin had tried to destroy countless times, the concubine grew even paler, and her nostrils flared. "I am keeping the imperial soldiers in a ring around Gondol. If that brat thinks she is going to come and claim the throne, devil at her side or not, she will not succeed. However…" Soo Hebin trailed off, a superior glint in her eyes appearing. "I have also heard that there has been an official notice that Her Majesty Queen Katarina Reyes and her mother, Duchess Annika Ashowan, are on their way from Daxaria."

Aradia stilled, then smiled widely. "Oh, how fascinating that is. Why isn't her father coming in light of my escape from my Troivackian prison?"

"It is *because* of your escape that he is staying behind in Daxaria. In the event you attack their kingdom personally."

Aradia scoffed. "I'm shocked they aren't aware I'm here. Though it makes perfect sense for them to send the Daxarian queen to Zinfera, what with our history. I take it the Coven of Aguas is sending their own representatives from Troivack?"

Soo Hebin took her time answering, and Aradia could tell it was because she was attempting to assert dominance in the conversation.

"They are sending their former coven head Mr. Kraft, and a knight who is allegedly going to return to Daxaria in three years to begin the process of taking over as the captain of military for Daxaria."

"I see." Aradia's eyes drifted toward the brilliant-blue mid-afternoon sky and the fluffy clouds drifting by. "Expect the coven leader of Giong to come visit me soon. Together we will start talking about collaborating with your men to look for my brother, the devil."

Soo Hebin's outrage seared forward in her expression. "Why did you summon them without speaking to me first?"

Aradia's eyebrows shot upward in mock surprise before she let out a soft laugh. "Soo Hebin." The concubine gritted her teeth at being addressed so casually by the first witch. "Those are not your people. The covens were my creation, and they obey me. The only other entities with authority over me would be my parents, the Gods themselves."

There was an eerie note in Aradia's voice that sent an unnatural echo through the air.

While she couldn't see it, Aradia was quite certain that Soo Hebin's hands were trembling within her sleeves. Regardless, she resumed speaking to finish her point. "You are a mortal. You do not command me, and while you may have thought you commanded my people, that is a very serious misconception I'm afraid was born out of your ego."

Soo Hebin's eyes bulged, but after a moment of staring murderously at Aradia's calm expression, she lifted her chin. "If I am nothing to you, then leave. I do not need your help."

Aradia's smile was toying. "Gladly. I'll go to the coven, reveal my presence, and alert everyone that *you* helped free me." Aradia stood, her hands finding her pockets as she stepped lazily over to the concubine. "I'll also share the fact that you have been abusing my creation, Witch's Brew, and have been dosing your dear emperor for years in an effort to control him. I'll even go an extra league and talk about how the only one you truly feared—because she was the emperor's chosen heir to the throne—was Elisara Taejo." Aradia inclined herself ever so slightly as she stared down at Soo Hebin. "Shall I show myself out now?"

The concubine was visibly struggling not to shrink back into her chair when a male voice called out. "Mother! Mother your servants said you are out here! Whatever could you be doing here?" Aradia straightened just in time for a young man in his early twenties to appear. He wore a long, plain royal-blue coat tied around his waist, and had a tidy bun pinned atop his head.

While he didn't have any adornments, the quality of the silk spoke to his wealth.

"Mother, I was wondering where we decided we were going to host my birthday this year?" the young man all but whined to Soo Hebin.

Aradia cocked her head to the right.

The young man was handsome, but only if he didn't talk. He had a sharp, square chin, broad cheekbones, and wide brown eyes.

"Jum, I told you to wait for me in the center garden. I have business to finish up here."

At being reminded that his mother was in fact talking to other people, the prince at last noticed that there was a seemingly young Daxarian woman standing over his mother, and a Daxarian man lounging in a nearby chair.

"Who are you?" he asked bluntly.

Aradia squared herself to the prince, her stare unblinking. "I am a guest of your mother's. And you?"

Confusion mixed with indignation on the young man's face. "I am Prince Jum! The next emperor to the throne! Son of Her Highness Soo Hebin, and—"

"Ah. Jum it is." Aradia turned on her heel and glided back over to the bench before seating herself.

Soo Hebin glared at Aradia who smiled pleasantly back.

At least she hasn't tried to stab me outright yet.

"My dear." Soo Hebin looked away from the first witch with great difficulty. She may have been wanting to see if she could kill Aradia simply with the acidity in her stare. "Please go inside and wait for me there. I need to finish this meeting."

"But that woman—"

Soo Hebin raised an eyebrow at her son, silencing him instantly, making him turn with slumped shoulders to trudge away.

Aradia would've bet money that watching Jum behave like a petulant child was irking the concubine horribly.

"What is it you want Zinfera's coven for, exactly?" Soo Hebin fired at Aradia, her gaze once more boring into the first witch.

Aradia let out a long-suffering sigh as she looked at Ansar, who merely bowed his head under her attention.

"I'm going to announce that witches have no business being nobles or leading countries, and then I am going to use the coven's influence to find my brother and send him home."

"The last time you did this, you started a civil war and failed," Soo Hebin reminded her with no small amount of satisfaction.

The first witch remained unflappable. "True. But I wasn't only trying to accomplish those two things. Back then I was trying to lend power to the Troivackian queen to improve the gender inequality of the kingdom while crippling her effort to restore the coven in court. I was also busy trying to overpower my brother with a human army and ancient beasts."

"So then how *do* you plan on returning the devil to the Forest of the Afterlife?"

Aradia looked at Ansar, and again smiled. "We're working on that. But I'll need the coven's full cooperation."

Soo Hebin rose to her feet, her body angled toward the exit.

Aradia watched the burning ire simmering in every inch of her proud being. "Your Highness?" Aradia called out politely—a small gesture of peace.

The concubine didn't look in any way placated.

"You will be free of Princess Elisara, and by the time I am finished, Daxaria's economy will be weakened. You can boast spearheading resuming trade that will happen as a result. Remember, this is a partnership."

Soo Hebin turned back to Aradia, peering down at the first witch with every ounce of superiority she possessed.

Unbothered, Aradia continued. "If you start attempting to be a tyrant, you will meet the same end as Aidan Helmer. I've seen it time and time again. In life you will have partners, and you cannot lord over them all. Tread carefully." She clasped her hands in front of herself and watched complicated emotions flex in the concubine, who then stalked away without another word.

Aradia looked back at Ansar, who was rubbing his mouth while hiding a smile.

"I never knew you to have a sense of humor," Aradia noted wryly.

At this, Ansar smiled more obviously at her. "My apologies. I simply am euphoric to have you back with us."

Aradia looked tenderly at the man, then stood to make her way over to him. Once in front of Ansar, she lifted a hand and gently touched his cheek. He stared up at her adoringly.

"I can't feel love, Ansar. But if I could, you would have all of me. As it is, guard yourself, my darling." A shadow of pain passed over her eyes. "Now tell me what you've learned about the other princes and princesses. That idiot son of Soo Hebin's shouldn't so much as breathe on that throne."

Ansar bowed his head. His warm expression dimmed but did not entirely dissolve as he relayed his findings to his mistress.

Aradia eventually seated herself as she listened, leaning back her head to enjoy the birds that sang around her. It was a rare moment of peace, but she knew she was going to have to prepare in more ways than one to properly receive the queen of Daxaria.

CHAPTER 8

A CONCERNING CONDITION

Tam cradled Luca against his chest and continued to feed him a spoonful of vegetable broth inside their tent. His face was tense and pale as he stared down at his son's bleary eyes.

Eli picked at her thumbnail from outside as she watched Tam huddle near the lantern they had risked lighting in order to warm Luca.

"It's been two days, and he is getting weaker," Jeong said gravely from beside Eli.

"We need to stop traveling and let him rest somewhere warm. Maybe even find a physician," she responded without removing her gaze from Tam and Luca.

"Do you think Eusa is a big enough town to have a physician?" Jeong wondered.

"Absolutely. The problem is, unlike Daxaria and Troivack, physicians here in Zinfera can sell what they know about another person. And with the imperial soldiers looking for us…"

Jeong nodded with a grimace.

It wasn't all physicians that acted so greedily, of course, but there were cases of noble or wealthy families being torn apart after they learned of a diseased partner, or a pregnancy that could not have come from the husband.

"I know a few teas that could help him, but we'd need to buy the ingredients, and—like I said—we need a place to rest," Eli added. Her hands fell to her sides.

"Perhaps we should try imploring help from some farmers. They rarely leave their land and may not have heard all of the rumors, and every earth-working man and woman I know would at least let poor travelers use a barn." Jeong turned gentle, sympathetic eyes to Eli.

She gnawed on her tongue, then let out a long breath as she watched Tam put down the bowl of soup and start to rock Luca while murmuring something she couldn't hear. He then picked up his son, wrapped a blanket around him, and set him down near the lantern before stepping outside the tent, his countenance grim.

"This is bad. He needs a fire at the very least. Gods… if he has an infection of some kind, there is no option but to find a physician," Tam lamented as he stared blindly into nothing as his anxiety and fear visibly tortured him.

"Let's give it another day. We can reach the outskirts of Eusa tomorrow morning, and I was just suggesting to Eli that we might ask some more remote farmers for assistance," Jeong explained softly. "It's risky, but I can't think of any other way. If we get reported, you may just have to take Luca and myself into your void, and Eli will have to run away."

"I don't know that I can take more than one person into the void," Tam said with a rasp.

"You took an entire wall and a desk once, according to you. I'd like to think I'm a bit smaller than that," Jeong reminded him with only a hint of humor.

"People are different, though. I care a lot more if I can't hold on to you in the void. With Lord Kim, we weren't in there for very long, and when I did it with Luca, I couldn't hold him there," Tam argued, his voice rising slightly.

"Tam." Eli's voice was hushed, and Tam's eyes snapped to her as she drew closer. "We don't have a choice. If he needs a physician because of an infection, we'll deal with it then, but he needs a full day of rest. I think Jeong's idea is a good one."

"What if they've seen your poster? The one with the reward?" Tam pointed out next, a sheen in his eyes only faintly visible thanks to the last vestiges of daylight.

"We'll run. We should be close enough to the harbor that we can steal a boat and leave that way. We're far enough from the coven that it'd take them a few days to catch up to us," Eli countered, one finger tapping the back of her hand.

Tam lowered his chin. "This is all my fault. I should have sent him straight back to Daxaria with you when I got here. Now you both are in danger, and I don't know what I can do." He shook his head.

Eli and Jeong could see that he was trembling.

"I'm going for a walk. I just… I need some time. We'll find a farm and ask for help tomorrow morning."

Jeong didn't say anything in response, and while Eli opened her mouth to try and offer some comfort, Tam turned and strode stiffly off into the trees.

Eli watched his back until he had disappeared in the darkness and foliage, then looked toward the tent. "I'll get ready for bed and stay with Luca."

Jeong nodded with a sad half smile pulling at his mouth.

Once Eli had crawled up beside Luca with her own blanket, she threw half of it over him and very carefully moved closer.

If I can give him some body heat, it'll be better than nothing.

Sensing her presence, Luca shifted in his sleep and slowly opened his eyes. "Eli… ?" he asked dazedly.

"Go back to sleep. You're still sick," she ordered awkwardly.

"Am I dying?"

The tears that sprang up surprised Eli, and she tried to hastily blink them back before Luca could see. "No. No, you are not dying."

"Dad's scared, though."

Eli found herself falling into a familiar internal debate over how much of the truth she should share with the boy. "Of course he is scared. He's never had a sick child before. All parents are scared when their children are sick."

Luca's eyes fluttered closed, and for a moment Eli thought that he had simply fallen back to sleep with remarkable speed. Then he opened his eyes again.

"Were your parents scared when you got sick?"

If Eli had thought she had any chance of controlling her tears before, she gave up on it now.

"No, they never got scared. But that's because they weren't good parents. Not like your father."

Luca stared blearily at Eli as tears fell from her eyes, and her right hand gripped the blanket over them tightly. "My mother never got scared when I'd get sick. She always said it wouldn't matter if I died," Luca confessed sadly.

Eli drew herself up onto her elbow in alarm. "That is just not true, Luca. It does matter!"

Luca smiled a little. "Thanks, Eli. If you get sick, I'll tell you… the same thing." Pausing, Luca appeared to struggle to stay conscious. "Eli?"

"Yes?" She tried to wipe the tears from her face with the back of her wrist.

"I'm glad you're here with me. Don't tell my mother, but… I wish you were my mom. Even if you do make me study a lot."

Eli broke. Her sobs overtook her as she lowered her face to her hand.

"Luca, it's my fault we can't get you a physician," she managed through the tears. "I'm barely a decent person, let alone—"

Luca shifted closer, then wrapped an arm over Eli's middle and pressed his burning cheek into her collarbone. "We have to stay together for as long as possible," he insisted. While he had clearly tried to deliver the words with great, forceful meaning, they were still weak and desperate. "And it isn't your fault. I can tell."

With shaking arms, Eli carefully returned Luca's embrace. She kept holding him until eventually sleep claimed both of them.

★★★

It was a cloudless day when the rows of raspberry bushes came into view. By this time, Luca was already slumped on Tam's back, and Eli walked alongside them in her human form; they hadn't wanted to risk her being seen as a beast.

"How are you this morning, Luca?" Tam called over his shoulder as he felt his son start to stir.

Luca had been half awake for the majority of the time they'd been walking, but Tam's heart soared when he felt Luca fully lift his sweaty head off his back.

"Where are we?"

"We're going to go talk to some people and see if we can get you a bed to sleep in."

"And maybe some tea leaves that will help bring your fever down." Eli reached up to gently brush Luca's damp hair off his forehead.

"I think I feel a bit better," Luca informed them with a yawn.

Tam, Eli, and Jeong exchanged tentative hopeful looks, prompting Tam to heft Luca with a little more muscle. The boy gave a laugh, only for it to be followed by a cough and a stream of snot from his nose.

Eli hurriedly produced a handkerchief and wiped his face before they set off once more down the rows of raspberry bushes.

It took a little longer than they had anticipated to find the house on the farm, but when they did, they were greeted with the sight of a wide expanse of pristine blue water stretched before them. There on the south shores of Zinfera lay the Tinoo Ocean. It was a peaceful day, and the water almost looked still under the early sunshine.

The house, in comparison with the grandiose view, was humble. It was perhaps four carriages long, with three small windows dotting its whitewashed sides; the roof was brown tile.

As they approached, they could see an old woman wearing a faded green wool sweater and a long flimsy white dress that most likely was her night shift. She tossed feed on the ground with fingers bent from arthritis to a cluster of chickens and a rooster. Her hair was braided with a lone tendril floating about her downturned face as she worked.

Seated under the shade of the house, fanning himself with a large ginkgo leaf in one hand and holding a cup of tea in his other, was an older man. Both of them had hair that was more white than black. The man's hair, what little he had of it, stuck up on the left side of his head, and his white shirt was loose, his feet bare. He also appeared to be in his sleepwear.

They looked meek enough not to pose an imminent threat, but Tam knew nosy neighbors or grown children might be nearby.

"Should I go and introduce us?" Jeong offered kindly.

Tam shook his head and moved forward. "They need to see that Luca isn't well so they don't think we're trying to con them."

"Most people wouldn't think—" Jeong started, but Tam was already setting off toward the couple.

The moment he set foot onto the dirt patch of the yard and off the thick grasses of the field, Tam spoke out, hoping that his respectful distance would help him seem more trustworthy.

"Excuse me?"

The old lady turned with shuffling feet to look in surprise at Tam's appearance, while the old man under the eaves of the house leaned forward in his seat.

"Hi there, I'm sorry I… um…" His voice was a rasp as tears suddenly warmed Tam's eyes.

In his life he had felt powerless and pointless many times before, but never, *never* had it been like this.

"My son is sick, and… the imperial soldiers keep wanting to arrest anyone who isn't Zinferan, and we… He can't keep going. He has a fever." Tam knew he wasn't making a ton of sense, but at the mention of his son the woman's eyes moved to the top of Luca's head, which was once again resting against his shoulder.

She stared into Tam's eyes as her husband stood and made his way over to his wife. He was shorter than she was, and Tam towered over her.

The woman reached out a hand and gestured him toward her.

He obeyed on legs that felt like they had rusted.

The old man shot a frown at his wife, but she merely pressed the basket of chicken feed into his hands and reached up with her thin arms to touch Luca's forehead.

The old woman's attention briefly turned to Eli and Jeong, then back to the boy. Her mouth pursed.

Luca coughed, then coughed some more.

The distrustful expression changed to sincere worry.

"Please, all we ask is a place where he can rest. We can pay you. We-We can pay for food, or tea leaves, but can you—" Tam's remaining composure crumbled. "Please help my son."

He was crying.

He hadn't cried in years, but the frustration, desperation, and fear that had been gouging his heart wrangled it from him.

Tam had handled everything that had happened on his journey since leaving Daxaria the best he could, the most logically he could. He had questioned himself, and grown stronger. He'd made friends and opened himself up in ways he hadn't ever thought possible.

But Luca was too sick, even if he said he was feeling better. And there was no one to save them. No one they could count on for help.

The old woman gently touched Tam's cheek, her brown eyes gentle.

"My name is Sua. Come inside. I'll make some tea."

CHAPTER 9

A FATHERLY FEAR

Finlay Ashowan studied Eric Reyes's profile. "Have you heard any word?" His son-in-law didn't even look at him."No."

"Have you eaten dinner yet?"

The candles flickered in the dark council room, and still, the king would not look at Fin. "No."

"Any news about Antony making it stop raining anytime soon?"

"No."

"It's still early, I'm sure Kat has arrived safely," Fin said with a sigh while lowering the paperwork in front of him and slouching back in his seat.

The two men were alone in the council room. The report on the first witch's escape as well as the record regarding the last time they defeated her spread out on the table in front of them to help them begin to strategize should another war break out.

However, the new Daxarian king had been in a Gods-awful mood ever since his beloved wife boarded a vessel set for Zinfera with his mother-in-law.

And it didn't help that the threat of the daughter of the Gods, the first witch, loomed over them as well.

Fin leaned his head back until it hit the chair. The relentless downpour that washed the windows was starting to become a concern. The riverbanks were buckling, and the farmers worried about their crops rotting.

"Eric, maybe you should take half a day tomorrow to spend with Antony. I'm pretty sure he would feel a lot better if you and he had some one-on-one time."

"Fin, I don't think it's that simple." Eric's bloodshot hazel eyes reluctantly drifted up from the pages before him. He hadn't slept well since Kat had left. "We only told Antony two weeks ago that Charlie would most likely be the only one to take the throne. He needs time to sort out his feelings."

"He needs guidance," Fin corrected, keeping his tone as gentle as possible.

"I tried to talk to him and be there for him, but all he did was scream and tell me to get out because I wouldn't understand as a human."

Wincing, Fin inclined forward again to better rub the back of his neck. "He didn't want to talk to me, either. Just said I got to become a duke, and that at least I was given a choice."

"So you see my dilemma," Eric pointed out wearily.

"He still needs to know we're there for him."

"Fin! I'm—" Eric's voice was loud and aggravated, but upon hearing how it came out, he paused. Closing his eyes, the king took a breath and then in a quieter tone continued, "I'm doing the best I can. With Kat away, everything is three times more difficult. For more reasons than one. I'm… Gods. I'm not right just now." Eric reached up and rubbed his eyes.

Fin gave a resigned half smile. "I'm sorry. I know how hard things are for you without Kat. Well. I don't exactly, but I know you are struggling a lot." He paused. "I really wish Tam were here. He'd be the perfect person to talk to Antony."

"I don't know about that. Tam wasn't all that thrilled himself that the coven is planning to take away the duchy from him."

"He'd put his own feelings aside to help Antony. I know he would," Fin affirmed.

Eric tilted his head over his right shoulder and didn't comment.

While Fin noticed the pointed lack of response, he once again chose not to bring up Eric's wariness when it came to both Tam and Annika. He had sensed it for years, but never addressed it directly. He had his suspicions about it, but knew Eric had still yet to finish making up his mind about Fin's family members. Which was rare for him, and showed how much there was for him to process.

A rumble of thunder crescendoed outside the window.

"I find it odd that the coven has become so particular about witches in power. I thought we should be able to take whatever role we wished, so long as we counseled others on the balances of our element."

"It's hard to counsel the balance of a mutated power," Eric pointed out swiftly, as though he'd had this argument one too many times.

"True, but even so. It seems oppressive."

"They are drawing a clear divide between witches and humans. Differences should be noted. I don't begrudge them for making that point. I mean, Antony struggling to control his mood is resulting in Austice getting drenched. Not many seven-year-olds can say that," the king argued reasonably.

Fin's mind drifted quietly through the arguments for a few moments longer, until he eventually shook his head. "Maybe you're right. I mean, I hate being noble—"

"Oh really? No one's noticed."

"—My real love is cooking and keeping a house happy. The only reason I can manage any of this is with constant reminders that this is all part of my home," Fin plundered on, ignoring Eric's interruption. "But maybe that's just it. Politics might be something we need to keep more separate from witches."

"The only problem with that? It starts to sound like religion. And religion building power is… tricky."

Fin cringed. "Definitely."

Shaking his head, Eric sighed. "Can you convince your wife and my wife to abandon our lofty roles so we can go farm or something?"

Fin grinned. "I wish. I didn't even win in the battle to keep my beard."

Eric nodded at the memory, though his shadowed eyes twinkled a little, which encouraged Fin to say more. "Who knows, maybe Tam finds an insight into things that we are missing while he's away. He did say he was going to talk to the Zinferan coven and possibly even travel to Lobahl after." The house witch watched as Eric rubbed his eyes. "Come on, let's take a break."

The two men rose to their feet, Fin's hands finding his pockets and Eric looking a little more relaxed, when all of a sudden the duke's vision filled with white and his knees buckled. His palms slammed blindly against the surface of the table, stinging his palms.

"Fin?" Eric moved hastily to his father-in-law's side, fear lacing his tone. Whenever this happened, it meant that one of Fin's family members was either terrified or dying.

Fin's legs started to give way, and he felt his face contort with pain. With Eric's arm going around his back, Fin teetered, as though about to fully collapse.

"What's wrong? Is something happening on the ship with Kat? Or with the duchess? Or—"

Fin shuddered, and as he closed his eyes, the white light disappeared and he felt his own tired blue eyes gaze out once more. He slowly returned himself into his seat while Eric tentatively backed up. "It's Tam," Fin rasped.

Eric's tense expression eased fractionally.

"Someone is sick. He's terrified they're going to die."

"What exactly did you hear and see?" Eric pressed while trying to suppress his own apprehension.

"A Zinferan woman was saying something about someone named Luca having an infection in his lungs… Eli was beside Tam."

Eric straightened and rubbed his mouth. "Was there anything about Tam's surroundings that could tell you where he might be?"

Fin squinted. His mind was already growing sluggish from using such a powerful part of his ability. "They were in a small cottage. I think they were by the sea or ocean… I could smell the salt in the air."

Blinking in confusion Eric couldn't help but blurt, "Tam isn't supposed to be anywhere near the sea or ocean while in Zinfera. He was supposed to be in the desert."

"I know." Interlocking his fingers, Fin dropped his gaze to the table and struggled to swallow down the hard lump in his throat. "He's more terrified than he's ever been in his life. Whoever isn't doing well is incredibly important to him."

Eric was quiet for a breath, as Fin felt his insides rattle with concern, fear, and sadness. His son was struggling, and he wasn't anywhere nearby to help.

"He's an Ashowan. Things will be alright," the king said in an obvious attempt to bolster his friend's spirits.

"Eric, imagine one of your own sons…" Fin trailed off and shook his head, unable to finish the thought. "Tam is different. Everything is harder for him because of his magic, and he just never seemed to find his own place. I was hoping this trip would help him, but now he's in some kind of trouble."

The king said nothing.

With his new insight into Tam's present, Fin realized that his son had perhaps found his own place if he'd discovered someone who meant so much to him, but still…

Eric rested a hand on Fin's shoulder and said, "Let's go to bed. Hopefully we'll hear word that Kat has arrived in Zinfera, and then she can help find Tam."

Tam sat outside the cottage staring at the Tinoo Ocean. His elbows were braced on his knees, his hands loosely clasped in front of himself.

They needed a physician.

Which meant they'd have no choice but to steal a boat and try to sail around Zinfera once Luca was better, even though Jeong barely knew how to sail and neither he nor Eli had the faintest clue.

Tam dropped his chin to his chest and tried to force another solution into his mind. But it was difficult to think of anything other than Luca. The old woman who owned the cottage, who had kindly let Luca rest in one of her children's old beds, had told Tam that if he didn't get help, the boy would die.

Jeong was already off in the town of Eusa getting the physician.

Eli, after resting a cold cloth on Luca's head, had gone to harvest vegetables for dinner with Hajung, the old man who had begrudgingly accepted them into his home.

Tam had parked himself on a bench pressed against the wall of the cottage, just below the bedroom window where Luca was sleeping. It gave him both a moment to himself as well as a place to keep a close ear out for Luca if he woke up or needed something.

The sound of the front door gently closing drew Tam's attention to Sua. She stood in a plain gray cotton dress; a vivid red apron tied around her waist had chickens embroidered on the bottom edge.

Tam's mouth almost twitched at the sight.

"Your son sleeps well. The physician will have him recovering quickly. He is a very good healer," she informed him bluntly.

Sua's matter of fact way of talking was both hard to take and yet simple enough that it was easy to digest what she said.

"Thank you again. For helping us."

"He is a kind child."

Tam's throat felt swollen as he nodded and looked back toward the ocean.

The old woman rounded Tam to sit beside him.

"It is frightening when the little ones get sick. He will recover, though."

Tam nodded again, but he felt the threat of tears building back behind his eyes.

"It is a different empire than it used to be," Sua started idly, seemingly changing the topic. "There is much fear, and people are not certain what is happening to the emperor."

Tam held his tongue.

"Have you been in Zinfera long?" she ventured mildly.

"A few months."

Sua didn't respond straightaway. Gulls crying overhead drew her attention upward.

"You should return home swiftly," she said in her same matter-of-fact manner.

"I know. It isn't safe for my son here."

"Do you need a boat?"

Tam's head whipped around.

She stared somberly at him. "My son is a fisherman. He can take you to Bani if you need to find passage home."

Tam's expression stilled, and Sua's sharp eyes caught it.

Whether or not she assumed they were wanted criminals, or that they could not risk traveling out of Bani, he wasn't certain, but he didn't feel like it was a good idea to offer clarity.

"I see." Sua became quiet once more.

Nothing more was said.

Tam could practically hear the pounding feet of Zinferan soldiers down the dirt road. In reality it was just his heart hammering against his chest.

If he wanted any chance of getting home, he'd have to hurt a lot of people and he would, without a doubt, be put on trial in Daxaria and possibly jailed as a result.

Or.

He let the Zinferans take him, and risk Eli and Luca getting hurt.

Something stirred inside Tam at that second option, and he discovered that if he was forced to choose, he knew what he would do.

"I am sorry we had to burden you," Tam said to Sua. Dark thoughts were swelling in his mind.

Sua regarded his profile then looked out over the sea. "I do not know much, but I do know you are a good father, and I can appreciate that. I hope whatever you choose to do going forward is a choice your son would be proud to see you make."

Tam's head slowly turned to her.

"I've seen my fair share of desperate men. And they are not nearly as fearsome as a desperate father," she explained distantly.

Tam couldn't comment, though he felt some unpleasant whirling guilt and dread in his gut.

"I'll go check on Luca." He stood.

"There is only one beast more fearsome than a desperate father that you should know of."

Tam glanced back at Sua, though it was surprisingly harder than he would've liked.

"A desperate mother is by far the most vicious of beasts. So whatever it is you choose to do, try to make it so that Luca's mother does not reach that point. Whatever sins you are willing to commit for your son, I guarantee your wife would go further. Empires collapse under such creatures. Just as ours is about to do."

Unable to process Sua's warning in light of his emotional turmoil, Tam headed back into the cottage, though he doubted he would be forgetting her words anytime soon.

CHAPTER 10
DINNERTIME DRINKS

Tam stared at the table laden with freshly washed carrots, bok choy, green onions, and celery. Beside the vegetables was some ginger root, and sitting in a pot, freshly caught and plucked, was a chicken.

The physician had only recently left, meaning Tam had just come back from hiding behind the shed, and Luca was fast asleep.

"You know how to cut vegetables?" Sua asked crisply, her hands on her hips.

A wry smile passed across Tam's face before he darted a brief look at Jeong and Eli. They pointedly looked elsewhere as they, too, fought back knowing grins.

They were all feeling significantly better. Luca had received medicine, and as Jeong had relayed to everyone, the physician believed the boy would be feeling right as rain within a few days, though he'd most likely have a lingering cough for another week or two.

"Sua, I was planning on making the whole dinner for you and your husband to show my thanks."

Sua's gaze narrowed. "You can cook?"

"It'd be incredibly strange if I couldn't."

The woman turned to Eli. She clearly wanted to ask about why Tam would say such a thing, but instead she said, "What about you? Do you cook?"

Eli shook her head. "Not at all."

Sua fell silent.

"How about you and Hajung sit outside with a glass of rice wine, or whatever liquor you have, and enjoy the evening?" Tam proposed with a half smile.

Sua frowned, but Hajung, who was still drying his neck off after washing it with a damp towel by the back window, interjected. "Come, Sua. It's not like there is anything to steal."

Sua's finger tapped her upper arm once, and then she turned to leave—though she did reach into a cabinet beside the front door and pull out a stack of cups before following her husband outside. The sun was casting its final moments of light over the water, promising a brilliant sunset.

When the door closed, both Eli and Jeong turned to Tam, who was already picking up the knife.

Tam looked at Eli. "Did you see where she keeps the garlic?"

She nodded. "It's in the bowl behind you."

"Great." Tam laid everything out before himself.

"Is there anything we can do to help?" Jeong asked with a faint chuckle.

Tam shook his head. "Oh no, I've been trained in cooking since I was seven years old. You two could probably just go join Sua and Hajung outside."

Eli and Jeong looked at each other and shrugged. Jeong gestured toward the exit. "Might as well."

Hesitating only a moment, Eli proceeded out of the cozy cottage, the rushing waves on the nearby beach growing momentarily louder as she opened the door and stepped over the threshold.

Jeong cast a wink at Tam then followed behind her.

Tam smiled back and started to work on peeling the garlic.

It was a nice, familiar task. Cooking a meal was something Finlay Ashowan had made his children do at least once a week for years. Sometimes they'd all cook as a family—save for his mother, the duchess, who instead sat nearby with a stiff drink in hand. Tam recalled how his father had always believed cooking to be a spiritual experience.

While not quite as reverent about the act as Finlay Ashowan, Tam did find it the perfect way to occupy his mind and busy his hands as a kind of meditative practice.

And so he lost himself to the task, humming on occasion or uttering things like “Oops, get back in there.” Or, “Get. Off. That.” when his chopped green onions stubbornly stuck to the knife’s blade.

The repetitive crash of the waves outside and the lowering sun all slowly helped Tam to breathe again. Soon he felt calmer than he had in days, and so he allowed himself to think over his present situation, as well as how best to plan for the future.

The physician may have alerted someone about a foreign boy being there, and so every day from now on was a risk. Hell, soldiers could already be on the way.

Tam’s anxiety hummed in his chest with renewed vigor, until the potent aroma of the broth he was stirring changed, and drew his focus as he removed the pot from its place over the fire using two towels that Sua had set out.

He stared at the colorful hearty soup with a satisfied smile before he grabbed a ladle and eased some liquid and vegetables into it. The sweet carrots, the zingy ginger, the savory chicken…

His mouth watered.

After weeks of roasting whatever wild animal Eli had hunted for them, to have such a well-seasoned meal was heavenly. Steam curled off the broth. After blowing on the liquid to cool it, Tam took a sip. “Hm. Needs more salt.”

“Dad?”

Tam nearly leapt out of his skin.

“Luca!” he gasped when he registered his son’s pale face staring up at him in confusion.

“What’re you doing?” Luca asked before reaching up to rub his right eye.

“Making us all dinner. How’re you feeling?” Tam hurriedly put the ladle back in the pot and gave Luca his full attention.

“Better!” Luca smiled up at Tam, and the future duke felt like he would cry again out of pure relief.

Crouching, Tam wordlessly pulled his son into a hug, then kissed the side of his head. “Thank the Gods,” he said, his voice hitching.

It took a while, but eventually the father and son were forced to part when the front door opened and Jeong stumbled in.

"Smells good in here! Is, uh, is dinner— Luca!" Jeong greeted after slurring most of his words with his cheeks pink.

Tam could tell the Zinferan was a tad inebriated.

"Dinner is ready, yes. I take it you all are enjoying the sunset?"

"We *hic* are!" Jeong's smile suddenly turned devious. "I've never seen Eli drunk before, but Sua keeps making her drink even though we haven't even been out there that long."

Tam barely fought off a snort of laughter as he straightened. "She's drunk?"

"Come see for yourself. Luca, how about you help me bring out bowls for everyone, hm? You look like you've gotten a bit of strength back!"

Sheathing his mouth with his elbow, Luca loosed a terrible wet cough before nodding.

As it turned out, the group had not been enjoying their beverages at the front of the house where they could watch the ocean, but were in the backyard sitting at a low table they must have moved over for the occasion.

When Tam found them, Sua waved to him happily. It surprised him, as the woman had generally been quite standoffish.

"Why don't you come join us for a drink! Your wife here is holding up quite well!" Hajung chortled as he tossed a handful of raspberries into his mouth.

Tam's eyes moved to Eli. She was flushed and swaying, her hair sticking up oddly as though she'd been running her hand through it.

"Dinner is ready," he informed Sua and Hajung. "Jeong can help fill your bowls if you'd like to go tell him how much you'd like."

Eli turned to face him, then squinted. He guessed she was seeing perhaps two or three of him.

"Help yourself to the drink. We always make plenty." Hajung pushed himself to his feet and shuffled past Tam. Sua followed closely behind him, wearing a coy smile.

Tam bobbed his head in thanks, then strode over to Eli, who was struggling to uncross her legs and set her feet on the ground. He watched her do this, and, once he was absolutely certain he'd heard the front door close, he drew closer.

"Are you a little drunk?" Tam couldn't keep the smile from his face.

Eli's head flopped back so that she could stare up at him, and her eyebrows twitched. "I'mm fiiiiine!"

"Are you now?" Tam casually plunked himself down on her left. "Luca's awake and feeling a lot better."

"That'ss so—so good! I'm so relieeved!" Eli declared exuberantly.

"Mm-hm. I'm glad for it as well.. I'm hoping that if no soldiers come for us, we can take off heading east and track down a fishing boat along the way."

"That'd be good." Eli reached up and scratched the side of her head clumsily before turning to stare at Tam again. "You're… really handsome."

He laughed. "Why do you sound annoyed by that?"

"Because it *is* annoying."

Unsure how to handle receiving such a strange compliment, Tam awkwardly reached up and pinched the bridge of his nose. "Sorry about that."

"You can't help it. But it'ss… It's *sso* annoying." Eli gave a derisive snort.

"Ah. I'll try to do better on that front. Is there anything else about me that annoys you?" he ventured while planting his palms on the table so that he could lean back and stretch his legs out.

"A loooot of stuff, but I shouldn't, shouldn't tell you that, because people who… who love each other don't, don't do that!"

Tam's humored expression froze as he looked at her in surprise. "Eli, are you saying you love me while being wildly intoxicated?"

"There you go! Being annoying! Can't just let me… Let me sssay stuff. You have to be the kind of… kind of guy that *listens* to women. Puh." She tossed her head.

Tam blinked and tried not to laugh. "I'll work on that flaw as well. Anything else?"

"You're juss' so… so… respectful! Don't you want to—to have sex?"

Tam was grateful that he wasn't drinking anything as he was certain he would've spit it out when Eli launched that question at him like an arrow straight for his heart, or maybe it was an arrow directed elsewhere.

"Uh. Yes. Yes, I do want to do that. With you. A lot. But you asked me to go slow. We are going slow."

"*You* want a thousand babies! So why won't you—"

"Oh. Oh, no. No, no. I do not want a thousand babies. I was teasing you before!" Tam leaned forward and tried lowering his voice in the hope that Eli would maybe do the same, though he could feel heat warming his cheeks.

"Nooo! You want that! Admit it! You looove having Luca, an' you want more. You're the type!"

"There's a type?"

"Yeah. The good-dad type. The happiest-being-a-father… type."

"Eli? Look at me."

The Zinferan princess took her time, but eventually she did manage to roll her head in Tam's direction and stare at him.

Well… kind of stare.

It looked like she was about to go cross-eyed.

Tam decided to help her, and so he lowered his face to hers and cupped her cheeks in his hands gently.

"I will have as many children as you want. And yes, I want you in my bed one day, and not with Luca between us. But we are on the run from an empire's army and a coven of witches, and we have only just started this relationship. So I am not rushing you. Especially when we have no… contraceptive measures."

Eli leaned her face into Tam's left hand. "What if *I* want a bunch of children?"

"Then Gods help you, you'll get them very quickly," Tam assured her, though he was starting to feel his struggle with reason and desire resurface as the conversation progressed.

"Well. I do. I want five."

Tam's mind went blank. "You want five children? Even though you are wildly particular and a bit of a perfectionist?"

"Mmm. Yeah. Yeah I do. Though Luca counts as one."

Tam sighed. "I'm going to have to ask you about this when you're sober."

"Go ahead! It's what I want!" Eli straightened herself and lifted her nose into the air indignantly.

Tam couldn't help it, he chuckled.

"You think that it's funny?" she accused.

"A little! Not that I won't be happy to oblige you, but can I ask why specifically four more?"

Eli stared up at the darkening sky and didn't answer straight away.

Tam wondered if she had maybe forgotten the question and was about to suggest they go grab some dinner when she finally responded.

"I didn't think I could be a good mother… 'cause of my mother bein' awful. An' then… then I spent time with Luca, and I think I could. And my-my parentsss had four kids, an' I just think… I could have the right family."

Tam listened, his heart aching as he recognized the longing in Eli's voice.

But then she decided to utterly undo him by saying, "Besides, there should be more people like you in the world."

Feeling both uncomfortable and appreciative of the compliment, Tam gently rubbed Eli's back. "You are an amazing woman."

"Tam?"

"Yeah?"

"I think… I might vomit."

"Ah." It was all Tam had time to say before Eli bent from her waist and was sick on the ground.

"Aaah." Tam kept rubbing her back as she retched. "When you're finished, we'll get you some water and soup and I'll put you to bed with Luca. Sound good?"

She vomited some more.

"Yeah… Yeah I think that's the best idea for now."

CHAPTER 11

PUSHING FOR PROGRESS

The cool porcelain pressed against Eli's cheek, drawing her back to her senses as a pained groan crawled out of her throat. Then a heavens-sent cold cloth was pressed to her forehead, and her groan turned to one of relief.

"I figured you'd be in a state this morning." Tam's gentle voice chuckled beside Eli.

She scrunched up her face and rolled onto her side with a grumble while reaching up to clutch the cloth to her head.

"Eli, I need you to be up soon. I want to try something with my magic, and I need you there. Jeong is off in the fields with Hajung helping him with his farmwork. Do you think you can manage to come with me?"

"How's Luca?" she mumbled instead of answering.

"He's helping Sua in the kitchen. He still has a cough, but his fever is staying down. I'll give him a bath later." Tam reached up and stroked Eli's hair as he spoke. Feeling this, Eli stilled, the soothing movements quelling some of the nasty sensations plaguing her. "Sua made a spicy pork bone soup for you. Hajung swears it helps you get through the worst of a hangover."

Eli's mouth instantly watered.

Something told her that this savory spicy treat would set her to rights.

"I also made a cup of ginger tea for you."

"Did you—"

"Yes, I boiled it in the pot. I did not just add boiling water to the cup. You taught me well."

"You're still a tea heathen," Eli grumbled while sitting up, and instantly regretting it as the world briefly spun around her.

"There is no pleasing you," Tam teased while reaching out to rub soothing circles on her back.

At first she wanted to bark at him to not touch her, but after she considered how good it felt, she decided to hold her tongue.

Though she still gave a faint rumble.

"I almost feel like since you've been turning into your other form more often, your catlike tendencies have become more apparent to me."

Turning her head slowly, Eli narrowed her eyes. It hurt to do, but she wanted Tam to see her annoyance.

He merely grinned.

She felt her thoughts sputter as in her weakened state she was confronted with his handsomeness. *Him and his stupid good looks..*

"What is it you want to try with your magic?" Eli asked, hoping to stay indignant for the sake of her pride.

"Well, I was thinking how Lord Kim raised a very interesting line of questions when he identified my magic as ether."

"Such as?"

"Such as, shouldn't I be able to control matter around me? Or the void? What if I can make people or things disappear through it? Is it still as taxing to me? Or can I move things rather than opening and stepping into the void myself?"

Eli's head throbbed, but her heart fluttered with excitement. "That *would* make sense if he was right about your magic."

"It's hard to explain, but I get the sense that he found the appropriate title for my power." As he spoke, Tam's hand casually found its way into Eli's. She gripped it tightly in response.

She normally wouldn't do such a thing. She blamed the hangover. "I see how this would make your abilities wildly powerful and helpful. So yes. Yes, I will get up and go outside."

"After you've eaten," Tam assured firmly.

"After I've eaten," Eli agreed while closing her eyes with a weak smile.

"And after your tea."

"After my tea."

"Thank you." Tam pushed himself halfway out of his crouch, making his knees crack, but he paused nonetheless to brush a kiss against Eli's forehead. "I'll see you out there. Love you."

Caught off guard, Eli blinked, then stared dumbly up at him, his hand still clasped in her own as she lowered the cloth from her forehead. He had every right to be annoyed with her. There was much to do and Luca still wasn't well. Yet here he was doting on her.

"Gods. I don't think I deserve you."

"You deserve someone even better than me," Tam murmured sincerely before once again kissing the top of her head. "How many other women would let me drag them through the wilderness with a seven-year-old, help me plan escape routes, battle corrupt covens… Should I go on?"

"You forgot putting up with your lack of tea knowledge."

Tam chuckled, the warm sound emanating from his throat and his breath tickling Eli's forehead. "Ah. My greatest sin aside from my alleged attractiveness, according to you."

Eli's eyes rounded. "Oh. Did I say that out loud last night?" Tam chortled again in response. "Oh no. Gods, no!" She buried her face in the damp cloth.

"Mm-hm. I'm still curious to hear confirmation about these four extra children you'd like to have."

"Nnngah!"

Tam, laughing heartily, gave his poor lady a final kiss on the head then headed toward the door. "See you outside, dear one."

Eli flopped back on the single bed and turned on her side, her cheeks burning against the cold cloth. She wouldn't have been surprised if there were steam coming from it.

Gods. And to think I chose the milder-mannered Ashowan..

Standing outside among the rows of raspberry bushes, far enough from the cottage and from where Hajung and Jeong were working so the farmers would not be able to see anything, Eli faced Tam. Between them sat an empty steel bucket.

"Alright. I'm going to first try to topple the bucket over," Tam announced, his skepticism of his own abilities apparent in his tone.

"How exactly are you planning on doing it?" Eli asked slowly, her eyes moving from the bucket up to Tam's uncertain face.

"When I'm moving through the void, I often feel, hear, and smell things in the surrounding area. It's how I slowly started to figure out where to go the first few times. But I've never tried interacting with any of the things I've felt."

Eli nodded thoughtfully. "That makes sense. Alright. Go ahead."

"Thank you for your permission."

Eli shot Tam an unimpressed glance while he grinned at her, and then in a fluttering of black, silvery wisps, he disappeared.

She watched the silver bucket, patiently.

Nothing happened.

She waited.

And then…

It shuddered.

Tam reappeared, lying beside it gasping on the ground but otherwise unharmed.

"So it was harder than you thought?" Eli speculated casually.

Tam managed to look up at her, still breathing heavily, unable to answer.

She scratched her nose idly as she waited.

"You know… some assistants… offer their… employers water when they see them… like this," Tam said between his deep breaths while pushing himself up into a sitting position.

"Most assistants don't serve a lord with magic that is still a little unpredictable," Eli reminded him curtly.

Tam draped his arms over his knees. "Holy antlers, that was difficult. Did it move at all?"

"It trembled a little, but that was it."

"Damn. I was really hoping I could do more with it." Tam hung his head, his breathing still quick.

Eli stared pensively at the bucket. "Can you make other things disappear without touching them?"

Squinting against the sun as he stared up at Eli, Tam processed her question before responding.

"Never tried."

"Could you try?"

"Now?" Tam's note of exasperation was not lost on Eli.

"Unless you're too weak, of course. My lord."

"How many people know that you are actually a very coldhearted woman?"

Eli's mouth twisted briefly. "Two? Everyone else just thinks I'm the perfect professional."

Tam gave a breathy laugh, then pushed himself up to his feet, closing his eyes. Eli waited. She knew he was centering himself, feeling out his power. A deeper sense in Eli suddenly bristled.

Then a small black dot appeared in the air six feet to her left.

Stepping back in alarm, Eli watched as it started to expand. It stretched wider, and wider, its blackness consuming her view.

"Tam, Tam, whatever you're doing, stop!" She grabbed his arm.

Tam's eyes snapped open, and he jolted at the sight of the gaping hole in front of himself.

"I-I don't know exactly how to—"

"Do *something!*"

"Give me a moment!" He closed his eyes again.

The hole spread an additional two feet wide.

"You just made it bigger."

Panic rose in Eli, along with the alarming sense that the fabric of the world around her was about to dissolve entirely.

"Tam!"

The void rushed at them, and Eli gave a short shriek as she flinched against it. Her body hummed with adrenaline. When they were consumed, however, Eli merely felt as though a cool breeze had ruffled her hair, though the loss of her surroundings made her dizzy.

Looking around, Eli gaped at the void she had heard so much about.

Nothing was beneath her feet, and she was surrounded by blackness. A light from an unknown source overhead illuminated Tam at her side. And he was glowing. His eyes were now open, his face shocked as he realized where they were. He turned to her dumbfounded.

Eli cleared her throat. "This is the strangest thing I've ever seen. It even *feels* disturbing. Almost like being squeezed through a tube and then evaporated. Oomph. The hangover isn't… helping matters."

Tam seemed to only be half listening, however, as he looked down at himself.

A golden, almost orange hue encompassed his being.

"Gods. I almost look like my sister," he murmured to himself softly.

Eli would've asked what he meant, but a cold flush swept over her. "Tam, if I vomit in here, where will it go?"

Evidently caught off guard, Tam didn't reply quickly enough.

Sadly, Eli couldn't wait any longer, and so she doubled over and emptied the contents of her stomach all over the nothing-ground.

And that was how both Tam and Eli learned firsthand that puking in the void was much like getting sick in the normal world, only you then knew that in some corner of everything on a Zinferan raspberry farm, there was a splatter of sick that was really difficult to find and clean up.

Eli also learned that spicy soup going down actually hurt quite a lot coming back up.

CHAPTER 12

A HELLISH HELLO

The duchess stood under the blistering Zinferan sun with her arms folded."Anything?"

"He's alive."

"Thank the Gods."

Katarina opened her eyes as she listened to her mother's sigh of relief and the sound of crew members' boots pounding down the gangplank as they unloaded the ship.

An impressively ornate carriage sat waiting, along with a long line of servants sent from the palace to receive the Daxarian queen.

It had been a particularly expedient journey to Zinfera to the three wind witches from the Coven of Wittica and a water witch to ensure that any storms they encountered could be managed.

"Have you received word from Jiho Ryu?" Kat asked as she turned away from the ship's rail to make her way over to the gangplank.

The moment the ship had docked, she had been trying to feel her magical connection with Tam. She'd struggled to feel it during their voyage to Zinfera.

"I did. But you know your father's friend. He did not disclose everything in the missive for safety purposes, but it sounds as though your brother and Eli are in a significant amount of danger. His second son, Jeong, is still with them as well."

Kat bobbed her head. "Will Jiho come to Gondol?"

"That would not be wise for Jiho, so I doubt it very much."

"Why is it not wise?"

"Her Highness Soo Hebin does not like him, and if we remind her that we are close with his family, it will not serve us well as we try to learn what is happening. By all accounts, Soo Hebin is prideful. It will be bad enough that she will have to lower herself to you."

A wolfish smile tugged at the corners of Katarina's mouth. "I do love terrible people with too much pride. They're easy to torment. And with *him* traveling to Zinfera to help us, it isn't like we'll be her favorite people anyway."

"You are a queen now," Annika reminded her sharply. "The fate of Daxaria's people, whom you protect, rests on how well you can conduct yourself. As for the man the king had join us, he is outside my control. It's good we traveled separately, and that he is in Bani now."

"I'm not going to be a pushover to this Soo Hebin woman," Kat interjected, drawing her mother back to the topic of the corrupt concubine.

"You leave Soo Hebin to me. Acknowledge her, but say as little as possible," Annika counseled, her voice still carrying an edge at the thought that her daughter might lapse into more mischievous antics.

"You really do know how to douse my fun," Kat said with a sigh as she touched down onto the dock then turned to offer her mother her hand.

The duchess's gaze narrowed at the gesture.

Kat waggled her eyebrows. "I get to wear trousers and help my aging mother down a gangplank. Deal with it."

"I will shove you into the sea and make it look like an accident," Annika informed her coolly.

"Pfft. I'd just grab a bit of seaweed and wear it as a scarf the rest of the trip. Try me."

Annika closed her eyes wearily. "I forgot what a calming influence your children have been."

"Yep. And now I'm a free woman on the hunt for your own favorite child."

"I have no favorites. I love you both." Annika's eyes snapped open furiously to scold her daughter for saying such an awful thing, but the sudden look on Kat's face stopped her.

"What?"

Kat slowly moved over to a young dockhand handing out flyers to sailors as they passed him.

Snatching one of them, Kat's eyes bore into the page intently before she looked up at her mother.

"Kat?"

"Mum… Did Eli or Brendan Devark happen to mention that she was actually a princess?"

The duchess's stricken face answered her daughter's question. Kat brandished the wanted page at her mother, who gripped it with her eyes flying over the picture and the text beneath it.

"I think my brother and his assistant are in a great deal more trouble than we bargained for."

"Godsdamnit," Annika managed breathily. "That was why. That was why Eli didn't want to come back."

"Why *did* she come back here if this was a risk? Eric offered her the chance to stay," Kat whispered urgently as she noticed out of the corner of her eye a royal Zinferan attendant drawing closer to greet them.

"I don't know. Bloody hell. This is… Godsdamnit, we need to find them quickly."

"Your Majesty Katarina Reyes, and Your Grace Annika Ashowan. I greet and honor you on behalf of our Zinferan emperor." The steward stopped a few feet in front of the mother and daughter and bowed deeply, his bright-orange shirt eye-catching amid the sea of dirty cream, white, and black tunics flooding around him.

Regardless of the shock Annika Ashowan had just received, her expression transformed miraculously quickly into calm composure as she lowered her chin in acknowledgment of the man.

He then gestured to the carriage awaiting them.

Giving her mother another look, Kat stepped forward, her hand gripping the hilt of her sword, her mood thoroughly blackened.

It didn't help that she could feel unseen eyes following her, and a little voice in the back of her mind started to warn her that things were going to be incredibly, *terribly* messy during her stay in Zinfera.

"Thank you, again, for helping us." Tam bowed to Sua and Hajung, who stood in their kitchen.

Sua had her arms crossed, a wooden spoon in hand, and Hajung appeared to just be waking up.

"We didn't help you. We just ignored a couple of strangers and took their money," Sua argued curtly.

"Bye, Sua." Luca darted forward from Eli's side and wrapped his arms around the woman's waist.

Tam, Eli, and Jeong all smiled as they watched Sua's resolute stoniness crack. She lifted her wrinkled hand to pat Luca's silky black hair.

"I'll miss your tarts," the boy murmured into her middle.

"It's good you're leaving. You've eaten through most of our stock. I take it you'll be as tall as your father one day." Sua gave a suspicious sniff as Luca finally released her then moved over to hug Hajung.

"Truly. Thank you. We'll continue our journey and steer clear of your village so as not to bring you any trouble," Tam added warmly.

Sua gave a short jerk of her chin in acknowledgment as Luca returned to Eli's side and grasped her hand.

"I do appreciate you helping Hajung with his crop," Sua said to Jeong, who smiled and bowed. "Now get on. And good luck getting home."

Tam turned to the cottage exit, cast a smile at Jeong to confirm he was also ready to go, and opened the door for Eli and his son.

"Are we going to do a lot more walking?" Luca asked, drawing Eli's attention at the faint whine in his voice.

"Yes. We already told you that—"

"Well." A breathy, indignant voice stopped Eli dead in her tracks.

Iciness filled her blood.

"Elisara, to think a child of mine should wed a peasant and bear his child. Gods… The shame."

Eli sensed Tam stepping out behind her, Jeong following, as they took in the scene.

A Daxarian woman whose auburn hair was heavily streaked with gray stood wearing a bejeweled purple dress very much like the styles worn back in Daxaria. Though the older Zinferan man standing behind her wore a matching color, his own clothes were distinctly Zinferan.

Beyond the couple there was a giant cage on wheels fit for moving something the size of a horse. Twenty armed men stood lined up in front of the pure white carriage that sat waiting.

"Pardon me, but who are—" Tam started, but he was interrupted by Eli who croaked.

"Mother."

Tam stiffened at Eli's side, and he turned to look at her. He instantly saw her soul-deep pain. Her watering gaze didn't leave the woman's face.

"Come along. If you come peacefully you can ride in the carriage with us. You—" Marigold Nam lifted her nose disdainfully at Tam. "—take your runt and forget she exists."

"He is not a runt!" Eli suddenly shouted. "He's my son, and you can go to *hell!* You aren't my mother anymore, remember? You sold me off to the emperor!"

Tam had never heard Eli speak so emotionally. He realized the intense trauma from her past had managed to break through the fortress she maintained around her feelings. Witnessing a portion of her broken heart tortured him a little inside to see.

"I made you a princess in a palace. Cry about it in the carriage. I brought a silk dress for you to change in. Her Highness Soo Hebin is very generous in allowing you to return to court. Now come along." Marigold waved her daughter's impassioned words off as though they were mere fruit flies.

"Soo Hebin is the one who *sold me* into slavery!" Eli moved forward, furious tears gathering thickly in her eyes.

"Enough with your theatrics. It's bad enough we had to leave Bani to come get you." Marigold sighed before leaning to the side to stare at Jeong. "You look familiar. Why?"

Jeong said nothing, but his eyes did move to Tam out of concern.

Back in the kitchen, Tam could hear Sua and Hajung whispering.

This was bad.

Horribly bad.

Tam immediately started trying to calculate if he could magic all four of them into the void, but he was still pretty tired from his experiment with the bucket from the previous day.

Oh Gods. He actually might have to reveal his identity. Which would raise all kinds of political problems as to why someone of his class was in Zinfera sneaking around. The incident at the docks would most likely be connected to him shortly thereafter.

Damnit. I could lie and say I wanted to elope with Eli. Or that we already got married. Or—

Marigold let out another irritated huff, then curled her finger lazily, drawing her husband forward.

Lord Geun Nam looked every bit as inconvenienced as his wife did, and he couldn't even bring himself to look at his daughter despite not having laid eyes on her in more than a decade. "Elisara, you will do as your mother says and get in the carriage, or we will make you ride in the cage."

Rational thought left Tam's head as he drew himself up to his full height and stared daggers at Lord Nam. He was preparing himself to tell Eli's parents that they could try to force her into the cage, but they wouldn't be alive shortly thereafter, when Eli spoke again.

"Gods. How can you be so awful at something so easy?" Her voice rasped.

Marigold's eyes glittered. "I beg your pardon?"

"You… You are the worst parents I have ever met. You once said you couldn't love me, Father, because I was a girl. And because I was your firstborn? I'd shamed you. Then you, Mother, said you couldn't forgive me for making Father angry at you. And when I got my magic, you said I was an animal and not allowed to be around my siblings."

Tam's murderous impulses were becoming quite potent.

"You said loving me was hard. And so you sometimes let yourselves forget to do it, because otherwise..." Eli paused, licking her lips that were becoming dehydrated from the tears and snot that streamed down her face. "Otherwise you'd leave me in a street somewhere and hope I'd die without adding dishonor to the family."

Luca looked up at Eli, tears rising in his own eyes. Behind Tam, he could hear Jeong's sharp intake of breath.

Tam was barely able to notice over the intense buzzing in his being how Luca leaned his head against Eli's side, tightening his grip on her hand. Upon seeing Marigold roll her eyes in response to her daughter's words, Tam brought himself back to stand at Eli's side.

He watched the way Eli's breath came out more slowly, and he could tell she wasn't through with them just yet.

"I have Luca now, and because of him, I see it isn't hard. It isn't hard at all to love a child. It's the easiest thing in the world. Unfortunately you two are just some of the worst people I know."

An impressive steadiness settled over Eli when she next looked at her mother.

"I have Luca and his father. I have my family. Don't ever say you're related in any capacity to me again."

"Are you quite finished with your tantrum?" Marigold tilted her head as Lord Nam jerked his chin at the armed men behind him, setting them into motion.

Lord Geun Nam reached out as though to seize Eli's arm. "Elisara, you really should—"

Tam's hand shot out and caught the man's throat in a vise grip.

"You will tell them not to move a step closer," he informed Marigold softly, his dark eyes ominously calm.

Marigold stumbled back in surprise and fear. It took her a moment to heed Tam's order, but it didn't really matter. The armed men seemed to have a decent enough understanding of the situation, and had already stopped their advance.

"You aren't going to be taking Eli anywhere," Tam continued evenly. "I will be taking her, my son, and our friend here with me. You can leave as well, and pretend you never saw us. *Or* things are going to get very, *very* unpleasant."

Lord Nam was turning purple as he tried to claw at Tam's hand.

Marigold gave a single nod, and Tam released the nobleman.

Coughing and gasping, Lord Nam stumbled back while waving his arm forward at the men, ushering them to attack.

Tam kept his sights on Marigold. "I'm assuming it was Yun, your son's assistant, who is responsible for alerting the concubine to Eli's presence. And I'm guessing it is because he thinks he can get something as a result. I'm *also* guessing that he told you I'm most likely a witch. So, I will say this again. We will leave here without any trouble. Or I will be your *last* problem."

Marigold sidled over to her husband, resting a hand on his back as he gradually managed to straighten and regain his breath.

The Zinferan nobleman openly seethed at Tam. "We did not come alone," Lord Nam spluttered haughtily. "Daxaria sent their own coven members, and as you are from there, I know you will have to answer to them. Besides, if you hurt a Daxarian duke, that would immediately give you the death penalty."

Tam had started getting excited at the news that members of the Coven of Wittica were coming. It meant they were saved! But then he balked. "Duke? Finlay Ashowan is here?"

Marigold's nose scrunched up as though someone had wiped poo on her upper lip.

"No. It is Duke Os—"

A new voice called out, "Well, well, well. I'll be *damned*. Fancy. Meeting. *You*. Here. And on the day after I arrive, no less!"

Tam's head snapped round to look to his right.

It turned out that there happened to be an additional twenty men surrounding the cottage that he hadn't seen drawing closer.

But he paid their appearance no attention, because swaggering casually over to him away from the other soldiers, with his sword sheathed and resting against his shoulder, was none other than Duke Oscar Harris.

One of Finlay Ashowan's closest friends, who also happened to know Tam *very* well.

CHAPTER 13
HARK THE HARRIS

"What are you doing?" Lord Nam barked at Harris—technically his brother-in-law—as he stopped in front of Tam, wearing his usual shit-eating grin.

"Taking in the sights!" Oscar Harris called breezily over his shoulder. "I haven't seen this fine fellow in what feels like *years!* Goodness! Do you know the commotion you have caused?" The Daxarian duke bopped Tam on the head with his sheathed blade, his hazel eyes sparkling with fun.

Eli stared skeptically at the man. He was shorter and in his early fifties with white curly hair and a slight paunch in the middle, wearing the most ridiculous set of mismatched clothes she had ever seen in her life: baggy mustard-yellow pants and a bright-red-and-blue-striped shirt that for some reason had small bells sewn on the lapels.

Tam didn't even need to look at Eli to know what she was thinking.

Is this person an idiot?

"You know this man?" Marigold asked in domineering tones. Her vulturish gaze locked back on Tam.

Lord Harris's attention on the other hand didn't shift an inch from Tam. "Oh yes. I've known this *delightful* man since he was a babe. Glad to see you've gotten into a bit of trouble! I was worried you'd miss out on life, the way you always kept to yourself."

"My sister lived enough for fifty people," Tam managed while staring dazedly at the nobleman who had dubbed himself Tam and Kat's godfather long ago.

"Nonsense! She's as docile as a newborn lamb!"

The situation was so absurd, Tam couldn't even laugh at such an outrageous statement. Though knowing Oscar Harris's antics, the man was most likely sincere.

"What are you doing here?" Tam asked faintly.

"Ah. Well, our wise former king made a special request that I accompany a few important family members to Zinfera, seeing as I have my own dear relations here. Don't I, Marigold?"

"Stop being aggravating and tell me who this person is!" Marigold all but shrieked before addressing their armed entourage. "Take them!"

Duke Harris held up his hand. The forty armed men around them only took a single step.

"Dear, darling, sister, that would be the stupidest thing in the world you could do. Do you really have no idea who this is?" Lord Harris pointed at Tam while casting a beaming smile at Marigold.

"No, because you won't tell me!"

"Really? You don't see the resemblance he has to some of your favorite people in the world?" Lord Harris taunted joyfully.

The look on both Marigold's and Geun's faces almost succeeded in making Tam laugh.

Lord Harris truly did love enraging his half sister, and in that moment, Tam was enjoying it quite a bit as well.

The Daxarian duke turned back to Tam, then looked down at Eli.

"I take it you are my niece? Elisara? Ah, that's why you avoided me like the plague back in Daxaria! No one knew who you were, and there was a possibility I would've recognized you. And here I'd felt bad that my godson's new assistant was too terrified to meet me, but now it makes all the sense in the world!"

"I beg your pardon; did you say godson?" Marigold interrupted, her eyes wild.

"Ssh. I'm catching up with my beloved niece whom you heartlessly abandoned, you wench. Anyway!" Lord Harris regarded Tam again, then dropped his eyes to the seven-year-old boy holding both Eli's and Tam's hands.

"Aah… Uh. Tam. I did not think I'd have a whole lot of fun on this trip, but I have to offer you my heartfelt thanks in advance. Apparently I was woefully wrong. Who is this young chap who just so happens to look just like you, hm?" Lord Harris batted his eyelashes at Tam expectantly.

Tam swallowed with difficulty.

Of all the things he had anticipated doing that day, officially revealing he had an illegitimate son to Lord Oscar Harris was not one of them.

"He's… mine."

"Aah! I see, I see. Yes. Well. Trouble I'm having with that is, last I saw you, say… What? Two months ago? Three, perhaps? You not only were unmarried, but you didn't have any children to speak of."

"He tracked me down on the ship with a letter from a former…" Tam trailed off and cleared his throat.

Even the infamously flippant Lord Haris's eyebrows shot upward. "Oh. Oh my. Oh, this is. By. The. Gods. Your father will—No! No, it is your mother! *She* will be the one to kill you! I've always suspected she was capable of outrageously awful things!"

Tam winced then glanced down at his son, who looked ten different levels of confused. "Luca, this is Duke Oscar Harris. He is a very good friend of our family."

"Oscar! What in the Gods is happening?" Marigold exploded and stormed forward. Eli backed away from her and wrapped her arm protectively around Luca's shoulders.

Lord Harris shot Tam a wry look. "It's always the quiet ones that surprise people," he murmured before holding a hand to stop his sister from advancing any closer.

Marigold was practically frothing at the mouth. "Are you jesting again? Trying to catch them off guard? If so, stop this! We need to—"

"Woman!" Lord Harris cut off Marigold's tirade. "Show some respect! You're looking at the future duke of the Ashowan duchy, brother to the queen of Daxaria, and… probably your son-in-law? I'm lost on the state of your relationship. We'll talk in a moment," Lord Harris added more kindly to Tam and Eli at the end.

Lord Nam drew closer as well, his eyes bulging as he looked at Lord Oscar Harris, then at Tam in disbelief. "What?"

"Come now, I know you're not deaf. You run from my bells when I try to join you for coffee. You hear me just fine. This is Lord Tamlin Ashowan!" Lord Harris swung back to address Tam, who was starting to feel a bit queasy. "By the Gods, everyone is worried about you! And here you are gallivanting around Zinfera on a backpacking trip with your new paramour, your son, and—I'm sorry, who are you?" Oscar squinted at Jeong, having finally noticed him standing just behind Tam and Eli.

Jeong looked at Tam, who gave his head a shake.

"From an important family, I take it? Don't want to be associated with whatever disaster this"—Lord Harris waved his hand vaguely around Tam's face—"has most likely caused?"

"Lord Harris. I wasn't supposed to let anyone know that I—" Tam began, but was cut off in short order.

"Lad." Lord Harris reached up to clap a hand on Tam's shoulder. "This kingdom, and everywhere else for that matter, is in utter chaos. The fact that you're suddenly here is not even going to stick out in anyone's memory."

"I doubt that very much," Tam responded weakly.

"You…" Marigold Nam's breathy voice drew everyone's attention once more. "You are the…"

"—the future duke of the Ashowan house and also viscount of the Jenoure house. That's right. He is. He is also a member of the Coven of Wittica, and last I heard, Elisara is under his protection, yes?"

Tam somehow remembered how to nod.

"Wonderful. Happy for you both. However, that also means"—Lord Harris looked back at his sister—"that unless everyone here wants to make an enemy of the Coven of Wittica, the Ashowan family, *and* the king and queen of Daxaria (which, you know, it's a package deal: If you make an enemy of monarchs, their kingdom is involved, too), we should all conduct ourselves *very* nicely."

Silence hung heavily over everyone.

Lord Harris kept looking back and forth among everyone involved, still grinning, his bells jingling with every turn of his head.

"If you are an Ashowan boy, then you must be a Ryu boy." Marigold nodded in Jeong's direction, but he didn't move an inch.

"You will still have to go to the palace and see Her Highness Soo Hebin! She has ordered—" Lord Nam started.

Lord Harris turned around shaking his head. "Mm. No, no. We are going to have a lovely luncheon right here. And I am going to have a nice, long, uninterrupted chat with my godson, and I will decide from there where he goes."

Lord Harris then made a shooing gesture with his hands, and Tam watched as Lord Nam's teeth clenched. "He tried to kill me."

"You did kind of start it." Lord Harris tilted his head side-to-side.

"He should have identified—"

"By the Gods, shut up and go away. You're amazingly lucky all he did was give you a break from breathing! I've seen this man with a sword! He once beat the Troivackian king in a duel!"

That claim to fame was not at all true, but Tam didn't see the point in saying so just then.

Incredibly, the Zinferan nobleman did close his mouth.

Geun Nam cast one last scathing look at Eli, a look she met head-on, and then he rounded back toward the carriage while gently tapping Marigold's shoulder to indicate she follow him.

Once they were out of earshot, Lord Harris let out a whoosh of air. "Gods. I'm sorry, Elisara. Marigold really is a cow. I should've figured out how to adopt you ages ago!"

This sentiment managed to bring another wave of tears to Eli's eyes. "Thank you."

"Harris?" Tam called out, summoning the duke's attention to him again.

"Hm?"

"I have never been so happy to hear you talk so much."

The duke's unbearably sunny smile returned. "That's the nicest thing you've ever said to me. I will tell your father all about it, too! Assuming my sister doesn't kill me in my sleep while I'm here."

Tam glanced at Marigold Nam, and he sincerely doubted that she would be docile with her brother after this public humiliation.

"So, Tam, care to tell me what you've been up to?" Lord Harris started bouncing on the balls of his feet.

"Er. Well. I was supposed to—"

"I know what you were *supposed* to do, but what did you actually do?"

"Got an army to go after Eli and me, and uncovered deep corruption in the Coven of Giong."

"Hm. Okay. So it wasn't all fun and games. I take it the 'devil' rumors have something to do with you as well?"

"That would be correct."

"Mm-hm, Mm-hm… Okay. Men! Set up a table for me and my godson! And please pour four goblets of wine!" Lord Harris hollered over the gathering crowd.

"Harris?" Tam cleared his throat. "Harris, they are probably going to alert Soo Hebin that I'm here. It'll be problematic. Especially with Eli. She can have her imprisoned."

"Very true. But you're an Ashowan! You'll figure it out! Besides, this outcome is probably better than whatever it was you were thinking of doing before I revealed myself."

Tam wasn't sure about that, but he didn't say so as he watched three servants leave the carriage and start to set up the table that Lord Harris had requested.

Eli tugged on Tam's sleeve, her gaze intent on the back of Lord Harris's head as he started asking what sort of libations had been brought along. "Are you sure we can trust him?"

"Completely. He owes my family a lot," Tam confirmed. "Are you alright?"

Eli's watery gaze turned up to him. "I think so. Though we need a new plan now. My parents aren't going to sit still."

"Excuse me?"

Tam and Eli jumped.

Sua had appeared in the doorway, her wrinkled face shadowed with a frown. "What is the meaning of this?"

"Ah." Tam winced at the mess of people loitering in front of the cottage. "It seems as though we might need the use of your front lawn for a little while more. Apologies, Sua."

The woman's mouth pursed. Tam couldn't blame her. He knew she was just as surprised by this excitement. There was no doubt in his mind that it was someone else that had reported their presence.

Clearing his throat, Tam held up a finger then walked over to Lord Harris, who was pulling golden goblets from a mahogany box. “Do you have any coin on you, Harris? The owners of this land are a bit concerned.”

Lord Harris’s mouth quirked upward ruefully. “Of course! And don’t worry! I will only charge a *modest* interest rate to my only godson.”

Tam sighed but didn’t argue as the man reached into his oversized pants and withdrew three silver coins.

Bobbing his head in thanks, Tam returned to Sua and Hajung and handed them the coins.

Looking only slightly mollified, Sua gave Tam a lingering look as though she were unsure of what to make of him, then turned back into the cottage with her husband and closed the door.

Evidently they were going to be taking the day off from work what with all the strange people milling about their property.

By the time he returned to Lord Harris, he found Eli and Jeong already taking a seat as Harris gestured them into the folded-out chairs.

Luca sat a short way off with one of his geography books, though Tam could tell by the way his eyes were darting nervously at the armed men that he wasn’t doing much actual studying.

“Now then, dear Tam,” Lord Harris started while uncorking a bottle of wine that Tam could tell was outrageously expensive. “Tell me, are you aware that in light of the first witch having escaped from her cell in Troivack, your sister and mother are now here in Zinfera?”

All color drained from Tam’s face. “I was not.”

“Makes sense. Don’t you feel better about having to go to the palace now?”

“Not really.”

Lord Harris’s hazel eyes drifted upward in confusion, until they slid over to Luca sitting on his own on the lush grass. “Ah.”

“Kat is going to assume he’s the devil,” Tam explained.

Lord Harris tilted his head as he finished topping up Jeong’s cup. “Possibly. But he does look incredibly like you, and he doesn’t seem like the source of all evil. He’s reading that book upside down.”

Eli straightened in her seat instantly. “Luca! Chapter four! And turn the book around!”

Lord Harris's eyebrows shot up at the mothering tone that exploded from his niece, then he proceeded to watch as Luca nodded hastily and turned the book in his hands right-side up.

The duke leaned his elbows onto the table. "Frankly, I'm really not feeling all that threatened by him. I'm sure the queen will feel the same."

Tam couldn't help it, he smiled at Eli.

She blushed. "He *is* smart. He's just struggling with reading. I thought geography would be a bit easier for him because of the maps," Eli defended.

Lord Harris held up his hands with a knowing look on his face. "I didn't say a thing. Anyway, Tam, Elisara, and… you?" Lord Harris raised an eyebrow in Jeong's direction, but he didn't receive a response. "We have a problem."

"We have more than just one," Tam pointed out glibly.

"We have a more immediate problem," Lord Harris clarified while lowering his voice even more. "Please tell me you actually married my niece."

Tam looked at Eli, a mixture of guilt and uncertainty in his eyes.

"Shit." Lord Harris sighed regretfully. "I can't protect her as easily without her being tied more closely to you. Soo Hebin can deny her involvement in Eli's abduction. As a princess, regardless of her next move as an heir, Eli needs to go to the emperor's palace. As your wife, that's a whole other matter."

Tam saw the outright panic in Eli's eyes, but luckily, so did Lord Harris.

"So… here is what I'm going to propose to the two of you." He leaned in closer and made his voice so soft that it was almost drowned out by the Tinoo Ocean's waves lapping at the beach. "You have informed me you had a whirlwind romance and got married in Junya. There will be an investigation on this claim, but while that happens, go get yourselves actually married. And I will sing my ignorance of anything to anyone who will listen to it."

Tam grimaced. "Eli doesn't want to marry me, Harris, and I promised my father I wouldn't get married like my sister did without him present."

"I think your father would acknowledge these are not our usual circumstances," Lord Harris pointed out before turning to Eli. "And you, dear Elisara, I am sorry for all you have suffered and endured. For being jerked around and trampled. No one deserves what you've had to put up with, and I do say that from some measure of experience."

It was the first time that day that Jeong, Tam, and Eli could tell he was being utterly serious.

"However, if you are getting out of this kingdom safely and alive? Marrying Tam is the best option for you. Yes, you are under Tam's protection as his assistant, so they won't put you in that cage. But once Tam goes to the palace, there are a lot of larger powers that will be sure to separate you. With Katarina Reyes here, it wouldn't matter if you were a princess as long as you are currently married to her brother, because then you are the next duchess of the Ashowan household, and with the marriage, you become an automatic citizen of Daxaria. Our queen will therefore have every legal tool at her disposal to keep you safe."

Eli swallowed with difficulty.

Tam could see the hesitation in her eyes, and hated it.

He hated how she was once again being forced into something.

He hated even more that it was something that tainted their relationship.

Things had been proceeding perfectly well. Slowly, yes. And sure, they talked about their future children, but talking and teasing in the happy early days of a relationship was very different from going and getting actually married.

But Harris wasn't wrong.

And Eli knew it, too.

So she lowered her chin, and with a croak said, "Alright."

CHAPTER 14
POSSIBLE PATHS

"Harris, I can't marry her."

Lord Harris turned slowly from his horse. He had been inspecting one of his saddlebags for a corkscrew to help them with their second bottle of wine for the afternoon lunch, and Tam had taken the opportunity to speak privately with him.

The duke looked briefly stunned at the sight of Tam's uneasiness. "Tam, you know that is the best way to help her. You know you—"

"No. She has… She has so much pain, Harris. She has so much grief and anger. You heard a fraction of it today." Tam paused. His throat was becoming uncomfortably tight. "I can't be a part of that pain. I can't be a part of that trauma. That will make things so much harder for her, and it will take that much longer for her to heal and grow in our relationship. And she has taken some very big steps. With Luca in particular. And if she starts to resent him? After she has helped him come to think of her as his mother and rely on her? Harris, that's… I couldn't live with myself after that."

The soberness in Oscar Harris's eyes would've terrified most who knew him as he turned from his horse and faced Tam.

"When will her trauma be something you no longer have to manage, Tam?"

Anger flashed across Tam's face, until the duke's next words.

"You are taking care of a seven-year-old you had no idea existed. You are in a tricky spot with not only the covens but also a foreign kingdom. You need a partner in this, Tam. Or at the very least someone who can manage their own lives."

"It's not her fault that—"

"Sometimes in life, the disasters we find ourselves in aren't our faults. But it's still up to us to figure it out. And sometimes, the best person to save us is ourselves. Look…" Stepping closer, Lord Harris rested a hand on Tam's shoulder. "I'm not saying she doesn't deserve time to heal. She has suffered and she deserves a bit of grace. What I *am* saying is that it isn't your job to take her burdens from her."

"She's thrown herself in with me, Harris. And I have messes everywhere. I don't want to make her take on more. And marrying me before she's ready? It'll hurt Luca as well."

"Tam, realistically? Look at everything *you* have going on compared with her. You have a child and some explaining to do with two covens. *She* has armies and royalty wanting her dead. You can't take all of that from her. You can support her, and can even help her set a few fires, whatever helps—"

"Who sets fires to deal with problems?"

"*Anyway.*" Lord Harris cleared his throat, rolling his eyes in mock innocence. It wasn't really a surprise. Among the Daxarian duke's many oddities was his particularly passionate and dramatic relationship with his wife.

Tam resumed his argument. "You had help when you had to face your own family. My da helped you. And my da had you and the other kitchen staff when he wanted to be with my mum, then he had the king when he went to war."

"Fin then went off to face his father alone."

"A rescue team went after him, and my grandmother saved him!"

"This is what I mean about helping her, Tam. Some things you have to step back and let her face. Or do you not think she is strong enough?"

Tam felt his insides turn to iron. "She's plenty strong, but a whole kingdom is against her, and—"

"You know who you remind me of right now?" Harris chuckled, but it didn't sound in any way good-humored. "Your father. But the way you're talking about Eli is the way he talks about you."

The shock that rushed through Tam froze him.

"I've told your da for years that you have to face things on your own terms. He kept trying to decide for you and help you, to carry your burden for you. I don't say that because he thought you were lesser or weak. He did all of that because he loves you. It's a terrible side effect of the affliction, I tell you."

Tam's hands were trembling in his pockets.

"Sometimes, Tam, we have to grip on bloody tight when our backs are against the wall, and sometimes we just have to say, *Godsdamn, I'm going to get myself out of this because I have no other choice.* It isn't necessarily a bad thing. It helps you learn what you're made of."

"So I shouldn't be accepting your help right now? I should save myself?"

"To save yourself without help right now would result in—I'm guessing—you killing a person or two, if you're lucky. You've grown up pretty sheltered from any real skirmishes, Tam. And do you really want to start killing people when you can just as easily spare everyone?"

Tam almost laughed before he could stop himself. He had been relatively open about his abilities while in Zinfera, and it honestly shocked him to hear that Harris thought that he wasn't strong enough to be an actual threat to more than one or two unaware soldiers.

And that pricked his fragile nerves more than it should've.

Sensing that his ego was going to make him do something stupid, Tam started to turn away and leave the conversation all together. But before he did, Harris dropped his hand from Tam's shoulder and said, "Tell you what, Tam. Let me play devil's advocate. Say you fight your way out of this, make a real name as a dangerous fellow. You defeat all of Eli's enemies for her, she stays safe, and you have had to become some kind of monster that toppled an empire. Do you think that's the kind of father Luca deserves?"

"Get help. Don't get help. What are you telling me?" Tam's voice was rough.

"I'm telling you to take my help today. Then I'm saying let Eli decide how she wants to deal with this. She can either marry you or face the concubine unmarried and without Daxaria being able to interfere. No one really knows how everything is going to wash out." Harris sighed wearily but then renewed his grin. "Though I will advise that you remember to have fun when you can, because who knows, you might find after all this that you've made some good friends, or had some good memories despite the shitstorm. I know I did when I found myself in the middle of it. Farts and all."

Darkness settled over Tam despite Harris's attempt at levity. "What if Eli wants to topple an empire?"

The Daxarian duke got a funny look on his face as he slowly took a step back. "You're acting a bit scary right now, Tam."

"Don't you know that farmers sometimes burn the fields to get rid of disease or insects?" Tam started, his eyes flitting to the ground. "Maybe—"

Harris grabbed the front of Tam's shirt with one hand and shook him. Hard.

"You're talking about some dark things there, lad. You're an Ashowan. You protect people. What the hell has gotten into you?" The duke's face hardened, and Tam noticed the way his free hand had moved instinctively toward his sword, which was once again clipped at his hip.

Tam blinked, a subtle frown between his brows. He felt nonplussed by his family friend's reaction. "I guess I should ask Eli first."

"What does *that* mean? So help me Gods, Tam. I'll put you on the ground myself and cart you to your father gagged and bound if you start doing something stupid."

The sudden calm that had come over Tam had him simultaneously relaxing his shoulders and straightening them.

Harris's eyes flit hastily over him. "You're a big man, Tam. You've always hidden it, and you are good at dueling with a sword. But—"

"I will not hurt anyone who doesn't attack first."

The words were chilling.

"*Tam!*" Harris shouted, again shaking the young man desperately. "There are better ways! Harder, yes, but so much better. Ways that will leave you whole!"

Tam turned and looked over to where Eli sat beside Luca, her arm around him. She eyed her mother and father in the distance warily, unaware of Tam's gaze on her.

"Harris… Luca and Eli? They're my family. *Mine*. And there is so much nonsense trying to destroy it. I just found them. We don't want power. Hell, I'll even give up my titles. I'll give up being a member of the coven if I can just—Wait."

His face lightened, and the frightening thoughts he had been descending into disappeared as though it had simply been a silly joke.

"If Kraken or Pina got in trouble with a foreign kingdom, would the coven have to help them?"

Flummoxed, Harris's grip on Tam's shirt slackened. "Err. I think… so? Why?"

Tam's heart pounded. "Lady Marigold said there were coven members from Wittica here, right?"

"Yes. Some will be here shortly, and a couple others traveled with your sister."

Tam smiled. "Great."

"Tam, did you eat something odd recently? Did Marigold give you something that tasted funny? Don't ever eat something she offers you."

Shaking his head, Tam patted Harris's shoulder. "I have to go ask Eli what she would like to do."

"So, my choices are: reveal I'm technically your familiar, or get married," Eli repeated thickly.

She had stopped crying shortly before lunch, but her eyes were still red.

"Well, there is a third option. But it involves a lot of…" Tam trailed off, his eyes dropping briefly to Luca. "Creative approaches to vanquishing obstacles."

Luca looked up with a frown. Internally Tam cheered that it hadn't been obvious to his son what he was suggesting. Eli, on the other hand understood, at least to a point, and so she blurted out, "What? *Vanquish* everyone?"

"Just the ones who say we can't leave."

"Tam!" Eli reached up and covered Luca's ears. "Are you suggesting we kill Soo Hebin?"

"I don't really like what I've heard about her so far, believe it or not."

"Tam, that… That's a lot."

"I know. And I'm sure it isn't what a good person would do. But aren't you sick of everyone just—"

"Yes." Eli locked eyes with Tam.

She most definitely understood.

"If we fail, we're dead."

Silence hung between them.

"Or I could just marry you," Eli pointed out mildly.

Tam's heart stuttered. "You could also show the Coven of Wittica that you're a familiar—"

"Then the debate of whether or not I have human rights would be brought up by some nasty people. It'd be even more complicated. And it very well might change nothing," Eli pointed out, as her emotional distress faded to thoughtfulness. "To be honest, I think our best card is the one you used to play all the time back home. No one knows anything about us. Not for certain. They know that you are rumored to be the devil, but they don't know why. They know I am a witch, but only a few people know I can turn into an animal. And only four of us know now that I've… grown."

Tam nodded along to her reasoning.

"So what are we going to do?"

Eli dropped her hands from Luca's ears.

"Well… I have an idea."

Katarina paced in the quarters she was given in Soo Hebin's palace.

She was waiting for her mother to come join her.

Despite having arrived earlier in the day, neither she nor her mother had seen hide nor hair of any royal family members, and the unnerving awareness of being watched only buzzed louder in Kat's senses.

Part of her wanted to start wandering around and poking her head behind closed doors to investigate this strange new place, but her mother had said to be patient.

Kat's fingers fluttered against the handle of her sword.

Maybe just a quick stroll would be fine—

A knock on the door interrupted her thoughts.

"Come in," Katarina called, while turning to stand with her feet braced apart.

She knew she looked like she was about to attack whoever walked through the door, but she couldn't bring herself to respond any differently when it felt like she was about to be surrounded.

The door opened, and in came four Zinferan maids with a tea cart that had a squeaking wheel. The cart was laden with a plain porcelain tea set and some simple pastries. Kat masked her expression as she watched the maids pour the tea without a word. When they were finished, they bowed to her.

"Your Majesty, we hope this will satisfy you for the time being, please enjoy these light refreshments."

Despite politicking and its many nuances being her weakness, even Kat knew that the plain tea set meant there was a subtle snub being given.

She raised an eyebrow.

The maids waited with their heads bowed to be dismissed.

Moving over to the tea, while intentionally putting more weight into her steps to make her presence seem even bigger, she plucked up one of the pastries and pretended to examine it.

"Who ordered this for me?" she asked airily.

"Her Highness Soo Hebin has—"

"A lowly concubine thinks she can cater to me?" Kat watched as the maids collectively flinched, almost seeming to shrink in fear.

"Where are the emperor's stewards and maids?" Kat allowed her aura to start simmering off her skin.

"Th-The emperor's servants are tending to—"

"Not all of them will be. Go fetch me his closest assistant or ally, or I'll go and find accommodations with the Coven of Giong."

Kat doubted these women knew that technically the covens would no longer receive her.

Predictably, the women sprang into action, scurrying out of Katarina's chamber.

Katarina grimaced.

Evidently she'd be engaging in her least favorite kind of battle.

A battle of egos.

She could also guess that two of those maids would be alerting Soo Hebin. Kat braced herself for the concubine to come herself to run interference, and most likely attempt to distract her guest from insisting on speaking to any of the emperor's people.

Sighing, Kat drew out her sword and stepped back two paces.

"Alright. It's just the two of us now. Come out."

The tea tray remained perfectly still.

Kat regarded it flatly. "I'll start taking test stabs if you don't come out."

Sure enough, a hand appeared from under the tea cart, followed by an arm, then a torso. Finally the young man stood straight and stared at Kat, whose eyes went wide with shock.

"Hi… Your Majesty. I-It's been a little while."

"Thomas Godsdamn Julian," Kat wheezed.

The young man before her barely looked like the fifteen-year old lad who had served under Eric Reyes, her husband, seven years ago before he betrayed them in Troivack. To make matters worse, he had committed the awful sin in order to work for the first witch.

But since then he had grown more than a foot. His face was sharper and his shoulders broader.

Kat lifted her sword. "What the bloody hell are you doing here? And you'd better explain quickly. I'm not really in the mood to give a warm reception to treasonous arsehats."

CHAPTER 15

A TRAITOR'S TESTIMONY

Tam stood with his hands in his pockets, Eli at his side with her arms folded stubbornly. Luca, Gods bless him, tried to imitate his father with a threatening scowl.

"It's ridiculous! Why would we travel by boat to Gondol? It's faster to take the carriage!" Lady Marigold trilled.

Odette Gilly, the Daxarian Coven of Wittica representative who had joined the group shortly after the luncheon hour, shrugged coolly. "The coven doesn't want anyone escaping while they travel to Gondol. We have to investigate whether or not Lord Tamlin's claims are true regarding his marriage with Her Highness."

"This wasn't mentioned to us before," Duke Harris noted, his eyes narrowing suspiciously at the Daxarian coven member. "Why now?"

"Because it is a whole new matter if Her Highness really is married to Lord Tamlin! If they are lying—"

"A very dangerous accusation," Tam observed evenly.

The Daxarian coven member's eyes flitted in his direction only briefly before returning to Duke Harris.

Tam's gut churned.

Something was wrong. *Very* wrong.

The Daxarian coven should be acting protectively of him.

"A ship is the safest place to prevent escape," Odette repeated dismissively. "Now, I have sent word with a member of the Giong Coven for two vessels. In the meantime, Lord Tamlin, Your Highness, you will wait here under heavy guard." She then proceeded to swing back around to give orders to the armed men that still milled about in the confusion.

Tam felt Eli stiffen at his side. Even Harris was frowning.

Odette was a water witch, though she wasn't one of the witches with unique physical attributes. She had shoulder-length black hair and clear blue eyes, with a sprinkling of freckles over her nose. She was near the same age as Eli, perhaps a little younger, but her haughty confidence worried Tam for a multitude of reasons.

Harris sidled back over to his nephew while Lady Marigold and her husband started to whisper back and forth to each other. "Tam, I don't like this. I didn't notice it on the ship when I traveled with the coven members, but things don't feel right."

"Now you see why I started talking about a revolt. The corruption in the Giong Coven might only be a fraction of what's going on," Tam said in a murmur.

"Easy there, Tam. Bloodshed is not a fun thing."

"I'm aware."

"Are you, though?" Duke Harris didn't mask his dubious tone.

Tam didn't comment further on his expertise with fighting. "Soo Hebin has ties to the slave trade. They might be trying to get us on the water to corner us and kill us."

"They wouldn't plot murder around you or myself lightly, Tam. Though I admit, it is questionable—this order that you be placed on a ship."

Movement a short distance away halted the duke and Tam's discussion. They turned to watch as Lady Marigold and her husband returned to their carriage, said a few words to the Daxarian coven member, then stepped into the vehicle.

Visibly concerned by this, Harris tilted his head and started walking toward the carriage.

Tam looked over his shoulder where Jeong loitered innocuously. "I think we might be making a run for it sooner than later."

The Zinferan cringed. "I don't know how good an idea that is right now."

"Getting on a ship isn't the worst thing depending how close to shore they stay," Eli contributed.

"You told me about one of the traders that worked closely with Lord Yangban. Aren't you worried they'll ask him to come?"

"Of course I am. In fact, it is almost too obvious." Eli sighed.

"Well, we can still try to escape by jumping in the water," Jeong suggested.

"Not with the water witch accompanying us. Not to mention the air witch," Tam reminded him while eyeing Harris and the aforementioned air witch, who had hung back during Odette's confrontation.

Harris appeared to be in a heated discussion with his half sister at that moment.

"That leaves my original plan, too." Eli looked at Tam expectantly.

"I don't like your plan. A lot can go wrong," he retorted firmly. "Besides, even if we all go into the void, when we eventually come back out, this area will most likely be crawling with guards."

"Tam, you took Lord Kim into your void and moved from his office to our room in Junya. We've never officially tested how far you can move with someone."

"There are four of us!" Tam interjected. "I fell asleep immediately after when it was just Lord Kim I was moving."

Eli made an agitated noise. "Right now, it looks like the Coven of Wittica and the Coven of Giong are in league with each other. And they are taking their orders from Soo Hebin."

"And/or the first witch," Tam added grimly.

Eli nodded. "The first witch wants 'the devil'; Soo Hebin wants me dead. I'm tricky right now because I'm tied to you. But they can't prove *how* I'm tied to you. Even if they summon Captain Woo, the leader of Soo Hebin's slave trading operation, to kill me, it opens up all kinds of vulnerabilities for Soo Hebin. The only threat that we have no insurance on are the other concubines who may see my death as an opportunity to partner up with the Ashowan family and bring Daxaria into the fold."

Luca stared between Eli and Tam, utterly lost.

"Do you think Soo Hebin will risk exposing herself like that? Especially if the other concubines could benefit from it?" Tam asked next.

"I think she will bide her time to double-check if we are married. If she finds out we aren't, there is less risk, and she hates me enough to go forward with having me taken out of the portrait. She'd probably send a bird to Captain Woo to do away with me while we travel to Gondol," Eli explained.

"We can become the pretentious nobles that we actually sort of are and dig in our heels, demanding better treatment and refusing to get on the ship," Tam suggested next.

"That'll go over better for you than it will for me, what with the well-planted rumors that I eloped with a peasant boy. My character is dubious to the Zinferans, at best, even with our alleged marriage. The other rumor has gained traction already. So I doubt people are placing much stock in this new claim."

Tam made a grumbling sound in the back of his throat. "Alright. We get on a ship. We make a break for shore at some point. I can practice vanishing into the void with all of you while we're on the ship."

Eli nodded glumly.

Jeong cleared his throat in assent.

"What if they try to split us up?" Luca asked suddenly.

Tam and Eli looked down then back up at each other at the same time.

"Then I have to resort to plan A," Tam said softly.

"What's plan A?" Luca wondered with a tilt of his head.

"Plan A means you close your eyes and hide with me," Jeong said, grasping Luca's shoulders, his defeated tone undisguised.

Tam gave an apologetic half smile at Jeong, who reluctantly nodded in understanding.

He realized how precarious their situation was.

Reaching over, Tam took Eli's hand and gave a reassuring smile. "If only I could tell them how seasick I get. Then maybe they'd think again about being trapped on a boat with me."

Eli laughed. "Do you think you'd be able to aim while getting sick?"

"The only way to find out is to try!" Tam grinned.

"Eww!" Luca slapped his hand over his eyes, though he was giggling.

Despite the precariousness of their situation, Tam took a moment to relish in the more lighthearted conversation. Especially as he doubted it would last much longer.

"You expect me to believe that you've been lying in wait for the first witch to escape this whole time?" Katarina scoffed as she stared down at Thomas Julian, who knelt before her.

She still had her sword drawn, though the tip rested against the wooden planks of the floor.

"It's true! I didn't want to betray His Majesty! But when I met Ansar, he told me that even if she failed, she had done enough work that once freed again, she would be able to finish executing her plans!" the young man argued passionately.

Kat rolled her eyes to the ceiling. "I have no reason to believe you, and I don't. You want something. Or you're trying to play both sides in the event things don't work out. Get up. I'm having you arrested."

"No! Please! Please, I really just want to help! I can tell you what the first witch is trying to do!"

"Not interested."

"No, Your Majesty, it is so much worse than you think! Even the Coven of Wittica has been corrupted!"

Kat had been on her way to alert the guards that there was an intruder in her room, but froze.

"Long ago the first witch started working with Louise Riddel to gradually persuade coven members to separate from serving the king, and instead create their own sect. A temple for the covens to reside in and operate under. It would govern its own independent land and hold records of all witches. The temple hierarchy would be in charge of sending out witches as they deemed fit. Not under the control of the king!"

Kat slowly turned her body toward Thomas as he spoke.

"It's already in motion! She's arranged for this in Zinfera regardless of whoever takes the crown. She knows Troivack follows Daxaria closely, so it is all set for this takeover."

"Then why—" Kat cleared her throat, which felt thick. "Why are you telling me? It sounds like a lost cause."

"Look I… I'm not a witch. I know I have no say over how this should go, but the kind of takeover she is describing will not be a peaceful one, and if your husband, His Majesty, refuses? It'll be a war of all the covens against humans. Especially if Zinfera sides with the covens, things will be…" Thomas Julian looked around the room as he searched for the words. "It's going to be bad."

"Not all witches can be in agreement with this. Otherwise they would've already brought this up to my father," Kat pointed out, her grip around her sword hilt tightening.

"Not all, no. Mostly it's the younger members that have sided with the first witch."

"How did the first witch do this?"

"She has followers, and she helped get them positions as teachers for the covens. And, well… if you control the education, you can control their point of view. She plotted this out for years."

Kat pinched the bridge of her nose. "Godsdamnit. So she wants the covens to lead some sort of religion? That opens up a huge power imbalance amongst normal humans and witches!"

"She thinks as the daughter of the Gods that she is more than capable of helping the kingdom's transition to this new era."

Cursing, the Daxarian queen dropped her hand. "So how do we stop her?"

Thomas Julian turned sheepish, suddenly seeming like the fifteen-year-old boy Kat remembered.

"You're you, Your Majesty. And you have your family!"

Kat's head dropped back. "My family is great, don't get me wrong, and we battled Aradia the twit before, but now we're talking covens full of witches and then kingdoms! That isn't just a couple of people we have to—"

"But it is! If you can somehow defeat the devil and the first witch again, things will be alright!"

Kat sighed. "What if I agree that witches should be separated from the monarchy or government? It's true that witches are a complicated group to manage. It would open a lot of tax coin back up to help support the other citizens—Gods, I'm so boring now," Kat lamented at the end to herself.

"But what if there are witches that don't want to belong to the temple?"

"So you're saying she would *enforce* that witches obey the temple?"

"Yes!"

"Like a monarchy forces its people to obey?" Kat's tone turned wry.

"No. It'd be worse! The hierarchy she is proposing would most likely surpass the human leaders, and the covens would act as overseers to all the kingdoms! The covens would use magic to enforce it."

"I agree that this is not good. But those are terms that can be dealt with during negotiations. If there is one annoying lesson I've had to learn, it's that a deal with teeth often turns to a gummy old dog by the end of a hellish amount of paperwork." Kat shrugged.

"Do you really think the first witch is going to bow to any conditions you make? She'll tell you it will have to be her way, or none at all!"

Kat's gaze rolled to the ceiling. "This woman just had to be a pain in the arse."

Thomas Julian stared at Kat. At first, he looked angry, and then bewildered. "Your Majesty, I thought you of all people would—"

"Would what, Mr. Julian?" Kat asked sharply. "Charge around this palace looking for the first witch? Declare war and rile the stakes even higher as I look for this bloody woman and the devil?"

"I expected you to do *something*," he finished wistfully.

Kat lifted an eyebrow. "I will do something. But I'm not going to be an idiot."

"What are you going to—"

A knock interrupted whatever it was Thomas Julian was about to say.

He attempted to dive back under the tea cart, but Kat had moved closer as they talked and seized the back of his collar in a vise grip.

"Come in!"

He tried to struggle until Kat's aura flared and she kicked out the back of his knees, sending him to the floor.

When the doors opened, a Zinferan woman dressed head-to-toe in gems glided in.

It could be no one else than Soo Hebin.

Kat felt a growl building in her throat.

She'd been behaving herself. So why was it that everyone had to test her patience at the same time?

CHAPTER 16
IMPRESSIVE IMPOSITIONS

"Your Majesty, I am Concubine Soo Hebin. It is an honor to meet you." The concubine lowered herself gracefully, the rubies in her hair catching the light from the candles around the room.

Her long dress was white silk. The hems and collar were sewn with glimmering silver thread.

Kat stared, unimpressed.

The outfit and its accompanying bangles looked heavy and annoying. By comparison, in her tan trousers and her tucked in navy-blue shirt, Kat looked like a commoner. But Kat had never really relied on clothes to make her presence felt—no matter how many times her mother tried to change this.

"Your Highness. I'm glad to meet you. Though we have an unfortunate set of problems already. This—" Kat hefted Mr. Julian up by his scruff as though he weighed little more than a sack of apples. "—snuck into my room."

The concubine's eyes had been downcast demurely, but at Kat's words she lifted her gaze.

It was brief, but Kat saw the hesitancy cross her face. "How disturbing." The woman sounded perfectly calm as she gave the barest of waves over her shoulder that summoned the guards to take Mr. Julian away.

Kat stepped back with a shake of her head. "Oh no. This man is wanted for treason in Daxaria, and is Daxarian-born himself. If your guards could go retrieve one of the elite knights I brought with me, that would be best."

Soo Hebin's thin eyebrows twitched. "Your Majesty, he broke into my palace where—"

"Which brings us to our *second* problem." Kat's voice rose as she interrupted the concubine. "I asked to speak to one of the emperor's attendants. Your serving staff had the balls—gall! The gall—to serve me inferior dishware to insult me."

Soo Hebin slowly brought her hands together, making the wide sleeves of her dress fall to cover them.

"Ah, my apologies, Your Majesty. I will see to—"

"And you yourself now insult me?" Kat's eyes flashed as her heavy boots thudded closer to the concubine. "Do you think I'm unaware that an apology from a *lower rank* should be done on your knees?"

The barest tremor ran across the concubine's lower lip as Kat bore down on her.

The maids surrounding the concubine even leaned farther away from her.

"A man breaks into my room, your maids insult me, and now you add to the offense. Since it seems there are all kinds of *ridiculous, childish* games afoot, I will have no choice but to seek the emperor's people out myself. Guards!" Kat barked. "You damn well better bring me one of the emperor's people now, or I will be forced to take matters into my own hands. With the Gods, and *this*—" She gave Thomas Julian another shake. "—as my witness."

The two guards looked nervously at each other, then tried to catch the eye of the concubine, but Kat's hand shot out and she gripped the woman's chin.

"Oh no. You aren't going to be telling them a thing. Especially while you still. Aren't. Godsdamn. *Kneeling*." The rumble in Kat's voice and her rising aura brought the maids behind Soo Hebin to all fours.

The concubine's eyes widened, and Kat could see by their tightening corners that she was furious.

When the guards came back to their senses, they clumsily rushed into each other, then had to sort themselves out before dashing out the room.

"Well?" Kat tilted her head as she stared at the concubine, still holding her chin.

She could tell that while the woman was trying to continue looking composed, she struggled with her rage.

"Your Majesty, to cause such a—"

"That does not sound like an apology from your knees. Are you aware that this alone can have you imprisoned while I negotiate your punishment with the emperor's officials?" Kat gave a cold smile. "Gods, listen to me. Preaching to a Zinferan concubine about Zinfera's laws."

Soo Hebin gently pulled her chin out of Kat's hand and lowered herself to her knees. She bowed her head. "I apologize on behalf of my maids, and for permitting a criminal to break into your room, Your Majesty."

"Wonderful. Get up." Kat turned to the maid who had been the first to lift her gaze from the floor. "You. Go bring me proper tea."

The maid scrambled to her feet and left.

Judging by the tension in her shoulders, Kat wagered that ordering Soo Hebin's maid to do anything without her consent was inciting an even deeper ire in the woman.

"Your Majesty?"

Kat looked up from the concubine lazily when her mother entered the room. "Yes, Your Grace?" she greeted lightly.

The Daxarian queen noticed the faintest of winks from Annika Ashowan.

Evidently she had been listening to the exchange and was quite pleased with her daughter.

"Has there been some trouble—Oh dear, Your Highness!" Annika gushed in a mothering tone when she noticed the woman on her knees. "Your Majesty, what is happening?" When the duchess's eyes landed on Thomas Julian, she momentarily froze and her eyes flashed with all the sharpness of an executioner's blade.

She gave a very quick look to her daughter, and the two of them shared an instantaneous grim conversation.

"You may stand," Kat said to the concubine, who rose swiftly.

"Whatever happened?" Annika used a breathy, delicate tone, casting her brown eyes wide as she dipped into a low curtsy to the concubine.

The show of reverence did little to placate the woman, and Kat almost grinned when she saw the subtle clenching of Soo Hebin's jaw.

"There seems to be a bit of misunderstanding on etiquette," Kat replied to her mother, keeping her tone imperial.

"Oh dear. Is it perhaps just because with everything going on, they are worried—"

"There's no excuse for lax security." Kat hoisted Mr. Julian up once more. The young man didn't so much as raise his eyes.

"Ah."

"Leave us," Kat ordered with a wave of her hand.

Soo Hebin bowed dutifully, and didn't linger any longer than necessary before departing.

Once the doors had closed, Annika stopped wringing her hands in false worry and stared down at Thomas Julian emotionlessly.

"We've been looking for you for quite some time," she informed him softly. "The pain you have caused Likon is immeasurable. Are you aware he has been forced to serve time under the Troivackian king because of you?"

The two women noticed that the young man's ears burned bright red and his shoulders hunched forward. Kat released him to kneel on the floor.

"I never meant for anything to happen to my uncle. I was just trying to make him proud."

Annika looked at Kat questioningly.

The Daxarian queen's lip curled scornfully. "He claims he stayed with the followers of the first witch to gather information."

With her mouth pursed, the duchess considered this information, then gradually crouched to be at eye level with Thomas Julian. "We will see what to make of you in the near future."

The duchess's words succeeded in sending a visible chill down the young man's spine, causing him to shiver. When the Daxarian knights showed up, they dragged Thomas Julian off without another word.

Kat looked at her mother expectantly.

"You didn't handle the concubine like I told you to," Annika began slowly. "But you handled her perfectly as a queen. I'm impressed."

A rueful smile climbed Kat's face. "I knew I had to act out of character. Especially once I heard what the first witch is allegedly up to."

The duchess frowned in concern as her daughter relayed to her everything she had learned from the nephew of their family member.

"Interesting."

"Mm-hm. Thomas was anticipating a reaction, but I remembered how you taught me that whenever someone is trying to lead you somewhere, try pulling them in an unexpected direction."

Annika smiled. "My Gods, to think my daughter would listen to me. And it only took twenty-eight years."

Kat rolled her eyes with a sigh. "What should we do now? The first witch is here. In these walls. We have no idea what she looks like thanks to her being able to change appearances anytime she dies."

"Well, hold on now." Annika held up a finger. "She always becomes a young maiden again when she dies. So that eliminates anyone older."

Kat tilted her head. "True."

"I'm inclined to believe what Thomas Julian has said about the first witch's plans about building a separate land and temple for witches to lead. It is in line with what we last heard about her when she wanted to mold Troivack," Annika continued.

"Why would he tell us that, though? Unless, as I already said, he wants me to do something."

Annika looked around the room thoughtfully. "If I were to guess? I would assume the first witch wants you to take care of the devil for her. She sees him as a bigger threat than we could ever pose to her. The most valuable variable to any plan is time. And both she and the devil have infinite amounts of it."

"So she doesn't know Tam is around the devil," Kat realized, her eyes bright.

"Most likely not. Though it's only a matter of time, what with everyone on the lookout for Eli, so we can't count on that fact remaining unknown."

"I still can't get over that Eric never realized Eli was a woman," Kat snorted.

"She lied to him when she was younger; it would've been easier to disguise back then. And need I remind you that you didn't have any idea, either, until your father and I told the two of you."

Kat's tongue poked her cheek as she scuffed her boot against the ground. "Well, it's incredible that she's also a princess, and you had no idea about *that!*"

The duchess made a funny noise in the back of her throat. "I'm surprised myself."

Kat smiled smugly. Her mother always knew everything, so learning something as big as Eli being royalty must have really irked her.

"Do you think they'll actually send for one of the emperor's attendants?" Kat changed the topic while eyeing the doors.

"One who is in Soo Hebin's pocket, yes."

"Right. Well, do you mind sending out invitations to all the concubines?" Kat looked at her mother. "I think it's time we start tipping some scales."

Annika reached out and plucked some lint off her daughter's shirt. "Any thoughts on how you would like to handle the first witch?"

"Yeah. Ignore her."

Blinking, Annika tilted her head. "Really?"

Nodding and moving her hands to her hips, Kat broadened her smile. "Yep. Because I am the queen of annoying. And I am quite certain that ignoring the daughter of the Gods is going to drive her up the bloody wall."

"So Katarina took the bait." Aradia tapped the tip of her finger on the garden table after listening to Ansar's report. "And she placed Mr. Julian under lock and key?"

"Yes," Ansar confirmed with a bow of his head.

"Then I suppose all I need to do is wait and—"

The sound of rapid footsteps stopped the first witch from saying anything more, as she waited with her eyes fixed on the entrance to her lonely square of the garden for Soo Hebin's appearance.

Sure enough, the concubine arrived, her cheeks flushed and the air around her crackling with tension.

"That lowly wench," the concubine spat.

Aradia raised an eyebrow.

"She made me bow—in my own palace! Tell me that I'll make her pay soon. You are going to have the covens gather here and ransom her to force the Daxarian king to sign the new division of witches and the monarchy? That will be soon?"

Aradia's eyes ventured casually to Ansar. "Once I have the devil in my grasp, yes."

Soo Hebin closed her eyes and took a steadying breath, which brought a sinister smile to her red lips. "I have good news then. We have located the man and boy who is believed to be the devil. They happened to be traveling with Princess Elisara!" Soo Hebin laughed triumphantly.

Aradia didn't rejoice as openly as Soo Hebin, but she did lean forward in her seat. "I see."

"And guess what?" the concubine continued in dulcet tones that nearly had Aradia's teeth on edge as she continued putting up with the noblewoman's grating personality.

Aradia took her time answering, and she didn't hide how tiresome she found the concubine's petty villainy.

"The man who was traveling with her? Is none other than Tamlin Ashowan, and apparently, he *married* that twit of a princess!"

Aradia's expression turned stony as she looked to Ansar, who was already watching her expectantly.

"You can eliminate the pesky Ashowan children and get your hands on your devil, while I can disintegrate whatever remains of the sham of a princess."

"Leave us," Aradia ordered.

The concubine opened her mouth in shock. "Excuse me? You are in my palace. You—"

A great surge of wind came out of nowhere and blasted against the concubine, forcing her to close her eyes and mouth and turn away as her dress flattened against her figure.

When it died down, the concubine rounded slowly to see a Zinferan witch she had been introduced to a week ago.

"Her Magnificence has ordered you to leave." The witch was an old man, with a long white beard and hair, wearing pants and a coat as white as Soo Hebin's own clothes.

She gaped in outrage at him, but when he lifted his hand again, presumably to summon back the wind, she made an aggravated noise, turned on her heel, and stalked away.

Once blissful quiet had settled back over the garden, and the wind witch retreated to his discreet guard post, Aradia spoke.

"Tamlin Ashowan traveling beside my brother… by chance. With the missing princess. This reeks of divine tampering," she said to Ansar without commenting on the concubine's dramatic exit. "Have we found anyone from the seer bloodline?"

Seers were handy beings. They weren't created by the Gods with the sacred magic waters of the Goddess's Pool, but rather, the waters of past, present, and future. Which meant that, unlike witches, their talents were passed down without variance in their talent level. All seers, upon touching someone, could see a moment of their past, present, and a year into the future. Which was quite useful, though they tended to speak vaguely as there was much that was still unknown surrounding their visions.

"Not yet. The last known one was in Troivack, but she died a year ago. There is the child that our people cared for that we presumed to carry on the legacy, but I have not inspected her myself."

Similar to witches, seers usually developed their skills by the time they turned eight.

"Damn. I want to know what the hell my parents are playing at." Aradia shook her head, her eyes growing lost in thought. "No matter what, my brother will pay. He will leave and I will set the world right, and everything—"

"Aradia." Ansar's warm hand gently covered hers. "Everything *will* be alright. I'll make sure of it. I know you repeat these things like a mantra, but… trust me."

The first witch gazed at her assistant for a long while, her emotions unclear.

Eventually she spared a smile. "I trust you as well as I can trust anyone, Ansar. Now let's find out where exactly my brother is and the soonest he can get here."

CHAPTER 17

PARTING WITH PEACETIME

Tam stood with his arms crossed, Eli lingering just behind him, and Luca at his side.

"Ms. Odette Gilly, could you please repeat that?" Tam's tone was polite, but there was a dangerous air in his posture that he knew should've given the water witch pause.

"We have sent an order for two ships to come. You will travel with myself. As for *Luca*..." She eyed his son disapprovingly, her lips curling as if she had bitten into a lemon. Tam's eyes narrowed. "The child and Her Highness will travel on the other vessel with her uncle, Duke Harris," Odette repeated coolly.

"I told you they might do that!" Luca called up to his father, a frown already wedged between the child's brows.

"You're a very smart kid." Tam nodded down at his son.

Luca scowled back up at Odette. "Does this mean I should cover my eyes and hide?"

The water witch raised a quizzical eyebrow in Tam's direction.

"Maybe. Stay close to Eli while I sort this out with Ms. Odette here." Tam stepped closer to the woman, who peered up at Tam defiantly.

"Nothing you can say will change this decision. It was agreed upon by both covens, and—"

"Oh, I don't know about that. *I'm* also a member of the coven, and I didn't agree to that. Furthermore, I have to wonder at being treated like a criminal. My wife and I have been hunted across a kingdom with our son. Why in the world would we need to be separated?"

"Lord Tamlin." Odette's tone was thick with insultingly forced patience. "There was a murder of a Giong Coven member, and an unfamiliar witch's symbol was found at the scene."

"And why is that related to us?" Tam asked, still looming over the woman.

"Because the covens have logged every witch's symbol. The only two in any coven that haven't been registered are your own as well as Her Highness's, and you both confirmed for yourselves that you were in Junya around the time of the murder."

"Not all witches report themselves to the Coven of Giong, or the Coven of Wittica. Are you telling me you also have every witch's symbol from Lobahl's own coven?"

Odette opened her mouth to say more, but Tam plowed on.

"I already know you don't. What you are doing is a gross abuse of power. If you attempt to press this matter, I will be forced to make things incredibly difficult."

Odette closed her mouth as she observed the ominous warning Tam did not mask in his face. Then she sighed and rolled her eyes.

Tam tilted his head in astonishment. The fearlessness. The lack of respect and concern for any consequences…

His gut twisted in trepidation.

The water witch shrugged regardless of the close appraisal Tam was clearly giving her. "Like I said before, nothing you say or do can change this order."

"And who gave this order?" Tam asked while folding his hands loosely in front of himself.

"Myself and—"

"And are you my superior in *any* capacity?"

Tam watched as at last the woman ruffled a little at his words.

"I am a current coven member working directly with the coven. You most likely won't become the next diplo—" Odette stopped herself as her lips pressed themselves shut.

"Oh? I most likely won't… what? Become the official diplomat for the coven like my father? That's strange. That was a confidential matter between the head of the coven, the Daxarian monarchy, and my family. The fact that you not only have knowledge of this but are also acting as though the decision has been made, when I know for a fact it has not, is grounds for a treason charge. Do you realize that?"

Tam noted the way Odette's hand curled into fists at her sides. And then her face twisted into a visage of anger and hate. "Who's going to believe you?"

He straightened.

"You Ashowans think the world revolves around you and that you have the final say in everything. Well, guess what? Your time is over. You were favored by the former king. Then you wormed one of your own into the bed of the current king. You're nothing but greedy, entitled, awful—"

Luca lunged forward and shoved the woman off the grassy ledge they stood on and into the shallow water a foot or two down, making her squawk in surprise.

Tam snorted and slapped a hand over his mouth to stop it from coming out. It wasn't a good thing to laugh at, and he knew it, even if the woman was revealing just how corrupt the coven had become.

"Luca," Tam managed to say, sounding stern.

Eli moved closer to peer down into the water. However, Odette was a water witch, so she was already rising up from the ocean with a water rope around her waist, her eyes burning with wrath.

Luca wasn't impressed with the magical display as he glared up at her. "Stop saying mean things about my family! You're just a bully!"

Tam gently rested a hand on Luca's shoulder and pulled him back. "Luca, go stand with Eli. Everything will be alright."

"What's happening over here!" Lord Harris's loud voice sounded just behind Tam as Odette ran her tongue over her teeth, her feet touching back down on the grass.

"It would seem the Coven of Wittica—after a very lackluster attempt—is revealing its true colors," Tam explained. "They are trying to separate Eli and me, and are saying there is nothing I can do about it."

Harris turned toward Odette, but the witch had her glower fixed on Tam.

Regardless, the duke was the first to speak. "Really? Are we now done with this political-intrigue nonsense and finally just saying what we mean? Odette, you're a stuck-up wench and you were a nightmare to travel with. Gods, that is lovely to get off my chest! I was trying so hard to be pleasant." Harris sighed with a smile while looking up at the sky. "Oh. One more thing. Do you ever wonder how the Coven of Wittica is able to afford to feed, clothe, and house witches? Or how they seem to have no trouble getting a magistrate to process qualms and other issues? Or how, when there is a magical outburst or fight between witches, there is never a bill for the repairs or settlement costs in the event of damages or injuries?"

Odette at last rounded on the duke, her nostrils flaring. "Your monarchy uses witches! It is the least they can—"

"Ah-ah! We *hire* witches. That *apply* for these jobs. I really must ask how much it is to feed that remarkably high horse you find yourself on."

"We can grow our own damn food! We have earth witches who—"

"Oh? On whose land will they be doing this? I don't know that myself or, say, the Ashowan duchy will be feeling quite so generous as we have been with these resources in the very near future."

The water witch's expression darkened, but the duke kept grinning. "Young lady, it is wonderful to have such passion. You have my sincere compliments on that trait. It's one of your few that I can say anything good about. But as you get older, you're going to find that things aren't so black and white, and you are also going to find that actions have consequences. Particularly the threatening kind of actions."

Odette seemed to be having an apoplectic event that stopped her from being able to speak.

"So how about we keep my niece and godson together, as they have been most cooperative in agreeing to be hoisted off on a ship."

The water witch practically quaked.

"I *dare* you to try and mess with us!" Luca hollered, shoving his finger up at the woman's face.

Eli hastily shushed Luca, but Harris turned a sparkling eye in their direction. "Love the little thug you're raising there, Tam!"

"We really should be more careful about what we say around him," Eli muttered from Tam's side as she, too, reached out to touch Luca's shoulder before casting the boy a chastising look.

Luca did not look chastened. He merely crossed his arms and continued glowering at the water witch.

However, the interruption seemed to help Odette recover her ability to speak. "You all will regret not being more—"

"Oh, for the love of the Goddess!" Remarkably, the outburst came from Eli. "You are more or less trying to take us as hostages! Did you really expect us to say, *Why thank you, of course we will listen?*"

A surge from the Tinoo Ocean rose up, and Odette's eyes glowed with flickering blue. "Yes. Because you are not in the position to negotiate."

"*Oh*. Oh no, no." Tam moved in between Eli and Odette. "Stop this, or you're going to find out how wrong you are."

Odette gave a derisive laugh. "I already know you can't manage your power! Stop thinking that—"

"What is that over there!" Tam burst out in falsified shock and horror as he stared at a spot just over Lord Harris's shoulder.

The duke and most people near them turned, hands flying to their weapons.

And that was all the time Tam needed.

He reached out and flicked Odette on the back of the head.

Suddenly, a seam of black appeared behind her, opened like a mouth, and swallowed her whole.

Having witnessed this sneaky maneuver, Eli's jaw dropped.

But by the time everyone else was looking back at Tam, the water that Odette had magically raised up like a threatening wall ready to crush everyone had collapsed back into the ocean with a magnificent splash.

"What the—" Harris blinked, and looked around at the empty space Odette had been occupying just a moment before. Then he looked down at Luca. "Did you shove her into the water again?"

"She just jumped in herself," Tam volunteered breezily.

The duke looked at the ocean for a long time. Then he slowly turned back to his godson.

"Tam. Did you happen to do something perhaps a wee bit magical?"

He shrugged ambiguously. "Did anyone see anything?"

Harris looked around then lowered his voice. "Tam, is she dead?"

"No."

"Can you… bring her back?" Harris asked carefully while squinting at the grass, as though he suspected that Tam had merely shrunk the water witch.

"Probably? Do you want me to?"

Harris emitted a soft groan then looked around at the Giong Coven member, an air witch who was already stalking toward them. Then just beyond the witch the armed men that Lord and Lady Nam had brought with them.

The duke looked back at Tam. "Are you able to do whatever you did again?"

"Yes."

Harris wrinkled his nose as he visibly braced for the answer to his next question. "Does this mean you are starting a rebellion against the covens and a war against Daxaria?"

Tam looked at Eli.

She sighed in resignation. "It looks like despite our best efforts, yes. That is what we're doing."

The Daxarian duke reluctantly drew his sword as the armed men caught on that something suspicious was happening, and started to move more purposefully.

"I'm too old for this kind of thing," Harris all but moaned.

"Luca." Tam looked down at his son.

"Go hide with Jeong?" Luca looked a little too happy with the way things were developing.

"Yes. And we're going to have a very serious chat about your behavior later," Eli announced sternly.

"As much as you want to help, it isn't good to shove people," Tam contributed.

"Tam, you really are your father's son," Harris called over his shoulder as he widened his stance and faced the nearing soldiers and air witch. "You still have time to lecture your child before a fight."

Ignoring this, Tam turned quickly to where Jeong was standing in front of the cottage. The Zinferan had been debating earlier whether or not he should try to slip away during the confusion and return home to update his own family on what was happening. But upon catching Tam's eye, he gave a nod of understanding.

Tam returned a somber smile of appreciation before sending Luca running over to him.

"What is the meaning of this?" the air witch shouted as he neared them.

"We're rebelling! What does it look like?" Harris hollered back indignantly.

The air witch, a man in his early fifties with short well-tended hair and a goatee, raised his hand as though intending to blow away the Daxarian duke. He didn't get the chance to do this, however, as a massive black cat with leathery wings suddenly launched itself over Harris and crushed him into the ground.

"HOLY BALLS!" Harris stumbled back, nearly dropping his sword while the armed men who had been drawing closer screamed and either fell over or backed away quickly. "T-Tam? Is that you?"

Tam clapped a hand on Harris's shoulder from behind. The duke gave a short shriek of surprise.

When Harris realized who it was, his eyes rounded and his mouth attempted to form some kind of word, but he was interrupted by the terrifying snarl that emanated from the black cat that was almost the size of a carriage.

Eli really is going through a hell of a growth spurt, Tam observed idly to himself before realizing how jaded he was about sparking a rebellion. *I wonder if I'm going a bit mad after everything that's happened. I feel oddly alright with bringing down two covens and a corrupt kingdom.*

"Tam." Harris pulled him from his thoughts. "W-What is that?" The duke pointed at Eli prowling closer to the men, who were scattering like spilled apples.

Smiling, Tam looked at the silkiness of Eli's fur in admiration and pride. "That, Harris, is your niece."

The Daxarian duke stared dumbly at Tam. Then he swallowed and looked back at the impressive beast before him.

"I'll be damned. Well… you two probably have this in hand. I'm going to open another bottle of moonshine." The duke sheathed his sword and walked hastily over to the abandoned lunch table just as the cage that had been brought to imprison Eli was flung into the ocean.

"That's for the best," Tam said aloud thoughtfully. "It's also nice to know they wouldn't have fit her in there anyway."

As he watched Eli bolt after each and every armed man, Tam briefly wondered what her parents would think when they eventually received word on what had happened. In a way, he was glad they had already left the scene. With his mind set on destroying the kingdom that had been a curse to his beloved's happiness, he was seriously considering having them join Odette in the void.

CHAPTER 18

PIECING TOGETHER A PLAN

Lord Oscar Harris sat swaying in his seat.

The infamous nobleman of Daxaria known for his utterly unserious nature, his problematically passionate relationship with his wife, and also his effectiveness in battle.

Yet when faced with the initial clash that was the spark of war and rebellion between two covens and the kingdoms of Daxaria and Zinfera, he was busy ensuring a bottle of moonshine didn't feel lonely.

"You alright, Harris?" Tam asked as he looked down at the nobleman, who was squinting to see the last soldier sprinting away from Eli. The man had tried to wield a spear at her, but all it took was one swat of her giant paw to nullify the danger.

"Yeah. I… I, uh… need some time to think this through."

Tam lowered himself into the seat across from the duke. "That is fair. Starting a war was probably not on your list of things to do today."

"Hm. Yes. I had: pick up my niece, tell Marigold she's a cow, enjoy some moonshine and wine. I mean… It was a packed day." Harris had counted down his list on his fingers, but having reached the end, he dropped his hand into his lap and at last looked at Tam. "How did things get to this point?"

"My money is on the first witch and our coven leader Louise Riddel having something to do with all of this."

Harris nodded grimly. "Sounds about right."

Tam watched as Eli loped back, having successfully dealt with the last of the armed men, which signaled Jeong and Luca to make their way over to where Harris and Tam sat.

"What happens now?" Jeong wondered, his hand still resting on Luca's shoulder.

As she approached the table, Eli shifted back to her original shape, prompting the boy to run over to her and wrap his arms around her waist.

"Well, those ships are coming from Bani. Geun and Marigold are going to find it strange when their men don't return, and the covens will most likely be alerted in short order. This means the army is going to swarm here. Most likely over the next two days," Harris speculated airily without bothering to comment on his niece's transformation.

"What're the odds Eli's parents relay to the palace and my sister that I'm here, do you think?" Tam wondered while Jeong picked up the bottle of moonshine and gave it a sniff.

"Not very high if they want her to remain… calm," Harris replied after searching for the right word. "Your sister is practically an army on her own, and everyone knows it. No use getting her riled up."

Tam lowered his eyes. "Gods. If I were them… No. Well, maybe."

"What is it?" Eli asked while gently patting Luca's back.

"If the first witch is now in control of the covens, in league with Soo Hebin, and she has my sister in a vulnerable position, she has very little real opposition. My sister can take on a lot but two whole covens and an army…?" Tam trailed off uneasily.

"It sounds like they've already won," Jeong voiced aloud somberly.

The group fell into a troubled quiet.

"What would happen if we got rid of Soo Hebin and the first witch? Is Soo Hebin's son as capable and problematic?" Tam looked up at Eli.

She shook her head in response. "He is not a good person, but he is more… placid. He isn't as conniving as his mother, and is pretty immature. Most likely it'd be Lord Yangban who'd step up to take over manipulating him."

"Lord Yangban, Captain Woo, Soo Hebin, Louise Riddel, the first witch…"

"Don't forget the Giong Coven leader, Hei Park," Eli contributed.

"Hei Park. Got it. Anyone else a problem?" Tam opened the question up to everyone.

Harris sighed. "Probably Elisara's parents. They've supported Soo Hebin for a long time."

"Ah, right. And most likely Yun Shik and his family," Tam concluded.

Silence fell as the long list of powerful enemies weighed on everyone. Finally Jeong reached over and started to inspect the bottle of moonshine with great consideration.

"Now, we can circle back to this discussion, but I would very much like to know what you did to that unpleasant woman, Odette Gilly, Tam." Harris reached for the bottle of moonshine in Jeong's hands, and the Zinferan dutifully returned it.

Tam looked at the sky pensively. "I don't know that Lord Yangban will still be a problem. We did start drugging him before we left Junya. If Lord Kim is true to his word, then the man may even be in shambles as we speak."

Harris raised his eyebrows, amused. "Did you just ignore me?"

Tam tilted his head innocently. "Will the ships arrive first, or the army, do you think?"

Harris scoffed. "Marigold will probably order both of them to come as soon as they return. So as of dinnertime, they are already on their way. The army is on foot, so they will take a while."

Tam nodded then looked up at Eli. "Do you think Captain Woo is with them?"

She regarded him bleakly. "If Soo Hebin had any say in the matter, most likely."

Tam then turned to Jeong. "Are you going to return to your father?"

Jeong nodded. "He's most likely being observed. The alliance between our families is well known. I want to check on them and let them know what is going on. We'll start rallying our allies and hiring any mercenaries to bulk up the number of soldiers serving our house."

Tam stood and offered his hand. "Thank you, Jeong. You've been an incredible friend."

Hearing the events unfolding, realization dawned on Luca, who instantly bolted to Jeong. "You can't leave yet!"

Jeong smiled down at the young boy, who was hugging him tightly. "Don't worry, Mr. Luca! I'm sure you'll see me again soon."

As Luca and Jeong exchanged their farewells, Tam locked eyes with Eli. They knew where they needed to go, but that didn't mean it'd be easy.

"Harris, are you going to stay with us, or return to Bani?"

The duke slouched a little. "I guess I have to go with you and help, or your father might kill me."

"I thought you'd be a lot more excited about the prospect of all the chaos. You could probably even set a fire or two," Tam mused.

"That's only fun if my wife is here," Harris lamented.

Tam gave the man a sympathetic half smile.

"So how exactly are you going to win?" the duke plundered on.

Tam looked at Eli, then at Luca, still smiling but allowing his thoughts to venture off on their own. "I'm working on that, but I think we're going to have to go to Gondol after all. We have ships kindly provided for us; we might as well use them."

Harris leaned back in his seat to look up wryly at Tam. "How do you think you're going to commandeer a ship? Are you going to take over both of them?"

Tam waved his hand dismissively. "Of course not. I was going to burn the spare one once everyone was off it, but apparently you aren't up to that task."

The duke balked, then rediscovered his smile. "What kind of godfather would I be if I left my godson when he had such a difficult goal to achieve?"

Eli raised an eyebrow. "So we lure them to land and fight them all?"

Tam shook his head. "We lure them, give them a great chase, and then maybe one of their ships happens to drift away on its own with us on it."

"But then someone is left behind if they are acting as bait," Harris pointed out.

Tam shrugged. "Don't worry about that. It'll be fine."

The duke's eyes narrowed. "Mm-hm. I see..."

"Are you just going to leave Odette as she is?" Eli asked, carefully avoiding any specific mention of Tam's void.

Tam glanced over to the edge of the water where the woman had last been seen.

"I'll see about getting some rope and tying her up before bringing her out of... uh..."

Eli nodded in understanding while the duke's incredulous expression only became more dramatic.

Crossing her arms, Eli squared herself to Tam. "Alright. Well, that's the plan for getting to Gondol. How are we going to deal with all the other people hunting us?"

"Get as many of them as we can in one place, and then I'll just give them a little nudge," Tam announced simply.

"Oh, really?" Harris's voice was starting to take on a subtle hysterical edge. "And what happens when you '*nudge*' people, Tam?"

Tam stared blankly at the duke. "We should probably talk to Sua and Hajung about us camping out on their lawn for a few more days while we wait for the ships. Did Marigold mention how they learned about our whereabouts? Was it the couple we were staying with, or the physician?"

"The physician!" Harris snapped. "I need a straight answer from you, Tamlin!"

Tam's eyes drifted toward Jeong after he purposefully avoided eye contact with the duke. "I'll try to explain it a bit later, but for now, let's get Jeong on the road. The more of a head start he has, the better it'll be for him."

The Zinferan bowed in response, though Duke Harris threw his hands in the air in irritated defeat as Tam rose and started sidling away.

After grabbing Jeong's travel pack, the two men proceeded to stroll toward the raspberry field behind the cottage that would take Jeong back into the Kaphe Forest. Birds chirped, the sun shone, and the sound of the gentle waves behind the two men echoed up to them.

"It feels oddly peaceful given we've just started a war," Jeong noted with a faint hint of awe.

"Yeah."

The two men looked at each other.

And both let out long streams of air at the same time.

Tam gave a slight smile. "Sorry. I never did try baking cookies to solve things."

Jeong opened his mouth, caught off guard by the reference to a request he had made months ago in what felt like an entirely different life.

Then he burst out laughing.

Doubling over, Jeong gasped and continued descending into hysterics, which eventually made Tam start laughing.

They knew it was fueled from residual adrenaline, but suddenly the insanity of the entire situation crashed down around them.

Tam barely managed to speak as his eyes watered. "Gods… I just wanted to stay home… and read! I didn't even want to get married!"

"And now you're practically *begging* a woman to marry you!" was all Jeong could get out.

They continued howling, unable to get a grip on their emotions for a long while.

When the pair eventually did, both of them clutched their aching guts.

"Thank you again, Jeong. You've been… I don't know how I would've done it all—especially with Luca—without you."

The Zinferan smiled. "He's a wonderful boy. I'm sure you two will be fine. I have learned a great deal from my time with you as well, Tam. As fun as I like life to be, I've come to realize my expectations of things were quite naive. I think Bong protected me from a lot of these lessons."

Tam shifted his feet as he listened. He felt guilty for exposing Jeong to such harsh situations—the man had been a pillar of sunshine when they'd first met.

Jeong continued speaking, however, without an ounce of resentment in his tone, only appreciation. "I understand now how hard it is for our elders to keep things fun and happy in our lives. It's much more complicated than I realized."

An ache seized Tam's heart as he realized that as they'd traveled away from Junya, Jeong had become quieter and more reserved. This prompted him to say, "We still have to try, though. As hard as it is, I think I should work on being more fun."

The Zinferan smiled once more. "It *would* be nice to have fun. I always found it helped with stress." Jeong gave a small, forlorn chuckle. "Well, I wish you the greatest of luck. We will see each other again one day soon, I'm sure."

Tam shook Jeong's hand again, but this time, he used the move to pull Jeong into a hug.

The two embraced, and Tam gave him another pat on the back. "Be safe."

"You as well."

The two men parted, and gave a final wave.

Tam watched Jeong disappear in the greenery, then turned to make his way back to Eli, Luca, and Harris.

As he walked, he started to wonder how he could possibly make starting a war and rebellion fun.

If he thought about the prospect of stealing a ship and burning another one down as new experiences he'd learn from, it wasn't such a bad thing.

Being absurd is how my da got to where he was. And if I'm stuck in an absurd situation, looking for any opportunity to have fun might just be the best way to go… Everything is so chaotic already, what would happen if we tried fighting chaos with chaos?

Biting his tongue briefly, he pondered how he might be able to pull off absurdity in an outrageously magnificent manner. Unleashing a flock of ducks, perhaps? As he sifted through his thoughts, Tam did concede that approaching his problems from this angle was already doing a decent job at diminishing his stress.

I guess we'll soon find out if my da passed along his talents for inciting madness that comes with a happy ending.

CHAPTER 19

A SALTY SIEGE

With his hands stowed in his pockets. Tam stood on the grass as the two ships dropped their anchors.

Eli, Luca, and Lord Harris were safely hidden from sight, and the elderly couple Sua and Hajung were off visiting their son. They had been grumbling about Tam and his friends' extended stay and the noisiness it brought until Lord Harris revealed a gold coin. The couple had then welcomed them with hot meals and even the occasional smile from Sua. With the amount of money they received, they could retire without a care in the world.

The lifeboats dropped into the Tinoo Ocean, and Tam could tell from the canary-yellow plume tucked in a high-quality dark-purple hat that the captain was coming ashore for his "passengers."

The air was salty and fresh, the sound of the waves rushing toward land interrupted only by the shouts of the sailors drawing closer. The heat was quite uncomfortable. Tam looked at his booted feet. If he wasn't about to battle some pirates, it would've been a nice day to dip his toes in the water. He rocked back and forth on the balls of his feet to his heels as he waited, occasionally blowing a lock of black hair out of his eyes.

He had tried to cut it a day or so ago, but Eli had insisted he grow it out a little more, and he didn't really feel the need to say no. Apparently she liked men with slightly longer hair that could be partially tied back. Though she hadn't liked his hair quite as long as it had been before, she had explained casually.

Her preference wasn't in line with Daxaria's current styles, but as long as she was happy he didn't really care.

Tam watched the progress of the pirates and noted that they had just about reached land.

It'll most likely take Harris and Eli even longer to get to the ship given that they aren't used to rowing. I'll have to try to drag this on a little.

"You there!" a grimy sailor—most likely a pirate—called out to Tam from the front of one of the three boats.

"Who?" Tam hollered back while shielding his eyes from the sun.

"Who else? You!"

Tam looked around himself pointedly before responding. "Hello!"

"Where is the member of the Giong Coven? Or the Coven of Wittica member?"

"Who?" Tam shouted.

Two men from each longboat splashed into the water to guide the boats the rest of the way to the shore.

"Are you an idiot or just looking to get a beating?" the sailor-pirate barked.

"Sir, I am just here to watch two boats come up to a remote spot on the shoreline!" Tam declared earnestly as the grubby man stalked up to him before any other of his crew members.

The Zinferan sailor was quite short, perhaps only five feet tall, and had no muscle on his body. His jaw jutted forward, revealing that he had large gaps between his teeth, but he did take care of them.

Tam tilted his head to stare down at the man. "Morning!"

"Where. Are. The. Coven. Members?" the sailor-pirate repeated while narrowing his eyes.

"What coven members?" Tam asked in return.

In truth, Odette Gilly was back in the void.

Tam had tried to free her, saying that as long as she didn't attack them he'd happily let her run off and rejoin her treasonous friends, but he hadn't even been able to finish the sentence before she had tried to kill him by filling his lungs with water.

Luckily Tam had reacted quickly enough that all he had gone through was a lot of coughing for the rest of the night. If he hadn't responded so swiftly, he would've died incredibly quickly.

As for the air witch from the Zinferan coven who had charged them on the first day of their rebellion, he was in a shallow grave back in the woods thanks to being crushed by a giant catlike animal, who just so happened to be Eli.

"Hoy, enough." The captain with his extravagant hat stepped up to Tam, and even the future duke wasn't immune to the chill in the man's eyes.

It made Tam feel nauseous as he was faced with someone whom he knew instinctively was evil.

He had no doubt that this was Captain Woo.

The urge to kill him instantly was potent when Tam recalled that this man was in large part responsible for everything that had happened to Eli.

"Hi!" Tam plastered a dumb smile on his face.

His mother had trained him. He would not reveal his true feelings or that he recognized the pirate.

"Who are you?" The pirate didn't quite match Tam's height, but he still tried to stare him down.

"Me? I'm Tam."

The captain raised an eyebrow. "I am supposed to be picking up Princess Elisara Taejo. You said your name is Tam? That's interesting. That means you resemble the half-breed noble Tamlin Ashowan not just in looks, but also in name."

Tam didn't bother rising to the insult about his commoner blood. "You've seen the future duke before?" he wondered instead.

The pirate captain didn't answer, and merely continued staring at Tam.

"You're Tamlin Ashowan, I see."

Tam blinked. "Oh? That's odd…" By then the rest of the crew in the lifeboats had started gathering around.

The captain didn't take his eyes off Tam. Instead he lifted his hand. "Search the area."

"Why would you do that?" Tam glanced briefly at the men leaving the group, but by the time he looked back at the captain, he found he had a sword pointed at his face.

"You're toying with me." The captain sounded bored. "What's going on here?"

"Ah. I'm stealing your ship and burning the other one. Do you have a preference on which is the one we burn and which we steal?" Tam leaned to the side away from the sword point so he could continue holding the captain's eyes.

The man didn't blink. In fact, he blinked so seldomly, it perturbed Tam.

The captain gave a quiet snort. "I see. Judging by your attitude, you must have something planned. Hoy. Rope and a blindfold for—"

The captain's eyes went wide as Tam smiled congenially.

Behind Tam was a black hole that was slowly widening. As it did so, Tam's eyes filled with inky darkness. "Pardon me, Captain, but I am not simply Lord Tamlin Ashowan."

The men surrounding him were drawing their swords and readying themselves, but out of the corner of his eye, Tam could see how fearful they were. Despite their terror and their weapons, Tam didn't look away from the captain, who was already winding back his arm, prepared to strike.

"You see, I recently have also been called the devil."

The sword dove toward his gut, but all Tam did was allow himself to fall back into his void, which surged forward hungrily.

Just as suddenly as the black hole had appeared, once it had wrapped its lips around Tam, it disappeared.

Tam shifted back into the physical realm farther away from the pirates, who were all still staring in confusion at the space he had just vacated. He gave a humorless half smile before he retrieved a sling that he'd earlier placed in preparation beside the pile of rocks. It wasn't only a child's slingshot he was reasonably skilled with.

He launched the rock and watched as the pirate he struck in the back of the knee collapsed with a shout. His kneecap was undoubtedly shattered. Tam grabbed another rock as everyone turned to stare at him while drawing their weapons.

When the men had registered his new position a reasonable distance away behind a small hill, Tam chose to launch the second stone, expertly hitting another pirate in the knee. He crumpled to the ground beside his companion. By this time, everyone had overcome their shock.

Tam watched it all calmly, though he could feel sweat prickling his neck.

He could see the rowboat that Lord Harris and Eli had acquired the day before sidling up to the ship on Tam's right out on the water. That was the one they were going to set ablaze.

Things were going to start moving quickly.

The pirates were already charging toward him, and so Tam released another missile that cracked against another sailor's head.

Tam eyed Captain Woo.

He had been standing so close to him, he could've attempted to kill him right there. But Tam knew that the pirate would've gutted him if he'd tried to attack. Even if he had disappeared and reappeared behind the captain, there were too many members of his crew surrounding him in close proximity.

It was fine. As the fighting proceeded, Tam knew he'd have another opportunity.

While Tam waited for the crowd of pirates to reach him, he knocked down three more men, mostly aiming for groins or chests.

Still the group bore down, coming closer, and closer, until…

The first twenty pirates tripped and landed in the shallow trench Tam, Eli, and Harris had spent the previous day digging.

His shoulders and back were still screaming at him over it.

Tam idly wondered if he could convince Eli to give him a back rub or if she would assume he was trying to make an advance on her.

Five more men fell into the trench, and Tam did his best not to look too hard at them. They'd filled the bottom with broken crates, glass, and nails that were haphazardly hammered into boards—compliments of Luca—and the screams told Tam that more than a few of them were not feeling all too special.

The pirate captain skidded to a halt, as did the rest of the men.

About fifty of the original sixty or so started to reroute around the trench to reach Tam, but the captain merely tilted his head and shouted, "STOP!"

The crew halted obediently in their tracks.

Tam arched an eyebrow. He watched as Captain Woo slowly turned around and, sure enough, discovered that one of his ships happened to be on fire. The remaining crew aboard were either frantically trying to smother the flames or diving off the deck—deeming it a lost cause as the flames rapidly spread.

Seizing the moment of distraction, Tam stepped back into the void.

He rested his arms for a moment, rolling his shoulders and stretching his neck; the physical activity really wasn't helping his already aching muscles. He dropped the sling and drew his daggers. Since he'd learned that time moved significantly slower inside the void, Tam had taken more and more opportunities to recuperate in the space when he practiced.

Letting out a breath that brought his heart back to a steady, even pace, Tam felt his way through the blackness. He pictured the spot right behind Captain Woo. Felt the wind, heard some groans from the injured men, smelled the ocean…

He reappeared behind the pirate captain, put his arm around the man's throat, and in the next instant stuck a knife in his back.

"This is for Elisara," Tam whispered.

He heard the wet, shuddering gasp from the man, and time seemed to stall in a way that had nothing to do with magic. Before any of the crew members could process what he had just done, Tam vanished again.

Not wanting to risk winding up stuck in between ship boards, Tam didn't try reappearing on the deck of the boat.

He could more easily move to a place he could see, or to one he knew very well less than a league away. He still couldn't do long distances without passing out instantly. Though he was sorely tempted to try disappearing and reappearing back home in Daxaria.

But that was too risky. He'd most likely get lost in the void and wind up somewhere else. Like the middle of the Alcide Sea.

At present, Tam reappeared by the edge of the ocean. He spotted Eli, Luca, and Harris climbing the side of the second boat. Luckily they had managed to start their ascent before the crew had raised the anchor in order to put some distance from its sister vessel that was aflame.

But the crew aboard this new vessel had already noticed they were gaining new passengers. It sent them dashing off, presumably for weapons. Panic seizing him, Tam fixed his sights on the ratlines and made the trip through his void to reappear there.

Once on the boat, he peered down at the men scurrying like cockroaches toward the side of the ship where Harris, Eli, and Luca were climbing up.

There were fifteen pirates.

Grimacing, Tam hoped that he'd have time to toss them off the side before Luca could see their injuries. He'd try to keep them alive at least.

"HARRIS! MOVE YOUR ARSE!" Tam roared as they at last hoisted the anchor enough that they could feel the natural current of the water start to pull them away.

He had dispatched the remaining fifteen pirates hastily with the help of his void. Which was a good thing, as Luca, Eli, and Harris were just finishing climbing aboard.

"YOU TRY CLIMBING THE SIDE OF A BOAT IN YOUR FIFTIES!" the duke shouted back.

Tam bolted for the sail lines, sweat pouring down his face.

Eli ran to the other side of the ship to help him pull up the sail. Though within moments she was struggling, and Luca wrung his hands worriedly at her side.

"Harris!" Tam called back over his shoulder toward the duke, who was slowly clambering up toward the helm. "Can you get to the wheel?"

"I *wheeze* can, *gasp* but… You aren't… That isn't the—"

The sound of longboats hitting the water pricked everyone's attention. The pirate crew Tam had left on shore had made it back to the shoreline, and they looked ready for blood as they started rowing toward their remaining ship.

"Shit."

"Language!" Eli hollered at Tam as she tried again to tug the sail up, only for it to slide down just as much as she had managed to pull.

"Not the time for manners!" Tam argued as he also worked to get the sail half raised.

He looked at Eli still battling the rope and felt his heart sink. He'd have to run over to fix the sail so it wouldn't be lopsided.

Seeming to sense that a greater effort needed to be made, Eli suddenly snapped out, "To hell with this!" She transformed into her massive familiar self, and she seized the rope in her teeth and yanked.

Luca backed away quickly to give her room.

The sail came up and matched Tam's side.

Letting out a breath of relief, Tam got back to work, and soon they were increasing their distance from the lifeboats.

Of course the other fiery vessel was starting to spray all kinds of smoke and ash, and one of the masts creaked ominously as the pirates in their longboats pulled closer.

Tam's lungs burned as he continued pulling up the sail, but as they moved farther away from shore, and the light breeze that touched his forehead bellied the sail, he finally allowed himself to collapse onto the deck.

He was drenched in sweat, red in the face, and desperately trying to get more air.

Eli was in slightly better shape than he was when she turned back to her human self, though she was still breathing heavily while resting on her knees.

Tam was just about to try and roll over to make his way up to the helm to speak to Harris about where they were going when Luca skipped over to him.

"DAD! THIS WAS THE MOST AMAZING DAY EVER!"

Closing his eyes, Tam silently congratulated himself.

He'd managed to successfully carry out step one of their plan, and he'd also been able to avoid Luca seeing anything too terrible aside from setting a boat on fire. That said, he imagined his definition of *too terrible* might not have aligned with that of most other parents in the world.

CHAPTER 20

A REMINISCENT REOCCURRENCE

The boat that Tam, Eli, and Lord Harris had stolen turned out to be stocked for a journey of seven days.

However, it was a journey of seven days for approximately twenty-five men as opposed to three adults and a child. There was a favorable chance that they would make the supposed three-week trip to Gondol without having to worry about restocking. Though the summer storms that occasionally plagued the land were known to add complications to even the best-planned voyages, particularly along the mountain range that cluttered the eastern side of Zinfera's shores.

Knowing that there was a great deal to strategize over not only in terms of sailing, but also when it came to food and water, Tam and Eli were taking inventory of the ship's cargo while Harris manned the helm. The pair were attempting to work through the crates hastily, as the duke was very clear about the fact that he expected both Tam and Eli to learn how to steer so that they could all take turns in shifts.

Eli nodded as she lifted the last crate lid up. "Beets in this one."

"Beets? Again? Those don't even grow here in Zinfera, do they?" Tam speculated while carefully moving a box of moonshine back in place. In total they had found five crates' worth of the root vegetable.

"They don't, but they keep a long time. So even if they received these in Troivack, it makes sense to have them aboard a ship."

"Hm. Guess I'll make some beets for dinner. Do we have any perishables I should cook sooner rather than later?"

Eli turned back to Tam, opening her mouth to respond, when Luca's pounding steps echoed down to them.

"Girl!"

The couple glanced toward the doorway of the hold, and saw Luca panting heavily, doubled over. He must have been exploring the ship.

"There's a girl! In a cage! A human girl!" Luca gasped, lifting his face to them.

Tam and Eli looked at each other in alarm.

"A girl? How old is she? Is she alive?" Eli asked while rising from her knees to a stand.

"Where is she, Luca?" Tam added more gently.

"Captain's room!" Luca panted.

Tam and Eli shared a look of tenuous dread, then both moved in sync toward the door.

"Luca, please show us where this room is," Tam ordered seriously.

Nodding, Luca turned and tried to resume running, but his steps were heavy and sluggish.

Eli caught up easily to him and placed a hand on his shoulder. "You haven't fully recovered from your cold. Don't push yourself."

Luca slouched. "But I feel fine!"

Eli cast him a stern look, making him groan in exasperation. Regardless, he did listen and trudged onward.

To get to the captain's quarters, they had to climb back up through the vessel, the temperature rising as they did so. Tam and Eli broke out in sweat as the summer heat outside roasted them.

When they reached the end of a particular passageway with the doorway framed in ornate, sharp-angled Zinferan-style carvings, Tam and Eli signaled Luca to wait outside. Tam took the lead, gently easing open the door, that with its well-oiled hinges didn't make a sound.

The Zinferan pirate's room, despite it not being on a particularly large vessel, still sported three walls of windows overlooking the water. There was a large comfortable bed and a heavy carved desk laden with papers and gold baubles. Built just below the windows were bookcases stacked tidily with rolled-up parchment and maps as well as some navigational devices. To add a touch of comfort to the space, there was a thick carpet with blue flowers and silvery thread outlining flourishing designs. It could have been a stylish cabin for the wealthy captain of a respectable ship…

But there, in the far-left corner, just as Luca had said, was a cage. A cage holding a little girl with her knees pulled up to her chest.

Blood roared in Tam's ears. He wished he had pummeled the pirate captain a few more times for good measure before ending his life.

"Gods," Eli breathed.

Tam rushed over to the desk, grabbed a silver-tipped quill and a backstaff, then hurried over to the cage. "Hi there, are you alright? What's your name?" he asked quickly while examining the heavy lock.

The little girl raised wide brown eyes to Tam, then to Eli, but she said nothing.

She had black hair and tan skin.

Her features indicated she was Troivackian, and she looked malnourished.

Tam pressed his mouth together and tried to swallow past the emotion that rose in him when he observed the hollowness behind the girl's eyes. He refocused his attention on picking the lock to help take his mind off of the palpable pain surrounding the girl.

Luckily, despite the rocking of the ship, the lock wasn't tricky, just large and awkward, and so with two satisfying clicks, he was able to yank it free and throw open the top door to the cage.

"Come on out," Eli coaxed, her voice soft.

The little girl stood, revealing a long dirty shapeless dress or tunic—it was hard to discern which—but she kept her hands clasped in front of herself and didn't take a step out of the cage.

Her hair was straight and a little mussed, but not matted. She had a freckle a couple of inches below her right eye.

Tam crouched down so that he was lower than she was. Seeing this, Eli followed suit, she must have understood his intention to seem less intimidating.

"My name is Tam, and this is Eli. We are… borrowing this ship and heading to Gondol in Zinfera. Where are you from?" Tam used his softest, friendliest tone.

The little girl's eyes moved to Tam, but she didn't respond.

"If you have family, we can try to find them," Eli said, her own expression serene.

The little girl's gaze shifted to Eli, but otherwise she didn't move.

Luca charged in, bolting right up to the little girl with a steamed bun in his hand. "Here! It's good!"

The little girl's eyebrows twitched at the sight of the food, then slowly drifted to Luca's beaming face. He tilted his head.

Tam opened his mouth to calmly tell Luca to maybe take a step or two back to give her some space, when she gingerly reached out and accepted the food.

As the little girl took a tentative bite of the bun, Tam watched the way her eyes lit up. She scarfed down the rest of the bun without much trouble thereafter.

"Thank you for bringing that, Luca." Tam smiled at his son, who gave his father a grin of his own.

"What's your name? I told you my name's Luca before when I first found you! I'm seven. You look younger than me. Are you younger?" Luca chattered excitedly while the little girl wiped her mouth with the back of her hand. "My dad says I should make friends my own age, but we haven't met a lot of kids. Do you want to be friends? I mean, I do have a friend. Jeong! But he's grown up. He can grow a beard. He's pretty great, but he had to go home. Where is your home?"

The girl's eyes moved to Tam. The look on her face was oddly mature, and it said, *What do I say to this kid?*

"Do you have a name? I could give you a name! My dad gave *me* a name! After an astronomer! Or an astrologer? Which one, Dad?"

"Erm, technically he was both."

"That's even better!"

The girl seemed to realize that if she didn't start talking she was going to be subjected to more of Luca's rambling-plus-questions, and so she finally spoke.

"I'm Penelope."

"Can I call you Penny?" Luca asked brightly.

"No."

"Oh… But your name is long. It's not short like mine is. Though I guess I could be called Lou—"

"Penelope," Eli interrupted while lightly grasping Luca's arm and pulling him back toward her. "You look like you're from Troivack. Are you aware you are in Zinfera?"

Penelope let out an irritated huff. "I guessed as much. That captain was Zinferan."

"I see. Penelope, do you know where your mother or father are…?" Tam ventured carefully.

"My father's dead."

"Oh. I'm very sorry to hear that. That's really—"

"He died three years ago. It's fine."

The quickness of her words as she cut Tam off paired with the tightness in her tone told Tam it was not at all fine.

"And your mother?" Eli asked regardless.

"Probably dead. She was sick the last time I saw her." There was a shiftiness to the girl that hinted at a half-truth there, or maybe just pure discomfort.

"We can try and find her or your other family members if you like. We're heading to Gondol, as I mentioned."

"You stole a boat. You aren't really trustworthy," Penelope pointed out with an appropriate amount of dubiousness.

"Well, uh… we stole the boat from the bad person who put you in the cage if that makes any difference," Tam offered bashfully. The little girl's directness and steadiness put him on the spot much the way his mother could.

"You're still criminals."

"That is *technically* true, but we are more the kind of criminals who just wanted to be left alone and found ourselves wrapped up in a bunch of trouble." Tam knew he had done a terrible job of explaining that, and yet remarkably, the young girl seemed to understand. She gave a slight shrug of her left shoulder and a tilt of her head.

"Are you still hungry? Want me to go get more buns?" Luca offered while squirming under Eli's touch. He was impatient to move again.

"I… I guess I could eat—"

"Wait. Luca, where did you get that bun?" Eli asked sharply.

Luca turned and smiled freely up at her. "The galley! The men that were on the ship before had some left out!"

"You don't eat other people's food! Especially not bad people!" Eli lectured.

"I didn't eat it, though! She did!" Luca defended while pointing back at Penelope.

"That's worse!" Eli reprimanded, then realized Penelope was staring at the two of them as if they had started meowing at each other and she hadn't a clue what was happening. Which, in fairness, she probably didn't.

"Penelope, I will find a tub, fill it with water, and leave you alone if you'd like a bath. Eli, would you be able to help her?" Tam turned to Eli, who was still staring in exasperation at Luca.

"I don't need help! I'm eight!" the girl exploded indignantly.

"Eight?" Luca looked utterly crestfallen. "Aw. I thought I was older… You look younger! Are you making it up?"

"No!" Penelope then folded her skinny arms and rolled her eyes while giving her head a bit of a toss.

Tam looked at Eli, and the two barely managed to suppress a laugh at the child's attitude. She must have started to feel safe and trust them a little—whether she realized it or not—if she was willing to act out.

Ideally they could continue easing her into talking more with more patience and kindness. They didn't know why she was there in a cage, or aboard the ship at all, or how long she'd been there. Neither Tam nor Eli needed to communicate this joint feeling, though. They simply set to work.

"Penelope, can you climb out of the cage by yourself?" Eli offered her hand. "I know it's hard to move when you've been cramped like that for a while."

The momentary lightening of the atmosphere dissipated at the reminder that Eli would've been treated similarly back when she had been a slave with Captain Woo, and Tam's mood once again turned black.

Then the sound of cracking knuckles had Tam looking down at Luca, who was scowling as he balled his right hand into a fist. He, too, appeared to be having some serious qualms about what he'd just heard.

Torn between proud and concerned right about now. Tam thought wryly.

Unaware of what was happening behind her, Eli carefully helped Penelope clamber out of the cage, the little girl winced the instant her knee bent.

"I'm not always in there," Penelope explained. "It's just when they go ashore that they lock me up so I don't cause trouble. Usually I'm washing dishes."

It wasn't exactly positive news, but it was better than many alternatives at least.

"Washing dishes is awful!" Luca declared seriously. "Back with my mother—not my mom here"—he gestured toward Eli—"but my mother in Daxaria, she would make me do dishes a lot. Sometimes my hands would get really dry and they'd bleed."

"And there are always more dishes," Penelope lamented with a sigh that someone many years her senior could've issued. She didn't comment on the oddity of Luca's history with his mothers.

"Always! Just when you think it's done, oh no, there's a fork! There's a frigg—stupid glass!" Luca cast a sheepish look in Eli's direction, as she was already looking at him in warning.

Putting his hands on his hips, Tam decided to stop the runaway dialogue before the two children wandered out of the cabin. "Alright, kids, let's go get some food. Then I'll get the bath ready for you, Penelope, so you can wash alone afterward." Tam's eyes met with Eli's. "Later we can let Harris know that we have another passenger."

Eli bobbed her head in understanding. Luca and Penelope gave vague nods. Amazingly, Luca's experience as a dishwasher back at his mother's tavern had earned him some begrudging camaraderie from Penelope, and so the two children walked out of the cabin talking.

"Cheese that was melted then hardened is the worst," Penelope said with great exasperation.

"Not as bad as a forgotten bread dough bowl where parts of it are still dough and other parts crust!"

"What about *burnt* cheese—"

When the two children had moved far enough ahead that they could no longer hear the grown-ups, Eli took in a long breath. "Tam, do you think that you might have a jinx? Or an odd fate that makes it so you find abandoned children whenever you travel on a boat?"

Tam stopped in his tracks. "Huh. Two times in a row—that *is* strange. Penelope isn't mine, though!"

"Mm, she wasn't entirely forthcoming about her parentage, so..."

"Oy!" Tam exclaimed in mock offense. "I don't casually go around—"

"Aren't you the one telling me all the time how you aren't as pure as you seem?"

"Well, that's different!"

"It isn't."

"I haven't slept with any Troivackian women!" Tam at last declared.

Eli stared at him flatly. Her thoughts weren't a mystery. "Dare I ask every nationality, as well as the number of your conquests?"

Tam felt himself turn a shade of ripe strawberry red. "Do I… Do I have to answer?"

Eli's jaw fell open.

And just when Tam realized how his words could've been interpreted, Eli turned and stalked off.

"Wait! That's not what I meant! It isn't a lot! Really! Only like… two? I think." Tam paused and once again, very belatedly, realized how *that* sounded. "It's bad that I'm not certain, isn't it?"

"*Yes, it is!*" Eli shouted back.

Tam grimaced.

And to think, he had presumed that after a battle with pirates, setting one ship on fire, and stealing another, they'd see nothing but smooth sailing.

CHAPTER 21

THE NUANCES OF NICETIES

Harris stared at the two children over the table, blinking very slowly. "Tam?"

"Yes?"

"How… are there two of them?"

Penelope's gaze shot up from her meal, and she eyed the duke much the way she would an idiot.

Tam had tried earlier to explain to Harris earlier that they had discovered a child belowdecks, but he hadn't gotten very far before getting bombarded with lessons on steering a ship.

Then Eli had come, and she'd had to learn how.

When dinnertime neared Tam had then left to cook, and so Eli steered and Harris helped himself to more moonshine nearby. Only the children hadn't come up to greet Harris during any of this—Penelope had been having a bath, and Tam kept Luca nearby to make sure he wouldn't try to eat any random food they hadn't cleaned up from the pirate crew.

All of this meant that it wasn't until the freshly scrubbed Penelope—who wore a long, clean white tunic with a rope around her waist—was seated across the table that the mildly inebriated Lord Oscar Harris laid eyes on her.

"You didn't notice her before? She's Luca's sister," Tam lied just to see how inebriated the duke was.

Penelope revealed how quick-witted she was as she stared at Tam flatly. Luca grinned.

"Why is it that every time you leave my sights, you have another child? I swear this one wasn't here before." Harris squinted at Penelope. "Though your mother, Tam, will be over the moon to finally have a granddaughter. She might even forget to kill you for having them while unmarried."

Chuckling and shaking his head, Tam spooned out the cooked beets and sausages he had prepared with some kimchi he had located belowdecks.

"What is that?" Harris asked, curling his lip at the brilliant-red beets.

"Vegetables," Penelope contributed while looking disapprovingly at the Daxarian duke.

Harris pointed a fork at the girl. "Name?"

"Penelope."

Harris squinted at her. "You're feisty. I like you."

"You're drunk." Penelope gave a derisive scoff.

Harris grinned. "Yep. You're exactly the kind of kid that goes places. Though tone down the rudeness just a bit around strangers."

"She's testing us, Harris. To see if we really are as harmless as we say we are," Tam reasoned while leveling Penelope with a knowing look.

She frowned back at him.

From her place at the helm, Eli glanced over her shoulder at them and gave the back of Penelope's head a very tense look.

Tam bit back a smile. He had a hunch that Penelope would soon be hearing the same lectures Luca had about manners and respectfulness.

"We found Penelope belowdecks as a prisoner. We'll try to get her back to her family. Kat can probably help," Tam said while cutting into his dinner.

Harris didn't answer straight away as he was sniffing the beets dubiously.

"Penelope, do you have anyone that you know in Zinfera? If not, you might have to come to Daxaria with us while we sort out where your family is in Troivack." Tam directed the question at the little girl who had tucked into her meal without complaint, revealing surprisingly polished dinner etiquette.

But at the mention of Daxaria, Penelope recoiled.

"Something wrong…?" Tam asked carefully.

"My… my mother and father hate Daxaria. And all Daxarians." Her dark eyes turned intent as her brows lowered into an ominous look. "Are you all Daxarians?"

"Eli is originally from Zinfera, but both Lord Oscar Harris and myself are from Daxaria, yes," Tam responded, keeping his tone even.

The little girl turned to Luca. "When you were talking about your mother's pub, you meant back in Daxaria?"

"Yes?" Luca looked perfectly confused as to why that came as a surprise. It didn't help that he had one cheek stuffed to the point of nearly bursting.

Penelope's nose scrunched up in disgust.

Tam leaned back in his seat and observed the child in silence for a time. "Have you ever met any Daxarians before?" He probed lightly in the hope of turning the discussion onto a more positive route.

Penelope's jaw worked and her attention grew fixated on her plate. "Maybe."

The future duke finished swallowing his food. "Well, I'd like to think I'm not the worst."

"That one's annoying." Penelope pointed her fork at Harris, whose lips were stained red as he made a healthy dent in his serving of beets.

"That isn't very kind of you," Tam said quietly.

She squirmed.

Evidently she wasn't used to being reprimanded by a stranger in front of more strangers. All of whom were Daxarian.

"So what? I only need to be nice to my family."

"That isn't true." This time it was Luca who interrupted. "Unless people are mean first, then you should be nice."

"Not everyone who is mean acts mean," Penelope retorted sharply while rounding on Luca.

"That may be true, but do *you* want to be mean?" Tam continued, staring levelly at the little girl.

He watched as she lowered her fork and shrank back in her seat. "I'd rather be mean and alive than nice and dead."

No one spoke.

The hurt and bitterness in Penelope's voice sobered the mood drastically.

Lowering his fork slowly, then plucking up his black napkin up to wipe his mouth, Harris turned to the little girl. "There are times to be mean and times to be nice. Being nice makes things happy. But you are right that sometimes it is better to be mean, Miss Penelope."

At this, the girl relaxed fractionally.

Seeing this, the duke leaned his forearms on the table and continued. "For example, there once was a young woman I loved very much. Her name was Hannah."

Tam tilted his head. Where in the world was he going with this?

"When she first got hired at the castle in Austice—that's in Daxaria—she was the opposite of you, Penelope. She tried to be nice and sweet to everyone so that other people would be nice and sweet back to her. It was her own way of trying to survive, because, you see, sometimes when you're mean it draws meaner people to you."

Penelope stilled as she listened.

"But then some not very nice knights started thinking they could do whatever they wanted to her, say anything they wanted to her, and she would just keep being nice."

Penelope glowered.

"Well. Tam there—yes, that man sitting over there—his father told off those knights. And he explained what they did was wrong. At first, they didn't care and wanted to bully him."

Penelope looked at Tam only briefly before she returned her attention to Lord Harris.

"But when they were mean first? Tam's da was meaner back, and they still thought it was okay to be mean to Hannah because, well, she wasn't ever mean back to them like Tam's father was. Until one day, she had enough, and she screamed at them and threatened them, and she was utterly terrifying." A dreamy smile took over Harris's face. "Soon, everyone was mean. But being mean takes a lot of energy, and so, eventually, the knights started being nice, and then Tam's father started being nice, and Hannah… well, she was nice, but she had learned to be mean at the right time."

The little girl gaped at Harris, her eyes wide, her feelings unclear.

"So, hearing this story, there are two things you need to learn. The first: being mean typically has two outcomes. Someone is going to be meaner, or you are going to scare someone off. Just like being nice means sometimes people are going to be nice back, and sometimes they are going to be mean."

Penelope waited patiently for the second point.

"The second lesson here is, depending on what you want from other people, you have to determine what you're going to be."

Tam wasn't sure how this wisdom was going to go over with an eight-year-old, no matter how mature she might seem.

"How do you want us to treat you?" Lord Harris continued. "Do you want us to be nice to you? Or do you want us to be scared off by you?"

Penelope's mouth twisted in thought. She didn't share her answer, but she didn't cuss out the duke, either.

The rest of the dinner passed by mostly in silence, until everyone's plates were scraped clean, and Tam started to fix a plate for Eli before taking over the helm of the ship to give her a break.

"Thank you for dinner. And for letting me out of the cage," Penelope said softly to Tam.

He smiled at her. "You are most welcome. Did you like the food?"

Her face scrunched up. "I don't like beets."

Tam laughed. "That's fine. I'll cook other things for you in the future. Besides"—he leaned down and lowered his voice to a whisper—"I think Lord Harris loves them. So we can just make him eat them."

Before she could stop herself, the little girl let out a giggle.

Tam straightened just in time for Luca to skip up beside Penelope. "Dad! Can we hear about the stars tonight?"

Tam glanced up at the darkening sky to see that there were indeed two constellations already rising above them.

"We could do that. But it will have to be later. I'm going to be steering soon."

"Aw…" Luca's shoulders slumped.

"Do you want to play a game?" Penelope ventured while feigning a careless air.

Luca rounded on her eagerly. "Yeah! What kind of game? I only know how to play hide-and-seek and tag."

"You also know how to leapfrog," Tam reminded his son fondly.

Luca grinned. "Oh yeah! Jeong and Bong taught me! Here, I'll show you!"

Penelope didn't look particularly enthused about this new game, but she still hesitantly followed Luca as he raced down to the main deck.

Smiling, Tam felt yet another knot in his chest loosen as he watched the two children depart. It was hard to believe seeing his son find a playmate would bring him such a measure of peace given the day they'd had.

Giving his head a shake, Tam turned to Eli and was reminded that they hadn't resolved their earlier discussion about past romantic partners. Ducking his head in what he hoped would appear a contrite look, Tam made his way over to his assistant.

"I got you some dinner. I can take over for the next while."

"The winds are changing," Eli informed him coolly.

"Ah… I'll watch out for that. Thank you for letting me know."

She said nothing, nor did she let go of the wheel spindles.

"I'm sorry for my jokes earlier."

"You weren't joking. You genuinely couldn't remember every woman you've bedded," Eli reminded him curtly.

Tam coughed and started to rub the back of his neck with his free hand. "Er… three. I've been with three women. Luca's mother was the first. I courted a girl a few months later who wanted to get married and have children, and it was around the time my first nephew was born. After seeing my sister give birth, I was relatively certain I was nowhere near ready for that kind of thing, so the relationship ended. Then years later, I—uh—I'm not proud of it, but I had a one-night encounter with a woman."

"So you *could* have other children out in the world?"

"No, no. I occasionally cross paths with the second lady. She works as a merchant in Austice. She's married with her own two children now. You actually would've met her when picking up moonshine for the—" Tam stopped talking as Eli's head whipped around at this new information. He decided the only way to make the moment end quicker was to conclude his sexual history as efficiently as possible while giving out very few details. "The last woman was, erm, older. She couldn't have children… anymore… when we…"

Eli frowned at him.

"She lives in Sorlia?" Tam finished awkwardly.

"Did you love any of these women?" Eli questioned.

Tam knew a smarter man would've lied. But he wanted to be a good man more than a smart one.

"I loved the second woman. Mary. We courted for seven months."

Eli looked ahead of herself again.

"Have you ever loved someone?" Tam dared to ask.

"Not really. I had an infatuation or two, but nothing like love."

"Ah." He couldn't think of anything else to say.

"It's intimidating enough—the idea that you… we… do *that*. But it is even more unpleasant to think how you have something to compare it with," Eli explained stiffly.

Tam moved around the helm to place himself directly in front of Eli, his expression stern. "Every person and every relationship is different. And the differences in ours have made it so that you're the first woman I've actually wanted to marry and have children with."

Eli blushed.

"Go eat dinner. I'll take the next shift." Tam jerked his chin toward the table, where Lord Harris was already asleep beside the lantern he had lit.

Nodding, Eli stepped back and accepted the plate Tam offered to her while he took the wheel. He gave her a warm smile and adjusted his focus to the compass on top of the wheel's post to ensure that the handoff hadn't put them too far off course.

"Tam?"

"Mm?"

"What if we… What if we shared a bed without Luca later."

"Ah, was he kicking you in his sleep? He did that to me a few times on our way here. I had to make him cut his toenails." Tam sighed at the painful memory.

"No, I… Maybe I want to try being… *closer* with you."

Tam went rigid.

His eyes widened.

How did breathing work again?

He cleared his throat and slowly turned to look at Eli.

She was fidgeting something fierce, but she locked eyes with him.

Tam vaguely remembered to inhale and exhale before speaking. "Uh… Are you… uh. Are you sure?"

She considered the question, then nodded.

Tam felt his face flush, then the blood started to make its way elsewhere.

"What about… Um…" Tam glanced over his shoulder at Harris. The man was snoring soundly, but Tam still dropped his voice. "What about contraceptives?"

Eli inched closer to Tam. "I know my cycle and… it'd be safe."

"Right… Ah. Right. Well. Later? Tonight?"

"I-If that's alright."

"More than alright," Tam reassured her swiftly. "But can I ask why now?" He sincerely hoped he wasn't slapping a gift horse in the face, but he really wanted to be sure she was ready for what she was asking.

"We just took in another child and we haven't even gotten intimate yet. It seems to me that we are all… backward."

"We don't have to adopt her. She probably has family."

"I know. But it is also that I… I've wanted to do *that* with you for a while, and I guess I don't have a better reason than that. I just want to."

Tam took in a heavy breath of air. "I am very happy about this, really. But I do want to remind you that my family has… err… a strong propensity to have an easy time conceiv—"

"I know."

"Right." Tam licked his lips, searching for his next words. "And if that does happen, you're okay with it?"

"Like I said, we should be fine with my cycle, but if it happens we can deal with it then."

Tam opened and closed his mouth. "We *are* in the middle of a war and a rebellion, so I just—"

"Do you not want to?" Eli started to shy away.

Tam instantly panicked. "No! I do! I *promise* I very much so do!" Realizing his voice had risen in volume inadvertently, Tam brought it back down to its previous hush. "I just want to make sure we are on the same page about everything."

"We're already parenting a child through this whole event. It wouldn't be ideal, but we seem to be doing just fine. Besides, we could always abandon our plans and run off to Lobahl and start a new life there." Eli shrugged.

Tam slid a knowing glance at her. "You've actually thought out a plan like that, haven't you?"

"I hear once you convince the Lobahlan government to let you in, it's a wonderful place to live," she answered innocently.

Tam grinned. "Alright. We share a bed. And if we wind up having a child, we leave the political fire we started and start a new life. Sounds like a plan with no consequences or problems whatsoever."

Eli drifted closer to Tam, rose up onto her toes, leaned in, and whispered, "You know how adept I am at planning."

Gods help him.

Tam's right knee buckled.

Only Eli could make talk about careful planning so seductive.

Tam coughed, and Eli smiled as she slid away from him. Apparently she knew exactly what she was doing.

His head swimming, Tam struggled to keep his eyes and mind on the very crucial task of steering the ship. Sensing his inner battle, Eli left him to take a seat at the table and eat.

Gulping down a much-needed dose of cold air, Tam discovered that, as adventurous as his day had been thus far, he was brimming with newfound energy.

It was almost impressive… though not entirely unexpected.

CHAPTER 22

A CERTAIN CONNECTION

By the time Tam let go of the wheel and passed it off to Harris, his hands were mildly paralyzed by the cold and the strength it had taken him to grip the wheel through changing tides and winds.

The duke was bleary-eyed at first, but after a few minutes chatting with Tam about their course—they were easing around Zinfera's east shores, headed north—he looked alert enough to take on the task. This next leg of their journey would see their ship climbing up alongside the eastern mountain range of Zinfera known as the Emperor's Crown due to its placement near Gondol.

Tam turned toward the stairs that would take him down from the quarterdeck to the main deck, his nerves scrambling. Eli was waiting for him in the cabin, where they would share a night together. He felt hyper-aware of his every movement.

Gods, he'd never been so nervous about such a thing. Even on his own first night, it had been with Rosaline, and she, being the more experienced one that night, had been incredibly patient and instructive.

The wind surged, and a chill skittered over him.

By this time, he was blindly making his way around the main deck toward their room. Then a very loud voice interrupted his thoughts: "I'm not lying!"

"You are! You're just saying that because I said my secret!"

Squinting through the shadows, Tam spotted two small figures sitting on the steps up to the poop deck.

Right.

How could he have forgotten he'd promised to tell the children stories about the stars?

Gods. How base can I be?

Shaking his head, Tam stowed his still-freezing hands into his pockets and headed toward Luca and Penelope.

"I'm never telling you anything again!" Luca hollered.

"You can't be serious! That's just… but it isn't normal!"

"What's happening?" Tam's voice was sharp.

He was prone to being a bit sensitive to terms like *normal*, especially when directed toward his son and how he might not be just that.

"Dad! She… I told her… I told her about my dreams with the beasts and people I've never met, and she doesn't believe me!"

"You told your father? That isn't a secret then!"

"I bet you told your mom your secret!" Luca argued.

By this time both children were on their feet, and Luca had his hands balled into fists at his sides.

"She's probably dead now, so it doesn't count!" Penelope said bitterly.

Tam folded his arms. "Who is going to tell me what exactly has just happened?"

In the faint light of the waning moon, Tam could see Penelope drop her chin to her chest stubbornly. So he looked to Luca instead.

His son squirmed, making Tam think of his nephews back in Daxaria whenever they had gotten in trouble.

"I told her about my dreams. And… and I had only ever told you about it. Even my mother in Daxaria didn't want to hear about it. And then she said—"

"Shut up!" Penelope shrieked, turning on Luca and revealing that tears had started to roll down her face.

“Hey,” Tam called out softly. “You don’t have to tell me your secret, Penelope, but do not tell Luca to shut up.”

“My dad’s a witch! He knows stuff! You’re probably just a witch, too!” Luca sniffed as he struggled to meet Penelope’s watery gaze.

Tam very much wished he could have asked what this secret was. “Kids,” he started.

Penelope whirled on him. *“I’m not a kid!”*

Frowning, Tam lowered himself down to be eye level with her. “You *are* a kid. And there is nothing wrong with that, and you know what?”

Penelope’s lower lip quivered as she shook her head.

“Just because you’re a kid doesn’t mean you are powerless.”

Both Luca and Penelope stilled.

“You have two very powerful things as a kid that you might not know about,” Tam explained, holding up his two fingers. “The first is that there are more people than you know in the world who are out there waiting to fight for you.”

Penelope’s shoulders sagged, unimpressed.

“The second is that when you are a kid, you learn faster than adults. So if you put your mind to it, you can outsmart any adult. It might take time and hard work, but you can figure it out. Even if an adult hurts you, you can learn how to heal yourself. You can learn how to be strong enough so they can’t ever hurt you again.”

Tam watched as both children struggled against tears, and he wished with all his might that his words did something to help whatever hurt they’d experienced in the past. Or at least made them feel a little better.

“Did anyone ever hurt you, Dad?” Luca croaked before wiping his nose on his sleeve.

Tam gave a half smile and reached up to brush away his son’s tears. “Lots of people. Honestly, both of you have probably had more people hurt you than I ever did. But it isn’t about how many people hurt you. It’s about how you learn from it. How you heal and become stronger.”

“How is it going to make me stronger if I just hurt all the time?” Penelope asked, traces of anger reappearing in her voice.

“Well, I bet you now know more about pirates than a lot of other eight-year-olds, right?”

Surprised by this point, Penelope slowly blinked.

"And I bet you would spot one really quickly."

"I know where they like to hide knives… You hide knives, too." Penelope gave a sly smile that made Tam smile back at her.

"I do. And see? Even Eli didn't know I had knives on me when we met."

The little girl bit her lip and twisted back and forth, evidently proud of herself for knowing such a thing.

Tam could tell she liked this new awareness of her own capabilities.

"You got one thing wrong, though…" Penelope trailed off, her movements stopping. "No one cares about kids. People only respect and listen to adults."

Tam shook his head. "There are a lot of adults that aren't respected or listened to. But I can guarantee you that *I* care. Eli cares. Lord Harris cares. I grant you it's harder to tell with him, but if you were ever in danger? He would do everything he could to keep you safe."

As though sensing he was being talked about, a very long, echoing belch echoed from the stern of the ship. "Those beets are making a ruckus, Tam!" Lord Harris boomed bawdily.

Tam pretended he didn't hear anything.

"So look, you have three surprise people in the world I bet you didn't know would protect you. And I can name a lot more off the top of my head. Remember that woman Harris was talking about, Hannah? Phew… If anyone messes with you, they should be terrified. She is indestructible when she has a frying pan!"

Luca giggled.

Penelope did not look convinced, so he changed his tactic a little bit.

"Penelope, I'm not saying there aren't horrible people, and I'm willing to bet that you have experienced things no child should have because of those people. I also think you've met more bad people than good. So you can doubt me as much as you want. Feel how you feel. But I am still going to protect you."

"I thought…" The little girl swallowed, struggling to maintain her strong front. "I thought the whole point of earlier was that if I'm mean, no one will help me."

"Mm, there's a difference in wanting to have a nice conversation with you and the fact that regardless of how much attitude you give me, I am going to protect you."

Silence rested over the trio.

"I still don't believe you," Penelope whispered.

"That's okay. It doesn't change that I'm going to protect and care about you going forward, and I hope I can prove it to you."

She couldn't say anything to that.

"I won't ever tell you my secret," she added, as though testing him.

"That's okay, too. Just don't speak disrespectfully to Luca like that."

Giving a sniff, Penelope twitched her mouth to the side for a moment before she leaned her head in Luca's direction. "Sorry."

"It's okay. But I *was* telling the truth."

Sensing that Luca's comment could reopen up the possibility for arguments, Tam stood up. "Alright kids, let's get to bed."

Penelope glanced at Luca then Tam. "Where am I sleeping?"

The three of them started walking back toward the stairs. "There are five of us on a ship for fifty people. I'm pretty confident we can find you something all to yourself," Tam assured her with a grin.

As they neared the stairs, Tam discovered Eli leaning against the railing, her gaze toward him warm.

The look in her eyes in the moonlight made his heart thud against his chest. Blinking quickly, he remembered there were children present. "I'm getting these two to sleep—Penelope, you can pick wherever you want to sleep, but make sure it's just a few doors down from everyone else at the farthest, alright?"

"O-Okay. I'm going to lock the door."

"Go right ahead, but I'll make sure your lantern is blown out before you do that," Tam explained reasonably.

Penelope nodded in agreement. The mood was still a little fragile, but not necessarily in a bad way.

Rather there was a sense among the group that something rather wonderful was just about to start.

Eli closed the door quietly.

Tam swallowed.

"Luca was a little upset about not being in the same room," he began conversationally.

"Mm-hm. He seemed alright by the end of your story."

"You mean dead asleep?"

"Yes."

Tam chuckled and looked down at his fingers, which had at last thawed from his stint steering. Eli crossed the small room and lit the lantern beside the bed.

Given that Lord Harris had been roped into the whole adventure, they had decided he could have the captain's cabin. They'd found a relatively comfortable one for themselves two doors down; it must have been for the first mate. Meanwhile Luca and Penelope were in the navigator's and the quartermaster's rooms.

Tam started to rub the back of his neck as the weightiness of the quiet settled over them. "We won't have a lot of time together, afterward. Just so you know. We really will need to sleep for a bit, with us steering in shifts. I can take the next shift so you can rest more, and, uh, I'll wake you up when it's time for yours."

Eli slowly rounded the double bed and approached Tam. His heart appeared to have shifted expediently into his throat.

"Yes, that scheduling makes sense."

She stood a mere inch from him. If she leaned forward, her lips could've brushed his collarbone.

Tam leaned back a little. "Are you certain that this is how…"

"Why is it"—Eli's voice was a mere hush—"that you seem more timid than me?"

"Because I don't want to mess anything up?" Tam tried to smile confidently down at her—though it was wildly difficult to meet her eyes right then—and could tell he hadn't quite pulled it off.

She gazed at him calmly in the faint light of the lantern. "You have given me absolute power over you by already saying you'd give me everything I want. If something goes wrong, I'll have to be the one to take responsibility."

Tam's knees were going weak. "Eli, once I stop… stop talking—"

"Which I hope is soon," Eli murmured as she leaned closer and brushed her lips lightly against his neck.

Thoughts and words became next to impossible for Tam. The smell of sea air and citrus lingered around her. He still hadn't quite figured out what that floral scent of hers was…

It was a struggle to finish his earlier thought. "It's going to be very hard to stop."

"I won't say stop, Tam." Eli paused her careful work moving her lips around his throat and inclined back a little. "You…" She sighed and settled back on the flats of her feet. Then she decided to torment him a little and started carefully sliding his vest from his shoulders.

"You are my favorite person, Tam. And everything is safe and good with you. The entire world seems to be falling apart around me, but I am steady here with you. With our family. And I know now that my feelings aren't because I'm indebted to you, or out of respect, or lust…" she added a little self-consciously. "I love you because you would become the devil himself for me and Luca. And even then, with you a devil, I'd still feel like everything was perfectly right as long as I was with you."

"You love me?" Tam rasped.

Eli stripped off her tunic, then her bindings. "Yes. I do. Even if you are being a little wasteful with the time we have right now."

Tam gave a breathy laugh, then didn't bother saying anything else. He kissed Eli deeply, a hand cradling her neck and another grasping her waist, pulling her closer to himself.

There were no other hesitations or words spared on the wisdom of what they were doing, and suffice it to say, there was no further wasting of time on either of their parts for the rest of the night.

CHAPTER 23

NIGHTTIME NAVIGATIONS

Tam and Eli had their backs to the headboard as the ship continued to rock back and forth—albeit with a more noticeable rise and fall as the night progressed and the winds shifted.

"That was…" Tam started to say, then found himself unable to complete the sentence.

"It was unexpected," Eli contributed dazedly.

"Good unexpected?" Tam asked, a frown creasing the space between his eyebrows.

"You were there. Yes. Good unexpected."

"You never know," Tam said with a light chuckle, still in awe of the experience they had just shared.

"Is it always like that?" Eli wondered while looking over at Tam as he continued to stare dumbly at the opposite wall.

"No. It is not."

"Oh… that's disappointing."

"I mean, it has never been like that in my experience in the past."

The sharp look Eli was giving Tam's profile motivated him to turn and apologize. "I just mean it was more with you! More meaningful, more intense."

Her expression softened again. "I can live with that assessment."

"Oh good." Tam laughed again before rubbing his face with his hand.

"So you said we should try to sleep now?"

"You can sleep after that?" Tam rounded on Eli, who was already reaching beside the bed for her clothes.

"Sure I can, and I bet you can, too. It's been a long day," she retorted casually.

Tam gaped at Eli as she sorted out her tunic and bindings, and set to work getting herself clothed again. When she failed to acknowledge the look he was giving her, Tam sighed, dropped his chin to his chest, and went about grabbing his trousers off the floor.

The pair had just finished setting themselves to rights when a knock sounded on the door.

Exchanging a brief look of uncertainty, Tam opened the door to find Lord Harris standing there looking dead exhausted.

"One of you needs to take over. I wedged my coat in the wheel to keep it on course to come get you, but I'm going toooo…" The duke trailed off.

He looked at Eli, then at Tam, who was masking his feelings as best he could.

A slow smile grew on the duke's face."So it's like that now is it?"

Tam blinked but otherwise didn't falter. "I don't know what you—"

"Oh, Tam. You don't survive the life I've had by being stupid." Harris's eyes glimmered in good humor. "Look, it's probably for the best. If we can't get you married, then her expecting your, er, second or third child—I don't even know anymore—it's probably for the best." Harris waved a hand.

"It isn't like that!" Eli put in, despite her entire face and neck turning a shade of red usually reserved for cardinal feathers.

"Come now. You'll make a lovely Lady Elisara Ashowan. I'm sure Fin's parents will be thrilled! Eventually!"

"Harris?" Tam began, placing his hands on his hips.

"Yes, godson?"

"Shut up."

The duke gave a dramatic gasp. "By the Gods! It's like your father is here in the room with us!"

"I thought we weren't supposed to tell people to shut up."

The three adults turned to find a sleepy Penelope standing and staring up at them, her hair mussed and her eyes not fully open.

"Yeah, Tam! You shouldn't tell people to shut up!" Harris chortled. "Thank you for coming to my defense, Miss Penelope. Now, if you all will excuse me, I'm going to sleep. One of you go steer the boat before we hit something."

Tam nodded, then addressed Eli over his shoulder. "You sleep. I'll get us through the rest of the night."

"The whole night? That's too long," Eli argued sternly.

"I'm used to working all night. Penelope, Eli can give you help if you need something," Tam gentled his voice for the little girl, who didn't look like she was fully back into the land of the waking.

She frowned up at him. "I don't need anything. You're all just loud."

Tam smiled and mussed her hair, making her growl at him. He laughed then continued on past her to take over steering the boat.

Issuing a long, loud yawn that sounded like a satisfied hound curling up in front of a crackling fire, Harris made his way down the passage to his own quarters. "Night, everyone."

Once the door to the previous captain's quarters closed, Eli looked down at Penelope.

"I'm sorry that we were too loud. Is there anything else I can get for you? Water?"

Penelope shook her head slowly.

"Are you heading back to bed then?"

The little girl didn't answer. Instead her mouth twisted and she bounced on the balls of her feet awkwardly.

"Are you scared to be alone?" Eli ventured next.

"No!" Penelope shouted heartfully.

Eli tilted her head patiently. "Then what?"

Penelope scowled up at her. "You aren't nice like that Tam guy is."

Unable to help herself, Eli laughed. "Not really, no. But I do want to help you."

Penelope considered this. "I don't always like nice people. They can be annoying. And of course I don't trust them at all."

A melancholy weight fixed itself over Eli's face. "I used to feel that way, too."

The sound of another door opening made both girls look to see Luca emerge, right in time for the boat to give a larger lurch.

"What's going on?" Luca asked before a yawn overtook him.

"Oh great," Penelope muttered at his appearance.

Eli stared down at the two children and came to a very clear realization. "Would you both like to sleep in bed with me? It might help us all stay warmer," she offered while making it seem like an afterthought.

"I guess if it helps me keep warm," Penelope sniffed indignantly. "Boats are too wet. All the time. It always smells damp."

Luca didn't utter a word of complaint, merely skipped through the doorway and hopped into Eli and Tam's bed.

"Luca, go bring your blanket before you settle down. With three of us, there won't be as many blankets."

"That's because you hog them all!" Luca pointed out with a faint whine.

Eli rolled her eyes to the ceiling. "I can't help it. It happens in my sleep. Go get your blanket. You, too, Penelope."

The little girl nodded dutifully and disappeared to retrieve her own bedding.

Eli watched Penelope slip back into her room and felt a smile tug at her face. She remembered being terrified around strangers. And she also remembered that she never would've admitted she was terrified of being alone, especially shortly after being freed.

Back when Captain Woo had been aboard with Penelope, his presence would've meant that he'd be the target of any threats that attacked the ship, and he'd be the one dealing with it.

Things were different now, and while it was a good change, odds were it left Penelope feeling more vulnerable.

Eli had had those exact feelings and experiences back when she'd been taken.

When the children returned with their blankets and crawled into bed, Eli joined after making sure that each little foot was properly wrapped in a blanket.

"I'm turning the lantern off; are you ready?" she asked, her eyes already growing heavy and her blanket still warm from Tam.

"I have to pee," Luca announced.

"I think I do want water after all," Penelope added.

Eli's hand dropped away from the lantern as she stared at the kids. She wanted to snap *"Too damn bad"* as exhaustion settled over her, but instead some hidden trove of patience unearthed itself and she said, "Luca, go use the chamber pot in your room. Penelope, wait while I get you a cup."

And thus began the second wave of bedtime preparations.

It wasn't quite morning, but a lighter hue in the sky hinted at its approach. Eli had been dead asleep, but then a high-pitched gasp had jerked her awake and she found herself staring at Penelope.

The little girl was crouched on her knees, holding Eli's hand, sobbing.

Sitting up, alert, Eli seized the girl's shoulder with her free hand while vaguely noting a pain in her lower back from her activities the day before. "Penelope? What's wrong? What happened?"

"She's dead! If y-you adopt me, she's dead!" she sobbed nonsensically.

"What? Who's dead?" Eli felt a dull headache pound behind her eyes.

"M-my mother! If y-you adopt me she's dead!" Penelope burst out in fresh sobs.

"I-I don't understand. Can you try to explain it better?"

Looking around the chamber desperately for a towel that the child could use to wipe her face, Eli spotted one lying over a small trunk in the corner she hadn't noticed the night before. Only she couldn't retrieve it, because the little girl had her hand in a vise grip.

"I-I can see things! And they always happen! No matter what! A-And you and Tam are going to adopt me!"

Flummoxed, Eli tried soothing her again. "It was just a nightmare. You don't know for certain that your mother is dead. Everything will be—"

"You used to be in a cage, too. B-But they had a collar on you. And whenever you tried to fight, they'd t-tighten it, and it hurt."

Eli felt her gut churn.

A cold, horrific memory came to her mind's eye. Back when she'd first been taken by Captain Woo and she'd first shifted into beast form, he had slapped a collar on her exactly like Penelope described, but he'd probably told Penelope that story, right?

"Y-You told Tam you loved him last night!"

Eli opened and closed her mouth. Had Penelope been listening at the door? "Penelope, look at me," she ordered quietly. She was mildly surprised Luca hadn't woken up.

The little girl listened.

"I want you to breathe with me. In…" Eli took a deep breath in through her nose. "And out." She released the breath. "Let's do that three more times."

At first Penelope's breaths were stuttering and mixed with sobs, and she couldn't stop shaking, but by the third breath, her face had at least stopped looking so anguished.

"Alright. I need you to tell me again what is happening, because I still don't understand. If you can't do that right now, we can wait until later."

Penelope performed an extra-deep breath in and out of her own accord, then nodded slowly.

Eli gave her hand a gentle squeeze, released it, retrieved the towel from the chest, and offered it to her.

Penelope set to wiping her face clean of the tears and snot, looking infinitely wearier and older than an eight-year-old should.

"Lie back down," Eli instructed softly, her eyes briefly darting to Luca's slackened sleeping face on the other side of the bed.

Again, Penelope listened.

"Close your eyes."

She did this, too.

Eli gently stroked her hair, pulling her dark hair free from her face.

And eventually, Penelope's body relaxed back into sleep, and Eli could stop brushing her hair.

But Eli couldn't let herself fall asleep. There was too much to think about.

At least that's what Eli believed until she found herself being gently shaken awake by a very haggard Tamlin Ashowan when the sun had fully risen, and her two wards were nowhere to be found.

Aradia stared at the missive the air witch had just handed her.

She raised an eyebrow at the man's bowed head. "So now they are headed Gods know where, on a ship they've commandeered?"

"Yes, Your Magnificence."

"And the concubine is handling this how…?"

"By sending out as many ships she can spare."

"And is that a lot?"

"I'm afraid they are limited. Her Highness Soo Hebin has great power in Zinfera, but her strength lies in her controlling the Torit Desert, the Ori harbor, and Captain Woo's men."

"So now that the captain has been killed?"

"There is great upheaval and a lack of organization."

Aradia stared at the air witch blankly before closing her eyes and giving a scoff. "Either the Gods love the Ashowan family a little too much, or they got damn lucky."

The air witch cleared his throat. "If I may offer my own insight?"

Aradia waved her hand. She knew she should remember his name at some point, but she wasn't sure how often he would be around her to bother with it.

"I believe there is a grander plan behind this than a simple escape."

Aradia leaned forward and slid a brief glance at Ansar. He was sitting across the wrought-iron table from her. "Oh?" She propped her chin in her palm.

"Yes. Princess Elisara was—is—known for her intelligence and planning. It was one of the reasons Her Highness Soo Hebin felt threatened by her. I wonder if this is perhaps the princess declaring war or starting to campaign for the throne."

Aradia smiled. "Well, that would be wonderful, wouldn't it?" She looked at Ansar. "That would mean she's on her way here along with the Ashowan son *and* the devil. How tidy is that? The only problem is that we aren't exactly sure of the nature of his magic and will have to start making preparations. Her power sounds interesting as well—transforming into a giant animal…"

"What will you have us do, Your Magnificence?" the air witch implored reverently.

The first witch slumped back in her seat with a smile. "Prepare a ship. I want to intercept them before they get anywhere near the capital and the concubine gets her claws into them."

"But you don't have the dagger or Chronos yet," Ansar asked worriedly.

The dagger was the blade capable of channeling the fragments of Aradia's stunted magic, while Chronos, with the use of a mage crystal could stop time for a short interval.

Aradia kept her smile as she answered him. "But unlike in Troivack, I have a very helpful coven at my back, and some of these covens have familiars, don't they?"

The air witch nodded carefully.

"Then I will be able to make all the necessary preparations. Please send the witches that have familiars to me, the ones who have the strongest bonds, if possible."

"Is there a particular number of witches and familiars you require?" the air witch wondered helpfully.

Aradia rose to her feet. "Let's say ten to be safe."

If the air witch found this number high, he did not show it. Instead he backed out of the garden, bowing all the way, to obey her orders.

Ansar looked up at Aradia curiously. "Is there something you haven't told me?"

Regarding her follower fondly, the first witch bent down until she was nearly nose-to-nose with him. "Ansar, I've lived more lifetimes than I can count. You can't live long enough to hear everything I haven't told you."

CHAPTER 24
A SLIGHT SNAG

Tam sat with his head propped up against his fingers, and his right ankle resting atop his left knee as he watched Eli.

After waking her to take over the helm, Tam had slept most of the day away, only waking shortly before he had to make dinner.

So he took the few brief moments of freedom he had to watch the woman he loved.

Oddly enough, she hadn't seemed to notice he was doing this as she stared off into the distance with a line deepening between her brows.

Tam wondered if she'd want to wear a wedding dress when the time came to get married.

He envisioned her wearing a proper white gown and found a half smile pulling his mouth up. Though something about the image didn't quite seem like Eli…

Maybe there was a different type of formal wear Zinferans wore for a wedding? Tam was surprised that he didn't already know this.

Wait… After they got married, Eli would have to live with him at the keep he grew up in?

Tam scrunched his nose. The dark keep with its damp smell didn't fit her. She would probably be happier with lots of light, and a forest nearby she could run through unencumbered when in her beast form.

Tam's mind turned to the keep his mother's first husband—Hank Jenoure—had loved in Sorlia. That would be perfect. The woods weren't large, but there were plenty of deer to hunt and a pond filled with fish, an apple and a pear orchard. Maybe they would add a cornfield. Luca seemed to really enjoy corn the past few times Tam had served it.

Living in Sorlia also meant Luca could grow up near the three princes, his cousins…

Excitement swelled in Tam.

The library at the estate in Sorlia was in a state of minor disrepair, but that only meant they could reconstruct it to their liking and—

"The winds are changing. They're blowing us inland," Eli suddenly announced, revealing that she was in fact aware of Tam's presence.

It took a great deal of effort for Tam to free himself from his lovely daydream. His mind was slow and sluggish as he stood and joined Eli at the helm. Her eyes were bloodshot from fixating on the compass and horizon.

The mountain range to their left soared majestically along the skyline. The sun, as it lowered toward the edge of the world, cast streaks of pale oranges and pinks that set the snow atop the peaks ablaze.

The skies had been clear for the first two days of their journey, which was very fortunate given how much Eli and Tam had had to learn about sailing. It was a miracle and a blessing that Lord Harris knew as much as he did, and this was entirely thanks to his beloved duchess.

Duchess Mackenzie Harris of the Iones dukedom had been the middle daughter of a wealthy baron who had earned the majority of his wealth by the ships he owned. When Harris—with all of his eccentricities and his illegitimate birth—declared his love for the man's daughter, the baron hadn't agreed at first. The old baron had believed Harris was a madman, and so announced that he would only agree to bless their wedding if his future son-in-law knew everything possible about the ships that would come as a part of Mackenzie's dowry.

Well, the baron had underestimated the sincerity of Lord Oscar Harris, and they were wed within a year and a half of the stipulation.

"I guess this is when we start tacking." Tam sighed as he stowed his hands in his pockets and looked out at the vast expanse of the Tinoo Ocean to their right.

The water still looked calm. Though sometime over the next fortnight they'd enter the storm season.

"PROBLEM!" Lord Harris's shout made both Eli and Tam jolt.

They'd never heard Harris sound any measure of panicked.

"What is it?" Tam started walking toward the steps the duke was sprinting up with impressive speed.

"Three ships behind us. Luca spotted them," Harris explained before thrusting the spyglass at Tam.

He instantly lifted it to peer off their bow, and after a couple of sweeps over the horizon found that there were indeed three tall-masted ships.

"Shit."

"Exactly."

"Is there any chance that they are merchant ships?" Eli asked, though her grim tone indicated she didn't have much hope.

"No. Their V formation indicates they're military," Harris responded ruefully.

Tam continued squinting. "The speed they're moving tells me they have air and water witches aboard helping. If I were to guess? I'd say they'll catch up to us within a day. A day and a half at most."

Eli's grip on the spokes of the wheel tightened. "We could do what we did before: hide and sneak aboard their own ship, or lure them here and take care of them that way?" She didn't sound certain of the plan.

"They probably brought more witches this time," Tam guessed before looking to the distant rocky beaches. "I wonder if going on land would give us a better chance."

"If we get trapped on land, we won't have enough supplies to navigate our way through the mountains on foot. It doesn't look like a lot grows here." Harris shook his head.

"There are some forests about a week and a half on foot due west," Eli pointed out. "And the maps in the captain's quarters I found are up-to-date. So we wouldn't be guessing where to go."

"It would give us some coverage, and they'd have to split up as well," Tam added.

"They will torch the ship to stop you from leaving. They won't be making the same mistake twice about leaving their own vessels unguarded. And all they have to do is see where we anchored to guess roughly where we landed on shore." Harris stared in the direction of the ships, which were barely visible to the naked eye.

"What do we do then? Go ashore, or wait here like a sitting duck?" Tam asked, both in irritation at this new problem as well as genuine curiosity.

Lord Harris, a seasoned warrior, pondered this conundrum.

"There are a few other options," Eli interjected, her gaze homed in on Tam.

Tam raised an eyebrow.

"One relies a lot on you, but what if you simply appear on their ships at night when they pull closer and sink them? Or at least damage them enough to slow them down?"

Tam tilted his head, a subtle grimace on his face. "They'd have to be a lot closer for me to be able to do that. I can only travel longer distances if I know the space really well, and even then it would still mean they'd be a lot closer than I'm comfortable with, given the air and water witches they have aboard."

"Sometimes, in war and desperate times, there isn't a perfect plan. You just pick one of your best one and pray to the Goddess it works out," Harris informed them somberly.

Both Tam and Eli fell quiet, both trying to find some magical solution to the coming threat, but their weary minds couldn't come up with much.

Until at last Eli spoke up. "Alright. Here's a plan that I think gives us a chance to avoid any fighting with children aboard. We just have to make it a little farther north to avoid any delay. This is not an elegant plan in any way."

Harris and Tam faced her earnestly, both hoping that she had indeed found a good option, otherwise things were going to get even messier.

Katarina had draped herself over the ornate chair as she stared over the faces before her.

There were four concubines present, along with their attendants. The concubines were seated around a large, ebony table in Katarina's quarters. The table had been laden with baked delicacies on beautifully painted porcelain.

The windows and shutters were closed, and all screens and long drapes had been removed from the room as per Katarina's orders.

This resulted in two successful outcomes.

First, the room was cooler despite the roasting summer heat outside. And second, Kat had managed to remove most of the spots where someone could hide or attempt to surprise her with an attack.

Soo Hebin was not among the women present, but that didn't mean the woman wouldn't try to send spies.

Even among the attendants accompanying the concubines, there could be someone in Soo Hebin's pocket, which was why Kat had limited the number of serving women permitted to join the event. One maid, one concubine. The concubines would of course pick their most trusted woman to remain by their side. While it didn't completely eradicate the threat of them being a spy for Soo Hebin, it did minimize the risk.

After a particularly infuriating exchange with someone who allegedly served the emperor after Katarina discovered Thomas Julian, she wasn't feeling fond of the Concubine Soo Hebin, and she wasn't afraid of letting it be known.

"Your Majesty, thank you for inviting us to this meal." The concubine that sat the farthest on Katarina's left spoke first, bowing her head.

Kat regarded her with an eyebrow raise, then looked around at the rest of the women, who all kept their faces downward.

They looked tense.

"Do you know why I've invited you here?" Kat tapped her finger against the ornate armrest of her chair.

The women didn't speak, and maintained a dignified quiet.

"Do you know why I've been summoned here to Zinfera?" Kat wondered if they were ever even told what was really happening in the outside world. The emperor's concubines were always well guarded.

"Your Majesty is here either because of the rumors, or because of the dead coven member," the same concubine that spoke before responded.

Kat fixed her attention on the woman.

Her name was Deoh Rin. She was in her early forties and wore a periwinkle silk shirt; there were bright-pink glass flowers on her hairpins.

"What rumors would draw me here?" Kat wondered with a feigned air of laziness.

"The rumor regarding how the coven exploited an ancient beast and has now incurred the wrath of the Gods."

Kat's cool demeanor cracked. *What? I didn't hear anything about* this!

Blinking rapidly, she shook herself back to the present and hoped the women merely thought she was surprised by the blunt response.

"And what sin is it that the coven committed against the ancient beast?" Kat did her best to make her voice sound confident, hoping Deoh would keep revealing the details of this rumor that the monarchy in Daxaria had most definitely *not* heard about.

"There are rumors of the coven and nobles associated with Soo Hebin experimenting on a sirin. Even going so far as to brew tea from her hair or drops of her blood to see if any humans could gain power."

"That's gross as hell," Kat blurted out before schooling her expression again with a grunt. "Where did this sirin come from?"

The room once again fell silent.

This time no one answered.

Sensing that she was about to get stonewalled, Kat sighed and leaned her forearms on the table in front of her.

"I'm here because of the dead coven member, but also because there are a lot of alarming rumors going around. This news that people are tormenting an ancient beast is newer information to me—"

"That happened decades ago. The reason we say that was what angered the Goddess is because of the beast attacks on our ships."

Kat's golden eyes glinted in the candlelight. "Oh?"

"The beast has destroyed most of the merchant vessels that try to leave Gondol. It's one of the reasons Her Highness Soo Hebin argues we should make Junya the capital once more. The attacks have not been occurring at that end of the kingdom."

"And you do not believe Junya should be the capital?" Kat ventured while sweeping her sights over the rest of the attendees.

The women didn't reveal their thoughts even in a twitch of their eyebrows. Which wasn't all that surprising. Doing so would reveal their own alliances and self-interests.

"The beast must be stopped or we will have no choice. Junya will have to become the capital. Supplies in Gondol are running low, and several merchant families are nearly penniless because of the attacks. Even Soo Hebin's own ships have been attacked, so it is happening indiscriminately," Deoh informed the Daxarian queen, an edge of passion coming into her voice.

Kat was willing to bet respectable amounts of gold that this woman was one of Soo Hebin's most powerful and outspoken adversaries.

"Tell me more about this creature, and who knows? Perhaps Daxaria can offer some kind of help. Assuming, of course, that there isn't something far more rotten going on here." Kat settled back into her chair, her fingers clasped over her toned stomach.

The women exchanged looks, but after a while, they most likely came to the conclusion: the Daxarian queen would hear about what was happening one way or another. So they relayed the very detailed information they themselves had gathered.

By the end of the discussion, Kat was pale.

She bid the concubines farewell and then waited in her chamber, her hand lightly covering her mouth as her gaze bore into the ebony table.

When Annika Ashowan eventually entered the room, having completed her own secretive tasks for the day, the duchess tilted her head. "What's wrong?"

Kat slowly pushed herself to her feet, the air practically crackling around her. "We need to write to Da. Now. Things are much worse than we thought."

CHAPTER 25

A WASTE OF WAVES

"The ship is no longer traveling north," the air witch relayed with a frown.

Louise Riddel raised an eyebrow and lowered her hand, waiting for the spyglass to be passed to her.

Once the cool brass touched her palm, she lifted it to her eye and discovered that, sure enough, the vessel carrying Tamlin Ashowan and the wayward Zinferan princess had changed course sometime during the night. They were now heading in a very straight line to the west.

"They are riding quicker on the wind," the air witch, a Zinferan woman with milky eyes that could still see perfectly well, relayed.

"They will be harder to catch. I suppose with the amount of supplies that would've been aboard their ship, they aren't afraid of waiting us out."

"Should we chase them?" another Zinferan witch asked. He was a fire witch with thick lips and a long face.

Louise Riddel lowered the spyglass and squinted after the ship thoughtfully.

Tamlin Ashowan was a soft noble who had everything handed to him on a silver platter. He most likely thought he could outrun them and wait for his father to catch wind of what was happening to save him.

Letting out a breath of disapproval, Louise lifted her chin. "No. We don't engage in this childish game of catch-me-if-you-can. This ends today. Let us reach them by this afternoon."

"But, Coven Leader—" A Daxarian water witch stepped forward, their expression tense. "That will use up the majority of every air and water witch's magic. We still need to be able to restrain the princess, and we aren't certain what magic Lord Tam carries. We saw his symbol all over the land in Eusa, and the pirates who saw him say he moved around abnormally quickly. They say he seemed to disappear and reappear at will with darkness swallowing him."

Louise took a deep breath, working to maintain her calm demeanor. "We have twenty witches aboard this ship. The fire witches and the earth witches will be enough to restrain Lord Tam. While we don't know the exact nature of his magic, we do know that it is more strongly aligned with air. He has not been using it much, so he will not be as strong or powerful. Fighting against his anti-elements works in our favor."

"The princess should not be underestimated, either," the highest-ranked Zinferan coven member interjected, stepping forward. A water witch. "Magic aside, she is clever. This is probably a trap."

That gave Louise pause. She looked out over the sparkling water.

"The devil is also with them. It would not be wise to rush a capture," the older Zinferan water witch, Ganum, pressed gently.

Louise folded her arms over her chest. "They are assuming we'll catch up to them in another day or two, which gives them more time to plan. I say we cut off any chance of escape or evasion and simply get within firing range, then set their entire ship ablaze. When they jump overboard, we can simply pluck them up from the water." She turned toward the Zinferan pirate manning the helm. "Hold steady. We are going to be moving much faster."

"Wait, Coven Leader." Ganum had remarkable blue eyes with dark flecks and streaks of lighter blue; they looked like magical whirling pools. "What if something happens to the devil when we set the ship ablaze? Her Magnificence will not be pleased."

Louise rounded back to stare at the man levelly. "I may think the Ashowans have too much power for their own good, but I can say with the utmost confidence that they will protect a child. Even if it is the devil."

"You have said before that this particular Ashowan family member is not quite like the rest of his family," Ganum recalled.

"Lord Tam still wouldn't leave a child to die."

"What if it is Lord Tam that ends up in danger and cannot save the devil? This is a very dangerous plan. We should be proceeding more warily."

Louise pursed her lips. "There is danger no matter what the choice is. This plan, however, gives us the element of surprise. And we eliminate any means of escape. We will proceed as per my orders."

The water witch stared at Louise, his blue eyes somber. His disapproval permeated the space between them far more efficiently than any further argument would have.

But he did not try to stop her again.

Louise nodded to the captain, then looked to the nearest witches.

"See it done."

It took nearly the entire day, but at long last, they caught the ship carrying Lord Tamlin, Princess Elisara, Duke Harris, and the devil.

As it turned out, it had not been as simple a feat as they had originally expected. The ship had gone on many impressive detours during the chase. By this point the Ashowan heir's ship had almost moved in a full circle, as though trying to come up behind the three ships.

"They must be nervous," the new pirate captain at the helm announced with a cold smile.

He had been one of the pirates who witnessed Tamlin Ashowan slay Captain Woo, and the man had more than a small amount of bloodlust to end the nobleman's life.

With another magnificent effort from the air and water witches, the ships rounded about and pulled their bows up to face the stolen vessel holding the Zinferan princess and Lord Tam.

"Alright, are we ready to go aboard?" Louise called to the witches lined up behind her. Most were fire witches, with a few earth witches carrying satchels of dirt and plants. There were three mutated witches as well. One could command their ankle-length hair to act as limbs to grab, tie, and bind as they wished; another could make someone suddenly feel as though their body weight had doubled. The last had the very odd ability to turn people into chickens. Though there were limits on how many people she could turn, particularly witches.

"We are ready," the group chanted back in unison.

Louise nodded to the bedraggled air witch that stood by the rails, who was already sweating from having pushed the ships as quickly as possible. Then she looked to the fire witch at his side.

A stream of fire ignited in the witch's hands, and he raised it carefully above his head, letting the flames spread and surge until sudden shouts interrupted the process.

"THEY AREN'T TURNING!"

"WHY AREN'T THEY DROPPING ANCHOR? AT THIS RATE WE'LL ALL CRASH! WITCHES, STEER AWAY!"

Louise's gaze snapped back to the enemy ship, which was indeed driving straight for them.

Frowning, she snatched the spyglass she had stowed away in her skirt pocket and lifted it to her eye.

She tried to find whoever was manning the helm. Most likely it was the machinations of the borderline unhinged Duke Harris whom Louise had always found a headache to speak with.

"What—" Louise felt her blood turn to ice as she squinted, hoping she was imagining things.

"What're they doing?" Ganum asked softly from behind Louise's left elbow.

She grappled heroically with her ire.

"I don't see anyone on deck. There is a… a dummy tied to the wheel."

And this dummy was a stuffed coat. A burlap sack packed with some kind of cloth acted as a head, complete with a hat.

The arms of the coat were tied at the halfway point under the spindles, so that the wheel could turn 180 degrees at most in the direction of the winds.

"Fire at the ship," Louise ordered.

If this was a trap to lure them aboard where Lord Tam, Lord Harris, and the princess fought them all, she wasn't going to fall for it.

The fire witch who'd been holding his hand up in the air, sweat pouring down his face, released the stream of fire with the help of the air witch. It made a direct hit with the main sail. But it only sparked, not fully catching thanks to the change of the winds that came, as the captain tried to swing their vessel to the starboard. Their other two ships veered in opposite directions to avoid collision.

"AGAIN!" Louise roared, her knees buckling against the rocking of the deck beneath her.

The fire and air witches both took a moment to steady themselves with the help of the rail, then issued another attack.

The more pressing danger came when they realized that the speed they were turning and the speed of the other vessel were not quite the same. Turning ate up time. Time that brought the bow of the stolen pirate ship closer to the bare side of their own vessel.

"WIND WITCHES, BUFFET US AWAY!" Louise barked as the sound of sails snapping in the wind echoed around them and sailors darted to the ropes to help the captain find the winds again.

"We don't have enough power to completely change course!" a Zinferan wind witch hollered back, the edge in her voice undisguised.

"EVERY FIRE WITCH TO THE RAILS!" Louise rounded on the witches behind her. Dutifully, they obeyed.

In the next few moments, a storm of fire blazed through the sky. The heat was powerful enough that Louise could feel it sting her cheeks, and it had the added benefit of generating enough hot air to fill their own sails, propelling them out of harm's way.

"HOLD!"

When the last of the fire witches ceased, Louise moved over to the rail to see if they had been successful, and felt a great measure of relief when she discovered they had.

"Excellent work. That succeeded in both slowing them down, and giving them nowhere to run. Now we simply have to watch for when they abandon ship."

And so they waited, circling the burning vessel as evening descended around them.

At first everyone waited, tensed and ready to attack, but by the time the first twinkling star appeared in the pale sky, and the bow of the ship was producing foaming bubbles as it sank beneath the surface of the Tinoo Ocean, everyone knew something was greatly amiss.

"Either we just killed the son of the house witch, or he isn't on the boat anymore," the witch who could turn people into chickens supplied helpfully.

Louise gripped the railing until her knuckles were white.

"I put that together, Henrietta," she retorted tightly.

One of the water witches stepped forward. "I can see about getting into the water and sensing for any life."

Louise nodded. "Please do."

"Erm… Miss Riddel?"

The Coven of Wittica leader was beginning to regret bringing Henrietta the chicken witch along.

"Yes?"

"What's that over there?"

"Over where?"

The coven leader turned and found that the captain and majority of the crew were already lining up on the opposite side of the deck.

As she walked, a low, terrifying groan echoed so loudly that the wood of the ship even hummed.

She slowed her steps to listen.

Then the deck beneath her feet rose on a sudden swell of water.

Holding her arms out to steady herself, Louise looked to the captain, about to ask if he could see anything from the helm, but she found that he had turned as white as their sails.

"Captain? Is that the—" one of the sailors called out uncertainly.

"Ssh!" The captain was staring at the water, his eyes round with fear.

There were similar shouts from the other ships, and Louise desperately wanted to know just what in the world was happening. Then the sound of rushing water reached her ears, and a sonorous cry that rumbled up to the heavens made her turn slowly around.

And as proud and capable a woman as Louise Riddel was, she was not too proud to admit that she screamed in horror at what she found looking back at her.

"Well?" Tam asked, his back resting against the stone wall.

"It worked. I can't even see them anymore; they must have overexerted the air and water witches hoping to rush us," Harris confirmed with no shortage of relief.

Tam turned to Eli with a beaming smile. "Another wonderful plan that worked. Gods, you are amazing."

Eli blushed but scoffed. "We got lucky. Now we'd better move farther into the mountains. Once they figure out that there's no one on the ship, they will most likely fan out and start plotting out what path we've taken."

With a sigh at her usual business-like tone, Tam rose to his feet with a grunt. He hadn't minded getting to rest after rowing ashore in the middle of the night. He had been pushing himself to the limits quite regularly as of late.

"Luca! Penelope! We're going to walk until it's completely dark!"

"Aw! But we just started playing!"

"You can play a little at the camp," Eli informed Luca, who had just been about to embark on a riveting game of hide-and-seek with Penelope.

The little girl popped up from behind a discreet boulder.

Tam eyed the shoes that were far too big for the little girl and hoped they didn't give her too much trouble. Not that they could do much about it right then and there.

Giving his head a shake, he decided to try to keep morale high. "Alright everyone, how about we tell stories to pass the time?"

Luca whooped and skipped, while Eli reached over to Penelope and tucked an errant lock of hair behind her ear, making the child squawk in irritation.

"I have a fantastic story!" Harris informed them all brightly.

Tam teased, "You always exaggerate your stories. Like how you told everyone I bested the Troivackian king in that duel. I didn't at all. So is this one real?"

"Godson, I was trying to give you more clout when you were surrounded by enemies!" Harris pressed a palm to his chest. "I was only looking out for you."

Tam sighed and rolled his eyes with a smile.

"Don't worry, this story is about how I single-handedly stopped your sister from assaulting not one, not two, but *three* esteemed and capable Troivackian men who annoyed her while in depths of labor with the second prince!"

The children turned to look at Harris wide-eyed, then Tam to see if he was telling the truth.

Tam pressed his lips together. "That one might be a little bit true."

With that, the group proceeded to journey deeper into the mountains, relieved that they managed to evade capture yet again, and hopeful that perhaps things would be a little easier now that they were back on land.

CHAPTER 26

LEARNING LENGTHS

Tam adjusted Penelope on his back, then glanced behind himself to ensure Luca was doing alright.

The children, like the adults, were drenched in sweat and exhausted to the bone.

They'd been walking from morning until dusk, in the mountains, for almost two weeks, and while the journey hadn't been all terrible, they were running horribly low on water, and there was little vegetation.

Eli was in her beast form carrying most of their things, but Tam could tell by the heaviness in her powerful legs that she was struggling as well.

"Hopefully we reach the woods soon." Tam tried to smile at Luca, but the boy had his eyes fixed on the ground ahead of himself in a daze.

Tam turned to Harris, who shared a look of concern.

They couldn't keep going like this.

At least they had been able to stay on the designated path that Eli had mapped out, and there hadn't been anyone coming after them, but even so…

They needed time for rest and recovery.

Tam was about to suggest they stop for a while to catch their breath when Eli's head rose abruptly.

Everyone stopped walking as the great cat's nose twitched and her ears twisted forward.

"Is something wrong?" Tam asked worriedly.

Eli gave no indication of what was making her react in such a way, but she trotted forward, her steps once again light.

Penelope gave a soft groan from Tam's back, but she didn't fully wake.

Adjusting his hold from under her knees carefully, Tam followed Eli while increasing his speed.

Harris placed a hand on Luca's shoulder, making him wait.

Tam continued following Eli until he caught up with her ropy tail swishing back and forth.

There, spread out before them like the divine afterlife itself, was a lush forest that wove its way through the mountains like an emerald ribbon.

Tears warmed Tam's eyes. "Thank the Gods."

He looked up into Eli's slitted golden gaze, and they shared in their relief.

"Can you smell water anywhere?"

"Hrm." Eli swung her head back to look out over the cliff, her nose and whiskers twitching. She stiffened abruptly, and her tail started to swish a bit more enthusiastically.

"What is it?" Tam wondered if there was perhaps some large animal they'd be able to kill and eat for dinner. Thus far they'd been surviving off dried salted jerky, cheese, and beets.

His thoughts were interrupted, however, when Eli did something she'd never done before.

A low, rolling purr echoed from her, and Tam found himself caught between a laugh and shock.

Just what had made her so happy?

"I've only ever read about these. Is it safe?"

"I tested it earlier; it isn't too hot."

"It *looks* like it's too hot!" Penelope announced warily.

Eli smiled down at the little girl, the excited gleam in her eyes just as bright as when she confirmed what she had smelled before. "You don't have to get in, and it might take a bit of time to get used to the temperature, but once you do I bet you'll like it a lot."

Tam, Eli, and the children all stared down at the steaming pool of water that sat nestled at the foot of the mountain they'd been climbing, right on the edge of the forest they'd been hoping to find. To make matters even better, there was an icy clear blue river gushing a short way off that would allow them to refill their water supplies.

Luca was on all fours in front of the water, raising a nervous finger to prod the gently burbling surface of the hot spring, when a shout alarmed all of them into looking up.

Harris came scrambling out from behind a boulder and some shrubs he'd found while still doing up the tops of his trousers and waddling awkwardly.

"Tam! Tam, I might be dying!"

Tam and Eli both turned, frowning to see that the Daxarian duke did indeed look quite pale.

"What's wrong?" Tam's panic was already climbing. They were in the middle of nowhere. Gondol was a week and a half away on foot. In other words, there wasn't going to be a physician around for a long time.

"Blood! I'm…" Harris looked down at the two children then back at Tam and Eli. "I seem to be producing blood when I… relieve myself." He cleared his throat, his hazel eyes shifting.

Tam's panic melted away.

He closed his mouth and turned around with shuddering shoulders.

"I know! I know this comes at a horrible time. I feel fine now, but if that changes, you can all leave me, and I will find my way. Or you can send for help when you find a town." Harris turned to Eli, who had her lips pressed into a thin line, her expression unreadable. "I know my wife said I should start drinking less. I suppose I didn't want to think I was that old yet! Gods… My youngest son is only eleven. There is still so much I—"

A peculiar snort sounded from Tam.

The duke stopped his grave speech and stared at Tam's back.

"Are you… laughing?"

Tam held up his hand over his shoulder without turning around, though the rise and fall of his shoulders was becoming more dramatic.

Harris then looked at Eli and found a telling twitch at the corners of her mouth.

"What is so funny about a dying man?" Harris snapped.

Unable to control himself any longer, Tam let out a very loud "HA!" before doubling over and laughing uncontrollably while clutching his middle, gasping for breath.

Even Eli had lowered her head as she succumbed to her own quiet laugh.

"Will someone please tell me just what is going on?" Harris demanded. Having finished belting his trousers again, he put his hands on his hips.

Penelope stepped forward looking thoroughly disappointed in the eldest member of their group. "Beets make you pee red. Everyone knows that."

"H-How," Tam wheezed from the ground. "How have you… only *just* noticed, Harris?"

"I was only going to pis—to take care of my business in the dark! And always off the side of the ship, or in the dark in some hedges!"

"You only pee twice a day? That isn't healthy," Eli noted sternly.

"I beg your pardon, but in case you haven't been aware, *we've been busy!*" the duke defended loudly. "And we didn't have a ton of water to go around! Good Gods! You laugh in the face of someone terrified for their life, and—"

"Have you pooped yet?" Luca interrupted, smiling up at the duke, who fell silent.

"Not… where… I can see—good Gods, is that red, too?"

Luca burst out in a fit of giggles.

By this time, Tam was lying down on the ground, unable to stop laughing, and even Eli was trembling fiercely.

Only Penelope was staring flatly up at the duke. "You're old. You should take better care of yourself."

Harris threw his hands in the air. "We're fugitives on the run! I don't exactly have the healthiest choices available right now."

Penelope sighed and shook her head before turning back around to investigate the hot spring. She stepped over Tam, who was only then regaining his breath while lying flat on his back and wiping the tears from his whiskered cheeks.

Harris glared down at him. "A little warning would've been nice."

"S-Sorry, Harris. I warned the children, but I thought you already knew." Tam allowed Luca to seize his hand and help him up into a sitting position.

"I don't buy it. This is exactly the kind of thing your father would've done."

Tam grinned. "Weren't you the one just saying how busy we've been? I genuinely thought you would've already heard what it does."

Harris's look of suspicion didn't abate. He didn't seem to have much faith in Tam's claims of innocence.

"I don't know about the rest of you," Eli began a little louder. "But I am more than a little excited to wash."

"You and the children go first," Tam called out, getting to his feet. "Harris and I will go after. I'm going to go scout the woods for firewood and any edible plants."

Eli nodded. "See if you can also find a spot by the river that would be good for us to make camp."

Tam waved in acknowledgment and set off to do exactly that.

Meanwhile Harris turned to look at the steaming water with an arched brow. "I've read about this kind of thing. Legend has it they came to be because of a fight between an imp and a dragon, long before humans walked the earth."

Both Penelope and Luca's heads snapped around. The two children, despite having polar-opposite personalities in most regards, shared a deep love of stories.

Eli gave a weary half smile as she set to removing her boots and socks. Her feet already had scars from the blisters she'd ignored during her weeks of traveling on foot.

Slowly, she dipped her toes in the water, and a rush of contentment coursed through her body. Stripping off all but her undergarments, Eli turned to see that Luca and Penelope were doing the same without additional questions.

It didn't take long for Eli to ease herself into the water, where she let out a soft moan of appreciation.

Luca sat on the edge with his feet dangling in and was soon joined by Penelope.

"Don't you want to come in?" Eli asked, though she was suddenly finding it incredibly difficult not to fall asleep.

Both Penelope and Luca peered over the stone lip at the water, then at each other.

"Can we stand up in it?" Penelope wondered in a business-like tone.

Eli glanced down and noticed that the water nearly came up to her collarbone. "It'd be a little deep, but you can lean against the edge or float."

The children again looked shyly at each other, then pointedly away.

"Can either of you swim?" Harris guessed. He stood a short distance away and had started clearing space to build a fire.

Luca shook his head first, and then Penelope followed suit.

"Well, alright. I guess we know what we're going to be doing until Tam returns," the duke announced. He, too, removed his boots and rolled up his pant legs. He sidled over to the children who, despite the cloudy day, still had to squint when they stared up at him.

The duke grinned down at them, then in one quick swoop he shoved both kids into the water, making them both shout.

Eli dove for them immediately, just as they came up spluttering.

"LORD HARRIS!" she roared as soon as she was certain she had both children out of the water, clinging onto her shoulders.

The duke continued smiling down at her. "Yes?"

"There are kinder ways of doing that!"

"This was a lot more fun."

Luca slowly turned in the water to stare up at him, while Penelope continued coughing out the water that had found its way into her mouth.

The duke proceeded to slowly sit down, looking entirely too pleased with himself to bother feeling guilty.

"Alright, Luca. You are going to kick your legs as hard as you can, then reach forward to scoop the water backward first with your left hand, and then your right. Eli, be a dear and stand on the far edge. We'll have these two swimming like carps in no time!"

Penelope was scowling ferociously, but Luca seemed to be rather interested in the idea.

Not knowing what else to do given that the children weren't outright objecting to the idea, Eli obeyed the duke's orders and made her way back to the other side of the pool. Harris slipped his legs in the water and let out his own breath of enjoyment at the blissfully warm water.

When everyone was set, Harris held out his hands. "Alright, Luca? Are you ready?"

The duke's exuberance was difficult to resist, and so despite the unceremonious introduction to the lesson, Luca smiled hopefully.

And thus began the two children's swimming lessons, where they learned to kick and hit the water as hard as they could, propelling themselves back and forth between the duke and Eli until the two barely needed any help at all.

As a result, when Tam returned, he had the great surprise and joy of getting to see both Luca and Penelope beside themselves with elation over their new skill, and even more thrilled to be able to tell Tam what they had accomplished.

All in all, it had been the best day any of them had had in a very long time, and it allowed them all a well-deserved wash and rest that eased the tense, worrisome journey they had embarked upon. Best of all, Penelope was acting more like the kid she was than ever before. And that encouraged Tam to start thinking about the possibility that maybe, just maybe, she could find happiness in a new family one day.

CHAPTER 27

A FUTURE FRET

Breathing in through his nose, Tam held his chest full of air. He listened to the din of bugs whirring and chirping in the summer forest around him. He exhaled while focusing on the rushing water from the river to his left. Then he inhaled and repeated the process of alternating his focus from his surroundings to what was happening in his body.

A snap of twigs alerted him to Eli's presence. He didn't have to look to know it was her. He could sense her. His blood filled with electricity and his heart started to race in excitement. How many of the sensations were because of their status as lovers and how much could be attributed to their connection as familiar and witch, he wasn't entirely certain.

"Breakfast will be ready soon," Eli informed him.

He could hear the grogginess in her voice. They'd all slept far longer than had become their norm.

After the soothing soak in the hot spring the previous day, they had enjoyed a dinner of rabbit and wild carrots that had filled them perfectly, along with several icy, refreshing waterskins. By the last few mouthfuls of their meals, everyone had nearly fallen asleep where they sat around the fire, but Tam and

Eli had herded the children into their tent under their blankets. They hadn't been quick or determined enough to do the same for Lord Harris. The man must have slept outside half the night.

Despite the haphazard bedtime preparations, everyone had slept a good portion of the next day away.

Tam was the first to wake up, and he had quietly formed the opinion that they should stay and rest another day or two before moving on through the woods.

Being the first one up, and not wanting to disturb anyone else's sleep, he had ventured off a short distance to center his mind. It had been at least a month since he had time to properly process his own thoughts and plans.

Despite the fact that Eli had arrived shortly after beginning this practice, he didn't mind.

Tam cracked open an eye and gave her a gentle smile. He was still feeling the weight of exhaustion in his own limbs. It had been an incredibly taxing adventure they'd found themselves on.

As she recognized what he was doing, Eli folded her arms and tilted her head curiously. "Who taught you how to meditate? Was it Bong?"

Tam chuckled. "No. Captain Antonio. The former captain of Daxaria's military was like a grandfather to my sister and me. He studied the Zinferan combat style, and this was one of the training methods he was forced to learn. Antonio would say it makes all the difference in the world when you know your mind and stop to take stock of your place in the world."

Tam had been happy to add the skill to his days. His sister, unfortunately, had never been able to implement the practice in her own life. Not that anyone was surprised. Being still for any duration of time was torture to the queen.

Eli strode over to stand in front of Tam, who was cross-legged on the ground. "He sounds like a very capable and levelheaded leader."

"He was." Tam still missed Antonio greatly. The military leader always had words of wisdom for Tam, and had been a wonderful teacher back when he'd learned to fight with a sword. "He was like family. It's why Kat named her first son Antony."

Eli smiled and crouched before Tam. "There's something I haven't had a chance to talk to you about," she began carefully.

Tam's eyes went wide. "Gods, are you pregnant?"

Eli's expression fell flat. "No. Are you always going to be this paranoid?"

Tam let out a whoosh of air and dropped his head before looking back up to respond. "Probably. Kat had a problem *stopping* getting pregnant after Antony. And allegedly my da and mum needed only one time—"

"You and your family share too many details about your personal lives."

Tam winced then laughed. "When you grow up close with a lot of people, it happens. Everyone knows everything and is in your business."

Eli's nose scrunched up.

Tam chuckled again while reaching up to rub the back of his neck. "Yeah. I figured you wouldn't be too happy to hear about that. After we get married, I thought we'd move somewhere away from my parents. I wondered about the castle in Sorlia my family owns for some space and quiet."

Eli blinked. "You've decided where we'll live after getting married? Already?"

Tam froze and dropped his hand. "Er—it's occurred to me, yes."

Eli sighed and looked at the sky. "And everyone says it's the women who are desperate for matrimony."

"Wait. You don't want to get married? At all? Ever?"

Her gaze drifted back down to Tam. Then Eli reached over and cradled his face in her hands. "Can we finish burning down a kingdom before planning something as stressful as a wedding?"

"Wow. You actually might have more in common with Kat than you realize," Tam teased.

Annoyed, Eli moved to take her hands back when Tam gently grasped them in his own. He proceeded to gently kiss the inside of her wrist and hold her gaze.

Eli's cheeks flushed, prompting her to stand abruptly, forcing Tam to release her.

Taking two steps away, Eli sat back down on a rock a short distance away as though to stop Tam from being able to distract her again. "Something happened on the ship I haven't told you about."

Tam's flirting ceased when he recognized the seriousness in Eli's face, and so he stilled and listened to the story she told about Penelope.

His alarm and surprise grew as the story went on, and by the end, his right index finger was gently tapping his knee.

"What do you think that's about? I haven't asked her about it since that night, but that was suspicious, right?"

Tam shook his head. "No. Not to me? It sounds like she's a seer."

Eli straightened. "A seer?"

He nodded. "Seers are rare. And the last known one was in Troivack. My sister met her there—her name was Esther. She claimed that she could see a bit of someone's past, their present, and then no more than a year into their future."

Eli's hands curled into fists. Tam could tell that the idea that Penelope had witnessed those pieces of her past, present, and future was bothering her.

"Tam, are seers ever wrong?"

Half of his face grimaced. "I've never heard it happening."

"It could have been just a dream! Captain Woo could've told her about my time aboard the ship, and she could have overheard us talking—"

"Did they really put a collar on you?" Tam's voice was soft.

Eli's mouth clamped shut, and her eyes shuttered. "Yes."

Seeing her reaction, Tam didn't pry any more than that.

"I suppose it could be a dream. We'd have to talk to her. I remember the report on the seer, and it sounds similar to what you experienced with Penelope. We could maybe see if Penelope has seen anything for the rest of us."

"If she is a seer…" Eli started slowly. "She might be able to tell us whether Luca is the devil or not."

"I don't want to know." Tam's firm tone gave Eli a small jolt.

"What? Tam, we—"

"No. He's my son. That's it."

"We should still *know* even if we aren't going to acknowledge it or mention it to others!" Eli argued intently.

"No. I don't want there being any risk of it changing a thing. We're happy as we are." Tam heard the steeliness in his words.

It was Eli's turn to recognize that this was not a matter she could press right then.

"Alright. That aside, Tam, Penelope says we adopt her," Eli reminded him.

"And?"

Her eyes widened before she threw her hands in the air. "What do you mean, '*And*'? Are we adopting every lost child in existence?"

Tam gave Eli a hard look and didn't reply straightaway, as he battled with his anger that began to stir. "If you don't like it, I'm sorry to hear that. But if she needs a home by the end of this, we're probably the best one. She'll have bonded with Luca and will hopefully feel comfortable with us by then. And Luca is not a lost child; he is, and always has been, mine."

"Tam, you're talking about parenting two kids! Two! And with one, you have no idea the family she is from, or if someone is looking for her!"

"I'm not saying I won't try to find her family," Tam informed Eli tensely. "I'm just saying if that was the future she saw, I have no issue with it, and it makes sense."

"It isn't that easy! Taking care of two kids for the rest of your life is a massive amount of work and responsibility and—"

"And I'm okay with that, Eli. Are you?"

The two stared at each other in a stalemate, not saying a word, until the sound of rustling foliage reached them from the camp, and out popped Luca, still yawning with his hair sporting two cowlicks.

"Harris says breakfast is ready," the boy announced groggily.

Shoving his emotions aside, Tam forced a smile on his face and moved to his feet. "Thank you for letting us know. Did you sleep well?"

"Mm-hm." Luca started picking the crust of sleep from his eyes.

"That's good. I was thinking that maybe you, Penelope, and I could play some games today. What do you think?" When Tam reached Luca's side, the boy easily slipped his hand into Tam's.

Looking over his shoulder, Luca smiled at Eli. "Are you going to play, too?"

She took a little longer to get ahold of her emotions, and so while she couldn't quite manage a smile, she did nod, making Luca beam.

The child held out a hand to her. "Come on!"

Staring down at his small palm, Eli hesitated, her cloud of thoughts seemingly taking her someplace else for a moment. Eventually she accepted his hand, and they walked back to the camp.

Evidently there were going to be more than political battles ahead for them, and these were the kind that unnerved both Tam and Eli the most.

"Are you certain?" Soo Hebin asked, wearing a dazzling smile.

Louise Riddel and five other witches remained kneeling on the ground with their heads bowed toward the first witch, who sat beside the concubine and looked significantly less pleased at the news.

"We saw no signs of them. We are assuming that they were hiding aboard the ship to attack us but got trapped."

The first witch's gaze bore into Louise Riddel, her annoyance barely contained. "Is it not possible that they simply went ashore?"

Louise Riddel hesitated upon hearing the stern tone of the first witch. "We looked all along the shore and saw no signs of any lifeboats. It's also doubtful they would have maneuvered it into any hiding points in the mountains."

The first witch stared over their heads without speaking.

"So the devil, Princess Elisara, that annoying Daxarian duke, and Tamlin Ashowan are all dead. This is quite the day for dramatic news." Soo Hebin eased herself back into her seat, not looking the least bit concerned.

"There is nothing the Ashowan family or the Daxarian monarchy can say on the matter, either, as we were barely able to save ourselves from the monster," Louise expounded gravely.

Soo Hebin nodded to one of her maids. "Of course. I'm sure you've had a treacherous journey. Rooms have been prepared for you all as well as some meals. Go rest, and we can speak more on this later."

The group of surviving witches stood and, still bowing, proceeded out of the concubine's quarters, leaving Soo Hebin alone with the first witch. She stared straight ahead.

Soo Hebin bristled with mild irritation. "Didn't you say you dealt with all the places the devil could be reborn? Doesn't this mean he'll simply spawn in the belly of the beast? Meaning he'll most likely die again and again and again for years to come?"

Aradia turned slowly to stare at the concubine. "I don't think they are dead. I think those witches are trying to give you the news you want to hear so that you are pleased and they are not held accountable for making a *gross* error in their work."

Soo Hebin's smile dwindled. "Where are they, then? In the mountains? There is next to no known water or food there. Even if they did make it to land, the likelihood of their survival is minimal. Besides, aren't you glad you heard the news before you yourself had to chase them on a boat? At times it is best to look at the blessings we've received, hm?" Soo Hebin glowed with smugness.

Aradia was ready to beat the woman to death with the nearest object she could lift, most likely the wooden chair she was seated upon.

She briefly longed for the days when all she had to do was drink an unholy amount of moonshine and occasionally say odd things back when she was disguised as a handmaiden to the Troivackian queen seven years back.

"There is one way we might be able to glean some insight on their survival." The first witch pushed herself out of her chair.

Soo Hebin visibly struggled not to roll her eyes in a most unbecoming manner, then forced herself to ask the obvious question. "And what way might that be?"

Aradia gave a humorless smile to no one in particular as she smoothed the black silk skirt she wore. "We tell Tamlin Ashowan's mother and sister he's dead, and see how they react."

CHAPTER 28

A POWER PUSH

Soo Hebin gazed at the Daxarian queen, Katarina Reyes, who stared back with undisguised dislike, while her mother, Duchess Annika Ashowan, wore a mask that was far more difficult to read.

They were alone save for the three maids accompanying the concubine.

"Your Grace, Your Majesty, I regret to tell you, Tamlin Ashowan perished on his way to Gondol due to an attack of the beast that has been plaguing our shores for the past few months. Your coven leader, Louise Riddel, was a part of the search team along with a handful of Daxarian witches, and they were not able to find any evidence that he was alive. I'm sorry for your loss."

During the speech, Katarina stiffened, and whereas usually some part of her shifted, tapped, or twisted, she currently sat completely still. Which was a large marker of concern to those that knew her.

However, the guttural, feral cry that came from Duchess Annika Ashowan was earth shattering in more ways than one and drew everyone's attention.

Annika clutched her abdomen, as though someone had just ripped her stomach out, and her free hand grasped her mouth, her back hunching as she coiled in on herself.

Katarina stared unblinkingly at the concubine whose head bowed respectfully to her, her face serene.

"Why are you the one telling us this horrific news?"

The concubine didn't flinch despite the venom in Kat's words.

"As you are staying in my palace, the duty falls to me to relay this grave information to you."

"No. It doesn't. It falls to the emperor." Kat stood, her presence filling the room as her hot, red aura started to flare out from her. If Soo Hebin had had her face lifted, she might be feeling a little bit worried.

"As the adviser you spoke to the other day told you, Your Majesty, the emperor is unwe—"

The deafening sound of something heavy and wooden smashing into the wall made Soo Hebin throw herself against the back of her chair in panic.

When she finally looked up at the seething Daxarian queen, she instantly started to tremble.

"Go get the emperor. Or I will single-handedly reduce your palace to rubble."

"Guar—"

Kat lowered herself, her hands gripping the armrests of the chair the concubine sat in, and gave a primal growl. "With the amount of dancing you've done around the rules and etiquette, Soo Hebin, I am *well* within my rights to kill you right here. So do you want even more people getting slaughtered on your behalf?"

Tears were involuntarily welling up in the concubine's eyes as her sights were consumed by the demon-woman in front of her. She gritted her teeth and glared up at Kat.

Lunging to the concubine's left, Kat made Soo Hebin shriek as she seized the empty chair beside her and threw it against the same wall, again with an explosion of splintering wood. The amount of effort Kat had expended was the same she might use to toss aside a dandelion.

"Get. Out. And pass along the message that if anyone bothers me, they'd better have their will prepared."

Soo Hebin was panting where she sat. The Daxarian queen bore down on the concubine, forcing the woman to try to sink into the wood of her chair like a frightened, cornered rodent.

The concubine's maids were hanging on to each other, quaking in fear.

Once they had all fled the room and the door had closed, Kat turned her sights to her mother, who had her forehead lowered in her hand. The duchess was the very image of a broken soul.

Kat rose back up, her aura dwindling down as she stared at her mother expectantly. "She's gone, you know."

"Just making sure no guards come in," Annika Ashowan explained quietly without lifting her gaze.

"After the ruckus I just caused, I doubt they'd risk it," Kat pointed out with a scoff before stretching her neck. "Gods. Do you think she honestly believes Tam is dead? Or is she trying to do something to us?"

Annika drew herself up in her seat, then leaned back and crossed her legs calmly, her former distress nowhere to be seen. "It is difficult to say. I think she wants all of us dead, but it could just be that she is testing us to see if we know anything about his whereabouts."

Kat nodded at this. "Did Da's last message say when he was leaving to come here?"

Annika tilted her head disappointedly. "He says it's difficult with the princes right now, and there is a lot of discussion on how wise it is to leave Daxaria undefended."

Giving a quiet grumble, Kat looked around the chaotic room. "Do you think that vase over there is expensive?"

"Yes. Excellent work, by the way, in pushing to see the emperor," Annika added with a bow of her head.

Kat managed a tired smile at this. "Does Soo Hebin have any idea that you've already been able to see the emperor?"

Annika shook her head. "She'd be a lot more careful if she did. Have you been able to discern if anyone is fit to be a ruler after the emperor?"

"Honestly, his concubine Deoh Rin is smart enough to do it. She has three daughters, though two of them went 'missing,' so she is more than ready to kill Soo Hebin with her own hands. Her youngest daughter is still a child, so she sent her to live with her own parents in Haeson, but she misses her and fears for her safety."

Frowning, the duchess considered this. "What power does Deoh Rin have that could help her hold on to the throne?"

"I'm not certain yet. But she cares a lot, has energy, is perceptive, and knows what to do with what she sees."

Annika winced a little. "Wonderful qualities, but depending on her support, it may not be enough to rise to the throne and restore stability."

Kat sighed.

"You're absolutely certain your brother is still safe?" Annika asked suddenly, the subtle tension in her voice drawing Kat's gaze to her.

Pressing her lips together in understanding, Kat closed her eyes to check. She couldn't imagine if one of her own sons were lost with a slew of powerful people piling firewood to burn him alive…

Searching for Tam's thread had always been easy. It was one of the strongest Kat had, and its presence alone gave her a great deal of comfort.

And there it was, waving away peacefully in the darkness.

She studied its glow. Did it seem brighter? No? Kat pushed a small bit of power down that thread. Tam had at one point told her not to do that, as it made his magic become unstable, but it gave her a sense of comfort. It meant that he could feel her supporting him wherever he was. Maybe if his magic got a bit of an extra push, he'd be a little safer.

"He's still alive," Kat reassured her mother.

Annika opened her eyes and let out a breath of relief. "I am beyond grateful that you are able to check on him every day," Annika Ashowan confessed, her face looking far more aged than usual.

"My dumb baby brother is probably fine," Kat insisted while looking around the room. In truth, her brother was only a few moments younger than herself, but that didn't stop her from lording it over him any chance she got. "Now I'm going to smash a few things. Are you going to keep pretending to weep?"

The duchess peered around the room, spotted the dainty teapot at her side, and casually backhanded it off the table to smash on the floor.

"I'll start my show again. Eventually."

Kat's eyebrows shot up in surprise.

Annika shamelessly met her daughter's look and shrugged. "Soo Hebin's a wretch who is trying to hurt our family."

Laughing, the Daxarian queen delighted in this new side of her mother, then set to work trying to find the most expensive items that the concubine owned to destroy.

The act was more than just simple defiance to Kat. If she were honest with herself, it was a welcome way to work out the many stresses and annoyances that had been building in her for a long, long time, and it was lovely to know that the act would have the perfect result of angering and insulting the concubine, whom Kat already had silently promised herself had limited days left in her comfortable palace life.

Tam flinched and halted in his tracks.

The group had just started their venture into the woods while following the river when he felt a very familiar jolt run through him.

"Penelope, I have to put you down now." The edge in Tam's voice stopped any protests from the child as he crouched and let her slide off. The poor girl was still building muscle and endurance after being malnourished for weeks and had no other choice but to make the long journey in shoes that did not fit properly.

"Why are your hands shaking?" Penelope asked, which in turn made Luca, Harris, and Eli in her large cat form turn around.

Tam wished he could answer her question. He could hear the disguised note of fear in her tone, but he couldn't get anything out over the dull roar of power that was filling his being.

Why is Kat sending me power now? Is this some kind of message? Is she just making sure I'm alive? His shaking worsened.

He knew he could simply disappear into his void, but oddly enough, the notion didn't feel like it would offer any alleviation for his discomfort.

"Tam? What's happening? I can feel something's wrong," Eli's voice sounded beside him. She must have shifted back to her human form and set down their things. How long was this shaking supposed to last?

"It's Godsdamn Kat," Tam offered in between pants as sweat rolled down his brow. "She pushed a power surge at me. Now my magic doesn't know what to do with it."

Eli looked around and spotted a nearby fallen tree branch that would've made for terrific kindling. "Try moving something again. Maybe it'll use it up?"

Tam tried to lift his head to look at Eli but found he couldn't. His body felt trapped in tremors.

So he instead closed his eyes.

He needed an outlet of some sort, so attempting to move a tree branch could help… Only his magic warred inside of him in response to this thought. That wasn't the answer it wanted.

Ether. My power is ether. Ether is a part of everything, and is in nothing…

Reaching out with his awareness, much in the same way he would while in his void, Tam found he could sense everything around him in a way he didn't quite understand.

He could feel the finest droplets of water moving through the trees, the worms tunneling deep down in the dirt beneath him, the rush of the air around them, the flowing of water in the plants through their roots into their leaves…

He was *a part of* all of these things, too. He could allow himself to get swept into the wind; he could join the droplets of water circulating through the trees…

The strain in his muscles reached a peak, and suddenly, Tam collapsed into his void. Only he didn't exactly.

He found himself feeling encased in wood.

He was inside a tree, or maybe even the stick Eli had pointed at.

But if he was a part of the stick, then why couldn't he move it? They all were a part of one another, and so they shared the same will.

Tension released in Tam, even though he didn't have his body in this peculiar space.

He wanted to spin and jump while encased in this piece of wood. Upon further reflection, he did confirm it was the very stick Eli had been talking about. He felt this instinctively, with no other clear reason.

It was amazing.

The very fact that Tam became conscious of it meant they had a relationship together, and therefore they could move together as one.

Something deep in Tam's soul stirred, inspiring heady elation to fill him.

He jumped, he spun. He felt free. The trembling stopped. The roaring power stopped, and Tam started to feel a little tired. So he tumbled back out of the void.

He found himself sprawled over some ferns and tree roots.

The wind rustled the leaves above him.

Incredibly, he felt completely at peace. Sure, he was a bit sleepy, but it wasn't because of the way he'd used the magic. It was because some part of him had let go of a barrier that had stood between himself and, well, the world.

A barrier that had taken a great deal of energy to hold in place. Now, with it down, Tam only wanted to rest.

He closed his eyes. Tam knew he should've gone to check on the others; he could tell they were nearby just by extending his senses through the earth.

"How did he make the stick dance?" Penelope's shrill voice cut through the air, making him smile, but Tam couldn't rouse himself just yet. Sleep was beckoning him in an all-too-alluring way.

And so, feeling completely at ease with his present state, regardless of the fact that he was technically lying upside down on a sloping rocky hill, Tam fell unconscious.

It'd just be a quick nap. He'd feel more refreshed once he woke back up again.

He was sure of it.

CHAPTER 29

THE DUTIES OF DAUGHTERS

"We're sitting ducks if we don't get moving," Harris informed Eli quietly.

It had been two days since they'd found Tam asleep near the stick he made dance.

Evidently he'd used too much power.

They'd decided to wait instead of having Eli carry him, but if he stayed asleep for much longer, it could become problematic.

"No one knows exactly where we are, they don't know how quickly we're moving, and the army was already spread too thinly before we left. It'll be fine." Despite the vehemence of Eli's words, there was a stress behind them that the Daxarian duke could hear and interpret perfectly well.

He didn't respond just yet, however, as they looked off to the distance to see Luca and Penelope attempting to skip stones off the frothing river. He glanced at his niece and watched the cacophony of emotions that plagued her before turning back to the children.

"In a way, I always felt better when Fin had to go unconscious after using his magic."

Eli's head snapped around, her gaze boring into the side of her uncle's face—though he pretended to ignore it.

"It made Fin feel more human. Like he wasn't all-powerful. He wasn't perfect. He was just someone who on occasion was amazingly strong and then could be amazingly weak. Like if he truly annoyed me, I just had to wait until he exhausted his power, and then a feather-stuffed pillow could be his undoing, you know?"

"Do you often think of ways to kill your close friends?" Eli inquired with only the faintest hint of sarcasm.

"It's a man thing. We consider how we could kill all our friends."

"I don't know that I believe that."

"Suit yourself." Harris shrugged. He waited another moment or two before springing into a new topic. "So what have you two been fighting about?"

Elie tensed at his side. "That is not your business."

"Of course it isn't. But you need someone to bounce your thoughts off, and who better than your favorite uncle?"

Eli emitted a soft grumble.

Harris smiled. "You're persnickety like your mother, but your kindness? Gods know who you get that from."

"I'm not kind. Even Penelope noticed that."

"Mm. That's true. A better description would be to say you're fair. And decent. Kindness is a luxury, and despite being a lady and a princess, you have not had much of that. At least not the type that counts."

Eli said nothing.

"Did your mother ever tell you the details of my birth and upbringing?"

"Yes."

"Do you trust her version of events, or would you like the honest truth of it?"

Eli's arms, which had been crossed over her chest, tightened around her middle, her fingers curling against her shirtsleeves.

Harris took her silence as an agreement. "I was a bastard. And not a bastard that was kindly taken in by his father. Or even one that was supported from a distance. As far as my father was concerned, he couldn't have cared less if I lived or died. The only reason he left any road of possibility for me inheriting his title was that he never had a legitimate son. Only Marigold, your mother."

"That doesn't count as a skip! It bounced off another rock!" Penelope's indignant shout interrupted the duke's story. Both he and Eli waited and listened to see if the children would manage the disagreement amicably or if intervention would be required.

"Did it? Oh. I didn't see. Where's the rock?"

"Aside from the one inside your skull in place of your brain? There."

"Oh."

Luca's innocent response made Penelope's shoulders visibly relax. She pointed to the subtle tip of rock that jutted out of the river.

Harris resumed his story.

"Marigold's mother burned my home down. My mother died. And all sorts of events managed by members of the Daxarian court saw that I met the wildly difficult criteria necessary for me to inherit the dukedom. I lived as a mercenary for a while. I served another duke's household for a time. Became a soldier, then a knight. When I was knight I became Finlay Ashowan's kitchen aide—Fin still doesn't trust me to peel potatoes. I thought I made rather charming sculptures."

Eli rolled her eyes, and Harris grinned while continuing. "Some of us don't get the luxury of waiting for good times to find joy. Sometimes we have to make it ourselves. And I'll be honest with you in a way I have only been honest with my wife and children, because you are family, and you desperately need family."

Eli's eyebrows twitched in response, but she didn't object.

"I'm angry. I'm so damn angry at so many people. It's so easy for me to be angry because I've felt angry more than a normal person should. And you want to know what pisses me off the absolute most? When people get mad at me for making a joke."

Eli rounded on him, most likely prepared to argue on why humor had a time and place, but the foreign look of iciness the duke allowed on his face stopped her.

"I get mad at people who don't recognize I'm doing the best I can to cope with how I'm feeling. Or the ones who think the best way to handle things is to be angry and hateful and unkind. Frankly? I'm constantly angry."

Eli's breaths stuttered, and the duke noticed it. He knew she empathized with how he felt. He could see it in her eyes. Despite the lack of warmth in the moment, he could feel a deeper connection forming between them.

"I still love, and I still try to be better every damn day. But it's harder for me, I think, than it is for others. It's hard to let go of what has been said and done to me. Because why should I? There are people who need to pay, and the injustices I've seen in my life? Gods. It makes me want to rip apart the world."

Harris felt his throat start to close. He hadn't had this sort of conversation in a long time.

"If I try to be funny? Or try to find the joke? It… it helps. I'm looking for good. Not looking for destruction. It's my way of finding my way out of my anger. Even though I know it won't ever fully go away. I know it's something I just have to live with, and I also know that, despite the efforts, I know I'm a quarter of the man I should be. Especially for my boys. I descend into chaos with their mother because she is the same as me: angry. And we find comfort in chaos—even though we both are working day in and day out to be better. It'd be unhealthy if it weren't for the fact we are both working to help each other and be supportive of healing our anger."

"Do you ever take your anger out on your boys?" The hardness in Eli's face made Harris turn to her somberly.

"Over my dead body would I ever lay hands on my boys. Same for my wife. My wife and I will fall apart in anger together about the world, never toward our children. But they have ears. And they see what we are… Children have glimpses of clarity no adult can rival."

"I also heard you traumatized some cows."

"That was unfortunate. The poor animals…" Harris trailed off with a wince before continuing. "Look. I can tell Tam makes you feel safe and happy. It's good. You have found solace in each other, but I also know that when you have even a small fight, it can feel much deeper on your side. That it's easier to feel angry, and to stay angry."

Eli was quiet. She weighed her next words, her jaw moving. "I… Tam… Tam says if Penelope has lost her family, he wants to adopt her."

Harris's eyebrows shot upward, but the rest of his face was still. Mildly surprised, but not entirely.

"I feel… toward Luca, that I can be a mother. I feel close with him, and I feel a bond. I thought about whether I was capable of stepping into that position for Luca for a long time. It wasn't easy. I don't… I don't think about having others close to me lightly." Eli let out a breath and dropped her head, her arms unfolding as she instead clasped her hands together. "Logically, I know I'm perfectly reasonable in not wanting to choose to parent another child. I'm not even married or betrothed. I've just started being… with Tam. I—"

"No details. Please." Harris held up his hand and cleared his throat.

Eli gave a brief half smile of relief before continuing. "It's new. With Tam. And yes, I'm angry. But I'm also broken, and I barely know how to be good in a relationship, let alone a mother figure to *two* children. One of which may be the devil, and the other who has enormous trauma. While I know it's reasonable that I'm hesitant, I feel especially guilty because Penelope is like me. I don't want to be like my mother. I don't want to turn away and be cold toward her. Hell. I even shouted at my mother before all of this about how easy it was to love a child… Right now, though? Gods, I'm just a damn hypocrite. A horrible person." Tears of frustration welled up in Eli's eyes.

Harris stared at her, his own eyes warming. "You aren't a horrible person. Even if you were to choose to walk away now, you would not be a horrible person, Eli. You would be cruel, but cruelty can be kind in the long term. Better the children and you don't suffer your regrets and resentment. You wouldn't be like your mother for choosing to leave. Your mother chose to have you. You merely chose to be in a relationship with Tam and his illegitimate offspring who may be the sweetest devil spawn imaginable. Honestly, Kat's children and my own make better candidates for the devil. It worries me at night."

Eli choked on a laugh at that.

"Tam needs to consider you in this decision. You signed on for who he was and his son, which was already magnificently kind of you. But if he pushes adopting Penelope on you while you are partners, he is in the wrong. You are not."

Eli took a shuddering inhale. She couldn't bring herself to speak, but she did nod.

"Tam wishes to be kind. But as I have long believed, be kind to your home first, and then if you can spare kindness elsewhere, spend it. Penelope will be put with a loving home should we be unable to find her family. She will be well looked after no matter what the choice."

Silence rested between the duke and his niece. A thoughtful, timidly warm quiet that eased some of the tension in Eli's posture.

Harris couldn't resist a small smile. "You know, daughters are… the greatest challenge and accomplishment in the lives of parents."

Eli laughed and turned imploringly toward Harris.

"People like to say women compete with each other naturally in order to be appealing to men, but you know what my wife clarified for me?" Harris was glowing at the mere mention of his dear duchess. "Women are wildly critical of themselves, and so they hold other women to the same standards they hold themselves. They are as cruel to others as they are to themselves. This makes them doubly more accountable than men. They encourage each other, yes. But they are quick to call fault. Whereas men will, for the most part, shy away from anything but joviality. Which makes us pleasant company, but troublesome partners and fathers at times."

Eli eased herself back on the rusty-rose wool blanket they had laid out on the ground for lunch a while ago. "You know, you would have enjoyed the study of philosophy here in Zinfera."

Harris chuckled. "I would've made a great many philosophers quit their profession. It's my wife who would thrive with them."

"Is it wrong that I think Tam loves me more than I love him?" Eli asked suddenly.

Harris chuckled. "No. But remember this time. Because to be honest, love always changes. It grows and ebbs. There will be times you adore him more than the air you breathe, and he will love you, but more in a content way. Then there are magnificent moments where it matches beautifully, and lo and behold you find yourself with an army of children as a result. It'll rise and fall. Effort is required, and thought, and struggles. And humility. All of it comes together to create the highest highs and the lowest lows of humanity."

"You should write a book," Eli noted quite seriously.

Harris snorted. "Ah. I'd fill it with terrible innuendos. I'm just sleep-deprived, missing my wife and wanting a nice dose of moonshine. It's making me strange."

"You mean wise and endearing."

"How insufferable."

"Even your complaints are dignified."

"Should I tell you the exact shade of red my poop has become? Will that break this awful streak of compliments?"

Eli laughed more readily than before. She looked significantly more at ease than she had before the conversation. "Thank you for agreeing with me about Penelope. I do like her. I like her a great deal, but I just worry empathy over trauma is the only thing bonding us."

Harris blinked rapidly at this astute assessment. "Trust yourself. Tam is generous in love and wanting to help people. It's the way of his family. Don't hold it against him, but it isn't what is best for everyone. He needs to hear you, really hear you as his partner. You are smart, and the way you proceed with caution is admirable. The Ashowan family desperately needs someone like you. Duchess Ashowan used to be remarkably good at maintaining *some* restraint in the family, but the poor woman deserves support or retirement."

Harris watched his niece's smile. Feeling perfectly pleased with his efforts, he sat back up. "I think I need to tell the kids that they need a flat stone if they're to make it skip on the river."

Eli rounded on him. "You didn't tell them that when you told them to go skip rocks?"

Harris grinned. "I needed to have some bonding time with my niece. Is that a crime?"

"I believe I would be interested in seeing all official documentation you've contributed to the Daxarian court when we return to double-check on things."

Harris pushed himself up to his feet with a grunt. "Suit yourself! My wife will most likely be thrilled to have someone else nagging me to behave. We are sorely without daughters, you see."

"I notice that the Ashowan family and your own all seem to be missing daughters," Eli observed casually.

"Yes. Which means that we are destined for feisty daughters-in-law, or Tam will give us women to rule all of us—which, you know. Whenever you feel ready, but us poor rambunctious souls most likely need some guidance from time to time."

With a scoff, Eli set off ahead of him toward the children, leaving the Daxarian duke to stare after her before turning toward the tent where they'd placed Tam.

Sighing, he found himself saying, "Gods. Just as your sister discovered she was much more like your mother than she knew, I bet you will discover you are terribly like your father. Wanting to do so much good even to your own detriment." Harris squinted against the sun back toward Eli, Luca, and Penelope. The backdrop of the mountains, forest, and river with the brilliant-blue sky above was something out of a heavenly visage. "I hope you can hold on to it, Tam. I hope you can find your peace. I don't even think your father ever fully found that balance. But maybe, just maybe… you will."

CHAPTER 30

ALIGNING THE ANIMALS

The first witch stared at the lineup of familiars and witches before her. She had originally intended for them to act on her behalf during the ship voyage to intercept Tamlin Ashowan and the devil. However, the plan had changed.

She did not believe for an instant that the son of the house witch and the Zinferan princess were dead.

Sure, Katarina Reyes was kicking up a wild fuss and destroying a staggering amount of valuable property in Soo Hebin's palace, but Aradia was willing to bet the Daxarian queen was merely using the alleged death of her brother to act as she pleased.

The first witch barely suppressed a smile at this thought.

Regardless of the fact that they were technically enemies, Aradia actually quite liked Kat. She wished she could join her in being a bloody nuisance to Soo Hebin, who had gone on a short, hasty vacation to her villa located only half a day's carriage ride away from the palace.

It seemed that Katarina was going to be successful in laying eyes on the emperor despite the concubine's best efforts. A notable feat indeed.

Aradia couldn't be bothered worrying about that, though. Frankly, an official meeting helped her plans tremendously.

Pulling herself back to her present task, Aradia lifted her chin.

"I need three familiars who can carry out my orders in the Forest of the Afterlife," she announced. "This important work is not for the meek-hearted or dull-minded. So if anyone has any hesitations about such an endeavor, I suggest you remove yourselves from the room."

Three witches turned with their familiars and sidled out.

Aradia took stock of the ones that remained.

There were a number of cats, a few snakes, some birds…

Her eyes landed on a small monkey that perched easily on his earth witch's shoulder.

"You."

The earth witch already had his eyes downcast, but at being addressed by the daughter of the Gods, he lowered himself into a bow.

"What is your name and your familiar's?"

"I am Kwang, Your Magnificence, and my familiar is named…" Kwang trailed off and cleared his throat. "His name is Ban."

The monkey grabbed a fistful of Kwang's hair and yanked while holding Aradia's gaze.

Kwang yelped. "Banana! His name! Is! Banana! I'm *sorry!*"

The corners of Aradia's lips twitched. "Banana. I am glad to meet you. Are you prepared to venture to the other realm?"

The monkey chirped his response.

Aradia tilted her head gracefully in gratitude. Her gaze slid over to the next beastie…

A white dog that was so fluffy he looked like a cloud, with a dashing black nose and eyes.

She stared at the dog. She stared for a *very* long time.

It wasn't until one of the witches stifled a cough that she continued her perusal of the animals.

"That one." She pointed at a red panda that had been sitting quietly on the floor that, hearing her address, rose to a stand on its hind legs. "What is your name?"

The fire witch at the panda's side curtsied. "Her name is Copper."

Aradia bobbed her head and issued another formal greeting before proceeding on down the line until she came to the second-to-last familiar, belonging to a water witch.

She stared at the animal.

It had sapphire-blue eyes that stared in opposite directions. Neither direction was at Aradia.

The cat's tongue stuck out a little, and its face seemed too wide and smooshed to be a proper cat. Its nose looked like it had been rubbed with coal, along with its tail and paws, while the color of its fur was akin to a milky tea. It had a small paunch but still looked nimble.

Aradia continued looking at the creature for a long, long time. Even longer than she had stared at the dog.

"This familiar," she started, her finger tapping the air over its face, "is integral to the task I am about to set for them."

Every witch in the room stared confusedly at the cat with its vacant, naturally stupefied expression.

Aradia didn't clarify what she meant.

"What is this cat's name?" she asked the water witch, who was a mite twitchy, as though she couldn't tell if the first witch were being serious or not.

"U-Um. H-His name is Oyster."

Aradia opened her mouth. Then closed it as she looked back at the cat that may or may not have started drooling.

Ignoring this, she lifted her head regally to speak once more.

"The three familiars and the witches I have selected, you will return to this room this evening, and I will give my instructions to you all then. The rest of you, I want you to focus your efforts on finding the missing Zinferan princess, Lord Tamlin Ashowan, and the devil. They would've had to row ashore, most likely at night. They were not quite at the halfway point moving from the south of Zinfera, so I imagine they are heading in a straight line near the middle to reach the forest and have water. If you are able to search around the river, I'm certain you'll find signs of them."

The witches all inclined themselves, and then wordlessly filed out.

"You. Hold on." The first witch waved her hand toward the air witch who owned the dog.

She stopped, turned, and curtsied. Her familiar sat back down, and panted happily at her side.

"I will ask that your familiar stay here with me until this evening, and I will most likely make similar requests again in the future."

The air witch's eyes widened, but she didn't object or question the order.

"What is your familiar's name?" Aradia tilted her head elegantly.

"His name is Goodo."

Aradia's eyebrows twitched closer together in confusion.

The air witch cleared her throat. "Because he's a Good-o boy."

A very quiet snort sounded from Aradia, though she didn't smile. "Very well. Leave Goodo here with me. I have an important matter to attend to with him."

The air witch curtsied again and slowly made her way out of the room, risking only a quick look over her shoulder at her familiar, who stared after her until the doors closed.

Once alone, Aradia peered down at the dog who had moved his attention back up to her.

"It is lovely to meet you, Goodo. I am the first witch, daughter of the Gods." Aradia knelt in front of the dog. "And you… are the *fluffiest* dog I have ever met."

She held out her hand for him to sniff, a smile already lighting up Aradia's face.

The dog's tail wagged, and so, unable to hold herself back any longer, Aradia wrapped her arms around him and buried her face in the piles of floof.

"You are the bestest boy, aren't you? Such a good, sweet, soft boy!" she murmured happily into the fur, making Goodo's tail wag even more furiously.

"Did you forget I'm still in the room?" Ansar asked from his discreet seat in the corner.

Aradia stiffened. "No, I did not. But how can I not tell Goodo what a sweet boy he is!" Her voice rose a half pitch up as she scratched behind the dog's ears.

Ansar rose from his seat. "You never cease to surprise me."

"I'm calculating and without all my emotions thanks to a curse. I'm not a monster," Aradia reminded him lightly.

Smiling, the assistant drew closer. "Are you going to tell me what you are sending the familiars to do?"

Goodo proceeded to lie down and present his belly, which Aradia was more than happy to nuzzle and comb through with her hands.

"No. You'll see soon enough. Do we have a leather ball we can toss for Goodo?" Her left hand paused over a spot on Goodo's belly that sent his right leg twitching vigorously.

Ansar's smile could be heard in his voice. "I can see about acquiring one."

"And a bowl of water," Aradia added as Ansar moved to carry out her orders.

"Thomas Julian is still being held in the Zinferan cell," Ansar announced abruptly.

Aradia paused. "We'll see about getting him out when Katarina Reyes isn't in the midst of destroying anything she can lift. Otherwise she may notice his absence, which might lead her straight to me."

Ansar lowered his chin respectfully. "It isn't like him to fail in his assignment. If he had been able to tip off Katarina Reyes sooner about your presence, that would have been best."

Aradia returned her attention to Goodo, unbothered. "We'll ask him what happened when we see him again. It would've been best if she had kicked up a fuss sooner as we had planned. I'd hoped to have more space from Soo Hebin."

Ansar didn't say anything else on the matter. It was quite obvious his mistress simply wanted to have a relaxed day before she sent off the familiars, and it was his duty to oblige her. Though even he had to admit, he never would've expected the first witch to have a soft spot for a fluffy animal. Not that it changed the way he thought about her in the slightest. If anything, it made her feel more human.

Which made him love her even more.

Ah, well. It wasn't like he could help it.

Kat paced furiously in her destroyed quarters, her heart pounding.

What the hell was happening to Tam?

The red thread of magic between them kept disappearing and reappearing.

Was he dying? Sick? Hurt?

The Daxarian queen hadn't told their mother about the change in Tam's state. She didn't want to worry her just yet.

Kat wondered with growing dread if the fact that she had pushed another two spurts of magic Tam's way over the past three days had done something horrible to him.

Her meeting with the Zinferan emperor had really just been her looking down at the face of a sleeping man. According to Annika Ashowan, he would wake again thanks to the herb concoction they had crafted back in Daxaria that lessened some of the immediate effects of Witch's Brew—though it wouldn't be enough to undo the years of damage.

However, seeing the man had left Kat feeling more restless than ever.

Gods… everything was a mess.

Kat started to experience a potent urge to hunt down the first witch and abandon her initial plan of ignoring her.

She needed to start *doing* something.

Her eyes glanced toward the letters on the desk she hadn't flipped over.

Back in Daxaria, Antony had managed to stop wreaking havoc on the weather, so that was good news. But the bad news was that anytime a member of the Coven of Wittica got near him, it would start all over again.

Her heart ached.

She hated being stuck in the middle of a web of politics. She just wanted to draw her sword and start solving problems in the basest of ways.

She wanted to go home and see her boys and Eric.

The door opened to her quarters. Kat's head snapped up and saw her mother entering, a bright glint in her eyes.

"What is it?" Kat asked without bothering with a greeting.

Annika pressed her lips together thoughtfully. "There's someone commanding the coven from within the palace."

"The first witch is still here? She didn't leave with the concubine?" Kat's eyes shone hungrily.

"It doesn't seem that way. A group of witches just left as well, but they are heading east. If I were to guess? It sounds as though Tam abandoned his ship for some reason, and then made it to land. He's hiding either in the woods or in the mountains."

Kat's throat fluttered. She really should tell her mother the concerning development in her connection with her brother…

"There's more." The duchess looked wildly pleased about something. "Lord Yangban, a cousin of Soo Hebin's and her greatest supporter, has gone mad. Rumors are circulating that the concubine is losing her most powerful allies left, right, and center."

Kat drew herself to her full height. "Things are about to explode."

Annika nodded. "People are saying that the Gods are angry with her. Even the most loyal citizens are losing favor for her as a result of the aggressive actions of the soldiers she has commanded. It's only a matter of time before one of the other concubines makes a move and has Soo Hebin and her son either killed or deposed."

Kat folded her arms over her chest. "I could get her deposed just fine, but I still don't know who would be a better match for the throne, or what the first witch is angling to do here. Are there any sightings of ancient beasts? Remember, the concubines talked about a sirin."

The duchess stepped farther into the room, maneuvering carefully around some glass shards of what had once been a particularly lovely wine goblet. "There have been no sightings. As far as I've heard, that sirin the coven harbored died sometime in the past few years."

Kat grimaced. While she wasn't particularly fond of the ancient beasts, she didn't believe they deserved cruelty. "Alright. Any word of Da coming to deal with that monster I told you about?"

"I received a missive this morning. He can't come. Eric refuses to leave Daxaria defenseless with everything going on, but your da did send us the next best thing," the duchess relayed with a bit of a weary sigh.

Kat lifted a quizzical eyebrow at her mother.

"He's sending us Kraken and Pina."

Kat's face fell. "We can't even talk to Kraken without Da."

The duchess slowly crossed her arms. "Are you really going to stand there and argue the fact that the two familiars are some of the best chances we have when it comes to dealing with mystical beings?"

"I mean… no. No, I won't argue about that. I just worry that they are going to make things even more chaotic."

"They normally just make more paperwork for your husband's assistant and father."

Kat squinted. "Are you forgetting that I now have to have Cleophus Miller in my castle for half a year, and go to scheduled visits with the rock golem that is obsessed with Pina?"

Annika smiled. "You know, I can't say I can feel much sympathy for you, my dear daughter. You now are all grown up and able to handle the consequences of your life all on your own."

"This is Pina's fault, not mine," Kat grumbled.

Annika laid a gentle hand on her daughter's cheek. "You're only grumpy because you are going stir-crazy. And you're jealous because the cats are going to go out and do things, aren't you?"

Kat's jaw dropped. "Of course not! I understand—"

"And something else is bothering you. What is it?"

Kat cut short her indignant response as she stared into her mother's keen brown eyes.

Of course she knew everything.

She always knew everything.

CHAPTER 31

PLEAS AND PROMISES

Luca stared at Eli's stony expression. Then he looked at his father's slack, pale face smattered with sweat. Then he turned to the funny duke. He didn't look funny at that moment. He looked frightened.

His stomach turned nauseous and tingly. It felt like something really, really bad was happening, kind of like when he had been sick.

But Eli kept saying that his dad wasn't sick.

Maybe she was lying?

Luca balled his hands up into fists before he started fidgeting with his pant leg.

"I don't think he'll die," Penelope announced while attempting to sound casual.

Luca swung his head around to stare at her. She always tried to pretend she didn't care and was confident, but Luca knew that she wasn't exactly sure of her own words just then, either.

"You said you see things before they happen. Did you see my dad alive later on?" he asked quietly.

Penelope shuffled her feet in the dirt and twisted her mouth. "I saw… I saw me calling Eli 'Mom.' And I… I saw her smiling at someone. I thought it was Tam."

"But you don't know for sure?" Luca's voice turned desperate and panicky.

Penelope grabbed his shoulders, forcing his wild eyes to meet with hers. "People die, Luca. My father died. My mother was sick and is probably dead. I couldn't see her future the last time I saw her. It just… happens."

Tears welled up in Luca's eyes, and his throat ached. "But I just found him. I don't want…" He trailed off, emotion choking him. "I don't want to go back to my mother in Daxaria. She didn't like me. No one liked me. She said I wasn't normal. Said she never wanted me, and I just had to be understanding that she wasn't—"

Penelope pulled him into an unexpected hug and began to gently stroke the back of his head. It felt like something she'd seen others do but had never done herself. Awkward, but not the worst feeling.

"What if this is happening because of me?" Luca croaked into her shoulder. "My uncle used to say I had devil eyes and I'd make bad things happen."

Penelope snorted. Luca pulled back, instantly angry by her reaction. Before he could shout at her for laughing, however, she spoke.

"You have your dad's eyes, and he's nice. Why would your eyes be the devil's?"

Luca stilled, a peculiar warm tingling filling him in the wake of surprise.

He fidgeted some more, but not because of bad feelings. "You don't think I'm scary or creepy?"

"Weren't your mother and uncle the ones who also said you're smart enough and don't need school? I wouldn't trust them," Penelope scoffed.

Luca's cheeks reddened. "I *am* smart!"

"Why do you think you're smart?" Penelope probed snidely.

"My uncle says I'm people-smart. He used to make me watch customers to see who would be bad, or if they are rich, or—"

"You can't tell if someone is bad just by looking at them," Penelope interrupted.

"Maybe *you* can't, but I can. I know my dad's a good person. I know Eli is good. I know Harris is good. So are Bong, and Jeong, and—"

"Am I good?" Penelope thrust her chin up with a superior air.

Luca let out a short breath. "I know that you're scared that I'll say you aren't, so you're acting like you're better than me."

Penelope flushed, and her composure wavered.

"You are good, though. You care; you're just mad and scared a lot of the time. That's why even when you're mean, I'm nice to you. Because I know you like all of us, but you kind of don't like that."

Penelope blinked rapidly. "That's stupid. You're stupid!" she shouted.

Luca didn't react to her insult and instead leaned a bit closer. "Everyone is a bit stupid, I think. My mother didn't know how to be a good mom like Eli. And my uncle didn't know how to be nice. And Harris… he's pretty smart actually."

At that, Penelope shot Luca a look of utter disbelief. "What about the whole thing with the beets?"

"He's dumb about beets. But not much else." Luca shrugged.

Silence rested between the two children.

"So…" Penelope started slowly. "You can tell people's emotions. Like I can see bits of their past, present, and future?"

"I guess."

Penelope nodded in understanding.

A loud grunt followed by gasping echoed from Tam, snapping both Luca's and Penelope's attention over to him to see him straining against some unknown pain. Dark shadows wavered from his skin, and the trees, tents, and even rocks around them all trembled as though an earthquake was starting.

However, the vibrations seemed to only be in a circle around their campsite.

It wasn't the first time this had happened, though each time it did, the area that was affected widened.

Luca watched as Eli gently laid her hand on his father's forehead and held his hand. It didn't make Tam's straining better, but it didn't make things worse. Eventually, as was the norm, he did settle back down to a dead sleep.

Swallowing with difficulty, Luca held out his hand.

"Do it."

Penelope looked at his offered palm, then back up at him, stunned. "You said you never wanted me to try with you."

"Because I… I was scared you'd tell me I was evil. Now I really need to know if my dad is… If he is…" Luca couldn't finish his sentence. Every inch of him longed to crumble into a sob.

Penelope grabbed his hand, her face scrunched up, and her eyes closed.

Luca waited.

At first he didn't feel anything, just Penelope holding his hand in a vise grip.

Then a tickle started in his chest, and a buzzing in his skull.

Luca gave his head a quick shake.

Something strange was happening, and whatever it was, it was oddly familiar.

He cleared his throat to stop himself from making a sound of discomfort. He didn't want Penelope to stop. The buzzing increased until his brain started to ache and colored dots crept into his vision.

Please see something. Please don't tell me my dad dies…

As the buzzing started to overflow into a numbing drone, Luca still didn't let go of Penelope's hands, though he did wonder if he might faint.

At last, Penelope released him.

Luca swayed on the spot until Penelope grasped his face between her palms. "You'll have a headache. You're probably a witch or something like that because they usually feel it worse, and you don't look good right now."

Luca swallowed, wanting the next words out of his mouth to sound in control. "What'd you—" He broke off in a cough. "What'd you see?"

His vision had mostly returned to normal, but there were still some bright patches.

"Well, you're weird. I only saw blackness at first. It wasn't easy, and it was almost like I had to force it, until it just popped up."

"What'd you see?" Luca repeated more irritably as his desperation got the best of him.

"I saw your uncle. He was… Uh, he threw things at you. Your mother told him to be quiet, and you went out to help with customers, but—"

"What about my dad?" Luca cut in to stop Penelope from reminding him of such an awful memory.

"I saw that last night he said your name in his sleep."

Luca swallowed. That was also true. He'd woken up hearing his father calling for him from the depths of his unconsciousness, and had been filled with hope, until he realized his father was neither better nor aware he was saying his son's name. "And the future?"

"I saw Tam and Eli," Penelope relayed carefully.

"What? What is it?" Luca could hear the hesitancy in her words, and he could feel her uneasiness.

"Someone is trying to hurt us. Someone strong wants us, and Tam and Eli are going to try to protect us."

"Does something happen to them?" Luca implored frantically.

Penelope shrugged helplessly. "I don't know. I couldn't see that far. I can't make myself see what I want or you want. I just get glimpses here and there."

Luca sat down on the ground and rubbed his eyes using the heels of his palms.

"Don't cry, you baby." Penelope attempted to scold Luca, though she sounded more caring than insulting as she said it.

"I'm not. My head just hurts. At least my dad's going to be alive later so he's not dying," Luca said seriously while dropping his hands away.

Penelope crouched to be eye level with Luca before seating herself. "That's true." The little girl paused, a foreign look of hesitancy and discomfort tightening the skin around her eyes. "Are you going to be okay when they adopt me?"

Luca lifted his head, and the right corner of his mouth and cheek hoisted up with a mixed grimace and smile. "Eh. I guess. I'd wanted a baby sister. Not a big sister."

"Why don't you want a brother? My Uncle Thomas says boys usually want brothers."

"You have an uncle, too?" Luca asked interestedly. Penelope didn't usually like to talk about her family, so he couldn't help but be curious.

"Kind of. He's not really my uncle. We all lived and traveled together from when I was a baby, so I just call him Uncle Thomas."

"Oh. You traveled together? Like as bards? Or performers?"

Penelope avoided his eyes. "No. We just… had to hide. My mother, father, Uncle Tomas, Mr. Ansar, and I."

"Like my dad, Eli, Harris, and I are hiding and traveling?"

At the comparison, Penelope perked up. "Yeah! Exactly!"

Luca nodded reasonably. "Is your uncle or Mr. Ansar alive?"

Penelope's lighter mood was short-lived as the question brought her shoulders and face back down. "Yeah, but they needed to leave for a job, and then Captain Woo found my mother when she was trying to take me to find my grandmother. She was too sick to take care of me by herself."

Luca leaned forward and put his hand on her head. "I'm sorry."

"What're you doing?" Penelope asked flatly.

"My dad does this to me and I feel better."

"Your hand is probably dirty. Take it off my head."

"It's not dirty! I just washed it!"

Penelope batted his hand away. "Shouldn't you go tell Eli that you know Tam's going to be fine?"

Luca looked over Penelope's shoulder at Eli's back. "Am I allowed to tell her? I thought you told me to keep it a secret."

"I already told her a little bit about what I can do. So it's fine." Penelope gave an impressive eye roll.

Luca leapt to his feet, staggered to catch his balance, then darted off toward Eli without another word. He couldn't wait to make her feel better. He could feel how terrified she was.

So he did just that, and while at first she seemed unmoved, as the moments drifted on, Luca watched her face soften, and he could feel the tiniest bit of relief from her.

Luca watched Eli glance over at Penelope, and give a nod of thanks.

Penelope nodded back.

Luca grinned.

Harris was off in the distance out of earshot, but he must have noticed the change in Eli's demeanor, as he straightened from his leaning position against a tree to look hopefully at Tam.

Yes…

Everything would be fine.

Tam would wake up, and then they could all start traveling again. Maybe one day, when Penelope was adopted, they could live together like a real family.

Jeong and Bong could visit, and maybe Luca could meet Harris's kids, though they sounded a bit scary.

Who knew? Maybe he'd even like meeting the queen and his cousins, though he was a little worried they'd hate him for being a bastard. That had been something his Uncle Liam had said over and over. How nobles hated bastards.

Luca looked at his father's face, once again still, and his complexion sickly.

Despite having Penelope's reassurance that everything would be alright, he couldn't help but do something he had only ever tried once before in his entire life.

He tried praying to the Goddess.

Please, Goddess. Can we all be a normal happy family together? Can I have that?

I'm sorry I was born without your blessing, but… I promise I'll be good. I'll take really good care of my dad and Eli—I'll even be nice to Penelope as my older sister! Even though she can be kind of a jerk. So even if it takes a little while, I hope we all can have a nice life. I'll work hard to make sure I earn it, so please, please, please, don't take them away from me.

Please. I need them. I love them. They don't have to love me back, but that's okay, as long as we're together. And happy.

Please?

CHAPTER 32

A ROUGH RISING

Tam's dreams varied from endless blackness to anxiety-inducing nightmares. When he wasn't fully unconscious, he was racked with a tearing sensation that reverberated down to his soul. It was only a matter of time before the pain would drive him over the brink into madness.

Worse, every time he thought it was getting better, another surge would overtake him.

At times, he felt hyper-aware of everything around him and how connected it all was. The spaces between the tiniest bits of natural matter where his void existed. Where nothing and everything rested. He could flex in these spaces, and then be a part of more of them. Spaces within bark, within leaves, within rich soil, within the mist off the river…

Over and over he bore the sensation of being shattered, ground to dust, then flung far and wide. It only improved when he would snap back together, becoming one with himself. Though the violent reassembly itself was hellish, when it was finished, Tam could relax. Briefly. Before it happened again, and again. Each time he'd be flung farther apart.

At the back of his mind, he knew this was all happening because of Kat.

She was sending him magic, and it was bolstering his own, making it unstable as it surged in power that should've taken years to grow.

He could occasionally make out Eli's presence through the haze of torture, her worried mood, her cool hand, her murmurings—not that he could understand what she was saying; only that she was talking.

Tam didn't know how long it had been since he had originally fallen unconscious. He wanted to wake up from the nightmare and start moving again, but every time he tried he felt his soul dissolve all over again.

It seemed endless, and Tam began to wonder—when he could spare any moment of clear thought—if perhaps he had accidentally released a curse and was dead.

Then at long, long last, he opened his eyes and found himself staring at a cool gray sky.

The light felt like a knife going through his eyes, making him wince and let out a garbled yelp.

In an instant, he felt Eli's reassuring hand on his forehead.

His eyes fluttered back open, and she burst out, "You're awake!"

Tam cringed away from the loudness of her voice, nausea brewing in his gut.

"He's awake?" Harris's voice sounded distant, but it made Tam roll over to his right side to get away from the agony.

"Tam?" Eli's uncertain tone made his heart ache, but all Tam could do was focus on breathing through the agony pulsing in his head.

"Can I get you water?" Eli lowered her volume, as though sensing what was plaguing him.

Tam barely managed to nod, and the movement almost had him throwing up. Though he doubted he had anything *to* throw up. His stomach felt horrendously empty.

He thanked the Gods that Eli's footsteps were silent.

A cold sweat broke out along his brow as he waited, and he barely resisted a shiver.

"Here."

The soft leather of a waterskin brushed against his knuckles.

He took it in shaking hands, and even though it caused blinding pain when he lifted his head, he took several gulps of cool water, then lay back down, his sense of balance as even as a ship deck in a storm.

Time elapsed, but Tam remained conscious. The wind, the birds, the dull rush of the river: he could hear it all, though he tried to ignore it. He managed a few more sips of water. Eventually the pain lessened enough that he could open his eyes, but it still made him squint.

"I have a broth for you."

After a fortifying breath, Tam slowly pushed himself up to a sitting position, then reached blindly for the wooden bowl she offered him. Accepting it gratefully, he sipped as much as he could before his nausea flared again.

"Thank you," he managed. He swallowed back a tiny bit of bile. "How long has it been?"

"Nearly seven days."

Tam's heart thudded against his chest. "Gods."

"I know. We need to move. Do you know what happened? Was this just some kind of sickness that affected your magic?"

Tam would've shaken his head if the mere notion of doing so didn't frighten him.

"Kat." He paused to lick his lips. "Kat can… bolster other people's abilities. Human and witch alike. For some reason, she sent three surges to me. It… did things. It made me lose control, and I am suddenly able to do more with my magic. It's like I went through artificial growth, but it feels permanent."

Tam dropped his head between his knees and took several deep breaths. Saying all of that had cost him.

Eli rested a hand on his back.

"Don't touch me. Please."

She withdrew instantly.

Tam struggled to inhale and exhale as sickening sensations plagued him for a few moments longer.

When he could bring himself to speak again, he said, "Sorry. I just… If I start feeling attracted to you right now amid everything else… it won't be good. My attraction to you might actually be the death of me."

He didn't have to look to know she was blushing.

In less dire situations, he knew she would be saying something along the lines of how base men were. He almost smiled over the fact he knew this.

"How are the kids?" he asked after taking another drink from the waterskin.

"Mostly good. Penelope confirmed she can see the past, present, and future, and said she saw you alive and well, so we at least knew you weren't dying."

"Someone should've told *me* the news," Tam noted drily.

Eli didn't respond to that. "How long do you think until you can travel again?"

Tam closed his eyes, despite it being evening as the light of the sky was already dimming.

"We can try for a bit tomorrow, but I think… No. I'm certain I won't be able to use any magic for a while. It's been overextended. I'm shocked I didn't die and cast a curse."

"It's alright. To be honest I… I've been affected by this as well."

Tam managed to turn and at long last lock eyes with Eli.

He could see the way her brown eyes softened and her shoulders eased down from the deep relief she felt at being able to talk with him.

"I'm even bigger now."

Tam blinked in alarm and lifted himself a bit straighter. "Even bigger? How big are you now in that form?"

"A lot bigger."

"How big, though?"

Eli bristled a little. "Bigger than a small shanty?"

"*What—ow.*" Tam's shout had released another burst of pain behind his eyes.

"I tried flying."

Tam had to focus on breathing for a time to even think coherently. Finally, he said, "How did that go? Wait, if you experienced a growth spurt, did you have any pain?"

"A bit. I was able to transform back to my human form, though. When I'd shift back, the pain would be better."

Tam still didn't like that she experienced any kind of hardship because of him, and, seeing this, Eli gave a tentative half smile. "It really wasn't bad."

Sighing, Tam continued rubbing his face. His migraine was steadily improving, but he started eyeing the river as he became increasingly aware of how pungent he was.

Eli rose and offered her hand. "Come on. I'll go with you to make sure you don't drown."

Tam grasped her hand with a raised eyebrow and, on trembling legs, managed to stand, though the world spun violently and he needed to grasp one of Eli's shoulders to steady himself.

"You're just… saying that so you'll see me without my shirt," Tam stuttered while shooting a boyish smile at her.

Rolling her eyes, Eli turned and started moving toward the river. "You're skin and bones right now. There's not much to look at."

"You're a tender woman."

"If you wanted tender, you should've bought a rib-eye steak instead of opting to court me."

Tam allowed himself a light laugh as they neared the riverbank. Fireflies were already dancing in the trees around them. "I thought I heard Harris earlier," he commented.

Eli lowered herself to help him sit. "You did. He saw you weren't well enough to talk yet and took the kids on a walk to get firewood for tonight."

"Is a fire a good idea?"

"Not at all, but you need a good night of rest and a hot meal if we're going to even attempt traveling tomorrow."

Tam made a disgruntled noise before he tugged his shirt off, then his boots—all in a very slow fashion—then tentatively dipped a toe in the water.

"Holy antlers that is freezing," he gasped while snatching his foot back.

Eli shrugged. "Dunk yourself, then come out."

"If I'm doing that, I'll need a blanket right after."

Eli tilted her head in acknowledgment, then made her way back to the campsite to find just that.

Taking the opportunity of being alone, Tam stripped his pants off next, and before Eli could see him embarrass himself horribly, he pushed himself into the icy water—which instantly dropped him into a new world of pain and earnest teeth chattering. He could barely haul himself out, goose bumps riddling his body. Luckily a blanket fell over his shoulders in an instant.

"As someone who smelled you a whole hell of a lot, I thank you," Eli declared while managing to sound cavalier.

Tam grinned. The shock of the cold water had cleared his head, though there was still a dull throbbing behind his eyes.

As they neared the campsite, Tam spotted Harris, Luca, and Penelope lighting the fire.

Luca, unable to contain himself for another instant, bolted over to his father and wrapped his arms around him. Tam staggered from the embrace, but Eli was quick in placing a steadying hand on his back.

Tam smiled down at his son and ruffled his hair.

Penelope sidled closer, looking like a wary kitten trying not to show she cared too much.

"Tam, my boy! Wonderful to see you up and about! We were worried we were going to have to leave you to the bears!" Harris called out jubilantly as he pulled out a pot that looked quite heavy. "We have some venison stew here, and we even sacrificed some ginger root to make you a nice tea. Eli, don't worry; I haven't made the tea. I won't make that mistake again," the duke assured her, a traumatized shadow passing briefly over his eyes.

"She's a bit particular about tea," Tam agreed while locating his traveling bag and pulling out a tunic and pants that smelled significantly better than his previous ones. He then utilized his blanket to hide himself while dressing.

"You don't say," Harris called out sarcastically.

Eli crossed her arms. "I barely burned you."

"It'll scar."

Eli made a tsking sound before grabbing the kettle, presumably to go fill it with water.

"Can I chop the ginger?" Luca asked excitedly.

"A little bit. I'll do the first cut," Eli said.

"What about me?" Penelope hollered indignantly.

"If you're careful, I will let you put the tea ball in."

The two children beamed happily and then trailed after Eli like ducklings after their mother as she returned to the river.

Alone, Harris looked at Tam, his typical jubilance fading to seriousness. "You alright?"

Tam lowered his head. "I have next to no magic right now. It'll take a while to recover, but I want us to get moving tomorrow morning as soon as possible."

Harris nodded. "Good. The hairs on the back of my neck are standing up these days, and I don't like it."

Seating himself by the fire, grateful for any extra warmth he could absorb, Tam shared the details of what had caused his recent problems. At the end of the story, Harris pressed his lips together thoughtfully.

"It sounds like your sister is getting worried."

"I know."

"But why exactly?"

"There are a few things to worry about right now," Tam reminded him drolly.

"Yes, but why now? Something has to be happening in the capital. Odds are all hell is breaking loose, and your sister is a part of the reason."

Tam rubbed the back of his neck. "Sounds about right. If only we knew more."

"Well, we don't. And we won't. Not for a long time. You won't know if we are going to be met with armies, or if the emperor is ransoming your sister, or—"

Tam snorted at the idea of anyone attempting to ransom Kat. He almost pitied them.

"—or if the first witch has managed to find some magical powerhouses again to help back her."

That certainly would be a problem. Especially if she tried to take Luca.

"I wonder if we should just head straight to Lobahl and stay there for a while until things calm down once we get out of these woods," Tam announced suddenly.

Harris stared at him.

"Eli and I joked about it before, but what can we do in this war? I don't even know that we could make much difference unless someone forces Eli to take the crown, and they use her connection with me and Daxaria to do it."

Harris considered this point. "So you wouldn't support your sister? As she tries to make Zinfera better? End slave trading? None of that sounds like something worth helping?"

"Not everyone is meant to save the world, Harris," Tam argued sharply. The duke looked at Tam levelly, prompting him to continue. "Look, we all get a choice. My da chose to protect the position and home he found. He hadn't wanted to be relied on by an entire kingdom. He'd wanted to be a cook and have a quiet life. He chose to seek more because of my mother. Then my sister seemed crafted for the role of protective leader. I'm different from my sister and mother."

Harris's eyebrows twitch. "You can take part in something bigger that doesn't consume your life."

"You can't half-ass fighting in a war, Harris. Besides, things might be made worse if we get involved."

"How so?"

"What if Luca—"

"Dad! Dad, it's a full moon!" Tam's words were cut off as Luca and Penelope bounded over to him excitedly.

Shoving aside the heavy topic he had been discussing, Tam drew up a smile and peered at the night sky. The moon was indeed large in the sky.

"Dad, are there any stories about the moon?"

"Lots."

"What's the best one?" Penelope asked while settling herself down in front of Tam. Luca did the same.

Smiling despite the anxiety in his chest and the ache in his head, Tam leaned his back against a nearby tree trunk.

"Well, my favorite has to do with an air witch and a sirin who tried to become friends with the moon…"

As the familiar story wrapped around the group, and a hot dinner was served, everyone reveled in Tam's return to the land of the waking.

Even though there was a creeping sense that danger was closing in around them, and it was closing in *quickly*.

CHAPTER 33

A DISASTROUS DAY

"There I was, staring down five armed men with nothing but a big stick and a hangover from hell, and the largest of them—real odd-looking fellow with no neck and skinny legs—shouts at me to give him my money."

"But I bet you didn't!" Penelope hollered with both indignation and delight over the story Harris was telling the children who skipped alongside him.

"Well, I told him the truth: I didn't even own the shirt on my back. So unless he was looking for a pointless beating, he should pick on a plump nobleman instead."

"Aren't you a duke?" Penelope asked sharply.

"I'm not plump, and I wasn't a duke back then," Harris explained without batting an eye.

"Then what happened?" Luca was starting to fidget from excitement.

"Then one of the gutless ones behind me tried to lunge at me, but I heard his boot in the mud. One shot to his family jewels with my stick had him down on the ground."

"Family jewels? Why was he robbing you if he had jewels and you didn't?" Luca looked at Penelope to see if she was having the same confusion.

She was indeed.

Harris glanced forward to where Tam and Eli were walking ahead of them. "Family jewels is another name for testicles."

"What are testicles?" Luca asked next.

Harris cleared his throat. This time when he looked at Tam's back, he was hoping the man would turn around and answer his child's question.

When that didn't happen, the old duke sighed. "Behind a man's shaft is a sack with a line running through it. Those are testicles."

"Oh, you mean balls!" Luca perked up in understanding while Penelope made a disgusted face.

"*That's* what balls are?" Her voice was shrill, and loud.

Both Eli, in her large cat form, and Tam swung around.

"Just what are you lot talking about?" Tam demanded seriously.

He still looked pale from his time unconscious. He wasn't moving as swiftly as he had been before, and Eli was too ladened with their supplies to carry him. Regardless, the warm glint in his eyes was the same as ever.

"Harris is being gross!" Penelope shouted while darting over to Tam.

Harris watched as she grabbed Tam's hand, and he briefly wondered when she had started doing such a thing naturally.

"Harris?" Tam called, drawing out the name.

"They asked me the meaning behind *family jewels!*"

Tam sighed.

"He's making it up, right? Men don't have balls like that, right?" Penelope demanded seriously.

Wincing, Tam shook his head. "He's not lying." He didn't elaborate further.

"Yuck." Penelope stuck out her tongue and gagged.

Tam smiled and looked ahead.

Harris sighed, then turned to Luca. "So after I felled the first one, another two lunged at my sides. I held the stick out, bashed the left one in the stomach, and then hit the right one with each end of the stick."

"But there were two more!"

"Very right!" Harris grinned down at the boy. "Your math skills are really coming along, Luca!"

The boy beamed.

"So there I was with two more robbers to take care of before I could get back home and jump in the lake."

"What lake?"

"The lake just outside Sorlia. It's crystal-clear, and I can't say I've been able to swim to the bottom of it. It has lots of fish to eat and is wonderful to jump into in the summer. Or, as in this story, when your head feels like it's being smashed open with a red-hot fire poker due to a heavy night of drinking."

"Does it always hurt like that when you drink?"

"No, no. Now, back to the story. The next one that came at me—"

Eli stopped walking, and her great head came up, ears twitching.

They all halted.

"What is it?" Tam lowered his voice and scanned the area around them.

A low rumble echoed from Eli. Tam gently pressed Penelope behind himself and drew two of his knives.

Harris gave Luca a nudge in the back and sent him darting toward where Penelope was.

Tam carefully sidled over to Eli. She lowered her great body—it was in fact a little bigger than a shanty—and Tam slowly reached under her to release the straps they had fashioned so that Eli could carry their gear. In truth, it barely fit her anymore.

She allowed the packs to slide off her back but then flexed her powerful body in a pre-pounce position.

"Where are you hearing them?" Tam murmured quietly.

Eli's ears twitched a few more times, her golden eyes fixed on the treeline.

"Can you tap your paw on the ground to let me know how many people you smell?"

Eli didn't quite do this, but she did extend two massive claws.

By this time, Harris was at Tam's side with his sword drawn.

"Tam," he whispered. "You really should've acquired a sword of your own on the pirate ship. Knives are only good in fights when the person is unsuspecting or otherwise unarmed."

"These were lighter which was better for traveling. And it's not the time for this conversation. There are two people coming toward us."

"Are they witches? Can you tell?" Harris asked, glancing over toward Eli.

She shook her head.

"Dad? Should Penelope and I go find somewhere to hide?" Luca whisper-shouted from where he and Penelope had backed away.

"Yes," Tam called back softly over his shoulder.

The three adults could hear the children's footsteps grow more distant, and so readjusted their attention and their grips on their weapons.

It was difficult to hear any sounds from the forest over the roar of the river at their side. But still they waited.

Tam's face paled the longer he crouched; his endurance was waning quickly. Licking his lips, he asked, "Are they coming closer or moving away? One claw for coming closer, and two for moving away."

At first, Eli extended one claw, but then she added a second.

"Are they separating?" Tam guessed.

Eli bobbed her head.

And that was when the screams echoed out.

Tam, Eli, and Harris whirled around to see a Zinferan man with long white hair and a long white beard grasping Luca and Penelope by the backs of their necks. He was already starting to rise up in the sky using wind magic from behind the large rock the children had been hiding behind.

"NO!" Tam roared.

He darted toward the air witch, adrenaline pumping through him. Eli had already taken two massive bounds toward the Zinferan when a massive wave of water rose from the river and crashed into Tam and Harris, dragging them into its icy depths.

The Zinferan princess pounced into the air, her wings pressed tightly against her body, when another massive wave of water grabbed her mid-jump and plunged her into the river, pushing her back and down. The air witch continued to ascend into the sky with the two shrieking children, who kicked and screamed against his hold.

The water witch stepped free of the trees, her hands flexing and sweat beading on her brow with the effort of pushing not only Lords Tam and Harris down the river, but also Elisara, who was significantly larger than they had been led to believe.

When she was certain they were long gone, she stopped forcing them against the current and merely allowed the river to flow as it should.

They would all eventually wash back—if they didn't drown, of course.

The water witch then ventured back into the woods to meet up with one of the others to find another air witch to bring her back to Gondol.

The first witch should be happy. They'd found the boy and confirmed that Tamlin Ashowan and Elisara Taejo were alive.

Eli hauled Tam out of the water, her fur soaking wet.

Harris, whom she had managed to pull out of the river first, was shivering on the ground and already rifling through his pack to find a blanket. It was a very lucky thing they had removed their things before they had been washed away, otherwise their gear would be soaking wet, and they most likely would've lost their food.

Tam, on the other hand, was in the fetal position, shivering and coughing, trying to draw a clear breath.

Eli shifted back to her human form, and dropped to her knees beside him, her own skin tinged with blue from the cold.

"H-Here." Harris tossed a folded wool blanket at them weakly.

Eli reached for it with trembling fingers that didn't want to fully straighten, but she grasped it and hauled it over Tam, then herself as she huddled beside him.

"Godsdamnit," Tam sputtered at last, his voice hoarse. "Gods *fucking* damnit!" he seethed, his hands closing into fists. "If only I wasn't weak right now. *Godsdamnit* they have them. They took them!"

Eli could see the tears in his eyes as he managed to sit up.

Her own throat was starting to constrict as she then looked at Harris, who appeared equally grim.

"At least we're alive," Eli started slowly. "It's a miracle we weren't bashed on any of the rocks."

"I'd rather be bashed to pieces and the kids still with us," Tam remarked bitingly.

"We're going to get them back, Tam," Harris called out, though he was looking far worse for wear himself.

"What if the first witch leaves Zinfera the instant she grabs Luca?" Tam speculated, his hand running through his hair anxiously, his eyes wide with fear.

"We will find them," Eli repeated firmly. Something was brewing in her chest. Something hot and prickly. Something with teeth that wanted to start tearing the world apart despite her calm outward demeanor. "We are going to get our kids back safe and sound or so help me I will burn more than just Zinfera to the ground."

Harris stared at his niece, understanding in his eyes, but she ignored him. He didn't try to calm the obvious rage simmering in Eli, or the soul-shaking panic that had clearly dug its claws into Tam.

At least the heated emotions were chasing away the last of the shivering from their dunking in the river. The blazing sun above was also helping.

"We need a plan," Eli ground out, her mind already racing. "I can try to improve my flying. Tam, you need to recover your magic as quickly as possible. Once we reach Gondol, we'll see what we can find out about where they've been taken, or if the first witch has left Zinfera. We can contact your sister, but not directly—"

A shrieking, monstrous roar echoed out through the mountains and forest.

The three of them fell silent.

Harris's eyes were wide. "Good Gods." He slowly rose to his feet, his eyes transfixed on the mountains, the expression on his face making him look like someone else entirely.

"What? What was that?" Tam demanded, turning in a full circle.

"I've heard that sound only once before in my life," Harris started, gazing at the nearest mountains to the south. "It was twenty-nine years ago. But there are some things you just don't forget."

"Harris, what are you—"

Eli stumbled back, grabbing Tam's upper arm, her face turned to the sky in distressed awe.

A great shadow passed over them.

"Oh. Oh, no, no, no! Why *today*?" Harris shouted.

Neither Tam nor Eli could say anything, as gliding toward them, its form only growing larger and larger as it neared, was a dragon.

A golden dragon, whose scales glinted in the sunlight, blinding them as its great wings, each nearly the length of six horses, flexed against the air, sending a blast of wind at them.

Despite its size, the dragon landed softly on the ground ten feet in front of them.

It lowered its long, glimmering neck until its snout was close enough to Tam's chest that he could've reached out an arm and touched it, if he dared.

The dragon breathed in deeply. Then continued to snuff Tam interestedly.

Its eyes were green. Dark green toward the edges, with faint white lines tracing through them, and bright green in the middle, where an inky black pupil slit stared down at them.

"I think I've pissed myself," Harris choked.

The dragon growled, making the earth rumble.

Something in Eli snapped. They had enough problems; she wasn't going to let a Godsdamn dragon become another one.

With a shout that sounded like a barbaric war cry, she shifted into her cat form and threw her head back, her shout transforming into a terrifying roar. Her wings snapped out, and her claws dug into the ground.

The dragon reared backward in surprise, rising up on its hind legs.

Snarling, Eli prowled closer, power coursing through muscles that still ached from her growth spurt. She didn't care. This was one of the worst days of her life, and it had gone downhill so *fast*, and they'd been completely powerless. And that wretched feeling of helplessness ignited something in her that smothered any exhaustion, wariness, or fear.

Eli drew closer to the dragon. She noted its black claws and scales that looked like closely woven sheets of armor while trying to find a weakness.

The dragon dropped back down to stand on all fours. A peculiar expression crossed its long face before its lips stretched back, revealing teeth as long as Tam's forearm and quite pointy.

Eli glowered, until a voice suddenly echoed from the dragon. A voice she heard *inside* her head.

"Well, hello, little one. I confess I've not met an ancient beast quite like you before. How is it you are a beast, and a human, and have the smell of chaos belonging to familiars in your blood?"

Eli's head came up, her mind wiped blank in utter shock. Did the dragon just *speak* to her? *How?*

CHAPTER 34

AN ANCIENT ACQUAINTING

Tam, Eli, and Harris stood in awe in the gigantic cavern the golden dragon had led them to.

As it turned out, the lair hadn't been far from where they clambered out of the river. It had appeared less than a quarter league into the woods, in the base of what had seemed like a solid rocky wall of a mountain. The entrance was a discreet lopsided triangle of blackness amid thick foliage, and it had been quite narrow when Eli, Tam, and Harris had entered. They weren't even sure how the dragon was going to follow behind them.

However, that mystery was solved when they stepped out into a massive open area. Several holes in the rocky walls let in pale streams of daylight, illuminating the space, and also providing a perfect dragon-sized entrance to the cave.

Speaking of the scaly ancient beast, a great flapping of air sounded from above a moment before a swath of light disappeared during the dragon's entrance into the cave. He glided in a neat circle before landing in front of the trio.

The dragon stared at them.

They stared back.

"I don't think he can talk unless I'm in my beast form," Eli guessed slowly.

Tam nodded in understanding, his face still pale and grim from the events of the day.

Stepping forward, Eli shifted back into her own beastly form and approached the dragon.

"You are correct. I can only speak with you in this form, but I can understand what the other humans are saying," the dragon confirmed.

Seating herself, Eli lifted her furry chin expectantly. *"You said I am an ancient beast?"*

The dragon let out a rumbling chuckle. *"You carry the blood of one, yes. Yet that is not all you are."*

"I quit being a familiar. So you were wrong about that."

"Little one, you cannot quit being a familiar. To quit is to die. You are soul-bound to your witch. If you are perhaps worried that you will be enslaved to them, or that this somehow takes from your free will, you could not be more wrong."

Eli felt iciness course through her blood at the dragon's words; he had guessed her fear so quickly and astutely.

"You have a witness and an ally for your life, and one who is incapable of being someone that you do not trust."

Her gut roiled.

"I see my words are not easing your concerns." The dragon let out a warm huff of air while settling down onto his haunches and wrapping his long tail around his body.

The gold of his scales glinted in the sunbeam where he had placed himself. The winking rainbow of lights that shone off him occasionally made Eli wince from its brightness.

"You also said I'm a human. How can I be a beast and a familiar as well as a human?"

"It seems you shift into these roles."

"But I'm also an ancient beast?"

"Yes."

Eli's head was starting to hurt. *"How can you know all this?"*

"From your scent, and from watching you change from one figure to the next."

"So am I only an ancient beast when I take on this form?"

The dragon tilted his great head and then extended his neck, his nostrils flaring.

"No. You always have the blood. The smell is only stronger when you shift. It is as though you have extra veins in your being. You are fully human, but your connection to the ancient beast is never far."

"I suppose I should be relieved that I'm only a familiar in this form."

"I am less certain on that. It is still possible for you to feel the echoes of such a powerful status in your human state. It is a connection and power that rivals even the greatest of ancient beasts such as myself. To be both? I must confess, you are nothing short of a mighty wonder."

Swallowing proved a difficult move that called for Eli's full attention. *"Why are you willing to tell me this? What do you want?"* she managed, her overwhelming emotions making the words taste bitter in the back of her throat, even though she did not speak them aloud.

"Ancient beasts are loyal to one another. We help one another. Even if we are on opposing sides of the feud between the children of the Gods, we will still offer some help—barring a battle, of course. Though even during a war, we do our utmost to avoid opposing each other and focus on threats more human–or witch–centered."

"You still haven't said what you want in return," Eli pointed out sharply.

"I want nothing, but should I need help, you will give it if you are able."

Eli thought back to the reports she had read on Troivack's civil war. Only one time did the ancient beasts actively fight one another and choose a side that was not the devil nor the first witch: when Katarina Reyes's familiar had become involved and somehow charmed a stone golem.

The fact that Pina was a familiar and somehow overrode these ancient rules became all the more impressive, Eli thought silently. Her ears twitched, and she allowed her mind to increase the scope of her questions.

"You're the rumored dragon of Zinfera. Why have you appeared?"

The dragon before had seemed elegant and wise. Not really emoting much outside of a sort of weary fondness for Eli, but at this question, he seemed even older. Grief made his eyes droop, and pain filled their brilliant green depths.

"I heard of the death of one of our kind. An ancient beast was killed at the hands of the coven here in Zinfera. Not in self-defense, but for the sake of greed

and cruelty. A sirin. I know Aradia has only just recently come to Zinfera and it is not her fault, but the people must be told that their leaders, the royalty they exalt, are being punished for this sin. For one such sin shall come thrice the consequence. I wield my presence as the threat of the doom that awaits them."

A shiver ran down Eli's spine, and some uneasy part of her started to wonder if she would play a part in this vengeance for the ancient beasts.

"*Can you help us?*" she ventured quietly.

The dragon's gaze moved over to Tam, then Harris, who still looked on the verge of soiling himself. "*I cannot help you save the devil.*"

Shock rocked through Eli, followed by potent dread. "*The… the devil?*"

"*Yes. I can smell him all over the three of you.*"

"*The little boy with us. Was he—does that mean he is—*"

"*I do not know what stage of life the devil is in now. Only that Aradia searches for him. She is about to set the world to rights, then take him home to serve his penance.*"

"*We were traveling with a boy. He had a letter from one of Tam's former lovers, claiming he is Tam's son. Is it possible—*"

"*The devil's followers arrange for his safe upbringing in each of his lives. Aradia thought she had dealt with all of the devil's contacts, but I believe she discovered an imp that managed to convince a raccoon—of all things—to save some ash from the devil's last death, allowing a safe rebirth. The imp most likely threatened or bribed the human to claim the devil as her own and name—Tam, you called him—the father.*" The dragon cut Eli off, staring gravely at her. He seemed to be able to sense her distress. "*I am aligned with Aradia and therefore cannot help you retrieve the devil.*"

"*But he isn't like a devil! He's a normal little boy! He's happy, and sweet, and–*"

"*Happy?*" This second interruption from the dragon would've irked Eli were it not for the quiet surprise in his voice. "*This boy you know, is… happy?*"

Eli managed to nod.

The dragon lifted his head, his eyes shining. "*He… our devil… has not been happy in centuries. Even with his many rebirths, he is never truly happy. There is an otherness about him that alienates him from others. A power that humankind senses. It turns them from him, even though he does not regain his abilities or memories until he is older.*"

"*So he himself wouldn't know he is the devil?*"

"Not if he is a child."

Eli's heart ached in her chest.

So Luca really was the devil.

How could she tell Tam?

Should she even tell him?

Tam claimed he didn't want to know.

"If the devil is happy as you say, then you have my greatest thanks. While I serve the first witch, it does not mean I do not love the devil as a friend. I side with Aradia merely because I believe our devil has suffered enough here on earth, when all he wanted to do was defend us. To keep this world safe for us ancient beasts. I believe he should go home to the Forest of the Afterlife to at long last be at peace."

Eli felt numbness overtaking her as the weight of this knowledge settled in her bones.

"If he is happy, then this Tam witch"—the dragon gestured with his eyes toward Tam, who was watching the conversation keenly—*"is remarkable, and I can see why a remarkable ancient beast like yourself would be loyal to him."*

Unable to say anything, Eli lowered her head.

"What is your name, child?"

"Elisara. Eli. For short."

"That is your human name. What is your beast name? If you wish to rise in your power, you will need a name gifted to you by your witch."

Conflicting emotions ranging from ire to grief continued to thrum against the protective barrier Eli had erected in her heart during the conversation.

The dragon continued, *"I am Wixim, and my hope is that one day perhaps we may speak again, and at that time you will have embraced all of your magnificence and will be able to see it as the gift it is, rather than a burden."*

"Can you help us return to Gondol? Or at least help us get closer?"

The dragon's magnanimous countenance fell flat. *"No. That'd be helping the devil. Not Aradia. I have been very clear."*

"You also said you have to help fellow ancient beasts," Eli argued.

"I have answered your questions and helped you realize your potential and the worth of your uniqueness. You are not in danger. You can return on foot. Or fly yourself. Your wings look large enough."

"I haven't been able to fly yet," Eli grumbled.

Wixim stared at her for a long, thoughtful moment. *"I will help you learn to fly. That is all. I imagine you should be able to carry these other two on your back."*

Pausing, Eli considered such an offer.

Would it be more expedient to spend time learning to fly and not traveling?

"How long will it take to learn to fly?"

Wixim lowered his head, his eyelids closing slowly. *"That depends. I've never seen a beast like you before. It takes dragon hatchlings a week to a month once their wings have fully grown."*

Eli weighed their options for a moment. They were already most likely a week or so from Gondol on foot, was this work the risk?

She shifted back into her human form and turned to Harris and Tam. Harris jolted, caught off guard by the abruptness.

"He can teach me to fly and I can take us back to Gondol, or we continue on foot. What do you think?" Eli looked first at Tam, then at Harris.

Tam's arms were folded over his chest, and his eyes moved to the dragon studiously. "He won't take us himself?"

"No. I'll explain why later."

"I imagine it might cause some distress if he's seen," Harris speculated with forced casualness. The duke was quite obviously still petrified of the dragon.

Ignoring this, Eli kept her eyes fixed on Tam. "What do you want to do?"

The future duke continued staring at Wixim, who, upon sensing Tam's gaze, had cracked open an eyelid to stare back.

"Do you think you can learn to fly quickly?"

"I'm going to try my absolute best."

Tam locked eyes with Eli, and she could tell that he read her sincerity.

"Alright. You'll learn how to fly. Then we're going to go find out where that woman took the kids."

Eli twitched her chin down in understanding. As she faced the dragon again, she returned to her beast form.

"If you are willing, I will greatly appreciate you teaching me to fly."

Wixim made a low noise of approval, then swiveled his slitted eye to stare intently at Eli.

"Your witch is powerful. His power may even rival that of the children of the Gods themselves. I'm afraid I will have to forewarn Aradia of this should I see her, but I confess… I hope we never will have to cross paths as enemies in a battle."

As though Eli hadn't had enough distressing news for the day. She glanced over her shoulder at Tam.

He was strong, sure, but was he really as powerful as Wixim said?

"I see now how the devil could be happy. He was put in the care of a being who would never become afraid of him. Only for *him. The Goddess truly does work in wondrous ways. May his good heart never bring out his power in the name of destruction."*

Eli leaned forward, wanting clarity and yet already sensing the meaning of this comment, when the dragon closed his eyes.

It would seem even the greatest of beasts required naps.

Moving back into her human form, Eli staggered, only to have Tam reach out and steady her.

"Well? What's going to happen?" Harris asked after Tam made sure Eli was alright despite changing back and forth so much in a day.

"I'm going to learn to fly. Probably once he wakes up, I'll start my lessons," Eli explained, her voice a croak.

The worry in Tam's face tripled when he spotted the tears rising in her eyes.

Eli almost couldn't tell him the truth about Luca. He had said he didn't need to know! But in her heart, in her gut… she knew she had to tell him. Especially if it meant they had to battle the first witch to get him back. He should be aware of just how high the stakes were.

"Tam there's… there's something I have to tell you."

CHAPTER 35

THE KIDS MAKE A KERFUFFLE

Sniffles sounded in the otherwise quiet room.

Aradia stared at the two children huddled together in the corner. She felt pleased but also a mite annoyed.

She always was when her brother, the devil, was in his child form.

He had no memories of any of his previous lifetimes, or his Godly parentage, and he couldn't even fully use his abilities.

"What do you want?" Penelope shouted. Ansar had told her the little girl's name.

Aradia rolled her eyes to the ceiling.

She had been hoping to go enjoy some lunch in the garden before spending the rest of her day watching two kids.

Stepping over to the children, she noted the way Penelope had her arms wrapped around the devil. As though she were the one minding him. Pulling out a chair, Aradia sat down a short distance from where they crouched, loosely clasping her fingers together.

"Penelope, you saw Ansar. You know I'm a friend of his. I'm not sure why you are so upset. Hadn't you wanted to be rescued?"

The little girl scowled boldly at Aradia, her arms still wrapped protectively around the boy. "I was fine where I was! And you didn't need to take him anyway! He should be back with his parents."

Aradia tilted her head interestedly, her eyes darting back to her brother. "His parents, hm? And is one of these parents Tamlin Ashowan by chance?"

Upon hearing his name, the little boy lifted his tearstained face.

"So what if it is?" Penelope snapped.

Aradia stared at her and the devil; he peeked back only a moment before he had to turn away and continue crying into Penelope's shoulder.

"Lord Tamlin isn't your real father. You are the devil. You are my brother. The son of the Gods. And you." Aradia's eyes slid to Penelope. "Are the only remaining seer alive right now. The blood of your father saw to it that you inherited such a gift."

"LIAR!"

Aradia regarded her little brother who had shouted and at last released Penelope, glaring at her with intense fury.

Aradia gave an unbothered shrug. "You don't have your memories yet, brother. When you start going through puberty, they will start coming back, and you will remember every horrible thing you've ever done. You will remember our feud, and that I am your twin sister whom you wronged."

"I'm not the devil! My dad is Tam! My mother is Rosaline, and my mom is Eli! You are just—you are just a bad woman!" The boy pointed at Aradia with a trembling finger.

The first witch gave a long sigh. "I will be sending you back to the Forest of the Afterlife as soon as possible so that you can start paying for your sins."

"I'm not going anywhere with you!" the little boy roared.

"You no longer have a choice. I admit, you were wildly clever—or perhaps I should be commending your loyal imp—for placing you in the care of an Ashowan."

"I *am* an Ashowan!"

Aradia blinked. Her cool mask didn't budge an inch.

"What name did he give you?" she asked softly.

"Don't tell her." Penelope's voice was like steel. "She needs your name to do anything to you."

Aradia's attention snapped to the girl. "And who told you that?"

Penelope stuck her tongue out in response.

Shifting her jaw, Aradia was reminded that she didn't have an abundance of patience for children.

Well, she didn't mind them exactly, but Soo Hebin had returned that morning and Aradia was already in a bad mood as a result.

"Penelope, I'm going to be sending you away first. My brother and I will be joining you shortly once we get things wrapped up here in Zinfera."

"Where are you taking her?" the boy demanded passionately while moving protectively in front of Penelope.

Aradia balked.

Had her brother ever been so thoughtful toward a human that wasn't a mate?

Whenever she had seen him in his child form, he had always been stoic. Emotionless. World-weary. Tired. Wise beyond his years. Yet this time, he seemed like a genuinely frightened, goodhearted little boy.

The Ashowan son must have really done a number on him.

Giving a scoff of disbelief, Aradia rose from her seat.

A loud commotion echoed out in the hall. Something broke, someone screamed. Then there was a great deal of shuffling of feet and men's voices.

It sounded like Katarina Reyes was wreaking some new havoc. Most likely she had learned of Soo Hebin's return and wanted to gift the woman a welcome-home headache.

Aradia smiled despite herself and turned to the door.

"My dad's going to come get us, and you're going to be sorry you took us."

Rounding slowly back to face her brother, Aradia stared down, unsurprised at his wrathful expression.

"I've been sorry for many things in my life, brother, but I've never been sorry for trying to restore the balance of the world, regardless of what doing so requires me to do. I'll be back shortly. There are no windows, and two guards will be standing inside this room to keep an eye on you."

Things were proceeding exactly as she had planned.

Which meant that in a fortnight, she would be heading to Daxaria, and by the time the autumn chill set in, she would have brought her brother back to the Forest of the Afterlife. The covens would be properly positioned as the religious powerhouses of the kingdoms, and with this all done, perhaps her parents would break her curse and allow her to go home at long, long last.

★★★

Penelope sat slumped against the wall, her eyes staring blindly ahead.

She had already been told by Tam and Eli about her abilities as a seer, but what good were those when she was being abducted again?

Luca wiped his face with his sleeve, his breaths still coming out in shudders. "She's lying, right?"

"Doesn't seem like it," Penelope admitted grimly.

"I'm not the devil! And why did she need my name?" Luca asked vehemently.

Penelope brought her knees up to her chest and pressed her forehead to them. "She doesn't have normal magic, and if she is using you to do something with or to you, she needs your name. That's what my Uncle Thomas told me," she explained quietly so that the guards couldn't overhear her and tell the woman who'd taken them.

"Oh… Did you know we were going to get taken?" Luca wondered carefully.

Penelope shook her head. "What I saw was us standing behind Tam and Eli in a room."

"Then that means we're getting out of here!" Luca perked up, his eyes filling with hope.

"Yeah." Penelope barely managed a half smile.

A particularly loud bang thundered outside the doors to the room the children sat in, making both turn to the guards, who were grimacing.

"That Daxarian queen is disgraceful," one of the guards muttered to his companion disapprovingly.

"I heard she has cost Her Highness over a thousand gold coins in repairs by now." The other guard shook his head in disbelief.

Luca stiffened at Penelope's side. "Did you hear that?" he whispered.

"What?" she mumbled.

"The Daxarian queen! That's my aunt! She's close by!"

Penelope's brow furrowed as she turned to stare at Luca. "Do you really think she'd want to help us? We haven't ever met her."

"My dad likes her! And he loves my cousins, so she can't be all that bad."

Clearly uncertain about this assessment, Penelope scrunched up half her face doubtfully. "How could we possibly find her?"

The sound of something delicate shattering made the two guards wince.

Luca smiled. "We just follow the noise."

"Are you forgetting about the guards? Or about the other people who will stuff us all back in this room the second we run for it?" Penelope reminded him warily. Though she was starting to look more quizzical than dismissive.

"We can always distract them. Or hit them in the family jewels!" Luca's dark eyes were sparkling.

Penelope couldn't resist a smile at this idea. "They won't let us get that close to them. Besides, if we do that, they'll tie us up."

"I'm sure I could just go up and ask for a water closet. Or say my stomach hurts! What do you think? Will you help me?"

While Penelope was far from confident in their getaway scheme, she had to confess, the sounds of destruction nearby really did seem close enough that it wouldn't be hard to reach.

"Even if we don't find the queen, we can scream for her," Luca persisted, making sure his voice was as quiet as possible.

Penelope tilted her head. That did increase their odds a great deal.

"Okay. Let's do it."

Luca grinned excitedly while hiding his expression behind his knees from the guards. Penelope couldn't help but smile in return.

The only reason she wasn't completely hopeless, in spite of her failed escapes from the pirates when she'd first been taken in Troivack, was this annoying kid she had come to like despite herself. And if he was going to go and get himself in trouble, she wasn't going to let him do it alone. Especially if it meant that maybe she could go back with him to Tam, Eli, and Harris, whom she had also maybe grown a little fond of.

Kat kicked over a bucket filled with dirty water the maids hadn't had a chance to empty after washing Soo Hebin's silk sheets.

The Daxarian queen stood with her hands on her hips, her fingers fluttering as she stared down the crowd that had thickened around her.

"Where oh where is Soo Hebin," Kat hollered out over them. "I have been trying to get in touch with Troivack's delegation to discuss the recent commotion in Zinfera, and *yet again* I have been given no information and stopped from leaving. Which makes me wonder if I am a prisoner here in this palace, which makes me rather *annoyed!*"

No one answered Kat, nor did anyone approach as her frightening gaze swept over them.

Duchess Annika had gone to nap, claiming a most unpleasant headache—at least that is what was told to the palace staff—and she was the only one capable of calming down the Daxarian queen.

In actuality the emperor had woken at long last, and she was in a private meeting with him. Which meant Kat had to create all sorts of distractions and commotions to ensure that their discussion was not interrupted. The fact that her brother's connection with her had returned—weaker, but at least steady again after days of flickering in and out—did wonders for helping Kat and her frustrations. It helped bring an almost celebratory energy to the destruction of Soo Hebin's palace.

Kat looked around the small courtyard, her eyebrows raised. She needed something else to smash. Maybe she'd rip up a shrub or two, though she felt bad for the gardener of the palace. It was bad enough she had had to terrorize the maids who, while they worked for Soo Hebin, were forced to clean up after Kat's bouts of destruction.

The queen was starting to wonder if perhaps she should start to be more creative in her approach to aggravating the concubine when a shrill shout pierced the air.

"KAT! AUNT KAT! KATARINA! TAM'S SISTER!"

Kat's head snapped around.

It sounded like a child.

Her aura burst outward, and without a moment's hesitation, Kat bolted straight toward the sound.

"KAT! PLEASE HELP US! KAT!"

She skidded to a halt at the far side of the courtyard, just in time to see some sort of scuffle taking place near the second-floor balcony.

Bending her knees, her eyes filling with golden light, Kat leapt up and soared inhumanly high. She seized the wooden railing of the second-floor balcony and swung herself nimbly over. She drew her sword when she spotted two guards wrestling back what appeared to be two children.

"AUNT KAT!" The little boy wrenched his body against the guard's hold as soon as he saw her, though she saw the nervous fear in his face at the sight of the blazing light in her eyes and her aura.

"HALT!" Kat boomed, her voice sending shudders through the air.

The guards, at last noticing her presence, faltered at the sight of the Daxarian queen.

"Put the children *down*."

The guards tried to readjust their grips on the children while sharing a nervous glance with each other, but the little girl bit down hard on the hand of the man who held her, and the little boy dropped a firm fist into the man's groin shouting, "FAMILY JEWELS!"

Kat pressed her lips together as she found she suddenly had to struggle against laughing. The boy then darted away from the guards behind the little girl, and they both skidded around to hide behind her.

"Your Majesty." The guard who had been bitten bowed, his injured hand clenched into a reddened fist, while the other remained doubled over on the ground.

Kat could've sworn she could've heard the man on the ground weakly utter, "Why… again?"

"These children are special guests of—"

"I'm Tam's son!" the boy interrupted, staring up at Kat with all the urgency and sincerity a child in danger could muster.

"It's true!" the little girl shouted. "We were with Harris, Eli, and Tam, and were kidnapped yesterday!"

Kat's heart pounded.

They'd been with Tam?

Wait… didn't that mean that this little boy was the devil?

Kat gazed down into the child's face and felt herself still.

He looked so much like Tam, but then again, the devil had looked very similar to her brother back when the devil had been a fully grown man in Troivack all those years ago…

Both guards were on their feet and stepping closer to Kat and the children. "These children are going to be returned to—"

"Touch me or these children and you will lose a hand each."

The terrifying aura around Kat surged, and the guards flinched back.

"These children are coming with me, and if Soo Hebin, or a certain bitch named Aradia wants them, tell them they can come see me." The demonic, hungry smile Kat gave the guards with a tilt of her head had the men paling in fear.

They shuffled backward on trembling legs, until they gave up on leaving the queen's presence with their dignity and instead bolted away as quickly as possible.

With her aura shrinking back down, Kat peered around their surroundings then, slowly, put her hands on each child's back protectively.

"You two come with me. I'm going to take you to my quarters, and I do not want you leaving my side for an instant. Understood?"

The two children looked at each other, then up at the Daxarian queen happily before nodding.

Kat let out a long breath of air.

Well, this was a surprising turn for the day.

"Excuse me?"

Dropping her gaze down to the young boy, Kat waited expectantly.

"My dad said when I saw you I should call you Aunt Queen and that you'd think it was funny."

A snort escaped Kat before she could stop herself.

"He's right. I like it," she admitted with a grin. A welcome bout of relief wormed its way into her heart. That was exactly something Tam would've said.

Then she remembered that the child she was now protecting was most likely the devil.

Though it was strange…

He didn't seem like the devil *at all.*

Which brought up a whole other disturbing possibility. The possibility that Tam *had* a son she had no idea about. But that was too bizarre, wasn't it?

"Erm. Hey." The two kids looked up at her. "You called Tam your dad. Did he tell you to call him that?"

The little boy smiled timidly, his cheeks blushing, startling Kat with his innocence.

"Uh. Yeah… I'm a bastard. My dad used to court my mother back in Daxaria, and I finally got to meet him when I snuck onto the boat going to Zinfera."

"W-Wait," Kat spluttered just as she reached one of the rooms to her quarters and pushed the doors open. "You… Wait. Tam had a lover, and she had *you?*"

The boy nodded slowly as he visibly shrank back from Kat's reaction.

The girl darted into the room while calling over her shoulder, "They also found me on a boat."

"A different boat!" Luca added swiftly as he, too, entered into the room.

Kat's mouth hung open, unable to form words.

"Tam's not my dad," the girl contributed helpfully. "Well. Not yet, really. He and Eli are going to adopt me."

"*Pardon?*" Kat squawked while moving into the room, then closing the doors firmly behind herself.

"Yeah. That won't happen for a while, though," the girl explained reasonably.

"Can I say you're my sister now, or later?" The boy faced the girl with genuine curiosity.

Kat's mind flailed.

"Ugh. I guess saying it now is fine." The girl sighed irritably, then fixed her big brown eyes on Kat. "Can you help Tam, Eli, and Harris? They're probably worried about us. They were trying to get here to Gondol. They're in the woods."

Kat's mind kept on spluttering. *How does this girl even* have *my mother's eyes? Just what the hell is going on?*

"Aunt Kat, are you okay? Oh. Sorry. Aunt Queen?" the boy asked worriedly.

"Are you allowed to say the word *bitch*? I thought it was a bad word," the little girl speculated as she drew closer to Kat with the boy. "I heard you call that bad woman Aradia a bitch."

The Daxarian queen stared at the two of them.

"Right… Right… I'm going to have a drink, and, uh, you two better start preparing yourselves."

The children shared nervous looks as Kat stumbled over to a discarded red dress, fished a flask from a discreet pocket, unscrewed its cap, and took several gulps.

"Prepare for what?" the boy wondered nervously.

Kat lowered the flask, wiped her mouth with the back of her wrist, and said, "For meeting your grandmother. This is going to be a lot, even for *her*."

CHAPTER 36

AN AGE OF AGONY

Annika stared, unmoving.

Her expression was unreadable.

Whether or not she was breathing was also questionable.

"Mum?" Kat called from her seat at the round table, where she lounged with her head propped up by three fingers.

Annika continued staring blankly at the two children standing before her.

"I know you're going to be adopted later, and you don't call Tam 'Dad' or Eli 'Mom,' but will you call her Grandma?" Luca whispered to Penelope curiously as they waited.

Penelope was gazing back up at the duchess with a little frown riddling her face.

Annika's attention had been homed in on the little girl from the moment she stepped in the room, her breath hitching.

Kat slowly pushed herself to sit up a little straighter. "Mum, are you going to faint?"

The duchess still didn't speak, nor did Penelope. Luca glanced at the pair, then eventually grew bold enough to stare blatantly at the older woman.

"Huh, you kind of look like her, Penelope. It's the eyes, I think."

"I thought the same thing!" Kat chimed in behind the children, making Luca turn around and grin at his aunt.

"Who is your mother?"

All eyes were on the duchess.

Penelope bristled a little. "That's not your business."

Annika slowly lowered herself, her knees visibly trembling. "You..." She cleared her throat. "You wouldn't happen to be Caroline Levin's daughter, would you?"

Penelope stumbled back as Kat rose to her feet. "What?"

Luca looked at Penelope with a tilt of his head. "Who's Caroline?"

While Annika didn't turn away from Penelope, she still answered Luca. "Caroline was my niece, and she had a daughter. She went missing shortly after the end of the war in Troivack."

"Whoa, whoa, whoa, now," Kat burst out, moving closer to the children. "That'd be too weird. This kid pops up and just happens to be—"

"I almost caught them. Three years ago," Annika explained dazedly. It was starting to seem as though the duchess really was about to faint. "I have been looking for them ever since they disappeared, and at one point, Her Majesty Queen Alina thought she had found them. They'd sent me a picture of Caroline and her little girl. Her little girl who looks..." She trailed off.

Penelope swallowed loudly and pressed her lips together tightly.

"Are you really telling me this girl is Caroline Levin's daughter, and that we're related?" Kat spluttered in open awe.

Luca's jaw dropped. "You're my cousin?" he asked earnestly.

"Technically you'd be second cousins," Annika explained distantly.

"Are you..." Penelope's voice croaked, tears glimmering in her eyes. "My aunt that my mother hated?"

Blinking rapidly as though she, too, were struggling not to cry, Annika responded with, "Yes."

"She hates you. *I* hate you!" Penelope shouted at the end, backing away.

Smiling sadly, Annika's next words were soft and vulnerable. "Well, I don't hate you, Penelope. Your grandmother and mother blamed me for your grandfather's death, and even though I tried to warn your mother when I met her again after decades, your parents still committed treason against Troivack's monarchy."

The little girl kept backing up, and most likely would've retreated all the way to the farthest wall were it not for the fact that she bumped into Kat's legs, and the Daxarian queen gently touched her shoulders.

"Penelope? Do you want to sit behind the screen away from the duchess for a little bit?" Kat asked gently.

Penelope didn't respond, only turned on her heel and stormed off toward the aforementioned screen, her mouth stretching in a silent sob as she did so.

The duchess sank back from her knees onto her backside, looking far older and more fragile than she had at the beginning of their introductions.

Luca sat cross-legged across from her. "Penelope thinks her mom is already dead. She was really sick when they last saw each other," he announced solemnly.

Annika's eyes flew to him.

Luca's mouth lifted in sad sympathy.

The duchess looked up at her daughter, who grimaced, then took in a long, deep breath.

Kat sat on the floor, placing herself beside Luca and her mother. "Hey kid, you didn't tell me your name."

Luca fidgeted. "Penelope said I shouldn't tell people my name because the bad woman could send me somewhere if she knows it. So if I tell you, do you promise not to tell her?"

Kat raised a puzzled eyebrow, which suddenly made Luca smile brightly. "You look like my dad when you do that!"

Caught off guard by this, Kat leaned back, while the duchess gave a quiet laugh.

"That's true. You do," Annika agreed with a subtle smile before returning her attention to the boy. "We promise not to tell others your name."

The boy stared at the duchess then the queen carefully before hollering, "Penelope, do you think I can tell them?"

"Do what you want! I don't care!" she shouted back.

Luca's chin dropped to his chest as he felt the twist of pain over her harsh words. So he stood and made his way over to the screen to peer at Penelope, who was curled in a protective ball, crying.

His mouth twisting, Luca approached her slowly, then bent down onto his knees and hesitantly put his arms around Penelope.

When she didn't pull away he hugged her tighter. "I'm sorry. You're probably missing your mom right now," he said quietly.

"S-She said that my great-aunt was a bad woman!"

"Why don't you ask her?"

"Because my mom's dead!"

"Not your mom, the duchess lady."

"I don't want to talk to her right now."

"Okay. But she doesn't seem like a bad lady. Remember my secret? You know…" Luca lowered his voice to be as quiet as possible. "About sensing feelings?"

Penelope stilled.

Luca smiled, "She really loves you."

Penelope shoved Luca off herself, making him fall on his backside and almost flat on his back. "*Go away!*"

Luca stared at Penelope, first in surprise, and then with watering eyes. His palms were smarting from catching himself.

"Okay… I'm here when you want to talk, though." Luca rose back up, still looking at Penelope who kept her face buried in her arms, then turned to leave her alone.

The Daxarian queen and her mother were still seated on the floor. Neither spoke as he returned to them.

"I'm Luca." He held out his hand to Katarina.

Blinking herself free of whatever thoughts she'd been mired in, Kat loosed a half smile. "Nice to meet you, Luca."

He bobbed his head at her. "Can we save my dad now?"

Kat glanced at her mother, who was beginning to regain her composure, before responding. "We'd like to, but can you tell us a little about what has been going on since you've gotten to Zinfera with Tam?"

Luca twisted his mouth and cocked his head over his right shoulder. "What kind of stuff do you want to know?"

Sighing, the queen seemed to be struggling with how to word her answer when her mother took care of it for her.

"Everything, Luca. We need to know absolutely everything."

"*Again.*"

Eli launched herself into the air, her wings flapping desperately to keep her body aloft, only to plummet back onto the rocky riverbank a moment later.

"*Stronger beats, not more beats. The objective is to rise up quickly so that you can find the air current and glide on those.*"

A low growl emitted from Eli's throat.

It was the day after the children had been taken. No one other than Wixim had been able to get a proper night's rest.

Tam had gone off into the woods, claiming he needed to think, while Wixim had reluctantly granted Harris permission to explore his cave with its various treasures and artifacts.

"*I don't think my wings are strong enough,*" Eli informed the dragon bitterly.

"*They are. Your wings are simply not accustomed to being used yet. Try a running start this time.*" Wixim yawned.

Lowering her head wearily, Eli stared down the beach.

And that was when it chose to hit her.

The thought, *Why won't this struggle and bad luck ever end? I'm so… tired.*

"*Your witch seemed to handle the news about the devil well.*" Wixim's voice interrupted Eli's thoughts, making her look at the dragon who was watching her with his eyes only partially opened.

"*He's not doing well. None of us are.*" Somehow, even though the conversation was happening in their minds, Eli's words still sounded choked with emotion.

Wixim lifted his long neck. He stared at Eli while sitting motionlessly.

"*You know… I wasn't alive when the devil and first witch first came to this world, but my father was.*" Wixim looked off into the woods to his left. "*He said the devil was nervous to meet the humans he was to help. The first witch comforted him as best she could. Kept telling him he'd feel natural doing it, because their parents had given him his gift for that reason."*

Eli lowered herself into a sitting position.

"The first time he met a bad human, it did more than scare him. It made him mourn. He mourned for all the souls that that one human had hurt. And he kept mourning anew every time he'd meet a new human that would be equally bad or worse. Aradia kept telling him it would get easier, but it never did." A breeze rushed over Wixim and Eli, making the dragon lift his head and close his eyes, as though relishing the gentle touch of the wind, before continuing his story.

"Eventually the devil became angry. Angry with his parents for putting him in such a painful position, and for creating humans that could be so vile. Then, when the humans turned their cruelty to us, the ancient beasts, we were told by the Gods we could return to the Forest of the Afterlife. The devil heard we were going to leave… And he broke." Wixim's gaze saddened.

Letting out a great huff, however, he continued. *"My father and other beasts were the ones who had stayed by the devil's side during all those years of heartache. He couldn't stand the cruelty that had already started to befall us. Then to learn we were to leave? He was beside himself. When he went to Aradia, he wanted her to join him in appealing to their parents. He wanted humans to die out, one by one, but Aradia… she had met and loved many humans. She even had children of her own. She didn't want to go against her parents. And so they fought."* Wixim lifted his great body from his stone and made his way closer to Eli as he continued the story.

"He wielded the feeling of fear over her. Tormented her with it. He wanted her to understand the kind of horrible feelings humans caused others. She tried to stop him. They couldn't finish the fight. They were too evenly matched. So the devil started warring against the humans all on his own. Again, Aradia tried to stop him, but this time they both lost. He managed to take away her feelings of love and, subsequently, fear. And they both lost the ability to return home, though it was a harsher punishment for the devil than Aradia back then."

Silence rested between Eli and Wixim for a while, but eventually the dragon locked eyes with her.

"I have never heard of any story where the devil was genuinely happy. I mentioned it before, but I don't know that you really understood the significance of that. Even in his very first life, before anything happened to him, the devil was never at ease. Never warm. Never understood."

"*Why did you tell me all of this?*" Eli asked, her heart aching in her chest as she imagined Luca scared and alone with no one to comfort him.

"*I don't side with Aradia because I disagree with the devil. I side with Aradia because I want the devil to go home, and to no longer be sad and in pain. I also don't think it's a bad thing that the humans and witches be separated a little more. They need to have a healthy respect for the balance that is nature and their world.*"

Eli's tail twitched. She didn't quite agree with segregating witches and humans.

"*If the devil is safe and happy with you? You and your witch mean more to him than you could ever fathom. It is my hope and sincere wish that you reunite and live in peace once more.*"

"*I want to. I want to just live in peace with them. I want this whole thing to be done. To hell with the Gods and terrible humans. None of that matters. Why did the Gods abandon a child like him? He needed them! He needs parents!*"

"*Because the devil is more a human than a God. And I believe it took the Gods a lot of time to create two other humans who could possibly be what he needed. I can tell that life has not been kind to you or your witch in many ways, but you two have what the Gods envy: an understanding of their beloved son, and the ability to give him what they failed to. They will be watching out for you. They want you to have the life you crave. So… try again. You have great powers that want you to succeed, so now it's simply a matter of finishing the work. It is hard, but by the end, you will have something remarkable, and something that is only yours.*"

Eli shifted her paws on the stones.

She let the story and the insight steady her.

She didn't feel less tired, exactly, but she did remember her resolve back when she had stayed in Lord Kim's home.

She would get the life she wanted more than anything, and she was going to make sure Luca and Penelope never had to experience loneliness without someone by their side again.

So when she looked down the rocky beach, Eli took a deep inhale and charged.

CHAPTER 37

A MAGNIFICATION OF MAGIC MATURATION

Tam sat with his legs crossed in the middle of a small clearing in a copse of maple trees.

He tried to settle his thoughts.

Tried to breathe through the ache in his chest.

But he could only succeed for brief moments before fresh waves of anger and panic overtook him.

His hands clenched into fists, his aggravation rising.

What if Luca was banished to the Forest of the Afterlife before he could get to him?

What if he was being tortured?

Then the recent confirmation of his identity as the devil crept up. The emotions in Tam's chest stormed even more violently. He was angry that the damn dragon had told him the truth. He was angry that the Gods left their son in a childlike state to fend for himself.

And he was livid that the first witch was no doubt going to tell Luca his origins, and his heart would break. Luca would feel the guilt of it, because that was who he was.

Eli relayed from the dragon that the devil had no memories from his previous lives in his child state, but how could he change so much? He had a good heart, and to think that centuries of horrible situations—situations created by the Gods—could turn him into the literal representation of evil was doing horrible things to Tam's own good nature.

Then there was Penelope. Why had they grabbed her?

Did the coven and first witch already know she was a seer and wish to use her for her abilities?

Tam had promised he'd protect her, and he hadn't been able to do *anything*. Would he ever see her again? What if she never forgave him? Never trusted anyone again, all because he had failed her?

All these horrible thoughts drenched him in fresh fury.

It was endless.

He reached for his magic, then felt the world around him shudder ominously. The leaves shook, the grasses bent away from him…

The cry of birds fleeing the area reached Tam's ears, forcing him to cut off the connection with his power that was barely starting to return. He only woke from his long magic-induced rest two days ago. He'd need longer to recover, and meditation wasn't doing much to help him. Which only fueled his impatience. What if when they left, he still couldn't do anything? What if he needed months to properly recover?

A sudden tingling of awareness skittered down Tam's spine.

Eli was approaching in her human form.

Interestingly enough, ever since Kat had shoved magic at Tam and he'd been unconscious, he'd been able to sense Eli more keenly than before. Previously she'd been able to sneak up on him, but it seemed now that if she was within fifty feet he knew about it.

"Tam?" she called out.

He could hear the weariness mixed with hesitancy in her voice.

Opening his eyes, Tam looked over his shoulder, sparing a half smile. "How did flying lessons go?"

Eli grimaced. "I was able to glide a few feet off the ground after a few running starts, but it's been slow."

Tam stiffened. "Do you think we'll still be able to try flying all the way to Gondol in a week?"

Sighing, Eli folded her arms over herself as she stood in front of Tam, who remained seated on the ground. "Wixim thinks I'll be fine. He says the hard part will be getting all of us up in the air, but once I'm able to find the air currents on a good day, I should be able to mostly glide there. I'll be tired, but… apparently it's still feasible, according to him. I'm hoping I can get high enough to clear the treetops in three days and stay up."

Tam managed a polite nod. "Thank you. Thank you for your hard work when I'm sure you're already tired."

Eli stared down at him. "I know we said we're starting a rebellion, but I want us to set ground rules so that we understand each other."

Tam raised an eyebrow.

"We do not kill civilians unless they attack," Eli started to list firmly.

"Agreed."

"You are not careless with your magic. Like opening a void, for example, if a crowd of people gets in our way at some point."

"I've never been careless like that."

Eli kept watching him, her thoughts unreadable. "You're desperate, and we both know desperate people get reckless."

"And you're not?" Tam retorted with feigned calmness.

Eli's eyes flashed. "I am, but I'm not as emotional as you are. Being emotional will get us nowhere."

Tam rose up from his spot on the ground. He looked down at Eli, his intense feelings bubbling higher. "I know. You might notice how right now I'm not currently shouting and smashing things. But I *am* allowed to have emotions about everything that has happened."

"I never said you weren't allowed. I just said that when we go to retrieve the children, we have to maintain said control."

Tam narrowed his eyes. "Why are you suddenly worried about this?"

Giving a small jolt, Eli faltered but eventually admitted, "Wixim mentioned something."

"Oh?" Tam slipped his hands in his pockets.

"He mentioned that you're incredibly powerful, and he hoped that you wouldn't use your power in a fit of anger or for anything else dark like that."

"Glad to see your faith in my character is so unwavering," Tam remarked coolly.

"Tam, I know you're a good person, but even good people can do terrible things in bad times," Eli argued, her own anger apparent by the frown pulling her brows down.

Tam held back from saying anything. He wasn't confident he'd be able to stop himself from showing just how much Eli's concerns had hurt him.

He thought she'd understood him better than anyone.

Yet there she was, worried he wasn't going to be able to control himself and would casually hurt people.

He turned away from her. "I'm going for a walk."

Eli made a noise of irritation behind him, but he didn't bother commenting on it. He needed to sort through his feelings of betrayal, hurt, and all the other nasty emotions before speaking again.

And then it happened.

Again.

The intense, hot burn of magic that sent Tam to a knee, his hand clutching his chest as he let out a yelp of pain.

"What is it?" The sound of Eli's feet hurrying toward him was distant in Tam's ears.

Heat rose into his throat, and pulses of tingling magic rushed down his limbs to the very tips of his toes and fingers. Blood roared in his ears as his power swelled in him.

"It's Godsdamn Kat. I don't know what the hell she's doing," Tam grunted, closing his eyes to try and ground himself.

Eli's hand rested lightly on his back.

While Tam knew she was merely offering a gentle comfort like she had the last time, at present it only added a sting to the pain he was feeling. His earlier frustrations had not dwindled, regardless of Kat's actions.

However, one thing was becoming clear to Tam as the intoxicating and potent power flowed into him…

Kat was being careful with how much magic she sent him. This was a smaller amount. A careful distribution, unlike before when she had simply sloshed out a bucket of power down their connection. This time, she was dribbling it in, bit by bit, and Tam could feel exactly what it was doing.

It was restoring his own magic.

But it was still making his head buzz. Whereas the magic before had broken down the walls of his magic's limitations, now it filled the freshly expanded magical stores that existed in Tam. It was an intense, heady sensation that Tam had never felt before. He hadn't even been entirely aware of the extent of what Kat's previous magic contributions had done to him. It expanded his awareness of the world around him, to the point that he started to feel the connections not just within the minuscule spaces of plants themselves, but also how the soil under his boots was conscious of the roots of every growth in the immediate vicinity.

Tam tried taking a deep breath, tried to focus on the texture of the grass beneath his palm, tried to focus on the scent of earth and the plants around him. The whir of cicadas in the forest…

It wasn't enough. He needed something more. Something to hold him in the world. He couldn't go unconscious again, but he already felt dizzy, his mind a little drunk on the power.

Eli's hand slid from his back to his shoulder, making Tam shiver.

His eyes snapped up.

He didn't know how he appeared to her right then, but there was a crackling awareness between Eli and himself when they locked eyes.

"Run," he growled.

She needed to get away from him or he would do something just as reckless as she had been worried about moments before, and he would never let that happen.

"What do you need?" Eli asked quietly, though there was a glint in her eyes that suggested she already knew.

That understanding from Eli could have been a trick from Tam's desperate mind, needing to hold on to the most solid anchor he had to the world.

"Get away from me, Eli." Tam's volume increased, and while her eyes rounded in surprise, she didn't budge. "If you stay it's a yes."

Tam gave her two breaths.

Two breaths to realize she needed to leave him the hell alone or be a part of whatever coping method he chose.

Her shoulders relaxed.

The subtle consent was given.

Tam roughly grabbed her around the back of her neck and kissed her.

The feel of her warm mouth against his settled his heart for an instant, but then another trickle of power came from Kat. His mind flitted to an image of a thick maple trunk just behind Eli.

He had barely thought about it when he had the sense of shifting through his void with Eli. When he exited, he had her pinned against the tree, his knee between her legs.

He was still kissing her, and the intensity of the kiss was battling back the magic.

As though sensing he was regaining control, another surge of power came.

Tam hoisted Eli up, her legs wrapping around his waist as he tore off her tunic.

A strange sensation started to take over then.

The sensation of the magic filling him and starting to leak over.

Whereas before this would've brought Tam to a state of unconsciousness, the power seemed to leave and find its way down the intangible connection he held with Eli.

An animalistic noise sounded out of her, and her thighs clenched Tam tighter.

He felt a maddening half smile pull at the corner of his mouth.

"Void," Eli gasped insistently before she sank her mouth back onto Tam's, one hand gripping his tunic in a bunched fist and the other clutching his hair.

Tam gave a low, dark chuckle, then fell backward, Eli on top of him, as he pulled her into the void with him where they proceeded to manage their way through the deluge of overwhelming power.

Tam happily shared with Eli this surplus for what felt like an eternity in the void without thought or self-restraint, but neither cared. They lost themselves in the flood of absolutely everything, in a place of absolutely nothing.

It wasn't until dinnertime that Tam and Eli came out of the woods to return to the dragon's lair.

Both crackled with power, and both bore a healthy glow on their faces.

Harris took one look at them from his place by the fire with his dinner and decided it was one of those rare moments not to ask questions or make any jokes.

The dragon, Wixim, who lay curled nearby, emitted a low stuttering grumble that sounded suspiciously like laughter, but otherwise he didn't react to the state of Tam and Eli, either.

Sometimes that was simply the best way to go about things.

CHAPTER 38

A BENDING BOND

With a book lying open in her lap, Annika Ashowan rested her head on her fingertips as she stared blindly ahead.

"Alright. So, he beat off the pirates. Then the thieves. Then scared off the two men following Eli. Then the people who attacked the carriage by the docks?" Kat repeated to Luca, who nodded while gulping down some sweet milk tea. "Wow. The lucky bugger. Sounds like he's been having a great time."

Luca giggled.

"Wait. You also said you found Penelope on a boat. What happened there?" Kat leaned her forearms on a table laden with food and drinks between herself and Luca.

"Oh. Well, I got sick, and then Eli's parents came, and they got in a fight. They wanted to take her away, and my dad said no, and then I think *everyone* was going to fight, but Harris came. Then more pirates came, and my dad tricked them on land, while we set fire to a ship!"

Kat gaped at the boy, then slowly lifted her goblet to take another mouthful of moonshine.

She had started playing a drinking game with herself as she listened to everything that had happened to her brother since he'd left for Zinfera. Anytime Luca said something that shocked her, she took a drink. She'd gone through three gobletfuls already, and were it not for her superior metabolism—which was enhanced by her magical ability—she'd most likely be falling out of her chair drunk.

"Who set fire to the ship?"

"Harris. I helped, though."

"Mm-hm. Mm-hm… Then what happened?"

"We climbed on board the other pirate ship. That's where we found Penelope!" Luca explained happily.

"Right. And… When did Eli and Tam start courting?"

At this, the little boy twisted his mouth to the side. "Um, my dad said she was pretty when we first got to Zinfera. Then they were always sleeping together."

Having just taken a sip in light of hearing that Harris had involved a child with arson, Kat sprayed out the liquor in her mouth. Even Annika, who had entered into a brief catatonic state, turned to look at Luca with wide eyes.

"S-Sleeping together? With you in the room or tent?" Kat asked incredulously.

"Oh! Not in the way where they could make babies—my dad explained how that works. No, they just slept *beside* each other!"

"There were a few nights on the ship you weren't with them."

Kat jumped as Penelope appeared beside the table. She hadn't heard the little girl approach.

Luca smiled at her appearance. "Yeah, but how can I know what they were doing?"

"I'm just saying." Penelope shrugged, her gaze fixed on the food.

Kat gingerly slid an empty plate closer to Penelope.

Luca looked back at Kat. "Anyway, they were kissing and holding hands by the time we left Junya and were in the woods," Luca concluded before turning to Penelope and pointing at the food on the table. "The dumplings have raspberries in them. These ones are honey cakes. They're really good!"

Slowly, the little girl started adding items to the plate.

Annika watched without moving a muscle, as though trying not to frighten off a fawn in the woods.

"Aunt Queen? I have a question." Luca settled back into his chair while Penelope started nibbling away on the desserts.

"Yeah?"

"What if the bad lady comes looking for us? They had guards."

"Mm. Well, I'm stronger than them."

"The first witch is smart, though," Penelope interjected. "Mr. Ansar used to talk about her a lot."

"Ah. Well, my mother is pretty smart, too. Plus, we should have other strong friends from Troivack here to help," Kat replied, leaning back to cross an ankle over her knee.

"Like Bong and Jeong?" Luca asked excitedly.

Annika interjected quietly, "The Ryu family has to be very careful, so they can't help us much more than they already have."

Penelope stiffened at the sound of the duchess's voice, and didn't look up from her plate. But Kat and Luca looked over at the duchess, who went on, "We are hoping our allies in Troivack have arrived in Zinfera and we can confer with them."

"Oh." Luca's disappointment over not getting to see the Ryu brothers in the near future was palpable.

"Any other shocking events to tell us?" Kat asked Luca, whirling what little remained in her goblet.

The boy pondered the question seriously. "Your coven has bad people in it."

"Louise Godsdamn Riddel," Kat growled, though she did so with a smile. "Even more proof of why I was justified for not ever liking that bitch."

Penelope sighed disapprovingly. "Language."

Kat looked wryly down at the child. "Good Gods, you sound exactly like my mother."

Penelope froze, and everyone instantly knew Kat's careless words could have a very bad effect on the child.

Everyone save for the little girl held their breath as Penelope slowly lifted her face to the Daxarian queen. "If you really do become my aunt, you should be a better role model in the future."

Kat maintained eye contact with Penelope as she slowly drained the rest of her drink in a single mouthful, then said, "You get what you get, kid. Welcome to the family."

The air was filled with tension.

Penelope continued gaping at Kat, Luca kept looking back and forth between them, and Annika's mouth had fallen open.

Then a snort of laughter erupted from Luca, snapping everyone's attention to him.

Annika stared in wonder at him, as did Kat…

His laugh was just like the Daxarian queen's.

Even the duchess wasn't immune to a smile then. "Yes. It would seem we have a couple of new additions to the family. Penelope, I must say that I am most grateful to have you as a new voice of reason in the Ashowan house."

Tam sat with his elbows braced on his knees, his hands loosely clasped as he stared at Eli, his expression hard.

She finished buckling the belt of her trousers and tying back her hair into the two-inch ponytail she was finally able to create.

With this finished, she looked over her shoulder at him.

He didn't say anything when they locked eyes.

It was the day before they were to leave for Gondol. Eli had successfully hit her flying milestones, including climbing into the air with Tam and Harris on her back, and gliding around the nearby mountain peak for longer and longer intervals.

And when Eli wasn't training? She was with Tam, helping him stay *grounded* as he adjusted to his surplus of magical ability. He used his power sparingly so that he had plenty in store for whatever they might need to do in Gondol, but he did train separately when Eli was away to get a better sense of what he could and couldn't do.

Despite the intimate nature of keeping Tam anchored to the physical world, there was still unresolved tension running between the two.

They hadn't brought up their fight again, and both had stubbornly refused to speak much beyond what was necessary every day.

At present, Eli faced Tam, her own countenance somber.

"We leave tomorrow before sunrise. Will you need us to do *this* again before we go?" she asked in a cool, business-like tone.

Tam didn't bat an eye. "I won't. If you feel the need, however, just let me know."

Just as often as Tam had partnered with Eli in order to steady himself, she had sought him out in fits of wordless frustration and anger that they'd work out together in his void or in the woods.

"I'm nearing my cycle soon. So it won't be likely."

Tam swallowed and gave a short nod in understanding.

A humorless half smile curled Eli's lips before she started to turn away from her employer.

"Do you know why I'm upset?" Tam called at her back.

She swung back around, anger and hurt glinting in her eyes. "With me? Not particularly."

"Really?" Tam's eyes searched her face skeptically.

"Is it because I advised you to be cautious in how you use your powers?"

Tam rose to his feet, his hands moving to his pockets. "It's because you trusted a random dragon more than me. When you know me. Intimately."

"A random dragon who is hundreds of years old, magical, and knows more than we can ever fathom," Eli reminded him frostily.

"So if Wixim said you would betray me in order to serve the first witch, I should believe him?" Tam shot back, an edge entering his voice.

"That depends on whether I've been behaving in a way that gives you reason to think that that could happen."

Tam's eyebrows shot up, his anger and hurt doubling. "I see. And when was it that I abused my abilities or took the lives of innocent people lightly?"

Eli opened her mouth, then closed it.

Tam clenched his teeth and looked away before speaking again. "I understand why you have trust issues. I just thought by now you would at least trust how well you know me—even in the face of a dragon's speculation. I guess you don't know me as well as I thought you did."

Frowning, Eli looked like she wanted to say a whole hell of a lot in response to that remark, until Tam moved his gaze back to her.

"If you weren't sure how I'd react or behave when things escalated in Gondol, you could have asked me how I was feeling or what I was thinking of doing before jumping to assumptions about my character." He paused, letting out a breath that made his shoulders slump forward. He could feel the anger ebb out of him. He was tired of holding on to it. "I'll be honest, Eli. I might need some space in our relationship."

"You're overreacting," Eli retorted sharply.

Tam's eyes widened in disbelief. He shook his head slowly. "I don't think so," he said evenly.

Eli waved a hand out, and her voice jumped in volume. "Then that's it? You're leaving me?"

"I just said I need space."

She scoffed. "We're about to go to war with divine beings. How do you propose we take this 'space'?"

Tam felt his expression morph as creeping discomfort made its presence known.

"Eli, you doubted my character when I gave you no reason to. I'm telling you that you hurt me. And you're saying I'm overreacting and being dismissive. Just because you don't understand it, doesn't mean it's wrong. Others often make misjudgments about me without talking to me, or just flat-out disregard what I say. You know this. It isn't a small matter to me."

"Oh, for the—I just wanted us to be on the same page when we faced conflict! Battles are messy, and you are protective to a fault of the children! It was worthwhile to discuss! I didn't come out accusing you of anything!"

"You didn't make it a discussion. You came here and said *Here are the rules* because you doubted I'd act reasonably. You said I am emotional, unlike yourself. Do you not hear how demeaning that was?"

Eli hesitated. It was the first flicker of understanding Tam had seen in her since the discussion. "Tam, we're all tense, and there is a lot at stake. Can we shelve the discussion of space?" she said more calmly.

Tam stared at her for a while. "We don't have to talk about it, but maybe we should just sleep separately for a while."

"Are you serious?" Eli's indignation sprang back up.

Again, Tam stared at her in surprise. Her complete disregard for his emotions and perspective was alarming in more ways than one.

"Yes. Seriously. I don't know why you think it's fine to talk to me condescendingly or dismiss my own feelings and thoughts, or to question my abilities. But I will say I have never and would never do that to you. If you can tell me what made you think this as an acceptable thing in a relationship with me, I'd like to hear it."

"Tam! I wasn't trying to be condescending! And you have to admit the inner workings of our relationship are not our most pressing issue right now!"

"Eli, trust is important."

"I *do* trust you! I just thought I should be clear—"

"I don't know that I can trust *you* right now," Tam interrupted softly. He felt his heart squeezing in his chest as he watched her anger be replaced with shock. "You doubted me the instant someone suggested you should. I'm not alright with that. So, yes. Space. And we can think and talk about these issues after the kids are back with us safely."

"Tam—"

"I'm going to go start dinner. I'll see you back at the cave."

Striding out of the clearing, Tam didn't allow himself to look back over his shoulder as he felt the chaos of his emotions darken his world. His surroundings were also quite bleak, as the day had been shrouded with thick cloud cover, and the descending evening dimmed what little light remaining there was.

What the conversation with Eli had revealed to him was that while he had thought she had come to trust him and rely on him like no other, that still didn't mean she trusted him very much.

And he foresaw a world of trouble with that fact.

CHAPTER 39

AN ENCROACHING ENDING

"And this? Junk. Pure garbage. You can tell they were trying to add variety to the offering, but just threw random things together in the end," Harris said knowledgeably.

"Rrr."

"You really haven't looked through all of this?"

"Mhrrrm."

"Even if you don't care about it, you should know what people are giving you."

"Rmr."

"Now, Eli mentioned you had one last cave filled with things."

"Hrm."

"Good timing, seeing as we have to leave tomorrow." Harris tossed the worthless bit of pottery he had found in one of the multiple chests of gold and treasure Wixim possessed, not caring when he heard the inevitable sound of it shattering.

The reason for the dragon's horde was simple. Soo Hebin's servants hadn't been able to communicate with Wixim, so they thought the best way to placate him was giving him valuable treasure. Wixim didn't really care about the treasure, but he found it funny to watch the humans cower.

At first, Harris had been terrified of the dragon, too. Then they found themselves spending large chunks of their seven days together sorting through the gifts while Eli either practiced on her own or was mysteriously absent with Tam.

In other words, this quality time between Harris and Wixim had led to an understanding developing between them.

Harris turned, his hands on his hips to squint toward the alleged final treasure-filled cave, when Tam swept in. His stormy expression and quick steps indicated that he was not in a good mood.

Ever since Luca had been taken, he'd been in a grim state, but there was a more frantic air about him at present that suggested something else may have happened.

Harris watched as Tam rifled through some of their remaining food and herbs, plucked up a few chosen items, then stalked off once more.

The Daxarian duke sighed. "Kids. Am I right?"

The dragon gave a low, throaty chuckle, his mouth stretching into a smile of agreement.

"He gets it from his father. Fin was a shit-head when it came to his love life."

The dragon tilted his head.

"Just your standard *man thinks he wasn't worthy of a woman who ranked above him and was the most beautiful woman in the entire kingdom* scenario. Even though Fin himself was rather memorable for his looks and has far too much power for his own good." Harris set off toward the final cave with Wixim ambling along at his side.

Upon entering the last discreet pocket of the cave, Harris tilted his head, spotting something in the corner that had him tilting his head with a lifted eyebrow.

He glanced at Wixim, who already appeared to be grinning knowingly.

Curious, Harris crossed the stone floor and plucked the item up.

"What the—*You had this the whole time and only told me now*? This should've been the *first* thing on the agenda!" Harris burst out excitedly, then bolted outside with the bit of treasure still in hand.

Tam stared at the first flames that flickered to life numbly.

Was he overreacting with Eli?

His stomach clenched.

No. No he wasn't.

She'd been acting callously and disrespectfully.

His mind flew through their argument—while also making a special note about the alleged proximity to the timing of her cycle. If her cycle was close, didn't that mean they'd done things during that risky window? He knew that sometimes that was all it took to accidentally conceive a child, and their intense bouts of intimacy as of late had been rather frequent…

Like we don't have enough going on.

"TAM! TAM TAM TAM TAM TAM! YOU HAVE TO SEE THIS! I DON'T KNOW IF IT'S AN ILLUSION OR WHAT, BUT LOOK!"

Startled from his thoughts, Tam turned around.

Then he rose from his crouch as shock coursed through him.

"Harris? What… How?" Tam asked, dumbfounded.

"I think it's a magic sword!"

Tam gawked.

The person in front of him was definitely Lord Oscar Harris… Except he was twenty years younger. His thinning white hair had crept back up and turned auburn, the deep lines under his eyes had filled back in, his paunch had given way to a toned middle, his eyes were brighter.

Dropping his gaze to the sword in Harris's hand, Tam noticed that it was wider than most swords by at least three inches, and it stayed as wide all the way to its tip—though its length was shorter than the Daxarian style. Tam studied the handle. It was wooden, in a spindle shape, with black inlays of stone.

"That's a Lobahlan sword," he concluded with undisguised awe.

Harris looked down at the weapon with glee still dancing in his eyes. "I guess that explains it! The only witch who has ever been able to imbue a weapon with magic was Theodore Phendor. And his weapons had to connect with a witch's own power. I'm magnificent in my own right, but I'm definitely not magical."

"I knew Lobahl was more advanced, but to do something like this… How do you feel? Is it merely an illusion?"

Harris shook his head. "I feel incredible. This absolutely does not feel like an illusion. Here, you try!"

Tam grasped the sword handle, and discovered…

He shrank.

Harris, once again looking his true age, roared with laughter. "So it's a fixed number of years it reduces!"

Tam looked down at his eight-year-old body. The sword suddenly felt ridiculously heavy in his hand.

"L-Luca? LUCA!"

A shriek ripped through the air, making Tam and Harris whip around as Eli flung herself down in front of Tam, her hands grasping his face as her eyes glistened.

"Oh Gods, we were terrified! Your father needs to see you! How did you get away? Are you hurt?" She was gasping as the tears spilled over. Then she hugged him tightly. "Thank Gods… Thank the Gods… Is Penelope with you? We'll get her back if not. Don't worry. Dear Gods, thank you, thank you…"

Tam's throat closed.

He felt like he couldn't breathe.

He stood in Eli's embrace stiffly, then released the sword, letting it fall to the ground.

Instantly, Tam shot back up in height.

Eli fell backward with a short shout, her wide eyes staring up at Tam, anguish and confusion written all over her face.

"The sword" Tam's voice rasped. "Wixim has this Lobahlan sword that makes the wielder twenty years younger."

Eli trembled on the ground.

Tam swallowed, lifted his gaze off to the distance, and walked away to get ahold of himself, tears starting to warm his own eyes.

Emotion overwhelmed him when he was faced with Eli's love for Luca. He was already a mess.

But seeing just how much she also missed his son was just… torture.

Aradia's fingers fluttered against her upper arm as she stared at Thomas Julian with her chin raised in the air.

The young man was standing behind thick wooden bars in his cell.

"You have my apologies, Mr. Julian. I thought you had failed to inform the queen of my presence. It would seem she did know; she simply didn't come searching for me. I confess, that surprises me."

The young man bowed his head in acceptance of her magnanimous pardon.

"Has Katarina Ashowan or her mother come to see you?"

"The duchess came down at one point to tell me about my Uncle Likon," he responded while still inclining himself subserviently.

"And what did you tell her?"

"What you told me to tell her. Which is the same as what I had told the Daxarian queen."

"Good. So they are aware of what we are aiming to do. Putting it in their minds now about our intentions on how to reform the covens will help the Daxarian king accept it later when he receives the ransom note. Though I wish she'd sent Soo Hebin running off sooner." Aradia dropped her arms back to her sides. "I will see that you are released the night I depart for Daxaria."

"Thank you, Your Magnificence."

Nodding in acknowledgment, Aradia turned and exited the dungeon.

At least that had gone to plan.

She was still wildly irked about the children escaping her so easily.

But no matter. They were still within the palace walls, and when the time came she'd take them back. She'd send Penelope off first, and then once she had toppled Soo Hebin's control and assigned a new heir for the Zinferan empire, she'd follow with her brother. If any of the Ashowans tried to interrupt the next step of her plans, she'd merely threaten to cut her brother's throat. Even if they knew who and what he was, she doubted the righteous family would let her cut a child's throat.

Aradia still needed to get progress reports from the witches who had loaned her their familiars to find out if there was any news on whether or not they had succeeded in the task she'd given them. Time was running out before the birthday party for Prince Jum. Soo Hebin was making it lavish as expected, with of course the added flourishes including poison, hostages, and other villainy.

Aside from hostaging the Daxarian queen and the duchess, Aradia was still on the fence about poisoning Lord Jiho Ryu, who would be attending, along with the other representatives from Troivack.

She wasn't worried, though. The most powerful witch in Troivack at present was a water witch. The young man was only fifteen years old, so there was no chance that the Troivackian king or queen would have sent him.

Climbing the stairs to return to her quarters, Aradia found herself letting out a breath. She was looking forward to sitting in the garden with Ansar for a restorative cup of tea. She couldn't remember the last time she had experienced such peace. Katarina Ashowan had been quiet ever since she'd taken the children, Soo Hebin was busy with party planning and welcoming guests for the event, and the weather was perfectly lovely.

After seven years in an underground cell, she relished being surrounded by nature and sunshine.

To make things even better, after centuries of misery, there was at long last an end in sight to the mess her brother had created. And with his powers dormant and his connections destroyed, he could no longer force her to suffer in silence.

She would soon regain complete safety, and all would be well.

Tam, Eli, and Harris stepped outside of Wixim's cave in the early morning. It was another gray day threatening a storm, but the winds were moving from the east, which was perfect for flying to Gondol.

"Thank you for letting me keep the Sword of Rejuvenation, Wixim. I wasn't sure what I'd do after my own old sword got lost in the river." Harris bowed to the dragon. He had wrapped the Sword of Rejuvenation in a thin sheet and tied it to his back so that when he drew it and reverted to his younger self, he would have the element of surprise.

Eli was already in her beast form with their meager belongings strapped on her back. "*Thank you for teaching me how to fly. And for teaching me the history of the first witch and the devil.*"

"*You are welcome.*" Wixim tilted his great head gracefully. "*However, I also have a gift for you, and another for your witch.*"

Lifting her great head higher, Eli watched as Wixim opened a clawed fist to reveal two items dangling from his grasp.

One was a brass whistle, the other a smooth brass circle; both dangled from chains.

Tam glanced at Eli, then the dragon's claws.

Wixim lowered his head, and Tam, taking the hint, proceeded forward to accept the two items.

"Should the first witch or one of her own commit the sin of harming you, an ancient beast and familiar, I will come to your aid. I will be near Gondol in the near future, so if the need arises, you may use the whistle—it is another Lobahlan-crafted item. The first witch's human has one in his possession as well. I am able to hear it from great distances."

At Eli's side, Tam inspected the mysterious circular item. Noticing the delicate button at its top, he pressed it. The cover of the circle sprung open to reveal a glass face, with numbers around the border.

"That is the predecessor to a device the first witch wielded during the war in Troivack. The device she used then was called Chronos. This device was not able to do what the first witch had hoped, but that does not mean it might not be useful for another. It still measures time, and it still accepts mage crystals, though I do not know to what end. Perhaps it has some purpose in the hands of another."

"Why give us these things? Isn't this helping those who oppose the first witch?" Eli asked bluntly.

Wixim yawned. *"I gave away a sword that makes the wielder young, a discarded experiment, and a whistle that is mostly useless—if you blow it and she has not harmed you, I will attack you."*

Eli swallowed at the casual threat at the end of Wixim's flippant retort. *"Are you banking on me getting attacked by the first witch in my beast form?"*

Wixim rose from his crouch to circle round the mountainside. *"I don't know what will happen. I simply think that the whistle might end things sooner than later, one way or another. Oh, please tell Harris that I would absolutely love to visit him. His wife sounds like a delight, and if I don't have to eat him later, it would be wonderful to meet his family and spend a summer in Daxaria."*

Too stunned for words, Eli momentarily shifted back and relayed what she had learned about the items to the two men. When she concluded the message with Wixim's response to a supposed invitation Harris had issued, the duke grinned.

"Ah, Wixim. What a jokester. The kids will love him. Mackenzie will be annoyed at first—he looks expensive to feed—but maybe she won't mind if he helps her set a few fires."

"Where are all these buildings your wife is allegedly burning down?" Tam asked flatly.

"Don't worry about it. The buildings are empty, and either I own them or they are due to be demolished. Sometimes I just build shoddy barns so she has something to look forward to." Harris smiled longingly.

"Right." Tam shot a look at Eli who, regardless of the rocky state of their relationship, shared the need to briefly communicate with a saner companion than Lord Harris.

Sighing without further comment, Eli shifted back.

It was time to leave for Gondol.

Which meant their time in Zinfera was coming to a very swift end.

CHAPTER 40

A MAJESTIC MEETING

Tam, Harris, and Eli halted in their tracks as they stared at the wall of Gondol through the trees.

Night was approaching, but the torches had not yet been lit.

They had landed a league and a half away from the city so that Eli's beast form wouldn't raise any alarms. They knew they'd still have to proceed cautiously, what with the imperial soldiers scouring the land.

Tam's gaze slid over to Eli.

She did not look well. Her body had been shaking terribly when she'd first transformed back into her human form. They'd rested for a short while before picking their way to the city. By now, however, Eli did not look better. Her skin was nearly gray, and while they all had a coating of sweat that was making them clammy as the air cooled, droplets still fell regularly from Eli's forehead.

"Alright, Tam, what now?" Harris asked patiently, his hazel eyes roving over the stone wall that stood four stories tall.

Moving his attention back to the city, Tam squinted.

"We time the guard patrols on the wall. Then once it's fully dark, I move us onto the wall, then onto a discreet corner below, in the city."

"Will you be alright moving three people in and out of the void so quickly?" Harris raised an eyebrow in Tam's direction.

A rueful smile touched Tam's lips. "Yeah. My abilities are much stronger now."

The duke tilted his head and squinted in the same direction as Tam. "Once inside the city, where are we going?"

"We're going to find one of the brothels my family has invested in with the Ryu family. There are three or four of them. Preferably we'll go to the one called The Opulent Opal."

"Why that one in particular?" Harris wondered as his gaze homed in on a small figure starting to patrol the line of wall they were to breach.

"It's one of the wealthiest brothels, and because of that, they can afford more discreet rooms and better security, and they know how to keep gossip from getting out. It also means they have nobles for customers, and the nobility will most likely have mentioned what is going on in the palace to give us a sense of where to go looking for the kids."

Harris gave a short jerk of his chin. "Makes sense."

With the plan explained, Tam turned back to Eli, whose eyes were starting to look a little glassy. "You go sit over there by the rock and have some water."

Eli's eyes flitted in his direction, and it was evident she wanted to give him some sort of chilly stare, but she also tried to take a step at the same time and stumbled.

Tam's hand snaked out and gently caught her around her middle. Once she had regained her balance, he ushered her over to the hidden spot he had observed.

"I'm fine," she informed him breathily.

"I'm sure you will be. But you just flew for most of the day and aren't used to it," Tam responded, his tone polite but distant.

Eli made a faint grumble of irritation as he helped set her down on the rock.

"Sleep if you can." He straightened and turned to Harris. "I'm going to risk going a bit closer to check the patrol times."

Harris nodded. "I'll wait with Eli."

Tam gave a half smile of appreciation then ventured farther into the woods, his footsteps silent in the thick brush and shadows.

His heart was a steady drum in his chest.

I hope you're safe, Luca and Penelope. I'm coming as quickly as I can.

Annika sat in the chair beside the grand bed, her arms draped leisurely over the armrests. "I am glad to see you awake, Your Excellency," she said, smiling.

The Zinferan emperor was sitting up in his bed for the first time in months. He coughed, his brown eyes bloodshot but sharp as he regarded the duchess.

"How did you send away my guards?" he asked warily.

Annika reached over to the nightstand, poured a goblet of water, and handed it to him. "I didn't. They are outside the doors. If you'd like to shout, you are more than welcome to."

The emperor's eyes swept over his room. "What of my attendants? Physicians? Maids?"

"Your attendants only come for the night. Your physicians come after meals. And your maids are all busy preparing for Prince Jum's birthday celebration."

The emperor's hand trembled as he raised the goblet to his lips and took a drink, his eyes settling on the perfectly calm duchess.

"Who are you?" he managed while handing her the goblet.

"I am Duchess Annika Ashowan of the kingdom of Daxaria. Mother of the Daxarian queen and wife of the house witch. You have met my husband before, Duke Finlay Ashowan. Though I believe the last time you two met, he was only a viscount."

The emperor masked his expression as Annika refilled his goblet and handed it back to him. He drained another cup before speaking again. "And why are you here, Duchess Annika Ashowan?"

"It would seem both the Coven of Giong and the Coven of Wittica are committing crimes against their crowns, and your concubine, Soo Hebin, has aligned herself with the first witch. The daughter of the Gods escaped her prison in Troivack and has come here, most likely with Soo Hebin's assistance. The first witch now lives within your walls, and Soo Hebin has also been drugging you discreetly for quite some time with Witch's Brew."

At this the emperor's eyes flared.

"I have given you an antidote that will help you overcome your withdrawal, but I regret to inform you that you will not live for much longer." Annika bowed her head.

"How long?"

"A month at least. A year at most."

The emperor gave a breathy laugh. "Soo Hebin… It is no surprise."

"Why has she been left unchecked for so long?" Annika wondered lightly, though her eyes were cold.

The emperor turned a dark look at the duchess. "Had you not woken me, I would have you on your knees for daring to question me."

The duchess didn't move an inch, nor was she particularly bothered. "You can try. But that would be a waste of time if you would like to set your court to rights."

The emperor stared at the duchess, his eyes searching her face before his lips curled upward in a humorless smile. "Your husband did not lie about you. He said you are the more fearsome one in your marriage."

Annika smiled, though she felt a twinge of sadness when she thought of her husband. She missed him.

"I did not interfere with Soo Hebin for a number of reasons. For one, she has powerful allies. She has to be dealt with carefully. It was one of the many reasons I didn't name an heir: to discourage her from attacking anyone viable for the throne."

"Ah yes. A plan that worked incredibly well given that dozens of your adopted and blood-related offspring have been abducted, murdered, and Gods know what else." Annika kept her tone breezy, but there was a steeliness beneath it she didn't bother to hide.

"Shall I holler for my guards?" the emperor bit out before another cough claimed him.

The duchess sighed irritably. "My understanding is that your mother helped run this empire for you in place of a wife. Without her, you have not been able to keep everyone and everything under control. And now your kingdom is on the brink of not only a civil war, but a war against Troivack and Daxaria because of this. Take responsibility. Name an heir. Execute Soo Hebin and turn this palace upside down to find the first witch. You will need to ally with Daxaria and Troivack to subdue the coming war with the covens."

"Must I?" the emperor mused drily.

Annika arched an eyebrow. "If you want your land to fall to ruin, then so be it. I will take my daughter, the queen, and leave."

"You think I'll just let you leave?" the emperor challenged.

Annika's smile was terrifying and she knew it. "You think you can stop me?"

The emperor's stare was hard. "My mother would've liked you."

Laughing genuinely, Annika relaxed a little. "I think she would've, too."

"You do not fear me at all," the emperor noted casually. "And you aren't afraid to speak your mind despite my threats. Why?"

At this, Annika leaned forward. "My husband's best friend is Jiho Ryu. I have heard a great deal about you, Your Excellency."

At the mention of Jiho, the emperor's face softened, and an astonishing blush warmed his otherwise sickly coloring.

Seeing this startled Annika. Jiho had said he was on good terms with the emperor. This look told her there was perhaps a little more to it than that.

"You are right about how things fell apart without my mother. I had intended on placing the child she took in as a close assistant to myself to keep the women in check—Princess Elisara was young but sharp. Efficient. Then when she disappeared, I had no one else that I would consider placing in such a dangerous position. I had hoped Elisara's magic would've helped her survive a bit longer regardless of her age."

Annika sat upright in surprise. "Do you mean to tell me Princess Elisara was that close in line for the throne?"

The emperor raised an eyebrow upon hearing the duchess's tone. "Of course. My mother had only taken in two adopted children. The first was a sickly boy. She adopted him mostly because he had a marvelous singing voice. He died four years before my mother. But Elisara she handpicked, raised, and taught for a reason." The emperor's eyes roved over Annika's face.

She knew she had gone very still.

"What is it?" the emperor pressed, a fraction of his imperial tone returning.

"Elisara is serving our household. She was sold to a Troivackian duke, but at some point during her time away from Zinfera she happened to endear herself to the Daxarian prince, Eric Reyes, who is now king. So she is working with my son while King Eric works to grant her citizenship."

The emperor leaned forward eagerly. "Elisara lives?"

"She does."

"And is now affiliated with the Daxarian crown…" The emperor looked away, his eyes bright and a slow smile climbing his wrinkled face as his right hand reached up and began stroking his long white beard.

"She has no ambition to be empress, nor any proper support here in Zinfera."

"Bah. I have a year to give her some," the emperor said dismissively, his gaze still fixed on his red comforter, his mind evidently reclaiming its former swiftness.

"She does not want it," Annika repeated, her voice a little louder. "And while she is under our protection, she will not be forced into a role she does not want."

The emperor's fury directed itself at Annika, and she met his gaze head-on without batting an eye.

After a tense moment, the emperor's shoulders slumped forward before he gradually leaned back onto the low wall of pillows behind him. "I will speak with her and hear that for myself."

Annika said nothing.

"First I will take care of Soo Hebin. Though her cousin Lord Yangban and that Captain Woo friend of hers are problems—"

"Lord Yangban has succumbed to madness, along with one of his more affluent affiliates, Lord Guk. Both Lord Yangban's and Lord Guk's wives are claiming they are now the guardians of the estates. As for the pirate Captain Woo…" Annika cleared her throat and settled back in her seat. "My son killed him."

The emperor shot the duchess an incredulous look. "Goddess's Pool. I go for a nap and the world has turned upside down."

"Your nap was several months long, and there is a dragon lurking in your land that is controlled by the first witch and Soo Hebin. Though I imagine they cannot do much with the ancient beast while they also reside in Gondol."

The emperor swore. "And you say the covens are rebelling?"

"The leaders are. I cannot speak for every member. My husband, for example, has no inkling of this, and we have a few friends in the coven whom I can say with the utmost certainty are not a part of the rebellion."

The emperor's expression betrayed his skepticism of Annika's claim, but then his thoughts appeared to gradually sift through the rest of the information. "How many soldiers are still loyal to me?"

Annika's head tilted. "I cannot say for certain, but two hundred at least. You might have even more who have simply fallen under the orders of Soo Hebin or one of the other concubines, but only because they had to go elsewhere until you woke. You may still have loyal nobles who would lend you their men as well."

"Soo Hebin needs to be deposed, and I need it to send a message." The emperor's fingers fluttered against his comforter as he fixed his attention back on Annika. "Jum's birthday. I will have his mother executed, and he will be banished and stripped of his title."

"That will certainly grab everyone's attention, particularly if you keep it a secret that you are once again awake."

The emperor's studious gaze returned to Annika's face. "How was it the concubine was dosing me?"

"She managed to have it mixed into one of your tinctures, claiming it was for your health. Once you fell unconscious, I imagine she expected to simply wait until you passed."

The emperor made a noise of disgruntlement.

Annika rose from her seat and curtsied.

The emperor raised an eyebrow. "Why is it you wear trousers, Duchess?"

Giving a weary sigh, Annika clasped her hands in front of herself. "It is easier to climb in and out of windows in pants than it is a dress, Your Excellency."

The emperor balked. Then his eyes darted to the four windows along the right wall of his room, and he noticed one of them was open. He gazed at the duchess without masking his bafflement. "Do all Daxarian noblewomen climb two stories and break in through the windows of monarchs?"

"The helpful ones do." The duchess smiled radiantly, then headed toward that very window.

"If you weren't already married, Duchess, I'd make an offer for your hand. Jiho Ryu was right to admire you," he called to her back.

Annika glanced over her shoulder. "You are too kind, Your Excellency. I will return later this evening with some food for you. Your physicians will come soon, so be sure to pretend to sleep. The prince's birthday is only three days from now."

The emperor's eyebrows twitched in somber understanding.

And then, with a nimbleness that did not at all seem usual for a woman in her later fifties, she vaulted over the ledge of the window and turned her attention to returning to her quarters where Kat, Luca, and Penelope awaited her.

Even though it was a warm summer day, Annika could practically taste a coming storm in the air.

CHAPTER 41
THE OPULENT OPAL

As luck would have it, it was quite easy getting over the wall into Gondol. The tricky part came when they had to inconspicuously ask the location of the brothel without alerting the patrolling soldiers.

However, thanks to a brief, *physical* conversation Tam took part in with a drunken merchant, they learned it was farther north in the city, and a bit closer than they'd realized to the palace.

The Opulent Opal was a discreet building, unlike most Zinferan brothels.

Instead of red lanterns hanging from the front of its eaves, it had a lone black Troivackian-style lantern, with glass windows right beside its door—a door that was painted black, with an arched top and heavy bolts.

A peculiar style choice unless one knew of the primary owner of the establishment.

There was no sign that the building could be a brothel on its street of quiet, respectable businesses—literally. There was no sign or painted lettering on its front to alert anyone to what sort of scandalous business was conducted within its walls.

The only indication of it being the right place was the hulking mass of a doorman who greeted everyone who knocked.

Tam stared up from under his hood at this man. He was Tam's same height, but twice as wide.

The doorman's beady eyes narrowed even more at Tam when he registered that Tam was not a Zinferan.

"I am the Shadow. Son of the Dragon. The cave will open for me."

The man's eyebrows shot upward, but he said nothing. He didn't move an inch, either, his thick form blocking the entryway.

Then another higher-pitched, squeaking voice whispered behind him, "Good Goddess, get out of the way!"

A scroll came up behind the doorman and clunked him upside the head. He flinched and shuffled away awkwardly.

Tam found himself staring at a man in an absinthe-colored coat, with bright-white lapels and cuffs cut in square designs. The smile he beamed at Tam looked like it was drawn up by fishing hooks—the deep lines of his small face climbed as high as they could.

"The Shadow! Of course! The Dragon did mention you might come! I am Mung, and it is an honor to make your acquaintance." Mung bowed low.

Tam gave no reaction to the news that his mother had already guessed that he'd make his way here.

"I come with allies," he said in a low voice. "We are not to be seen and our presence is not to be shared with anyone but the madam. Understood?"

The man only then noticed Eli and Harris standing off to the side in the shadows. He jolted a little, and his smile faded briefly before he swung back to face Tam. "Of course, Shadow."

Tam said nothing else, merely stepped inside, with Eli and Harris following closely behind.

The door swung shut on squeaking hinges, and the group found themselves in a narrow hallway. Its walls of white plaster were bare, and the width of the hall barely permitted Tam and Harris to walk side by side.

"Why is it so narrow?" Eli murmured.

"In the event of an imperial investigation or attack, this slows the intruders and buys everyone inside time," Tam explained gruffly.

The group rounded the corner to find another long narrow hall, this one with a series of wood and paper sliding doors running along the left wall. Colored slats were hung outside each room. Some were red, some yellow, others green. Most likely they were there to indicate the service or the status of the customer.

Music and murmuring voices could be heard from within the rooms. There was the occasional giggle, and the odd moan here or there, but otherwise it was quiet in the dimly lit hall.

Even the scent of perfume was not overpowering as it often was in brothels.

When they'd all reached the end of the corridor, Mung took another left and headed down another straight white hall much like the entryway.

When they reached that end, they took another left. This time, there were sliding doors on both sides of the hall.

It was moderately louder down this new row, but not by much. There were also some rooms marked with white slats, and some were painted in silver and gold. At the end of the hall, they came to a narrow set of stairs on the right.

Mung climbed them as they followed, their boots thunking heavily against the wood despite any effort to mute them.

They reached the third story—most likely an attic that had been refurbished into a luxurious office. A large, ornately carved desk sat facing the stairs they climbed. To its right was a seating area that was somewhat obscured by privacy curtains that were only partially tied back. Two chairs and a couch were covered in rich jewel-toned cushions, and there were thick rugs and a fireplace. Opposite the seating area to the left of the desk were two closed Daxarian-style doors.

"Pardon me, mistress, but the Shadow has graced us with his presence."

While Eli and Harris looked around to see where this elusive brothel owner was, Tam stood perfectly still.

Slipping free from the shadowed corner behind her desk, a tall Zinferan woman appeared.

She was in her late thirties, wore a black wide-brimmed pirate's hat, and held a long carved pipe in her hand. Her lips were a glossy red, her dress a vivacious purple. An eyepatch with gold designs covered her left eye.

"Do you wait in dark corners all day? Just in the event you have to make a dramatic entrance?" Harris asked loudly, breaking the mysterious mood in the air.

Tam was grateful for his hood as his lips twitched.

The brothel madam's eye cut to Harris as she slowly raised her pipe to her mouth and took a long inhale, making the embers in its bowl crackle and glow. She stepped closer to the trio of newcomers and released a long plume of smoke.

"Shadow. I am Madam Sao. The Dragon recently mentioned that you might pay us a visit. How may I be of service?"

While her words were polite, her gaze was cold and calculating.

Tam held his ground. "I require a place to rest and to gather information on the palace."

Madam Sao raised an eyebrow and shot one quick look at Mung, which sent the man barreling down the stairs out of sight.

"I see," she told him, rounding the desk to seat herself behind it comfortably. "And would you like to stay here with your entourage, or would you like more respectable accommodations?"

"Here will be fine. You are well known for your mastery at keeping things hidden," Tam retorted.

The madam tilted her head over her shoulder. "Very well. Here it shall be. I'll arrange a bath for all of you, beds, and meals. Will any of my women be required?" Her eyes darted to Harris, then to Eli. "Or men?"

"No," Tam returned swiftly.

Sao's index finger tapped the side of her pipe. "And would you like news from the palace now or later with more privacy?"

"Now."

At this, the madam drew in a long breath and began knocking the singed tobacco from her pipe onto a silver tray. She then reached over to a gleaming maple box with a beautiful inlay design, and opened it to reveal more tobacco, which she began to pack in the bowl of her pipe.

"There are children in the custody of the Dragon and the golden one, and there has been great upheaval brewing for Prince Jum's birthday. Some expect the guests to be poisoned, others a simple massacre of the ones who oppose him," Madam Sao explained—*the golden one* of course being Kat.

"What news of the first witch?" Tam persisted. He refused to let himself show any relief at the news that Luca and Penelope were apparently safe.

"She hides in plain sight. There have been ships preparing to leave Zinfera operating under the command of the Giong Coven, and there are members of the Coven of Wittica somewhere in the palace as well."

Tam watched the leisurely movements of the madam restocking her pipe. "How can I be placed in touch with the Dragon?"

"I can see about sending a note with one of my customers. But make your message discreet. There isn't a true ally in sight of the palace these days."

"And who are you allied with, Madam Sao?" Tam asked mildly.

"I'm assuming you are asking in terms of royalty, as I'd have to be a fool to name anyone other than the Dragon."

"Of course." A cool smile lifted Tam's mouth.

"I do not align with Concubine Soo Hebin for one simple reason: She wishes to change the capital from Gondol to Junya. This would hurt my business. Her power is crumbling even as we speak, and the people are angry." Sao paused, and took her time lighting the new bowl of tobacco. "There is talk of the downfall of the empire. Zinfera may break off into pieces depending on how evenly matched the nobles are. The extent of the breakage will become clear with the outcome of Prince Jum's birthday in two days."

"You haven't answered my question," Tam rumbled.

The madam smiled wryly up at his shadowed face. "I'm getting to the point. Which is this: I side with no one but myself. I have survived as long as I have because of that mindset. Now, I won't bother asking why you probed my political views, because it's evident you are concerned about me reporting your presence to a concubine or two for some gold. But my coffers remain full because of Daxaria, your home. I do not know how powerful you are there, and I do not tempt an unknown power to become angry with me."

Tam could've argued to the heavens and back why she could find other possible self-serving reasons to betray him, but he was tired. They were *all* tired.

"I will write my note for the Dragon. Send fresh clothes. You will be compensated."

The madam inclined her head before saying, "Does the lady with you wish for pants or a dress?"

"Rude of you to assume I myself wouldn't care to enjoy a breezy skirt," Harris scoffed.

The madam's expression fell flat. "You are an annoying man."

Harris shrugged. "I've been called worse."

"Pants would be appreciated," Eli cut in, her voice tight.

The madam's eyes settled on Eli for a while, then, appearing bored, she stood. "I will go arrange everything now. Stay here. You are welcome to sit over there." Sao jerked her chin toward the sitting area.

"Is there a water closet I could visit?" Harris called out, his left hand resting on his middle with a wince.

Sao didn't hide her dislike of him. "The door on the right. The one on the left is my private quarters. Stay out."

"Thanks!"

Without further ado, the duke waddled off in the direction of the water closet, and the madam, rolling her eye, headed down the stairs. Her heeled black boots made an even bigger ruckus than the three of them had caused on their climb up.

Once stillness rested over the space, Tam rounded the desk and stared down at some correspondence that lay open. He saw only an order for moonshine, and one for food. Neither was in his mother's handwriting, so he knew it wasn't a code from her—though any such messages were probably located somewhere in Sao's private quarters.

"Who are the Dragon and the Shadow?" Eli's quiet voice pierced through the hush.

Tam paused. This was not the moment to share the details of his underworld dealings with her.

"It's a long story. Go take a seat. You still need to rest."

Lowering her hood, Eli gave him a hard stare.

For a moment, Tam thought she was going to try to resume their argument. Then her shoulders rounded and she stalked off toward the couches without another word.

He watched her go, his heart feeling both icy and sore.

Later. We will deal with it later. We'll get a good night's rest, a hot meal, and then strategize how the hell we're getting everyone out of the palace without getting involved in the bloodshed of the prince's birthday. Though knowing my sister, she won't want to leave.

Tam's thoughts were interrupted by a horn blast of a fart echoing out from the water closet. Startled, he snapped his head around to stare at the closed door. But as the trumpeting stutters of gas persisted, he dropped his gaze, caught between a laugh and a sigh.

"Pardon me!" Harris shouted through the door. "I tell you, Tam, those beets never fully left me!"

Tam opened his mouth to say something, but closed it again when his sleep-deprived brain couldn't think of any response. He made his weary way over to the couches, plopped himself down, and dropped his head back.

It was a good thing that Harris hadn't been expected to be stealthy for very long. If in the near future there was a situation where subtlety was required for a greater duration of time, Tam decided the man could only be allowed to eat meals of carbs and cheese to keep him sated and his bowels silent.

CHAPTER 42

TERRIBLE TIMING

The first witch gazed at the vials with a pleased smile. Seven glass tubes were carefully set out on the low table, though one was set apart from the others.

"You have done well," Aradia looked at the three familiars that sat just beyond the table and gave a nod of approval. "I thank you for your efforts."

Two of the three bowed. The cat with its eyes stuck staring in opposite directions named Oyster gave no indication he'd heard a word.

"I have arranged for your preferred treats to be prepared for you and sent home with your witches. Please return to them."

All three familiars filed out of the first witch's quarters, leaving Aradia alone with Ansar. He moved to stand just behind Aradia's left shoulder, peering down at the vials with a tilt of his head. "Whatever is all this?"

"Water from the Goddess's Pool from the midday waters," Aradia informed him lightly while rising to a stand.

Ansar raised a quizzical eyebrow.

Aradia sighed. "With these vials I can once again wield magic of the four elements. The midday waters are the waters used when the Goddess creates witches."

Ansar straightened. "Wouldn't you simply need the mage crystals if you know the language of the mages?"

The first witch shook her head. "Not with my curse cutting off a part of my humanity."

A pained look crossed Ansar's features. "Is there really nothing that will break the curse?"

Aradia's calm expression stiffened. "No. I have had this curse for centuries. If it came about because of a simple overextension of power, like a regular witch, it would have faded after a hundred years."

"Aradia, I… I know you are reluctant to share the details of the fight that took place with your brother, but could I please ask about it?"

The first witch raised an eyebrow. She did not want to talk about the battle that had left her stranded and powerless in the human world. But something gave way when she saw the warm worry in Ansar's eyes.

"I cursed my brother to be stuck here, and because I cannot die, the consequence was that I locked away my magic and lost certain emotions. It is simple. It is why I had Theodor Phendor, the witch blacksmith, try to create a blade for me that would unlock my abilities. Really, it acted as a powerful mage crystal. You may recall I could add ingredients or mixtures to the blade to change what it could do as well. That was how I was able to cut a hole and force a doorway to the Forest of the Afterlife back during the civil war in Troivack."

"Why didn't you simply use the water and mage crystals when you were in Troivack? Why reveal the blade?"

"I can't go to the Forest of the Afterlife on my own, and that is where the Goddess's Pool is. I needed familiars who are able to traverse that realm. Troivack's coven was in hiding while I was there, and no one was going to take risks with their familiars. Very few of them even had familiars since they were quite literally underground for so many years."

Ansar nodded slowly as he listened. "I see. So now that you have the vials of water and the crystals, what is your plan?"

Aradia relaxed enough to give a confident half smile. "This afternoon, I'm going to retrieve the children. I will then immediately send Penelope away to board the ship with the remaining Coven of Wittica members. My brother and I will leave tonight during the prince's birthday with the Coven of Giong witches and Wixim."

"Wouldn't it be best to send the devil and yourself off sooner rather than later?"

Aradia shook her head. "I need to stay behind in order to help occupy Katarina Reyes. The Daxarian king most likely has received the ransom letter."

A rueful quirk curved the corners of Ansar's lips. "I know that she is minding the children, but I'm rather surprised that she hasn't already declared war."

Aradia's eyes darted to the morning sky as two magpies darted across the rich blue scene. "That's because Katarina Reyes has no idea she is being ransomed. This way her husband goes into a panic, and she doesn't act out."

Ansar's eyebrows rose. He was visibly impressed.

"No, this evening Katarina Reyes will be problematic because the children will be gone, not because of the ransom. She'll likely make a scene trying to find them, but because she won't want any harm coming to them, she will behave. Not to mention Soo Hebin is poisoning a great deal of her guests tonight. It will be fine, though. Wixim will come to transport my brother and to board the other ship, and one or two witches from the Coven of Wittica will remain behind as well, just in case Soo Hebin has found a way to craft another deal with the Giong Coven behind my back." Aradia turned toward the doorway.

She wanted to have a relaxing tea before she went ahead and took the children. It'd be her last time in the garden since she would be leaving that night and she'd be busy guarding the children in the meantime.

"Have you decided who is going to be the next person to inherit the Zinferan throne?"

Aradia paused in her journey. "I'm torn between putting in some extra effort and somehow placing Jiho Ryu on the throne, or the concubine named Deoh Rin. None of the children that remain are capable or bold enough. That is most likely why Soo Hebin hasn't been too worried about them."

"Neither of those people would be able to hold on to the power of the throne for long."

Aradia shrugged. "Maybe they would, maybe they wouldn't. Jiho Ryu rose up from the position of a lowly dockworker, and he has gained more power, wealth, and connections with every inch he has been given. The common people love him, and many of the nobility have come to respect him."

"Isn't he one of the party attendees this evening who is slated to be poisoned?"

Aradia nodded. "He and his eldest son, Lord Bong, are attending, and both are supposed to die… But I'll decide if I should let that happen after our tea."

Aradia left with a spring in her step while Ansar carefully collected the vials, stored them in a locked box, and carried it with him into the garden.

It was going to be a very busy couple of days.

Annika looked up from the missive a maid had discreetly slipped into her palm while claiming to be cutting a loose thread from the duchess's dress.

She looked to Kat, who was seated cross-legged on the floor while Penelope added a fourth braid to the queen's hair. Luca contented himself on the floor by the window with a plate of tea cakes and a book.

"Tam's in Gondol."

Everyone looked up with a jolt.

"My dad's here?" Luca jumped to his feet and rushed over, the book still in hand.

Penelope inched forward a little, too. "Is Eli with him? And Harris?"

"I believe so. They are hiding in one of the brothels we own. However, he also is warning us that he has heard about something terrible happening tonight at the birthday celebration."

Kat arched an eyebrow. "I'm going to pretend to be sick so that I can stay behind and protect the children. So we should be safe."

"I want you to make sure you eat any food that arrives before the children do. If I were to make a guess? I would say Soo Hebin wants to poison people. That seems her style, given that she doesn't have many muscled forces remaining."

Kat nodded in understanding. "Have you already warned the Ryu's?"

"I have," Annika responded calmly before leaning over to a nearby candle and lighting the missive on fire. Once the flames began licking closer to her hand, she dropped the remaining corner into her teacup, where the flames flared with new life.

Kat grinned at her mother, who brushed away imaginary lint from her skirts.

"Do you have alcohol in your tea?" Luca asked with an innocent tilt of his head.

Annika cleared her throat delicately. "I do. How did you know that alcohol is flammable?"

"My mother told me. She owns a tavern."

"Ah, yes." Annika nodded demurely.

"Luca, Penelope, do you mind going behind the screen for a bit? I want to talk with my mum about something." The Daxarian queen gave the children a kind smile.

The children shared curious looks, but retreated behind the painted screen to the left of the window.

"Mum, I have to say… I… I kind of think Luca is actually Tam's son. I know it just didn't seem plausible before, but the more I've gotten to know that kid…" Kat trailed off and gave a quiet laugh. "I think my brother really did have a little surprise bundle."

Annika leaned her elbow on the table, wading through the complex emotions that seized her when faced with her daughter's opinion.

"There are an alarming number of similarities, but we assume nothing," Annika said firmly. "Why do you bring this up now?"

Kat hesitated then glanced over her shoulder at the screen before leaning closer to her mother and dropping her voice even more. "If Luca isn't the devil, then where *is* the devil? What if Luca was a distraction and the first witch already has the devil locked up somewhere? What if the only thing Aradia is worried about is starting a war with the kingdoms and the covens?"

Annika tilted her head. "I doubt that very much. Otherwise she would have already left the palace."

"She didn't leave when she had captured the devil last time during the war in Troivack," Kat argued.

Annika settled back in her chair, the last of the flames from her teacup finally dwindling. "It would be risky to leave without a distraction when tensions are so high right now."

Kat sat up straighter. "You think she's going to try to kidnap the children back so she can leave when the party takes place?"

"Yes. I do."

Kat pressed her lips together. "How can we get Tam here with us?"

Annika had opened her mouth to say something when a knock on the door interrupted her.

"Who is it?" Kat came to her feet and instantly crossed the room to the screen where the children were hidden. Her mother moved to the door.

"The representatives from Troivack have arrived, Your Majesty," a maid announced.

Kat perked up. "Oh, thank the Gods!"

Annika held up a hand, signaling her daughter to wait. "And who are the representatives?"

"It is a Sir Hugo Cas and Princess Kezia, the Royal Court Mage."

Kat's jaw dropped. She had known Sir Cas would be coming, but to hear her close friend from the Troivackian court was news to her.

Annika warily opened the door to find herself staring behind the maid at a clean-shaven blond man with soft cheeks and blue eyes, who inclined himself to her. At his side stood a woman with long, silky black hair, olive-toned skin, and the most exquisite blue eyes she had ever seen.

"Thank you," the duchess said to the maid curtly, which had the woman taking her leave before Annika aside. "Won't you two come in? Her Majesty has been looking forward to seeing you."

The Daxarian-born knight bowed as the woman swept into the room, then followed suit.

When the door was closed, Kat descended upon the Troivackian princess, who was married to the king's younger brother, Prince Henry.

"KEZIA!" Kat flung her arms around the woman, who laughed musically and returned the embrace.

"*Ryshka*, I've missed you, too," she said affectionately.

The Daxarian queen finally released the woman only to lean away and cup Kezia's face.

"Gods. Still far too beautiful to be mortal."

The princess laughed again. They had once served the Troivackian queen, Kat's sister-in-law, together seven years prior. During that time the two had bonded closely, and Kezia had even revealed that she herself was a mage.

While mages and witches didn't typically get along, Kat had barely batted an eye over the discovery.

"It is good to see you again as well, Your Majesty." Sir Cas bowed again, a broad, warm smile of his own lighting his features.

Kat punched him in the shoulder before pulling him into a hug next. "Still breaking hearts over in Troivack, you big softie?"

"Oh, I've been far too busy for that," Sir Cas chortled.

In truth, Kat had already heard from the Troivackian queen how the knight had been the object of the affections of many women. He had never reciprocated, choosing instead to focus on his career.

"Mum," Kat addressed the duchess. "You remember Sir Cas and Kezia."

The duchess smiled. "I do indeed. It is wonderful to see you both in good health, though I wish it were under better circumstances."

At the mention of what had drawn them all to the same place at the same time, everyone's joyful expressions faded.

"What have you learned about the alleged devil sightings?" Kezia asked quickly.

"Uh… First of all, wasn't Mr. Kraft supposed to be coming? Why isn't he here? I'm shocked Henry let you come." Kat changed the subject quickly while fixing her attention on Kezia.

It was indeed strange that the Troivackian prince would allow his wife to go to a foreign kingdom that was on the brink of utter chaos.

Kezia's eyes lingered on Kat's face. She seemed to sense there was a reason that her old friend was dodging the question but indulged her regardless. "Mr. Kraft was struck with a terrible flu around the time we needed to leave. Part of the reason for the delay was that the Troivackian king had hoped he would recover. However, Mr. Kraft remained significantly weakened, and so I volunteered."

Kat raised her eyebrows expectantly.

Seeing this, Kezia spared a brief guilty smile. "Henry has been in the north overseeing the development of a large coven and mage school. We are trying to merge the two disciplines."

Annika jumped in. "That is a very innovative approach. I'll be interested to hear more about that. I'm surprised Their Majesties did not mention this when they were visiting for Katarina's coronation."

"The newly recruited apprentice mages have taken some persuading to join the witches, so it was not a confirmed plan when they were in Daxaria."

Kat folded her arms patiently and tilted her head, making Kezia at last confess. "Henry did not know I was going to volunteer to come here. But it would be ridiculous for no one of magical inclination to come to investigate. Now, what is happening here with the devil? I've also heard rumors that your brother, Tam, is dead? But given how… *yourself* you seem, *ryshka,* I somehow doubt that is true."

So Katarina enlightened Kezia on the status and influence of the corrupt concubine, the two covens that had fallen in line with her, and the first witch.

Hearing how widespread the trouble was, Kezia's beautiful face paled, and Sir Cas looked more than a little concerned. The Troivackian princess was just getting her wits back together, when out from behind the screen stepped Luca and Penelope.

Kezia's eyes dropped to the two children, but they quickly homed in on Luca with great alarm.

"*Ryshka,* who is—"

A blast of stone and air blew everyone off their feet and into the back wall.

Dust clouded the air, the crashing and crunching echoing loudly, followed shortly by a dull ringing.

Coughing ensued, followed by Katarina's aura flaring.

"MUM? MUM? ARE YOU ALRIGHT?"

In the debris of the destroyed quarters, Kat could gradually make out what had happened.

The entire wall where the window was had been blown to bits from four boulders that had smashed through.

Kat had managed to shield her mother at some point, but the duchess seemed to be disoriented and was struggling to draw breath.

Scanning the room in a panic for any additional danger, Kat noticed that Kezia was lying unconscious on the ground underneath bits of rumble, while Sir Cas was bleeding from the side of his head.

"The children," Annika gasped before her eyes suddenly flew to the ceiling. "Fin."

Shivering, Kat knew that her mother was terrified.

Whenever any of the Ashowans were extremely frightened, her father's magical connection to his loved ones gave him a vision of what was happening. Only Annika was able to see a ghost of Finlay when this happened.

"LUCA? PENELEOPE?" Kat shouted as her mother's breaths stuttered.

She dropped her golden eyes to Annika and pushed power down their magical connection, urging her mother's strength to restore.

It took an agonizing moment, but she did feel her mother's breathing start to even out once more. Mortals were physically improved when Kat did this. Witches experienced surges of magical power.

"Sir Cas?" Kat called next.

The knight squinted at her, his gaze unfocused.

"Shit. Shit, shit, *shit!*"

Annika slowly pushed herself up to a sitting position, her fingers trembling as she gingerly poked and prodded herself. "I'll live. But, Kat… the children. Did they…?"

Kat's magic flared as she gently set her mother to the side, then started sifting through the rumble.

A fraction of relief filled her when she didn't find their bodies anywhere.

"I'm going to kill that Godsdamn witch," Kat seethed.

"Kat," her mother coughed. "Get… a physician for the princess and Sir Cas."

"We can't trust a royal physician!" Kat peered over the jagged edge of what remained of the wall to the ground, but the land her window overlooked was empty of people. "We need to get the hell out of here. Now."

"They'll follow us," Annika explained while taking slow, deep breaths, her hair and face covered in dust and wood chips.

"If they do, I'll take care of them," Kat ground out before swinging around toward where Kezia lay. "But right now we need to retreat and come up with a new plan. Now, where is that brothel you said Tam is at?"

CHAPTER 43

A ROCKY REUNION

Tam sat on the couch and lit the cigar wedged in his mouth before he leaned back into the comfortable cushions and let out a long rushing stream of smoke.

Eli had been studying one of the paintings hanging on the wall when she smelled the burning and swung around in alarm. Then her eyes widened in surprise as she noticed the vice in Tam's hand.

He held her gaze, not batting an eye.

"I didn't know you smoked," Eli remarked stiffly.

Tam stared at the lit cigar, then back at her. "When inspecting brothels I do. And on special occasions. Or, apparently, highly stressful situations."

His somber face lowered as he took another puff and leaned forward to rest his elbows on his knees.

Eli fidgeted.

He noticed. "Do you not like me smoking?"

"I… I don't mind it on occasion. The smell can be nice when it isn't excessive."

She eyed the cigar again.

"Have you ever tried one?" Tam asked slowly while trying to read the thoughts behind her eyes.

She colored at the question. "I did. Once. Lady Chin preferred a pipe, but she would occasionally enjoy a cigar when she was alone before bed. It was the Winter Solstice… the last one she was alive for. We shared one by the fire."

Tam smiled despite himself. "Did you like it?"

"It made my head spin, but it was alright. It changed the taste of my tea, which was interesting."

Chuckling a little, Tam nodded to himself. "That is true. It also changes the way wine and liquor taste. It can be nice."

Eli rounded the couch across from Tam and sat down slowly. "Not too surprising that one vice compliments another."

Harris had gone down to one of the private rooms they had been given for a nap, and so the couple partook in another day of quiet in the brothel.

They all had slept soundly after the hearty hot meals, baths, and reintroduction to clean, comfortable beds. And while there was a restless tension as the time of the prince's birthday celebration neared, they waited patiently for more news from the palace.

Eli suddenly broke the silence. "Tam, you… you were right. I wasn't approaching my concerns about you as a partner. I was approaching them already defensive, and I… I was dismissive of your side. I'm sorry."

Tam blinked then turned to set the cigar down in the porcelain ashtray before clasping his hands.

"I am worried about how far you will go when it comes time to take back Luca and Penelope. And I guess I thought I knew you well enough that I made assumptions. I didn't even know you smoked cigars, or that you had another name when inspecting brothels." Eli's fingers curled into loose fists atop her knees. "I'm on your side, Tam. You're still the best person I know, and if I'm doomed to be anyone's familiar, I can't think of anyone else I'd rather be tied to."

Tam rose from the couch wordlessly and rounded the low table between himself and Eli before seating himself on its surface and holding out his hand to his assistant.

She stared down at it, then gingerly reached out and grasped his fingers with her own.

"I will only dispose of anyone who attacks, or who has been explicit in their abduction. Civilians? Children? I'd never hurt on purpose."

Eli's throat bobbed as she swallowed, then jerked her chin down in understanding.

"I don't know if you want to hear this," Tam said, "but I… I think I've thought of a name for you as a familiar. I've been thinking about it since you told me what Wixim said about it."

At first, Eli froze, and a glimmer of hesitancy rushed through her eyes. Then she lowered her walls, her shoulders easing down. "Okay."

"There is a constellation in the stars of a cat that protects the world from the people who have turned to evil. She was said to have originated as a house cat belonging to a beautiful young woman who lived alone. One day, she was murdered by robbers who had broken into her house. Her cat, brokenhearted, beseeched the Goddess to help her seek vengeance, and to stop such evil from ever harming another good person."

Eli visibly relaxed even more as she fell under the enchantment of Tam's story.

"The Goddess acquiesced to the cat's wish, as it was around this time that the first witch had lost her powers, and therefore could not do much to help humanity. And so this cat prowled her village, keeping the innocents safe from those corrupted with evil. Even the devil is said to be scared of this cat."

Tam paused, but Eli was hanging on his every word.

"I have always thought of this story when I've seen you change, but I didn't want you to feel uncomfortable."

"What's the name of the cat?" Eli whispered.

Tam smiled warmly. "Kasha."

A humming warmth spread through the air, and both Tam and Eli blinked in surprise as the room seemed to grow hazy, and an ethereal glow surrounded them.

The couple stared in amazement down at their joined hands, then back up at each other. Both broke out in nervous smiles before Eli bent forward and wrapped her arms around Tam's broad shoulders. They had thinned in recent weeks, but were still firm.

"I love you, Tam. I'm imperfect, and I'm working through my issues, but I… I do not want to lose you."

Tam returned her embrace and buried his face in her neck. "I love you, too. Thank you for talking to me, and for your apology."

After an extra-firm squeeze, Tam released Eli and leaned back, though he still held her hands. Some of the great weight that had been pressing down on his heart lifted, and a fraction of calm returned to his being."You and I, Eli? We're going to get the kids, and we are going to be happy after everything. Together. I promise."

★★★

Kat kept her face lowered as she stalked through the streets of Gondol. The dark hood she wore covered both her hair and her eyes.

Her mother limped at her side with a sickly pale Sir Hugo Cas following along. The knight appeared to be a light breeze away from collapse, but his blue eyes—normally bright and warm—had turned to steel. They looked the same when he wielded a sword.

Kezia was in Kat's arms, but she was covered with blankets and a coat to look like a pile of laundry.

They'd had to stop twice on their journey away from the palace so that Kat could go and dispatch those who attempted to follow them. The first group had been human, imperial soldiers. The next two groups had consisted of witches.

Kat didn't bother hiding the bodies.

By the time they had reached the door to The Opulent Opal, the sky burned with orange and red.

Annika was the one to knock on the door, her own hood drawn up.

A guard built like a brick outhouse opened the door.

"I am the Dragon. You will take me to the madam and the Shadow, or the brothel will burn."

The man let out a snorting huff, but he stepped aside without a word of objection. His overall attitude suggested that he had experienced this sort of interaction rather recently.

Kat hefted Kezia in her arms and hunched her shoulders, hoping to the Gods that she was not imagining the steady breathing of her friend.

It had been incredibly fortunate that Kezia and Sir Cas had been wearing their traveling cloaks when they'd gone to visit Katarina and her mother, and that both Kat and her mother's cloaks inside the wardrobe were undamaged, as more and more people flooded the streets lit with lanterns strung up between the houses to celebrate the prince's birthday.

Regardless of the cloaks, they swept into the building hurriedly. They couldn't risk being seen. Sir Cas closed the brothel door behind them.

The doorman stalked ahead of them and called gruffly over his shoulder, "Mung is dealing with important customers. You lot come up. The madam is with the Shadow and his company upstairs."

No one said anything. They proceeded onward and upward, passing the narrow corridors, catching swaths of voices and music, scents of liquor and sizzling meat, until at last they came to the top of the stairs.

Annika leaned heavily at the banister once she'd rounded the main spindle to allow the others past her, while Sir Cas lunged toward the small span of wall across the top of the stairs, his knees buckling and his eyes fluttering from the climb.

Only Kat walked without so much as a boot scuff toward the Zinferan woman seated behind the ornate desk.

She wore a black lace dress and a leather corset. Her hair was in a low bun, and her eye patch was made of leather with gold detailing.

She puffed on a pipe as she surveyed the newcomers dispassionately. "It would seem I am a popular establishment as of late."

"We need a physician," Kat growled. "I have a woman here in my arms. We were attacked. She's unconscious. The man behind me has a head injury, and my mo—the Dragon—has an injured knee and most likely fractured ribs."

The madam took her time reaching over to set her pipe down. "Once my assistant returns to my side, I will send up our physician. Though I must say, I will need to start accepting payment for all of this charity I've been expected to give as of late. I was under the impression the Dragon did not demand much of her business associates."

"I'll give you gold," Kat snapped. "Where can I lay this woman down?"

The madam rose to her feet and sauntered around the desk.

"Probably on the couch where the Shadow is sitting. Assuming he is fine making some room."

Kat had been so focused on keeping track of Kezia's breaths that she had completely forgotten her brother was somewhere in the building. She whirled around.

Her eyes widened.

She watched as he stood from the couch.

What… had happened to him?

Kat watched as, with long steps, her brother… her brother who had always slouched in poorly fitted clothes, her brother who had always lowered his eyes… her brother who had been missing and reported dead came closer.

She had expected him to be battered. Frail and frightened.

He was not.

Kat stared up into his face.

Had he always been that tall?

His dark eyes stared down at her, and Kat saw something in them that nearly made her recoil…

Shadows behind his brown eyes flickered like a dark flame. It was much like their father's ethereal white light, which revealed the time he spent in the Forest of the Afterlife. But whereas Finlay Ashowan's made him seem heavenly, this darker flickering made her brother seem… dangerous.

"Kat?"

His voice was low and gravelly, his sharp face intent as his gaze bore into her.

Why did he look so intimidating? He was in simple black clothing, and was a bit thinner than before, but Kat could tell there were even deeper changes within him.

Was this really her brother?

Tam neared her. *Loomed* over her…

"Kat, where are my kids?" His tone was deadly.

It took Kat a moment to overcome her shock, but instead of responding straightaway she moved past Tam and lay Kezia down on the couch her brother had vacated.

She spotted a lit cigar sitting in an ashtray as she uncovered Kezia's face and checked on her breathing, but the sight of the vice her brother had obviously been partaking in only unnerved her more.

So when she started to turn back around and found herself staring at Eli—who must have been watching from her place leaning against the wall ever since they'd arrived—she startled.

Eli, too, was different.

The young woman she had first met had been disguised as a boy, so of course there was longer hair that reached past Eli's chin, and her distinctly womanly shape. But as with Tam, there was a hardness in her. A confidence and strength that made Kat's senses prickle.

"Dragon, where are my kids?" Kat ripped her eyes from Eli to look at her brother with a large measure of outrage. Their mother was gazing up at her son with eyes so pained and uncertain, Kat froze.

"They were taken. By force. As you can most likely see," Annika informed her son softly.

"Where were they taken?" Tam persisted, his voice low.

No one in the room dared to breathe.

Even the madam wasn't foolish enough to so much as roll her eye.

"I do not know," Annika responded. She seemed to come to a conclusion as she continued to stare up at Tam.

Kat broke in, "Why are you being such an arse, Tam? I know we're worried about the kids, but a lot of people nearly died!"

She half expected this new version of her brother to wither away and his regular silly self to reappear.

But when Tam locked eyes with Kat, she could tell he never would be the same again. This trip to Zinfera had done too much to him.

His fierceness did soften a little when he met his sister's furious stare, but the steeliness in his face did not fade for an instant.

"Wait for the physician. Send word to Jiho Ryu when you can; he will help. Eli and I are going to be leaving now."

Kat watched dumbfounded as Eli pushed off the wall of the brothel and headed toward the stairs with Tam.

"Tam! Do you have any idea how dangerous the palace is right now? Both covens are—"

"We know," Tam interrupted but didn't stop.

Kat moved after her brother and his assistant. "Kraken and Pina are on their way, too! Hang on, can we talk? And where is Harris?"

"I need to go get my kids, Kat. We can talk later." Tam was already halfway down the stairs.

"Like hell we will," Kat rumbled, her eyes cutting to her mother, who was staring after Tam, her eyes filled with anguish. "Mum?"

Annika gradually turned toward her daughter, her mind obviously elsewhere.

"Mum, I'm going with him. I think my brother got dumber while he was away. Can you please keep an eye on Kezia?"

Annika nodded slowly.

"Thanks. And you!" Kat pointed a finger at the madam, who did not look impressed by the rude gesture, but when Madam Sao finally noticed the burning gold of Kat's eyes under the hood, she balked.

"We are not a family you want to cross. Get these people help. You'll get your gold. But if you betray us, I will be the last face you see on this earth, and I won't make myself pretty for the occasion. Understood?"

It took the madam a moment to regain her composure, but when she did she bowed her head magnanimously.

"I understand… Your Majesty."

Kat let out a guttural noise at hearing the formal title. At times it was annoying how recognizable she was.

However, she couldn't complain about it just then, as she hurried after her brother and his assistant. Uneasiness was burning a hole in her gut. She had the unpleasant notion that her brother was about to do something more than a little reckless.

CHAPTER 44

THE COMING CALAMITY

Kat felt her agitation start to burn through her, her fingernails digging into her palms as she wove nimbly in and out of crowds that were growing more and more jubilant with every passing moment.

She was forcing herself to keep her hood down and her eyes hidden. It added to her difficulty plowing through the bodies between herself and her brother.

At least Tam was easy to spot. His straight back kept his head above the majority of the street occupants, and the way he continued striding purposefully down the middle of the road forced people to clear a path for him.

With a snarl, Kat darted forward, though she almost loosed her aura in doing so.

When she finally reached her brother's side once more, she was a little surprised and impressed to find that Eli had managed to stick close to the other side without issue.

"Tam, what the hell is your plan here?" Kat barked, unworried that she would be overheard; the chatter and opening thrums of music continued to rise in volume.

The smell of frying oil and pastry started to permeate the air: the scent of a rousing good celebration.

"I'm going to walk into the palace and get the children back," Tam responded evenly, his eyes not moving away from the street for an instant.

"Yeah, you mentioned that, but *how* do you plan on doing that?" Kat pressed.

"Tonight is Prince Jum's birthday celebration, yes?" Tam asked mildly.

"What about it?" Kat's eyes narrowed as she stared at her brother's eerily calm profile.

"We're going to walk right in, and I'll do whatever I have to."

"That answers a lot of nothing—TAM!" Kat seized her brother's arm and yanked him back, pulling him to a stop. Her aura momentarily flared, making one or two people around them flinch. The passersby gave their heads a shake as though they assumed it had been a trick of their eyes, then continued on their way.

"You can't just waltz into a palace and turn it upside down without a plan! I can take on a lot of people, but I'm still only one—"

Tam pulled himself free and continued walking ahead.

Kat cursed, then used an extra flex of magic to place herself in front of him. "There are two covens working together, along the Zinferan imperial army. You don't know the layout of the palace or how many civilians are in there. The first witch might already be on a ship leaving Zinfera!"

Tam's dark eyes were cold, and for a chilling moment Kat thought back to the few people who had confided in her that they saw something horribly dark in her brother.

"We'll look in the palace, and if the children aren't there, then we'll go to the docks. If the first witch has left, that means there will be fewer witches against us. But one way or another, we are getting the kids back," Tam informed his sister. He lowered his chin, the black flickering in his eyes glinting in the dim lantern light of the street. "If you aren't fighting at my side, then stay behind."

"I'd love to fight with you *if you'd just take a Godsdamn moment to explain your plan!*" Kat threw her hands in the air.

Tam let out an impatient breath and opened his mouth to respond when they were interrupted.

"TAM! KAT! BY THE GODS SLOW DOWN!" Harris managed to skid to a halt between the siblings before doubling over, taking heaving breaths. "I go for *one* measly nap and you lot take off to do something terrible!"

"Harris! Great to see you. What the hell has happened to my brother? Did he get kicked in the head by a horse at some point?" Kat demanded while pointing her finger at Tam and staring incredulously at their old family friend.

Harris gradually managed to right himself again, though his cheeks were still pink. "Oh, Your Majesty, you have no idea what we've been dealing with."

"Ssh!" Kat hissed upon him addressing her formally, then leaned in closer. "Did you get a chance to hear from my mother what happened?"

Harris's expression turned grim. "I did. I passed the physician on the way out of the brothel. I hope Princess Kezia will be alright."

Tam suddenly turned to the duke. "Harris, are you going to help us?"

"Well, that depends what we're doing here, Tam!" The older man placed his hands on his hips. He wore a plain white tunic and black pants, with the sword Wixim had gifted him sheathed on his back.

Tam's lifted his gaze from Harris to sweep over the crowd. "We're buying flour and moonshine. As much as we can carry. Kat, get your hands on a bow, arrows, and flint. We're burning down the palace. There are going to be empty spaces while the main party carries on."

Kat's jaw dropped. Eli's eyebrows rose though she gave no other significant look of alarm. And Harris…

Harris looked like the Goddess had just offered to give him the best foot rub of his life.

Aradia sat in her inconspicuous spot at the end of Soo Hebin's long table overlooking the main palace courtyard.

At the seat on her right was her brother, who had set his little jaw the instant he had finally stopped screaming following his separation from Penelope and hadn't said a word. On his other side sat Ansar.

She sighed. "Ansar, have we released Thomas Julian yet?"

"Yes, mistress. He should already be aboard the ship with the seer child."

"Good." Aradia took a sip from her goblet. "Have you found where the Daxarian queen went?"

Ansar continued leisurely enjoying his grilled fish as dignified music drifted over the prince's birthday-party guests, seated in two rows of long tables that ran around the perimeter of the courtyard. "Most likely one of the brothels the Ashowans and Ryus jointly own."

"Which of their brothels is the closest?"

"The Coy Koi," Ansar answered. He took a sip of wine.

"Have the imperial soldiers been sent there?"

"They have half a unit casually surrounding the building. If anyone matching the descriptions of the queen or the others appear, they will send a message. They have direct orders not to get in Katarina Reyes's way."

Aradia nodded to herself reasonably. "I do feel badly about Princess Kezia and Sir Hugo Cas getting mixed up with the assault. I always liked them."

"It was the best time to attack. The queen and her mother were distracted, and the children were near the window," Ansar said, consoling her without any emotional inflection.

Aradia continued eating, then glanced again at her brother in his child form, who sat with his hands curled stubbornly over his knees. "Eat something. This is far finer than what will be offered here on out."

His breath hitched, then he lifted his furious gaze up to her. "My dad's going to come get me, and then we're going to save Penelope. You're going to be really sorry."

The first witch raised her eyebrows and pursed her mouth while looking at the child with pity. "Even if he does, I will steal you back. Again and again. You will know that I am always chasing you. Always coming for you. And that will place Tamlin Ashowan and anyone around him in danger. Do you understand?"

Fear and agony played across the boy's face, and his eyes glimmered with the promise of tears.

Aradia gave a soft laugh of disbelief. "My. I've never seen you truly so vulnerable in our millenia or so of knowing each other, brother. I can't wait to torment you with this when you finally remember who you truly are."

Aradia looked back at her dinner plate, her mind already drifting back to the matter of the cooked turtle on the table and how she had never really enjoyed this Zinferan delicacy, when the child spoke again.

"A lot of people were scared of me where I grew up." Aradia only partially turned toward the boy, with a bemused quirk of her lips. He was staring at her, his face fading to a calmer expression, though his eyes still stormed. "Sometimes even my birth mother and my uncle were scared of me. I didn't like it. But you should know something." His dark gaze settled and locked with Aradia's. "People are more scared of my dad than they ever were of me."

Aradia's amusement faltered.

"I didn't want my dad to know this, but I've heard a lot of people call him the devil."

A creeping chill started to press itself into Aradia's chest. Even Ansar stopped eating to look with a frown at the back of the boy's head.

"I don't know about you, lady, but… I don't think there is anything scarier than the devil."

After a beat of heavy silence, Aradia turned to face the child more squarely. "That was quite a sophisticated threat for a seven-year-old."

The boy's face scrunched up. "I didn't threaten anybody!" he exclaimed heartfully. "I'm just telling you that my dad's going to save me, and you're probably not going to wanna mess with him again."

Evidently pleased with himself, the boy plucked up the bowl of broth on his left and slurped at it obnoxiously.

Aradia's eyes drifted up to Ansar. He was already staring at her with steady concern.

The tip of her tongue poked at a molar point in her mouth as she leaned back in her seat and lifted her wine goblet. She allowed her gaze to rove over the party pensively.

Tamlin Ashowan was a witch, so there was no way he was actually her brother. The timing wasn't right. It wasn't possible.

But the boy's words still stuck in her mind like a pesky thorn.

"FIRE! THE PALACE IS ON FIRE!"

Aradia's attention snapped up. Over the outer wall of the courtyard was a faint orange glow that could almost be a trick of the light.

The shout had come from the doors to the courtyard, where beyond lay the west and south wings of the palace that were closest to Gondol.

"Good thing we have a few water witches still here in the palace." Aradia chuckled while taking another leisurely drink. She observed that even Soo Hebin from her place at the center of the table beside her son didn't appear all that bothered.

Then she noticed the smile on the boy's face as he peered at the doors expectantly. Eyes narrowing, Aradia set down her cup. "Ansar."

Without needing anything more explicit to be said, her ally grabbed the boy by the shoulders and hauled him up as she, too, rose to her feet. "I'll summon Wixim."

The child opened his mouth, a shout of *No* rising in the back of his throat before Ansar's hand came up and covered his mouth, silencing him.

The three of them headed back into the front building of the palace. Aradia gave a brief jerk of her chin in Soo Hebin's direction when the concubine shot an irritated glance her way.

She raised an unbothered eyebrow in return.

Though as Aradia, Ansar, and the child approached the doors, the first shrieks within the courtyard echoed out.

Aradia swung back around, her left hand rising. She had a vial of the water from the Goddess's Pool stowed away in a leather satchel tied discreetly around her waist, along with a small pouch filled with powdered Witch's Brew.

She relaxed when she realized that the screams had merely come because the first wave of nobles poisoned by Soo Hebin had started either collapsing or coughing up blood. From the few glimpses Aradia could catch from her position at the back of the stone terrace over the courtyard, she observed that the concubine had been rather thorough in selecting multiple types of poison to really strain the physicians that might attempt to heal the nobles.

Aradia turned back toward the doors.

She'd decided that the other concubine Deoh Rin would be the easiest replacement for the throne, but that would not come to pass until after Aradia had departed from Zinfera. The Giong Coven would take care of it.

For now, it was time to leave. Aradia had wanted to be present when the Daxarian king's response to their ransom note arrived, but alas. It just didn't work out this time.

Oh well.

CHAPTER 45

A DARING DEVIL

Eli stared at the back palace wall in all of its grandeur, then turned to her right. "Tam?"

"Yes?"

"I want to go somewhere before we break in."

Tam looked down expectantly, and on the other side of his assistant, his sister and Harris peered at her curiously.

"Where is that?"

"The shrine just over there." Eli jerked her chin to the left where a separate building stood alone. There was a fountain in front of it, and only two guards, who hadn't looked at them as the flurry of people flowed by.

"What's in there?"

"It's the shrine dedicated to the former empress. Chin. Before we burn everything down, I want to take something."

Tam raised an eyebrow. "We don't have a lot of time."

"It'll be quick. Most of the guards will be at the party."

Tam could see the resolve in her eyes, and how important it was that they make this quick stop. "Alright. You and I will go. Kat, Harris, you start the fire along the wall in between the guards. We'll be right back."

Kat looked uneasy and didn't respond to Tam's order, so he squared himself to her.

"Leave or help. But make up your mind." Then he stalked past his sister with Eli at his side to retrieve whatever item Eli wished to grab. It didn't really impede the plan; it'd take time for the fire to really be deemed a concern. They had first set fire to the back garden closest to the street, which, after a quick inspection by Kat, proved vacant except for a few guards at the far end by the doors to a small wing of the main palace.

When they were perhaps fifty feet from the shrine, Tam felt Eli turn her head toward him as they wove through the bodies that all seemed to be traveling in the opposite direction. "You seem angry with your sister."

"I'm angry at everything right now, Eli," Tam returned evenly.

"I know, but she is helping us without having much of a reason to."

"I've helped her many times. It won't kill her to do the same. Plus I think it makes her more receptive when I tell her to do something as opposed to asking."

Eli made a noise of disbelief but stopped talking as they neared the guards.

Neither Tam nor Eli slowed their pace as they climbed the stairs purposefully.

The spears the two guards held lowered to a cross in front of them.

"Halt. This is the shrine of Grand Lady Chin Taejo. It is not for public access. Turn around and return to the street." The guard on the right spoke without moving from his position by the jade-shaded pillar.

Tam turned slowly to look at the man, his eyes filling with blackness. "We won't be long."

The guard flinched and backed away involuntarily.

Eli meanwhile tilted her head at the second guard. "I am Princess Elisara Taejo. You will lower your spear now."

Tam heard the man splutter. "Th-the *princess?* You must come with me at once! You—"

Tam leisurely pulled out two daggers and redirected his stare to the second guard as dark, smoky silver started to waft from him.

The guard's mouth hung open in horror.

Tam didn't even raise his voice when he said, "Move."

The two men stumbled away, their eyes widened fearfully, their faces paling.

Eli glided forward and pushed open both doors to reveal a long hall filled with more jade-colored pillars and black marble floors. Vermillion drapes were parted and tied with gold rope to reveal treasures in the alcoves lining the hall.

Eli walked purposefully, her head not turning once, but Tam watched her hands curl into fists as she approached a display at the very back of the room.

He followed, daggers still in hand as he heard shouts from behind him alerting whoever was nearby that the devil had come.

His mind drifted to that thought.

A humorless smile tugged at a corner of his mouth.

Perhaps that moniker was more fitting than he wanted to admit, as he was feeling a great deal of his power thrumming under his skin, and a great deal fewer reservations about using it than he'd ever had before.

"Tam, stay back. I'm going to break the glass."

Pulled from his thoughts, Tam looked up and realized what it was that Eli had come to retrieve from the shrine of the emperor's mother, who had raised her for half of her childhood. Protected her…

He smiled. "I didn't think you'd be the type to wear something like that."

Eli didn't respond as her heel shot out and she shattered the glass. "I wouldn't usually, but I think tonight calls for it." She looked over her shoulder and smiled.

There was a nervous yet excited glint in her eyes that made her seem… different. As though she was about to finally free herself from all the fates that other people had heartlessly tied to her.

Tam felt his heart skip a beat. "You know… I think you're right."

It was only a few moments later, but by the time Tam and Eli swept out of the shrine, everything had fallen into utter chaos.

From their vantage point at the top of the shrine stairs, they could see Kat fighting guards with her sword drawn and her cloak discarded. Off to the side, Harris was laughing maniacally while tossing a bottle of moonshine at the blazing top of the wall.

The civilians in the street were screaming, running away from the scene, and already the road was mostly empty. The two guards who had been outside the shrine were nowhere to be seen.

Tam looked at Eli with a raised eyebrow. "Now that the alarms have started on this side of the palace, how about you and I take a walk to the front doors. It makes sense that the first witch would try to leave that way if she's heading toward the docks."

Eli frowned up at him. "Did you always intend your sister to be the distraction?"

Tam shrugged. "No one makes a distraction quite like her." He then offered his assistant his arm.

"Shouldn't you help her?" Eli put her hands on her hips.

Tam's gaze flitted back upward toward where his sister, with her aura blazing, effortlessly kicked one man and sent him flying back into four others. "Nope. She's fine."

Unable to argue the point, Eli accepted Tam's arm and they made their way up and around the west palace wall. As they strolled, Tam breathed in the smell of the fire that, judging from the brightness in the sky, was rapidly spreading. "You said it was only the gardens in that area of the palace, right?"

"Yes. And I imagine the coven members are going to try to put it out. Which is another reason I figured your sister could use some help."

Tam reconsidered the suggestion of offering Kat assistance. "No. She'll be fine. They can't even dose her with Witch's Brew."

Eli blinked and stared up questioningly.

Tam smiled. "She's built a tolerance over the last three years. With the help of my mother, she carefully worked up an immunity to it so that her outburst in Troivack would never happen again."

The shocking news had Eli falling silent as they continued up the street, which was empty… except for the fifteen soldiers coming toward them.

"Hm." Tam paused. He gently prodded his power stores. "Since we're hoping to cut off the first witch from leaving, I'm just going to take us through the void to reach the other end of the street. Are you alright with that?"

"That does sound more efficient." Eli smiled permissively.

Tam smiled politely back as the roar of the men approaching them grew louder.

Then he grasped her hand, and with the familiar flicker of silver and black, the two of them whooshed out of the physical world.

In the void, Tam closed his eyes, feeling the stone of the street around him. He could even distantly hear the shouts of alarm from the soldiers.

He glided over them, then imagined the far corner that would take them to the north side of the palace, and was just about to shift them out of the void when he turned suddenly to Eli.

"When we find the first witch, I'm going to do something, and… you need to know about it."

She looked at him expectantly. The eerie calm that had seized them both since Kat had arrived at The Opulent Opal was still prevailing. It was as though they both knew the time had come to face the higher powers that had tormented them. Any anguish or worry that had plagued them had simply evaporated.

They would get the children back, and they would be finished with Zinfera.

Simple as that.

"I think it's time I fully embrace the rumors."

Tam watched the confusion rise in Eli's eyes.

"I'm going to announce myself as the devil to anyone who asks."

She blinked rapidly but didn't show any kind of other alarm.

"I want the first witch coming after me. Not Luca."

A low, reverberation started to rise in Tam as he spoke. And he could tell by the way that Eli stiffened that she must have felt it, too.

"You won't hurt innocents or children?" Eli asked carefully.

"Correct. I think I can convince a lot of people without doing much. You already know how skilled I am at spreading rumors about myself." He smiled charmingly.

Eli's expression fell flat, but a reluctant smile of her own pulled her mouth up. "Are you planning on trapping her in this void?"

"That would be best. Then we can deal with the coven and Soo Hebin without worrying too much."

Nodding, Eli looked forward at the infinite span of blackness. "Alright. They surprised us with moving quickly when they stole the children, so I'd advise you to do the same once we see her."

"I love you," Tam declared, his chest warm.

Eli looked back at him, a slow, tender look filling her eyes. "I love you, too. And even though I wasn't sure about adopting Penelope before… well…" She sighed. "She has more common sense than most adults. I think I might like her being Luca's sister."

Tam laughed, then lifted their clasped hands to his mouth to kiss the back of her hand. "Don't worry. We can still have three more girls anytime you want."

Eli's cheeks flushed. "Stop flirting when we're in the middle of an uprising and bring us back to reality."

"As you wish." Tam grinned, then obeyed his beloved's persnickety request.

They reappeared exactly where he had anticipated. The soldiers, now behind them, were busy looking around the spot Tam and Eli had disappeared, unaware that the pair were resuming their stroll toward the front doors.

"Why aren't we running?" Eli asked next as the large rust-colored front doors came into view. Another crowd of soldiers was flowing down the front steps.

"It'll take the first witch time to decide to leave."

"She might have already left."

Tam nodded. "Then we'll fly to the ships."

A funny expression claimed Eli's face. "Gods. We really are doing this."

As the new wave of soldiers descended upon them, Tam wrapped an arm around Eli's waist, startling her as he then spun her as though they were on a dance floor back into the void.

"Doing what? Winning a war?"

"Yes. I feel it. We will win tonight."

Tam smiled. "I feel that, too." He waltzed them through the void, feeling his way easily over the stones, down the street, over the second group of soldiers, and up the stairs.

Eli tilted her head quizzically. "Why are you in a good mood?"

"Well, you are wearing a dashing red dress… And maybe I'm a little scared for Luca, but I keep thinking of the advice Harris and Jeong kept trying to give us. To have a bit more fun."

Eli laughed quietly, though she continued dancing with Tam without objection.

Tam didn't pay a second thought to where his feet went. Only to how warm his palm felt in hers, and how with every graceful sweep of their feet against her skirts they were drawing closer to their children.

"I think we've both gone a bit insane," Eli said softly, though she sounded sincere.

"More than likely. But you know, it's the ones who've lost their minds that I think have the most fun no matter what situation they're in," Tam speculated as they reappeared in the physical world directly in front of the open front doors to the palace.

The soldiers were behind them once more, and before them lay a rich entrance. It was rectangular with two large staircases running up the sides to a second-story balcony. The balcony itself was ornately carved from wood, while the ceiling and pillars were stenciled in vivid blue, red, and jade, with details in black, gold, and white. The walls were white in contrast, and the polished chestnut floors gleamed in the light of the braziers. Three doorways on either side of the ground room led off in various directions, as did three large doorways on the second-floor balcony. All had their double doors firmly shut.

"Huh. No welcome party. I'm a bit surprised." Tam released his hold on Eli's waist but not her hand as they walked into the vast room that lay empty.

"It is rather quiet. Though a lot of men just bolted to the street. Plus the fire," Eli observed.

"Ah yes. The fire… Almost forgot about that."

A loud roar followed by an earth-rumbling thud made Tam and Eli look over their shoulders to see in the frame of the open doors a familiar golden dragon with bright-green eyes.

"Wixim! It's been a while!" Tam called out jovially with a wave.

The dragon tilted his great head at Tam. Then, in the next instant, the middle doors on the second-floor balcony opened, and out stepped a short Daxarian woman with strawberry-blond hair, clear blue eyes, and pale skin donned entirely in black. At her side was a man of average height with brown hair and several earrings, wearing a silver vest, a blue shirt, and a plum tie. Over his shoulder was a squirming young boy Tam recognized instantly, prompting him to release Eli's hand.

"Ah." Tam vanished back into the void without Eli and reappeared directly in front of the man holding his son.

Before either the Daxarian woman or man could react, Tam jabbed his fingers into the man's eyes, grabbed Luca, and pulled the boy back into the void with himself just in time to hear a startled "Wha—" from the woman on the right.

Once safely back in the void, Tam spun Luca around and instantly spotted the gag in his mouth.

He watched Luca's teary eyes widen in shock as he gazed at his father's face. Relief visibly swept over him, followed by more tears.

Tam removed the gag and hugged Luca as the boy released a heart-ripping wail. "I was s-s-so scared!" Luca sobbed into his father's shoulder.

Tam took deep, shuddering breaths as he relished the feel of Luca's head beneath his hand and the frantic, small heartbeat against his chest, while tears of his own gathered. At last, he emerged from his dazed madness, the darkness that had been lurking in his mind ebbing away. He pulled free, framing Luca's face in his hands, his resolve from earlier only reaffirmed.

Luca… would no longer be the devil.

Tam brushed away his son's tears with his thumbs and kissed his forehead without a word.

No.

Luca would forever be his son.

And nothing more.

"Luca," Tam murmured, grateful that time in the void moved significantly slower than it did in the tangible world. "I need to leave you here in this safe space, okay? But I'm going to be right back."

Luca gave a quiet choking cry but nodded as he grasped Tam's forearms. "T-They took Penelope away!"

Tam nodded. "We'll get her back, okay? Don't you worry. Can you be brave just a little longer and wait for me here? That woman can't get to you here."

"W-Where are we?" Luca asked, finally realizing what a vast emptiness they stood in.

"It's just my magic. It's nothing to be afraid of. I didn't want you to see it before because I thought you'd find it scary, but nothing will hurt you here."

Luca gulped. "You'll be right back soon, right?"

Tam nodded. "I just have to tell that woman who took you that she shouldn't do it again."

Luca gave a weak, watery smile. "I told her you would come for me."

Tam smiled back and gently brushed his son's hair away from his tearstained face. "You were absolutely right. I'm always going to come for you, Luca. You're my son. And I'm your dad. Nothing and no one is going to change that or take you from me, got it? No matter where you are, I'm going to be there for you."

Luca nodded, his breaths calming.

"Alright. I'm going to be back, Luca. Wait right here. Just sit down and don't move, okay?"

"O-Okay… Dad?"

"Yes, Luca?"

"D-Don't tell her my name! Penelope says she shouldn't know it!"

Tam paused, then gave a reassuring half smile. "Alright, thank you for telling me, Luca. Now, please sit and take some deep breaths, and I'll see you very soon."

The boy gripped Tam's shirtsleeves again but gradually lowered himself to sit obediently.

Tam gave him one last affirming smile, the ache in his heart that had torn away at him every day since they parted at last releasing him.

With a single step back then to the side, Tam removed himself from his void and reappeared in front of the alarmed face of the woman he knew to be the first witch.

A cold smile climbed into place as he assumed the role that seemed to have been inevitable for him.

"Hello, Aradia." Tam heard the first witch's breath catch. Seizing her shoulders, he gave the woman who had stolen his children and caused so much pain and suffering a shake. "What? No hug for your brother? I hear you've been looking for me. Well… Here. I. *Am!*"

CHAPTER 46

CONFRONTING A CONCUBINE

Wixim let out another loud roar behind Tam, and the man at their side that had been holding Luca reached for something at his side—presumably a weapon.

But they weren't fast enough as Tam, still holding Aradia's shoulders, launched them both into the void.

Tam kept his gaze locked on hers, and once they were surrounded by total darkness, he released her. The all-encompassing void did exactly what Tam had hoped it would when he caught her by surprise.

It shocked her into motionlessness.

"Wh-where are we? You aren't my brother! How are… You can't be!" She spun in place, looking at the endless span of nothing.

"Of course I'm your brother, Aradia. What better place to put myself than with the Ashowans?" Tam called, casting his most sinister smile at the woman who had caused them all so much suffering.

She started to fumble with something.

Tam ignored her.

He saw Luca off to the side, waiting for him, his eyes wide as he looked at his father uncertainly.

Tam didn't waste another breath.

He launched himself out of the void, then immediately back in, reappearing in front of Luca to grab him before catapulting them both through the void, sensing the palace's materials as he went. He wasn't going to give the first witch another chance to stop them.

Tam felt the stone, could feel the wood…

And that was when he noticed the red thread coming from his chest. It had appeared again, leading him back into nothing. Tam frowned as he felt Luca's grasp around his neck tighten.

The grip helped bring him back to reality, which was when he reappeared in front of Eli. She had her back to him as she faced Wixim, who was starting to open his mouth as heat gathered in the back of his throat.

The dragon *had* told them he would attack if it ever came to this.

Wrapping his arm around Eli, Tam ignored the desperate shout behind them that must have come from Aradia's servant. He rushed back into the void, but did not move them into the street where Wixim sat waiting; rather, he sent them all careening down the second story corridor he had glimpsed when he had confronted Aradia.

He could hear the fire blast from Wixim echoing down from where they all reappeared.

"Come on," he murmured urgently as he pressed his free hand against Eli's back. "We'll have to take the back exit and meet up with Kat."

"How are you?" Eli asked, shaking her head to reorient herself.

"Going in and out with all of you is a quick drain on my power, but I still have a great deal left. Come on."

As they moved through the palace, Eli took over as she was the only one who knew the layout, though she still needed to pause now and then to remember. At last they found themselves faced with another pair of grand doors painted the same dull-rust color as the front doors. Eli looked up at Tam and let out a short breath.

He met her gaze. "We're about to enter the party, aren't we?"

"Most likely," she confirmed grimly.

"Ah. Do you want my help for this?"

"I'll let you know if I do… But Tam?"

He raised an expectant eyebrow. Luca slowly lifted his head from his father's shoulder.

Eli spared him a heartbreaking smile before she reached up to the little boy's face and gently touched his cheek. "Tam, the promise I made to Lord Kim? The reason he agreed to help us?"

Tam stiffened at being reminded. "Yes?"

"I promised him that if I needed to take the throne for a time, I would. At least in an emergency, until I found a more suitable ruler."

He swung around to face her with alarm and fury on her behalf surging through him.

Eli held up a resigned hand. "We'll figure something out. I just thought you should know."

Tam took a steadying breath. "You won't keep the throne if you don't want it."

"I don't. And I won't. You and I are going to build a brand-new home. But for now, we really should go and finish this."

It took Tam a little longer to process this new bit of information. But Eli reached under Luca's arms and tickled him, making him giggle, and Tam couldn't help but smile from the pure happiness of hearing his son laugh again.

"Come on, my heart," she said to Luca. "It's past your bedtime, and we still have to go get your sister."

Luca beamed, joy seeping out every pore of his face.

Then Tam and Eli put a hand on the doors and pushed them open.

Rather than a celebration, however, what they found was an execution site.

Soo Hebin stood at the edge of the terrace landing overlooking a sea of frightened party guests. Several of the attendees were crowding around bodies of nobility that littered the ground of the courtyard.

And in the middle of the chaos were Jiho and Bong Ryu, their heads lowered as two soldiers with swords raised their blades in the air.

Without needing any words, Tam seized Eli's hand and swept them into the void.

Tam rushed them through pure air in the void. When he had them steadied to reappear, he turned and saw Eli already starting to shift into a beast—but he was instantly distracted when the red thread appeared as her familiar form did.

He didn't have time to process what this meant, as the threat of their friends' death was still imminent.

When they fell free of the void, they landed between the two Ryu men.

Eli let out a sky-shattering roar, her form larger than ever. Tam marveled that she was nearly the size of Wixim, as if she'd had yet another growth spurt in a matter of two days.

The two soldiers who had been about to decapitate the two Ryu men fell back in fright. And the courtyard went silent as Eli's roar rang out.

Tam stared up at Soo Hebin icily.

Luca stuck his tongue out at her.

Neither Bong nor Jiho had been able to raise their eyes from the ground, cringing away from the terrifying appearance of Eli—now Kasha. So when Tam's palm lowered in front of Jiho and he slowly looked up, his eyes went wide in shock.

"Good to see you again, Jiho. I've really enjoyed getting to know your sons." Tam gave a half smile to his father's oldest friend.

Jiho, with his long black-and-white-streaked hair coming out of its half-tied bun, slowly accepted Tam's hand and managed to find his feet.

Tam looked over at Bong, who was gaping at Kasha with his jaw dropped.

"Hi, Bong!" Luca hollered excitedly.

The Zinferan nobleman barely managed to tear his eyes away from Tam's familiar. "T-Tam? Luca?"

Tam offered to help Bong up next, and he accepted. Though Bong couldn't help but swivel his eyes back to Kasha. "W-What is… that?"

"Oh, you'll see."

Turning to stare up at the concubine, who was pressing her son behind her and inching back to the doors, Tam stalked forward.

"Concubine Soo Hebin!" he shouted. "You had me, Tamlin Ashowan, a future duke of Daxaria, hunted after an assassination attempt. You kidnapped *my son*, you attacked Her Majesty Queen Katarina Reyes, Duchess Annika

Ashowan, Princess Kezia Devark of Troivack, and her escort! You aided the escape of the first witch from Troivack!"

No one moved as Tam proceeded toward the stairs and started to climb toward the concubine, who was still backing toward the doors.

The smell of smoke was heavy in the air, and distant screams echoed.

Kasha leapt toward the sky, her wings cracking in the wind high above.

"Worst of all, you have been trafficking and selling your very own people! The people of Zinfera you are supposed to serve! The people who put food on your table, who lay down their lives for you, and you have ground them under your heel! Stolen children from their parents, stolen the goodness out of Zinfera!" Tam paused, a cold smile tugging at his mouth. "I would say you should pay for your crimes, but I don't think there will be anything left of you once you've paid for one particular crime." By this point Tam's arms were shaking after holding Luca for so long, so he put his son down on the stairs but kept a firm grasp of the boy's hand.

The concubine turned to the doors as soon as Luca touched the ground.

However, her path was blocked when Kasha landed between her and the doors, Prince Jum's hand clasped in the concubine's own.

The beast let out another roar that sent the concubine scrambling backward.

That is, until Kasha shifted back into her human form, and Eli stood in front of her.

Soo Hebin froze. "*You!*"

Eli strode forward, the red dress she'd donned dragging behind her as she stared into the concubine's eyes calmly.

"That's right. Me."

Eli continued moving closer, but the concubine didn't budge as she stared down her nose at the estranged princess.

Tam sidled up right behind Soo Hebin and her son to make sure they were properly cornered.

"I'd say your life is mine, Soo Hebin, for what you've cost me. But I don't need something as worthless as that," Eli informed the woman calmly.

Soo Hebin reached into her sleeves, as though preparing to draw a weapon out but Tam casually seized her forearm.

"No, no. None of that."

"FAMILY JEWELS!"

Both Tam and Eli jumped at the shout that came from Luca. Both then turned to discover that Luca, their sweet boy, had punched Prince Jum in the testicles.

"That's new," Eli observed suspiciously. "I'm beginning to think your sister was the one to teach her sons all of their bad habits."

"It might not have been Kat," Tam argued as though they weren't in the middle of overthrowing a concubine whom they had interrupted in the middle of a killing spree.

Eli arched an eyebrow. "*I* certainly didn't teach him that, and I know you didn't—"

A loud wailing of hinges and splintering wood called everyone's attention to the doors on the opposite end of the courtyard. Then Katarina Ashowan pushed the heavy barricade open with one hand.

Splattered with blood, both her eyes and aura glowing, Kat glared around the scene before her with her sword in hand. She looked ready to continue her utter decimation of what remained of the imperial soldiers.

Until she spotted Tam, Luca, and Eli at the top of the stairs.

They all stared at one another for a beat of silence.

"WHAT THE HELL?" Kat roared, throwing her arms out to her sides. "HOW'D *YOU* LOT GET IN?"

"We danced in!" Tam shouted back. "The front door was unlocked!"

Kat dropped her head back and let out an annoyed shout just as Harris ambled in behind her, a dreamy smile on his face.

"Alright, Harris?" Tam called while adjusting his grip on Soo Hebin's arm as the woman tried to yank herself free. Eli seized her other arm.

"This was my greatest work yet!" Harris cried. "I dedicate this burning to my wife, Mackenzie!" He pumped his fist in the air.

Kat sighed, then proceeded into the courtyard, eyeing the bodies darkly. As she passed their family friends, she spared a pat on the shoulder of the patriarch. "Jiho, nice to see you."

"Kat, good to see you in fine health."

The Daxarian queen grunted in response as she, too, climbed the stairs.

Eli moved her gaze back to Soo Hebin. "Kneel."

The concubine's scarlet lip curled. "You are not Chin. Even if you wear her dress—"

Eli slapped the woman across the face with enough force that blood pooled on the woman's lips.

"Of course I'm not Chin. I'm your judge. And the Daxarian queen? She might be your executioner."

"I'm the what now?" Katarina Ashowan approached the confrontation with her one free hand on her hip.

"Executioner. If I say so," Eli repeated evenly.

Kat scoffed, though there was a glint of amusement in her eyes. "Bossy little thing, aren't you?"

Tam gave a rueful half smile at this.

Eli didn't respond. She did, however, catch everyone off guard by slapping Soo Hebin again. This time hard enough that the woman did drop to a knee.

"Mother!" Jum cried out.

Luca raised his fist again with a menacing scowl.

Tam gave his son's arm a slight shake, barely suppressing a laugh as he gave Luca a look to keep him from further violence.

"Harris!" Tam suddenly called out, as though having come to a sudden realization.

"Still working on the stairs!"

"No—no, sorry. I meant it was Harris who taught Luca about the term *family jewels*. From his story," Tam reminded Eli.

"Ah, my apologies, Your Majesty." Eli nodded solemnly to Kat, who looked all the more bewildered.

There was another breath of silence before Eli slapped Soo Hebin again.

No one said anything as they took stock of Eli's tranquil face as the concubine gasped on the ground in pain.

Which was around the time Harris's panting breaths could be heard perfectly clearly as he approached them all. "What'd I miss?"

Eli paused thoughtfully. "Nothing. I was just about to inform Soo Hebin she is going to be stripped of her titles and forced into indentured servitude for the rest of her life. Prince Jum will be removed as a possible successor for the throne."

Though neither Soo Hebin nor Jum said anything, Eli abruptly added a slap for good measure across Soo Hebin's cheek, which was already showing signs of bruising.

"Feeling better?" Tam asked, wondering if he should cover Luca's eyes.

Nodding, Eli furrowed her brows then looked at Tam. "How many was that?"

"Four."

She tilted her head. "Let's see… Kidnapping royalty, enslaving me, and spreading slander about my reputation to the kingdom… ah yes. Kidnapping Luca." The next slap that Eli dealt to the concubine knocked the woman out.

Eli shook out her hand and then turned to Tam with the same casual air of someone who'd just swatted a mosquito. "Shall we go pick up Penelope?"

Tam bowed his head and offered his arm. "Let's."

"Hang on here!" Kat held up her hands, her sword hilt still clutched with her thumb. "Just what in the hell—"

"Kat, we really do need to go, but there are a lot of people here that look like they've been poisoned. You might be able to help them," Tam reminded her softly.

At this, Kat whirled around.

"Oh. And there is a dragon but try not to kill him. Harris likes him."

"Wixim is here? Oh lovely!" Harris smiled jovially.

"*I beg your finest pardon—*"

And that was all Kat was able to get out before that very dragon came down with a loud bang onto the ground of the courtyard, letting out a screeching roar of his own.

Kat flipped her sword into her hand, but when Eli shifted back into beast form, the queen stumbled back in shock. "WHAT THE *FUCK* IS HAPPENING RIGHT NOW?"

"Kat! Language!" Tam chided. "That's Eli. But she's a familiar right now, so you can call her Kasha."

The redhead's jaw dropped as the cat leapt nimbly over them and landed firmly in front of Wixim.

Thankfully, Jiho and Bong had already moved to the side of the courtyard to start tending to some of the poisoned nobility.

“Tam, you have a lot to tell me,” Kat called. “But first, please tell me that that dragon is a friend of yours.”

Tam gave a grimace and tilted his head. “I could, but I don’t know if that’s true.”

Kat shot him a look of incredulousness but was already jogging to the stairs when she shouted over her shoulder, “I think you have me officially beat on getting yourself into nonsense!”

Tam shrugged. “You’re not dead yet!”

Kat scoffed and continued down the rest of the stairs.

Things were not quite finished, but with any luck, this particular fight would be over quickly. At least with both Kat and Eli working together, Tam thought the odds of this were rather high.

CHAPTER 47

WHEN FAMILY FACES THEIR FOES

"*Where is she?*" Wixim's voice rumbled in Eli's head.

"*Who?*" she returned innocently.

Wixim snarled. "*Aradia. What did your witch do?*"

"Protected the devil. You already know my witch is powerful," Eli answered vaguely.

Wixim prowled around the courtyard, which was rapidly emptying of its humans.

"*Her human companion isn't going to rest until he finds her.*"

Eli started to join Wixim in circling the courtyard, leaving the Daxarian queen with her sword drawn just past them, her golden eyes tracking both their movements.

"*It's good to have goals. I'm sure she will appreciate how dedicated her companion is to the task,*" Eli retorted flippantly.

Wixim bared his long, pointed teeth. "*I will not let you leave without bringing the first witch back.*"

"I'm afraid that won't happen. We need to go retrieve our other child. The Daxarian queen here can continue this discussion *with you."*

The dragon's great head tilted, and his long neck twisted with him. *"Is Aradia being tortured?"*

At this question, Eli stopped moving and stared levelly at the dragon. The tension in the air was thicker than stone, but she ensured she answered with the proper amount of levity.

"She is not being tortured."

The ferocity behind Wixim's gleaming green eyes softened a little at this response. His attention slowly slid to Tam and Luca at the top of the palace stairs. Tam still held Luca's hand, and his dark gaze bore into the dragon's profile. Luca, meanwhile, was inching closer to his father nervously.

Eli watched as Wixim's scaled face twitched. He almost looked… confused.

"Hm. Interesting." The dragon turned back to Eli. *"I am going to keep you here, little one, until Aradia's human comes. You will have to deal with him."*

With her head drooping, Eli realized that there would be no talking their way out of the fight. *"I'm sorry it has to be this way, Wixim."*

"I am, too, little one. I hope we both survive to the end of this war so that we might become friends."

"I would like that as well."

Eli and Wixim shared a nod, then Wixim reared back on his hind legs and opened his mouth, heat and sparks rising in the back of his throat. Eli tensed, preparing to dart out of the way, when a blazing figure launched itself off the ground and landed on Wixim.

The Daxarian queen's sword was pressed against Wixim's throat. Katarina was as bright as a small sun with her magical aura, her eyes filled with golden light, and her sword gleaming with red magical twinkling.

Eli's heart dropped. She knew deep in her bones that the Daxarian queen was perfectly capable of decapitating Wixim right then and there. She almost looked away. She didn't want to see the dragon's death.

But Wixim surprised everyone by fanning out his wings and launching both Kat and himself into the cold night air, forcing Kat to focus on keeping her grip around the dragon's throat.

Eli watched them as they soared across the sky, frozen with indecision. Would it be helpful to chase them? Or should she simply wait in the event the queen was thrown off and needed to be caught? Eli wasn't even certain if she could launch herself straight into the air as Wixim had; she still required more of a running start.

Her inner debate was interrupted as Wixim barrel-rolled in the air, then nose-dived toward the ground, the glowing queen still latched on his back.

"TAM! ELI!" Kat roared right as Wixim pulled up at the last second before crashing into the courtyard. "GET PENELOPE! I'LL HANDLE THIS SCALY BASTARD!"

Again, Eli hesitated. Was that really wise?

That said, the Daxarian queen had single-handedly taken on the majority of the imperial soldiers in the palace and didn't have a scratch on her.

I've heard she's practically an army all on her own, but she feels more like a beast than I am.

A warm hand on Eli's furry shoulder made her jolt. She relaxed when she saw that it was only Tam, with Luca already hoisted up in his arms. They must have moved through the void when she wasn't looking. "Let's go. Harris will stay behind with Kat."

Another roar from the skies above made them look back up. Wixim continued to try to dislodge Kat, but the woman seemed to have wrapped her entire body around the dragon's face—including his eyes—her sword still in hand.

Letting out a huff, Eli dipped her head in assent. Tam placed Luca on her back. She then lowered herself so Tam could climb on as well. It distantly occurred to her to feel bashful as she felt Tam's thighs grip her sides, but she flexed her claws and forced such thoughts from her mind before she charged toward the palace, then launched them into the cold air.

The wind whipped around her, and she felt Tam lean over her back, Luca's heart thrum against her spine; she could even hear him squealing and giggling in awe and delight.

The stars glinted above them, the full moon beamed; they were free.

While Eli was sad that Wixim would most likely be killed, she couldn't help but be happy to have Luca back safe. As for Concubine Soo Hebin and her son… well, Harris and the Ryu family would see to her punishment. Besides, Eli had gotten to do exactly what she had dreamed about doing during her darkest, most hopeless nights. She had slapped the woman into the ground and towered over her wearing Chin Taejo's iconic red dress. A dress that Chin had worn when she, too, had risen from the dirt of her poor circumstances.

Somehow, Eli knew that from the Forest of the Afterlife, Chin was watching, and she was proud.

★★★

Fin's left hand gripped his head while his right remained fisted. He sat at the council table, unable to hear anything over the ringing chaos in his mind.

Was Annika dying? He had seen her lying in his daughter's arms amid the rubble of a destroyed room.

She had been pale, disoriented… his wife, who was so formidable. Strong. Brilliant. But in that vision, she had looked like a limp doll.

His throat felt like it was closing.

"How can we even trust that the message was delivered properly? Let us just send a hawk the old-fashioned way without any interference. I know it will take longer, but—"

The sound of a fist slamming against the table at last pulled Fin from his terror ridden thoughts.

Eric was glowering at his council.

Keith Lee, who had been the one suggesting a follow-up message be sent, cowered. Captain Taylor stared at the king grimly. Morgan Linsey avoided eye contact. The former king, Norman Reyes, sat with his retired assistant, Mr. Howard, staring at Eric somberly. And the new chief of military—who had been appointed a week earlier, when Duchess Annika Ashowan's last concerning missive had been sent—Duchess Mackenzie Harris of the Iones dukedom, regarded the king with a raised chestnut eyebrow.

"We already sent them our response to the hostage situation," Eric rumbled. "We presumed they would not mistreat Her Majesty and Duchess Annika, but what Lord Finlay has reported to us is not in line with that assessment. The duchess is injured after an attack."

Mackenzie leaned forward, her bright, sea-glass-green eyes calm. "We only sent the response this morning. It won't arrive until this evening. There is most likely something else happening."

"More than likely it is something to do with the first witch. Or our queen may have…" Morgan Linsey trailed off when Eric's eyes cut to him.

Mr. Howard saved the king's poor assistant. "Your Majesty, it *is* possible the queen may have started a fight. Particularly if she discovered she was being held as a hostage."

"You don't think she knows?" Mage Keith Lee leaned forward with an eyebrow raised.

The duchess shook her head. "Telling the queen and duchess they are hostages would be the dumbest thing they could do. Her Majesty's temperament and propensity to be a problem when she wishes to be is well known," Mackenzie pointed out bluntly. "I imagine she'd be a lot more amenable to being a well-cared-for hostage if she had no idea it was occurring."

"Well, whatever has happened, we now know the queen and her mother are in danger," Eric reminded everyone darkly.

"Agreed." Mackenzie nodded and folded her hands atop the table. "At present, we cannot trust any coven member. Even if they say they had no idea about the hidden agenda of the Wittica and Giong leaders. We can't afford to trust anyone other than Lord Finlay Ashowan and the queen. We have told the covens that while we are happy to enter into negotiations, they are to release the queen and duchess before any sort of peaceful talks can occur. Otherwise we find ourselves at war with two covens, and most likely Zinfera," the noblewoman summarized tidily before cutting her gaze to Fin. "I am sorry, Your Grace, but you cannot leave Daxaria now. We must simply trust that your wife, your children, and my husband can find a way to return safely."

Fin felt his insides turn to ice. He didn't look away from Mackenzie. Nor could he bring himself to speak. Annika might be dying. It was beyond difficult to be reasonable.

However, he was saved trying to find an appropriate response by the unmistakable sound of a sniffle—one that clearly belonged to a child.

Everyone's heads snapped around.

Eric swung toward the rows of shelves and folded his arms. "Boys. Come out. Now."

Sure enough, the three young princes appeared, though not from the shelves. Rather, they appeared from three different locations. Asher was hidden behind a tall decorative vase, Charlie popped up from a chest that was normally used to store blankets, and Antony stepped out from behind a tapestry.

The trio of boys slowly drifted toward the table.

Asher was crying, while Antony sported deep lines under his eyes that no newly turned seven-year-old should have had, and Charlie was staring with his golden brows furrowed and his tiny hands curled in fists.

"You should not be here," Eric started, his tone firm, but less furious than when he'd been addressing the council.

"Is Grandma going to be okay?" Antony asked tightly.

Fin's heart constricted. He stared at his grandsons' faces wishing he could think of something comforting to say. "We are trying to find out what is happening with her."

"Our mother is a hostage?" Antony ventured next, with an audible hitch.

"She is, but she's fine right now. You know your mother is the strongest person in the world. Now, go to bed, and I will be up to talk to you all soon." As he spoke, Eric's mood continued to mellow as he stared at Antony's bright-blue eyes, shining with tears.

Asher burst out into fresh sobs.

At last Fin was able to react. He pushed himself to his feet then crouched and pulled all three boys to himself in a hug.

"I want Mama and Grandma home!" Asher gasped as he clutched his grandfather's coat sleeve.

Tears of his own welled up in Fin's eyes as he rested his cheek atop Charlie's head. He could feel the last of his grandsons start to tremble with barely contained emotion.

No one tried to hurry the princes or the duke as they embraced. Eventually, Fin heard Eric's footsteps round the table before he, too, knelt beside his sons and rested a hand on Antony's back. "I want them home, too."

Asher choked. Slowly, they all pulled apart.

By this time, Norman had also risen and made his way over. His hand gently brushed Asher's, only to snap it back in shock as a large black spider climbed over the back of his knuckles. "Gods!"

"CAREFUL!" Asher shouted as the spider leapt from the former king's hand to his own shoulder.

"Asher? What's this?" Eric asked, his gaze fixed keenly on the arachnid.

Fin was watching as well, and was already wondering if the massive thing was poisonous and how best to remove the spider from Asher's shoulder without causing the child any distress.

Then Antony spoke up. "It's his familiar."

The room fell so silent, they could have heard a drop of ink fall on parchment.

"What?" Eric stared at his eldest son dumbly.

"Asher wanted it to be a surprise for Ma when she came back, but… Asher's magic came out a week after mine," Antony explained tightly.

"What is your magic?" Eric's voice was quiet as he faced his youngest son.

Asher gently prodded the spider on his shoulder, but he kept his tearstained face turned to the floor.

"Bugs," Antony responded for his brother again. "He is friends with all the bugs and can give them things to do."

"Is that why I kept finding flies in my soup the past month?" Mage Keith Lee interrupted suddenly.

All emotional distress vanished from the children's faces as they pointedly avoided eye contact with all the adults.

Eric stifled a snort that came most likely out of a sense of relief that his children were not entirely changed.

"A weather witch and an insect witch…" Fin trailed off, his weary mind sifting through what he knew of mutated witches of the past. "There have been witches with those powers before. Usually they help farmers, but it is very important that both of you learn to control your powers, because you can disrupt ecosystems."

"Unfortunately, Your Grace, I don't believe now is the time to find a teacher for the princes. Prince Antony's last teacher has already left, and as we were just discussing, we can't exactly trust the coven," Mr. Howard put in from his seat.

At the reminder of the more serious issues at hand, Fin, Eric, and Norman all shared bleak looks.

But the interlude with his grandsons had helped pull Fin out of his spiraling fear, so he rose and gently touched the top of Charlie's head. Charlie's gaze was fixed on the ground, and Fin had a hunch that he may have been feeling a little left out by not having powers of his own. Eric would need to have a one-on-one chat with him soon.

"Everything will be alright, boys. We are all going to handle this, and we are going to figure out what is happening with your grandmother, but these are matters for the grown-ups to deal with. Could you please go upstairs and wait a bit? Your grandfathers and I will be up shortly," Eric said softly. While he addressed all three of his sons, he locked eyes at the end with Antony, who was still staring stoically at his father.

Asher murmured something to his spider familiar and turned to leave, with Charlie following closely behind.

Antony waited, his mouth twisting as he struggled to risk disobeying his father and asking his next question.

"Is Uncle Tam okay?"

At this, everyone in the room balked.

The last they had heard about Tam was that the concubine was telling the Zinferan public that he was dead, but Annika had assured Fin in her missive that this was not the case. Fin already knew it as well. He would've felt something if that horrible event had come to pass.

That said, he didn't know where Tam was, and he felt fresh guilt over not worrying more about his son.

"I don't know where your Uncle Tam is, Antony, I'm sorry," Eric said truthfully. "But I have a hunch that he might already be trying to help your mother and grandmother. After all…" He raised his gaze to Fin, a steady knowingness filling the space between them. "Tam is an Ashowan, and there is nothing he wouldn't do for his family. So if I were to guess? I think we're going to hear something about him very soon."

Fin gave a slow nod. He knew Eric was trying to comfort both his son and himself, and he sincerely wished the king was right. Though he did also send an additional silent prayer to the Goddess, hoping with all his might that in the next message they received he'd find out that every single one of his family members was safe and sound.

CHAPTER 48

POULTRY PROBLEMS

Kat landed with so much force that the stones cracked beneath her boots. The hand not holding a sword braced against the ground.

She was barely managing to stop her magic from overtaking all her senses as her battle with the dragon raged on. Tam and Eli had left a while ago, but she could not gauge how long it had been.

The dragon—Wixim, she'd heard—was clever at deflecting her attacks, but she could tell by the way his movements were slowing that he was starting to struggle as well.

Kat's attention snapped up to the ancient beast's face as he landed in front of her heavily, even more stones shattering beneath his claws. Then a whistle sounded, and his head turned toward it.

With a low growl, the dragon cast one final look at Katarina. She braced herself for the beast to open his mouth and attempt once again to burn her to a crisp, but he didn't.

Instead he launched itself into the air and flew away, leaving Kat almost completely alone in the courtyard that was ablaze thanks to both fiery blasts from the dragon during their fight, and her own efforts to burn the palace down.

Scanning the heated area, Kat noted that Harris stood atop the steps to the palace, his eyes fixed on something to the right.

Kat swung her gaze over and saw two water witches successfully dousing the flames. The witches appeared to be members of the Wittica Coven.

Briefly debating whether to knock them out for questioning later, Kat double-checked the skies to ensure the dragon wasn't returning. Once she had confirmed that he was not, she made her way up the stairs to Harris, where he was standing guard over the unconscious concubine and trembling Zinferan prince. Cracking her neck, she shot a blazing warning look at the prince as he gaped openly at Kat with her aura still burning brightly around her.

"So. Eli is a giant cat."

"Technically an ancient beast," Harris clarified matter-of-factly. "Oh, and your brother's familiar."

"Come again?" Kat swung around to stare at the duke, her aura dissipating instantly.

"You heard me." Harris sighed.

She vaguely recalled Tam referring to the winged cat as a familiar before he left, but hadn't properly processed it until now.

"And Luca mentioned that they are together?" Kat ventured slowly.

"That they are. They had a bit of a fight just before we got to Gondol, but from what I saw this evening, it seems as though they've made up."

"Huh."

"Eli is also my niece."

"Wh—Wait. Your half sister? Marigold Nam? That's her mother?"

"The one and only!"

Kat grimaced. Everything she'd heard about the Nam family had been absolutely awful.

"Anything else I should know?" she managed to ask.

"Your father made Tam promise not to get married without him there. But given how far Eli and Tam's relationship has progressed…" Harris trailed off. "They should probably get around to it soon, knowing your family's propensity for reproducing."

Kat's face scrunched up in disgust. "Too much information, Harris!"

"And you assume I, *her uncle,* wanted to know about it?" the duke asked dryly. The two of them watched as the water witches finally noticed Kat was no longer battling the dragon.

"Do you think I'll have to fight some more?"

Harris sighed again. "Well… they don't look happy; that's for certain." He made a quick scan of the courtyard. "Say, where did the Ryu family go?"

The water witches were just starting to climb the steps to the palace, their expressions dark. Kat tightened her grip on her sword when the massive doors behind them creaked open, making both her and the duke swing around.

They found themselves staring at an older man with a long white goatee that reached his chest, and gold and purple silk robes. He was being pushed in a wheelchair by none other than Jiho Ryu, and at his side… was Annika Ashowan.

"Mum! What're you doing here?" Kat rushed over to her mother, ignoring the witches who froze on the palace steps, their eyes wide.

The duchess gave a slight smile; her face still pale from the attack earlier. "I had to come. I'd promised His Excellency I would be here. Princess Kezia is being tended to by the physician as we speak. Sir Cas has received some stitches and is concussed, but otherwise fine."

Kat nodded grimly. Then the first part of her mother's words registered, and her attention dropped to the older man in the wheelchair.

"Your Excellency." She bowed.

Once she straightened again, the Daxarian queen found that the emperor was looking over her shoulder at the smoldering remains of his back palace.

"Your Majesty," he responded with only a small incline of his head. "Is this a customary greeting in Daxaria that I'm unaware of? Burning down someone's home?"

Kat gave a polite smile, but her gaze was sharp. "Apologies for the destruction, Your Excellency. Your people have been committing some grave offences, and I don't like unfinished dealings hanging over my head."

Annika tilted her head and shot her daughter a warning look.

Kat cast one right back that said, *I sounded polite while saying it at least.*

The emperor's reaction was thoughtful silence. He lowered his gaze to Soo Hebin, who remained unconscious on the ground. Their son Prince Jum flung himself down beside his mother in a bow.

"Father! These heathens from Daxaria have—"

"Silence." The emperor's voice was soft, but his dark eyes glittered dangerously. He focused on another spot just past Harris and Kat. "The two of you will kneel and explain yourselves."

Kat glanced over her shoulder to see the water witches frowning, evidently unsure what to make of this sudden shift of events.

"Try anything funny and I'll cut your feet off," Kat informed them casually.

The two women jolted in alarm, glanced at each other, then drew closer to the emperor cautiously. Eventually they stopped before him, but didn't kneel.

The witch on the left with walnut-brown hair and deep-blue eyes clasped her hands and stared down the emperor, while her fellow witch, a blond woman with identical eyes, stood silently beside her. Kat was willing to bet coin that they were related.

"Emperor, we serve the first witch. The Covens of Giong and Wittica will be separating from the rule of the monarchs and will operate independently. If you do not agree to this—"

"Let's say I do," the emperor interrupted. His voice sounded light, but there was something predatory in the way he stared at the women.

The brown-haired water witch didn't catch this. "Then we look forward to a fruitful partnering in the near fu—"

"Oh no, no, my dear." The emperor waved a hand. "The instant that this separation is made official, then we are declaring war. Violent acts, instances of espionage, and a long list of other crimes have been committed. So wherever your coven leaders may be? You can go tell them this. The instant they separate from their respective kingdoms, every imperial soldier belonging to Zinfera will be pointed in their direction. Your Majesty?" The emperor looked up at Kat.

"Yes?"

"What do you think Daxaria's position will be once this happens?"

Kat made a show of rolling her eyes thoughtfully to the sky. "Let's see. There was the attempted murder of my brother, an attack on myself and my mother, my nephew and niece were abducted. Oh, and I'm sure the Troivackian king and queen will also take exception to their sister-in-law being injured and in dire condition right now as well. So… Can the covens fight against three kingdoms?"

The water witches exchanged solemn looks before the blond replied, "The Goddess will protect us. This is how it should be."

"She wanted you to go around supporting a concubine who enslaved people?" Kat snapped, her eyes homing in on the woman.

"Speaking of my concubine," the emperor interrupted while eyeing Soo Hebin, who remained on the ground. "What happened here?"

"Princess Elisara slapped her at least once or twice," Harris supplied casually. "She was within her rights in my estimation. She also declared the concubine's punishment for her many crimes. Soo Hebin is to endure slavery for the rest of her life, and her son has been removed as an heir to your throne."

The emperor's eyebrows rose up at this. For a moment, it was unclear whether or not he would take exception to a supposed punishment being decided without his say.

But then he smiled. "I am amenable to this sentence—I already had my own in mind, but it wasn't so different. Tell me. Where did my daughter, Elisara, go?"

"She went to retrieve the other child that was taken from her and my brother's care," Katarina supplied.

"Ah… Once she returns, I'll have what servants remain attend to her. She will be quite busy in the near future." The emperor settled farther back in his wheelchair, his hands lacing over his belly as his intense stare shifted back to the witches. They seemed to be having yet another silent conversation. "You two. Are there other witches remaining behind that I should be aware of?"

The water witches said nothing, but they did meet his eyes.

Harris jumped into the conversation then. "Why is it Elisara will be busy?"

The emperor lifted an eyebrow at the duke's interjection. "Because I plan on naming her the heir to the Zinferan throne."

Harris grimaced. "Oh, I… I can say with the utmost certainty she does not want that."

The emperor leaned forward in his seat, his expression hardening. "That will be between the princess and myself. You are that duke who is related to Lady Marigold Nam, aren't you?"

Harris inclined himself slightly in confirmation.

The emperor was just opening his mouth to reply when both the water witches moved in sync, arms extended. One aimed for the emperor, one at Annika Ashowan.

Kat had been waiting for something like this and instantly stood in the way of both of them—right in time to get blasted by two powerful jets of water that sent her aura flaring.

The two witches braced themselves as Kat allowed her aura to feed off the magical attack. The more magic was directed at her, the stronger she became as she pressed forward, sword in hand, until she reached the two witches and made good on her earlier threat. Both women collapsed in a heap on the ground with shrieks of pain.

Kat turned from them grimly, only to see another young Daxarian woman creeping up behind her mother.

"MU—"

The duchess swung around, a knife already in hand, making the mousy-looking woman squawk, throw up her hands, and...

The duchess was suddenly gone.

Kat moved in a blur of aura. She seized the young woman's throat and hoisted her up. "Where. Is. My. *MOTHER?*" she thundered.

The young woman gasped beneath her hold.

After a moment of nearly depriving the woman of every wisp of breath in her body, Kat dropped her in a heap on the ground.

"What a perfect time for us to meet again, Your Majesty."

Kat's eyes snapped up to find none other than the man named Ansar approaching her.

She hadn't seen him since her time in Troivack.

The man's eyes were darkened with hate as he proceeded down the hall to the small group. "You see, your brother, Tamlin Ashowan, made Aradia disappear. And I would very much like her back."

Kat lifted her sword, her tip aimed at Ansar's throat, stopping him in his tracks.

He held his hands up, but his expression remained steely. "If you manage to return the first witch, then I'd be happy to ask Henrietta here to return your mother to her true form."

Kat glowered. "True form? What the hell are you talking abo—"

A cluck cut her words off.

The Daxarian queen's eyes slid to the ground.

There was…

A chicken.

A chicken with a dome-shaped tuft of black feathers atop her head, and lean silky black feathers with some white spackling the rest of the way down.

No one said a word as the chicken clucked two more times and took a tentative step forward.

Kat's sword lowered as she turned to look at the young woman, who was gently prodding her bruised throat.

"Did you turn my mother into a chicken?"

The young woman nodded slowly.

Kat looked back at the chicken.

"Now if you—" Ansar started.

Kat held up a finger, silencing him. She kept staring at the chicken. "Ansar… I don't like you. And my mother being a chicken is a problem. However, I'm incredibly angry about the fact that I really want to laugh about this right now, and I know I shouldn't. Is my mother in any kind of pain? Does she have the mind of a… of a chicken?"

Ansar moved forward. "It does not matter. Now go retrieve your brother and—"

Kat used a backhand punch to hit Ansar in the family jewels without batting an eye. She faced Henrietta expectantly.

"Th-the duchess is still herself… and she's not in pain. She's just… She's just a chicken."

Kat bit down on her lip. A long, whining breath streamed out of her nose. "Can she…" The queen cleared her throat. "He said she can be turned back?"

Henrietta nodded slowly.

"Good. Good…" Kat nodded idly.

Harris joined the queen. He peered down at the duchess in her new form.

"I think your father might take exception to this."

"You think?" Kat rasped. "Tam's lover might *eat* her!"

"Much like your mother the chicken, Eli retains her mental faculties. She won't eat the duchess," Harris said with a dismissive wave.

Kat pressed the tip of her sword into the floor, her chin dropping to her chest as her eyes closed. Then, despite the fact that she knew this was a horrible development at the end of a particularly gruesome day…

She burst out laughing.

And despite her best efforts, she couldn't seem to bring herself to stop.

The chicken clucked angrily, but that did nothing to help the Daxarian queen stop even a little.

CHAPTER 49

THE SPOILATION OF A SHIP

The air was crisp over the Alcide Sea.

The skies were clear, the moon illuminated the world, and the winds favored the vessel that glided through the shimmering water.

By the bow of the ship stood Thomas Julian, staring mournfully at a child's back.

"Penelope, I said I'm sorry. You know I'm not going to hurt you."

"Why did you leave us?" she whispered without turning around.

"I had to go help the first witch with Mr. Ansar, and your mother wanted to take you to your grandmother's home!"

"Well, my mother is dead," Penelope spat bitterly. "And I like Tam and Eli. You should have just taken me back to them!"

"What… you don't like me anymore?" Thomas said, attempting to cajole her.

Penelope was quiet for a moment, then slowly turned back around. She stared up at Thomas. The lines under her eyes were deep, and the weariness that lay in her features made her seem old beyond her years.

"I like you, Uncle Thomas, but the first witch… that lady… she's going to just use me anytime she wants. And she was stupid and mean to Luca."

Thomas couldn't say anything really to that point, but he tried again regardless. "Things will work out, Penny. I promise. Worst-case scenario, you live with me for a while! You liked it when we shared that house for a couple years, right?"

Penelope scoffed glumly. "You don't want to live with me."

Perplexed, Thomas tilted his head. "Why wouldn't I want to live with you? I'm your uncle, aren't I?"

Penelope gnawed on her tongue briefly before deciding she may as well answer. "You always talk about your family back in Daxaria. You talk about seeing them again, but you never talk about taking me with you."

Thomas's stricken reaction made Penelope's eyes lower.

Blinking himself out of his stupor, Thomas knelt down, his rumpled tan coat fluttering in the wind. "Penelope… I never thought I'd see you again. I thought you were going away to live with your own family. I'm sorry if I hurt your feelings."

Penelope's mouth twisted. Then she mumbled something that Thomas couldn't quite hear.

"What was that, sorry?"

"I'm related to Tam. They *are* my family," Penelope repeated without looking up.

Thomas's eyebrows shot upward. "What? How?"

"My mother. She is Duchess Annika Ashowan's niece," Penelope clarified slowly.

Thomas Julian lowered himself to sit on his heels as he stared at her thoughtfully. "Wow. That's pretty incredible."

She nodded.

"Did you look into their future?" he asked.

She nodded again.

"And?" Thomas pressed gently.

Penelope's lips pursed.

Thomas smiled. "It's fine. You don't have to tell me. But… can I ask you a favor?"

Penelope tilted her head expectantly.

He reached out, gently clasping her hands in his own. "If something happens to me… can you tell the duchess or her children something?"

The two shared a private conversation as the ship continued sluicing through the waves, at least until the boat abruptly dipped more deeply in the water.

Once Thomas had steadied Penelope, he rose and turned to see if the winds were shifting, or if the captain was handing off the wheel…

But he didn't get the chance—he was quite abruptly grabbed, backed up, and pressed against the railing.

Reaching up, he tried to defend himself against the man with the black hair and dark eyes, but he didn't get the chance.

He was thrown overboard into the cold water.

Shortly after he resurfaced, he heard the shouts and screams of the crew on board, but he couldn't quite make out what was happening. He didn't see another ship around them, so how had someone snuck up on them?

Thomas continued treading water.

He knew he wouldn't be able to keep up with the ship, but there were witches on board. They'd sort out whatever had happened and come get him. He just hoped Penelope was alright.

Something brushed against Thomas's ankle in the water, making him flail. He squinted at the inky sea but could see nothing… until he noticed trails of water in the moonlight. Something ginormous was moving toward the ship, which was still heading north.

Panic seizing him, Thomas started swimming as quickly as he could toward the ship. He had a bad feeling he knew what was about to happen.

"You're alright?" Tam asked Penelope with a smile.

The little girl was staring up at him looking wildly annoyed.

Luca had his arms around her in a tight hug and was crying.

"I'm *fine*! Luca! Stop being a baby! Tam? Is Uncle Thomas okay?"

Tam straightened in surprise. "Uncle Thomas? You knew him?"

Penelope frowned and shoved Luca off herself. "Yes, I knew him! I didn't want to be taken, but I know him and he wouldn't have hurt me! I swear if you hurt him I'll—I'll—"

Tam dropped down to a knee and gently grasped her upper arms. "He's swimming right now. He's alive, and once we get off the ship, I'm sure they are going to go get him."

Penelope's angry expression eased back in relief, until a new realization dawned on her. "There are witches aboard! *You're* going to get hurt!"

Nodding sternly, Tam rose back up. "There are. Eli's distracting them, but we have to go. We have to get on her back and return to Zinfera. We should be able to get our own boat and head back to Daxaria tonight."

"Why aren't we just stealing this one?" Luca asked bluntly after wiping the tears from his face with the crook of his elbow.

Tam paused as he stared down at Luca blankly.

Right... We really need to engage in fewer illegal activities around the kids.

"We need to leave this ship for Penelope's uncle, remember? That way he won't freeze to dea—He'll have a place to sleep tonight." Tam caught himself quickly before saying something else that could concern Penelope.

All too aware of how urgent it was that they leave before things turned too violent, Tam set to ushering the children back down to the main deck.

Eli guarded the stairs to the bow, snarling at a Zinferan witch who had a fireball in her hand.

Tensing, Tam quickly said, "Start moving toward Eli. Call her name so she knows it's you two."

"Got it, Dad!" Luca hollered.

Giving a hasty smile to his son, Tam slipped back into the void and reappeared behind the fire witch. Grabbing her by the back of her silk dress, he launched her over the railing of the ship into the water.

A sudden gust of air slammed into Tam's side, making his eardrum ache and his vision spin as he was blown ten feet away from where he originally stood.

He looked up in time to see an air witch, her hand extended, her long black hair fluttering in the wind.

Eli—now Kasha—looked as though she was about to pounce at the woman, but Luca and Penelope's shouts halted her.

Tam blearily watched as Kasha darted to them, then lowered herself so that they could crawl on her back.

The air witch, seeing this, turned her attention to them.

Tam vanished back into the void, though his head was aching from the last attack.

He reappeared behind the air witch and attempted to haul her off the ship as well. She seemed to be expecting this, however, and shot another powerful blast backward, catching Tam in the gut. He was thrown brutally against the stairs that led to the stern.

Nausea swept over Tam as he felt the telltale signs of a rib fracture.

The air witch swung back around to face him, her hand coming up—presumably to choke the life out of him. Then the ship was suddenly pitched onto its side.

Tam was slammed into the railing, his head receiving another sharp crack. The air witch was thrown clear across the deck, and seawater sprayed over the entire vessel.

Fighting against the excruciating ache in his head, and clinging to the banister to hold himself steady, Tam squinted through the spindles of the railing to make sure Kasha and the kids were alright.

They weren't on deck.

Tam lifted his gaze, and relief caught his heart. They were airborne.

They were safe.

Struggling to steady his gaze, Tam tried to mark where he should reappear on Kasha, when a large tentacle exploded from the water and wrapped itself around the ship.

Shock rendered him immobile as, in an instant, yet another massive tentacle appeared and curled itself around the mast of the ship.

Pushing himself up unsteadily, Tam looked to the right to see a giant, glistening, yellow eye that was as wide as he was tall peering at him.

"Holy *shit*," Tam spluttered.

The creature snapped the mast like it was a twig.

Tam was scrambling backward up the stairs when a third tentacle appeared behind him—this one was covered in feathers.

A roar above Tam pulled his gaze up. Eli was over him!

Falling back into the void, Tam didn't try to line himself up with where Kasha would be flying but rather, pitched himself out of the thin air above where she was circling.

As Tam fell from high above the Alcide Sea, he could see the mind-boggling monstrosity that was crushing the ship beneath its tentacles, but he couldn't let himself get distracted again.

"KASHA!" he roared.

Like a magnet attracting its opposite, Kasha swept upward and Tam landed with an *oomph* on her back. A fresh wave of pain made him break out in a cold sweat as his rib protested the extra bashing.

Eli must have sensed how rigid he became, as she began to glide over the water, away from the destruction of the ship, without flapping her wings while Tam gasped for breath.

"UNCLE THOMAS!" Penelope shrieked out into the night air. "UNCLE THOMAS IS IN THE WATER WITH THAT THING!"

Tam, with shaking arms, slowly slid his body up Eli's back toward where Luca and Penelope sat.

"Penelope… I… I don't know that Kasha is strong enough to carry all of us all the way back to Zinfera!"

"PLEASE!" The little girl stared up at Tam as he managed to move himself into a seated position. Tears ran down her face as the wind whipped her hair into a snarled mess.

Tam gritted his teeth and scanned the water behind them.

He noticed several fireballs glinting by the wreckage as one of the fire witches attempted to ward off the ancient beast. Still in pain, he tried to think of a solution. There had to be a way to save the man Penelope cared about, but to go back would be putting them *all* at risk.

"Kasha, do you think we can do it?" Tam shouted over the wind.

Eli turned her head slightly in his direction. Then she let out a low, disheartened rumble before lowering her head.

"NO!" Penelope sobbed.

"We'll come back!" Tam called desperately. "We'll take you both back and come back for him! He just needs to swim away from the ship!"

"THE MONSTER WILL EAT HIM!" Penelope persisted.

"He might not! The monster seems to be busy with the ship and—"

A flash of gold caught Tam's eye in the distance as it dove through the air toward the sea beast. Squinting, he could make out the telling lines of a familiar dragon. Relief filled him.

"I think your uncle is going to be fine, Penelope! I see a friend of his is going to help him!"

Penelope, turning to see the help that Tam was describing, let out another horrified scream. "THAT'S ANOTHER ANIMAL THAT WILL EAT HIM!"

Tam reached forward and rested his hand on Penelope's shoulder. "No, he won't. That dragon is a friend of your uncle and the people aboard that ship. I promise!"

Penelope looked dubiously at him, but when she saw the sincerity in his eyes, she turned forward. "You better be right!"

Tam allowed his hand to drop away. The ache in his head made him struggle to stay conscious. At least if he fainted this time, it wouldn't be due to a depletion of magic. It would be entirely due to the head injury he'd just sustained.

Bracing himself, Tam still managed to call out one more time. "Kasha! We better hurry! I think Wixim is going to start searching for Penelope sooner rather than later!"

Eli's ears perked up. She began flapping her wings quickly, bringing them higher to find swifter air currents.

Tam rested his hands on her silky fur and continued to fight to stay in the realm of the waking. Though he did remember to thank the Gods that he'd managed to retrieve the children. He also sent up a new prayer that when they returned to Zinfera, Kat wasn't too angry about the dragon getting away from her.

At least he hoped that was what had happened…

Tam sincerely doubted that his sister would allow herself to be killed off by something she would most likely describe as a fancy-looking lizard.

CHAPTER 50

AN ASSEMBLY OF ALLIES

By the time Kasha landed on the docks of Gondol harbor, the throbbing in Tam's head was making his continuing effort to stay conscious feel like torture. As he dismounted, he noted the clumsy heaviness of his limbs, but he still set about helping Luca and Penelope off Kasha's back before she shifted back into her human form.

A quick glance at Eli's face told Tam she wasn't feeling her best, either.

Penelope sniffled at Tam's side, drawing his attention back down to her.

"It'll be alright," he managed, though speaking made the world spin.

Penelope looked up at him, hurt, anger, and weariness warring behind her dark eyes.

Eli's hand appeared on her shoulder. "We need to get moving. Wixim will return when he learns she is not there."

Tam would've nodded, but he was relatively certain he'd go unconscious.

"Should we go back to the palace?" he wondered aloud, his voice quiet with fatigue.

The sky was starting to lighten. Streaks of pink and pale blue were aglow on the horizon.

The air smelled of salt and fish. Boats bobbing on the water was the only sound in the morning air as Eli took a moment to reply.

Which was when they heard the commotion taking place farther down the docks.

Tam turned and stared dumbly. Farther down the dock, the braziers were lit, and a great many sailors were scurrying about near where the docks met the short span of road that led to the gates of Gondol.

"I guess they saw me land," Eli noted grimly.

Tam blinked.

Right. A giant flying cat was not the norm. He'd completely forgotten.

He reached up and rubbed his face.

"Are you alright?" Eli asked, concern tinging her voice.

"I hit my head pretty badly on the ship when that monster first attacked," Tam explained. He relished the moments when his eyes were closed.

"Are you concussed?"

"Most definitely."

Tam felt a small, warm hand grasp his own. His son peered up at him worriedly.

"I'll be fine, Luca. I just need to rest."

Regardless of the reassurance, Luca didn't let go of Tam's hand, and he was perfectly happy with that.

"Do you think they'll attack us?" Eli stared at the cluster of men off in the distance that were gesturing over to them and waving their arms rather frantically.

"Probably." Tam sighed and looked over his shoulder at Penelope, whom he realized was staring at Eli's hand thoughtfully.

Despite the raging pain behind his eyes, Tam smiled and glanced at Eli, who raised a confused eyebrow.

Tam nodded his chin in Penelope's direction and lifted Luca's hand a little bit to indicate what he was getting at.

Eli blinked down at the little girl then back up at Tam, puzzled.

Dropping his head back with a loud sigh that instantly reminded Tam of his nephew Asher, Luca then said aloud, "Penelope wants to hold your hand but she's too shy to ask!"

Stunned, Eli's gaze dropped to the little girl, who scowled at Luca. "No I don't! That's for babies like you!"

Luca stuck his tongue out at her.

Eli shot him a warning look that had Luca shrink into Tam's side. She then reached down and grasped Penelope's hand. Before the child could yank it back or argue, Eli said, "We need to stick together through whatever is happening over there."

Tam smiled at Penelope, then moved his sights over Eli's head. Beyond her was the end of the dock, which dropped off into the Alcide Sea. To their right was a rocky wall. Tam leaned backward, trying to spot its top, but found he couldn't.

He could appear in the air above the clifftop, and then, once he'd spotted the surface, vanish and reappear there. He was confident he still had enough magic to do it, though he might vomit if he experienced that falling sensation again.

"What is that?"

Eli's question drew Tam's attention back toward the sailors.

Tam squinted and spotted something small, dark, and low to the ground moving toward them, and it was moving quickly.

Caught off guard momentarily, Tam's eyebrows shot up as he belatedly remembered something his sister had said the previous night.

He gave a short laugh in disbelief as his shoulders relaxed. When he sensed Eli's quizzical look he said, "What? You don't recognize him?"

At this response, Eli turned back to the darting figure and tilted her head. Then realization filled her face.

"Isn't that a cat?" Luca asked curiously.

Tam started to walk forward, his free hand moving to his pocket. "It is. In fact, that is your grandfather's familiar. I'd forgotten he was coming here—oh. There's your aunt's familiar as well, Pina."

A flash of a feline white chest swiftly caught up to the fluffy dark cat, who slowed to a quick trot then sat down and peered up at Tam.

"Why hello, Kraken," Tam greeted with a grin. "It isn't like you to miss all the excitement."

The familiar gave him a slow blink as Pina joined his side. "I take it we'll be fine to approach the sailors now that you've made it clear you know us?"

Kraken once again blinked up at him. It seemed as much of an assurance as they were going to get.

"Pina, would you like to ride on my shoulder?" Tam offered, lowering himself.

Kat's familiar was known for enjoying resting on people's shoulders as they moved about their day.

However, the pretty muted calico didn't move. Her green eyes instead locked on Luca.

"Ah. Right. This is my son, Luca, and that over there is Penelope," Tam introduced.

He was grateful that he couldn't understand the cats.

Both Pina and Kraken continued staring at Luca. After a moment they both turned and proceeded back up the dock.

"I don't think they like me," Luca declared sadly.

"That isn't it; don't worry," Tam consoled as they all followed the cats.

In truth, Tam wasn't exactly sure why both familiars had had such a reaction. He silently worried that they already knew Luca was the devil.

His frets were interrupted, however, by a fresh stab of pain to his head. He needed to lie down. Hopefully Wixim wouldn't return anytime soon.

Eventually the group made it to the sailors, who had all backed away nervously from Tam's path, their silence only emphasizing the fearful air around them as they watched the small group walk by. Once they stepped off the dock and were back on Zinferan land, they found a lavish carriage waiting for them with its door open. Kat and Harris leaned against it. Kat's arms were crossed and her expression was serious. Something was wrong.

But apparently not wanting to alarm the kids, all the Daxarian queen called out to say was, "Took you lot long enough!"

Harris smiled down at Luca and Penelope. "Why, hello again! Glad to see you are well!"

Luca released Tam's hand and bolted over to the duke and queen, throwing his arms around both of their legs. Kat reached down and patted Luca's head.

Tam felt relief ease the residual tension from his body. At least if Wixim returned, Kat could protect the kids.

Kraken and Pina leapt into the carriage. Kat lifted an eyebrow at the familiars. "Jeez, Kraken. You must be getting old. You missed the dragon."

An indignant meow sounded behind them as Eli handed Penelope into the carriage, then Luca.

"When did Kraken and Pina arrive?" Tam asked conversationally while rubbing his face in an effort to stave off the urge to be sick.

"You look like shit," Kat observed rather than answering his question.

Tam waved off her words. "Concussion."

"You only have a concussion and you look this terrible? Wow. Now I *know* Mum went easier on you than she did on me growing up," she grumbled.

"Kat, I'd like to sleep soon. Is something wrong?" Tam ignored her insult and folded his arms as Eli stood at his side silently.

"Yeah… We have a, uh, small problem." Kat cleared her throat.

Tam tilted his head. Why did it suddenly look like his sister was trying not to laugh?

Even Harris looked to the sky with an innocent wheeze.

"Mum's a chicken."

Tam stared at her blankly. "This concussion might've done some kind of serious damage." He turned to Eli. "I think I need a physician."

"I believe I heard the same thing," Eli declared, her eyes fixed on the Daxarian queen, whose leg was starting to vibrate and her mouth purse.

"You both heard me just fine, Tam. Mum's a chicken. There is a mutated Daxarian witch here who is helping Aradia's assistant, Ansar, and, well… Mum came to the palace to wheel out the emperor—who is awake and of sound mind now, by the way—and she got turned into a chicken." There was a laugh in Kat's voice, though she visibly continued to battle it back. "This Ansar arse is refusing to order the witch to turn her back until you retrieve the first witch."

Tam continued to gape at his sister, then at Harris.

He genuinely couldn't tell if this was a prank or not.

The Daxarian queen sighed then gestured to the carriage. "Come see if you want. Oh, and Eli?"

Eli faced Kat expectantly.

"The emperor has officially named you his heir."

Tam's jaw dropped, and Eli's eyes went round with horror.

"Oh, I know. We tried to tell him you wouldn't like that, but you're going to have to tell him yourself. Now come on." Kat waved again toward the open carriage. "We still have a lot of work to do."

As it turned out, Tam wasn't able to stay awake during the rest of the ride. He fell into dreamless darkness the instant the carriage started moving.

It wasn't until it had pulled to a stop and Eli gently shook him awake that his eyes flew open again. The headache had lessened in intensity a little, but it still lurked unpleasantly at the back of his forehead.

Upon stepping down from the carriage, Tam noted that the front of the palace still remained unaffected by the fire, though the smell of smoke clung heavily to the early morning air.

As Harris guided the children into the palace, Tam leaned over to his sister. He was surprised to find that she was already staring at him. There was a sort of expectancy behind her golden eyes, but also a large amount of calculation.

Tam gestured Eli forward. Her gaze darted to the Daxarian queen before she nodded in understanding, then ventured up out of earshot, though she halted outside of the doors to the palace. Presumably to wait for him.

"I'm surprised you haven't already killed Ansar," Tam mused as the carriage pulled away.

"Pretty sure that if I kill him, the chicken witch is going to double down against changing back Mum."

"Would killing the chicken witch lift her spell?"

"Maybe. I don't exactly want to gamble on that." Kat sighed.

Tam nodded in understanding, then continued to wait in silence.

He watched as his sister stared him up and down a few times, then eventually crossed her arms over her chest.

Tam lifted an eyebrow expectantly. "Will you just say it already?"

"Say what?" Kat lifted her chin defiantly.

"Whatever it is you want to say."

"There's a lot I want to say." Her eyes narrowed for a moment.

Tam rolled from his heels to his toes, repeating the movement as he continued waiting for Kat.

It didn't usually take this long.

"What did you do to the first witch?"

Tam stopped rocking. "I left her somewhere dark and inconvenient to escape."

Kat frowned. "I need to actually know the answer, Tam."

Tam leveled her with a serious look. "I put her in a void of nothing. A void that sort of exists in the palace."

Alarm filled Kat's face. "What? How?"

Tam shrugged before saying, "It exists everywhere. Between everything. It is everything and nothing. It's the void."

Annoyance riddled Kat's brows. "Did you start taking drugs recently?"

"I *am* concussed. But no. It's my magic. I can go to a nothing place, and I can take people with me if I'm touching them."

Kat blinked as she fell into stunned quiet. "Take me there."

Tam looked over at the palace doors. "Don't we have to go deal with Mum being a chicken?"

"She isn't going to become more of a chicken if she waits a bit."

Tam grimaced. He wasn't exactly in the mood, nor did he have the energy to start getting into his magic.

"You're different," Kat announced suddenly.

Tam let a wry smile lift half his mouth. "Oh?"

She smacked his chest with the back of her hand. "Don't *Oh* me! You met and talked to a dragon! You have a giant-ass familiar who can fly—will she let me go for a ride sometime?" Kat interrupted herself, her eyes glinting with excitement.

"She barely lets *me* ride her."

Kat's shoulders drooped before she continued talking. "Anyway. I think I also forgot to mention, oh yeah. *You have a kid!* And Penelope seems to think you're adopting her, too! You left Daxaria childless! What the hell?"

Tam cleared his throat and squinted at something obscure in the distance. "I had someone I was seeing years ago, and, uh… she sent Luca to find me when I was aboard the ship. So he stowed away."

Kat gaped. "I thought you were a virgin!"

Tam gave her a flat look. "Why in the world would I tell you anything about that kind of thing?"

"Well, I… Ugh. You're right. I don't like knowing this." Kat shuddered.

"Did Mum like Luca?" Tam ventured on, trying to sound casual, but in reality was a little nervous.

"Of course she does. He's a sweetheart. But you do know, Tam, that he might be—"

Tam held up a hand. "He's not the devil."

Kat gave him a hard look. It was almost as though she knew he wasn't telling the whole truth. But she must've recognized that he wasn't going to tell her whatever it was he was keeping from her, because she changed the topic and started to trudge up the steps to the palace.

"So… Eli as empress…"

"She's going to pass on the crown."

"But just think! The Ashowan family ruling half the continents!"

"What are you talking about? Kraken rules everything."

Speaking of the fluffy familiar, Kraken and Pina sat atop the palace steps next to Eli, waiting for the siblings to join them.

Kat opened her mouth, about to say something else that was jesting or ridiculous, when Tam halted abruptly. "Kat, there's something else. Did you hear about the monster attacking the ships?"

Caught off guard by the new conversation, she nodded. "Wasn't that just that dragon Wixim?"

"It attacked the ship we rescued Penelope from. It wasn't a dragon. It was…" Tam trailed off and stared up at his father's familiar with his magnificent chest fluff blowing in the wind.

"It was a kraken. An honest to Gods kraken. Tentacles and everything."

Kat balked and continued to do so for a long, long while, until eventually bursting out with, "Great! You know a dragon *and* have seen a kraken! My kids are going to absolutely listen to you over me until we die!"

Tam grinned. "They already do. Now, come on. I still don't fully believe you that Mum's a chicken."

CHAPTER 51

THE VALUES OF THE VOID

"Bok."

"Hrr?"

"BokAAAA!"

"Me-ow?"

"Bokbok."

Tam sat watching the very intense exchange between Kraken and his mother, who was, indeed, a chicken.

Kat stood with her hands on her hips, Pina perched happily on her shoulder, occasionally nuzzling her witch's hair affectionately.

"I wish we could understand what they are saying," Tam said with a sigh while shifting Luca in his arms.

The poor boy had been up all night. Once they were shown into a receiving room to wait for the emperor—who apparently was taking a much-needed bath—Luca's eyelids had drooped, and his body began to sway on the chair he sat upon. Tam had gently lifted him into his own lap and rested the boy's head against his chest. "Sleep," he'd murmured to his son, dropping a quick kiss over his head.

Luca obliged in a near instant.

Even Penelope was struggling to stay awake in her chair on Tam's other side.

Eli eyed the little girl, then gave a slight smile as she reached over and stroked her hair.

Meanwhile, across the long dark wood table from where Tam and Eli sat, stood Kat. At the head of the table was the duchess-turned-chicken, and beside her, Kraken.

"Eli, do you think in your beast form you'd be able to understand them?" Kat wondered.

"Possibly. It's a bit small in here for me to change, though."

"You *are* huge."

Eli gave an uncertain frown in response to the queen's note, as though she suspected she was being teased.

Tam grinned. "Mum?" he called out, his attention moving to the chicken with the dome of feathers around her head fluttering about. "We're going to try getting Eli to talk to you." He then raised an eyebrow at his sister. "Where is the witch who turned Mum into a chicken, by the way? Or Ansar?"

"Both of them are waiting in separate locked rooms," Kat explained.

A particularly loud snore echoed from Harris, who sat with his head resting on the back of his chair by himself on the other end of the table.

"How are they being guarded?" Tam leaned forward in concern.

"There are Zinferan soldiers, but I doubt Ansar or the witch will do anything until they talk to you and find out where the first witch is so they can bring her back."

Tam made an agitated noise and resettled in his chair. "I'm relatively certain that if we just bring Mum home, Da could change her back."

Kat's mouth twisted thoughtfully. "That makes sense. Though… You know Mum is going to be raging mad if we leave her as a chicken for the entire trip back to Daxaria, right?"

"BOK!"

Everyone turned to the chicken, who hopped up on the table and strutted over to stand in front of Kat.

"I don't know. I think keeping the first witch far away is much more important. We'll just take the chicken witch and Ansar back to Daxaria and go from there." Tam shrugged.

Kat's eyes snapped up to his. "Mm-hm. And what about the D-E-V-I-L?"

"Why is it no one thinks Luca can spell?" Tam put the question to Eli, who shook her head in equal exasperation. When Tam looked back at his sister, his expression turned serious. "I'm serious, Kat; Luca isn't dangerous."

His sister let out a long breath, her hand wrapped around the hilt of her sword out of habit. "Alright. So we take Ansar and the chicken witch back to Daxaria. What makes you think she won't turn you into a rooster?"

Tam pondered this. "Maybe she has to be touching the person to turn them into a chicken. Or maybe she has to see them. We can take precautions that way."

Kat grumbled. "I want to hear what Mum has to say. Can we please go outside so they can have a discussion? I want to go out there anyway to wait for the carriage bringing Kezia and Sir Cas back."

Tam yawned. "Can we do this after some rest? Even that Ansar guy and Henrietta don't need to—"

A bell clanged.

Without even needing to ask, Tam closed his eyes as weariness soared through him. "Wixim came back. I knew it."

Kat turned to the door, her shoulders already straightened. "Godsdamn lizard."

"Will Uncle Thomas be with him?" Penelope asked earnestly, sitting up straighter.

Tam glanced over at her, uneasiness and guilt brewing in his gut. "Someone can go take a look to see, but… Penelope, they are going to try and take you away again."

The clanging of the bell grew more frantic.

Penelope paused, her excitement dwindling as this realization visibly settled on her.

Seeing this, Tam knew what he had to do… But his stomach clenched at the thought of it.

Turning as much as was possible in his seat with Luca still sound asleep in his arms, Tam stared levelly at the little girl. "Penelope, if you want to go with them, you can."

"Whoa, wait—" Kat started. One sharp look from Tam cut her off.

By this point Harris was gradually waking up and looking around himself bewildered before rubbing the drool off the corner of his mouth.

"Penelope, it is your choice. Regardless of your status as a seer, we are not keeping you prisoner. I took you from your Uncle Thomas not realizing he was someone you knew and cared about."

"He's still wanted for treason, Tam," Kat contributed darkly. "Likon has been serving a seven-year sentence because of him."

Tam didn't bother responding to Kat's point, and just kept his eyes locked on Penelope.

She stared back at him for a long time.

Then she held out her hand to him.

At first Tam thought Penelope was saying they'd stay together… But then he realized she was asking for something else.

He gave her his hand, and the instant her slender fingers grasped them, he felt a pressure around him building.

His magic was reacting to whatever it was Penelope was doing. Even though she looked perfectly normal, Tam had to start fighting against his power filling his eyes with blackness or drawing him back into the void.

The moment went on… and on…

Until Tam was starting to worry that he would fall unconscious again, but just as soon as it started, it stopped.

Penelope stared up at him with wide, hopeful eyes.

She looked awed. Almost excited…

She glanced over at Eli and raised an eyebrow before giggling; only her giggle sounded closer to a cackle. It made Eli's eyes narrow in suspicion.

"I think I'd better stay with all of you," Penelope announced matter-of-factly while easing back in her seat, her shoulders wiggling happily.

"Do you think you might share with us what you saw?" Tam asked, biting back a laugh as his hand returned to his lap.

"Nope!" Penelope said with a grin.

"Alright. As interesting as this discussion is, do you hear that bell? Dragon!" Kat gently put Pina down on the table and stalked over to the door.

Only she wasn't the first one to reach it.

Kraken bolted through the doors the instant she opened them, his fluffy haunches disappearing around the bend as he headed in the direction of the courtyard, still in shambles after the previous night.

Exchanging a look, both Tam and Eli rose from their seats. Tam adjusted Luca in his arms as he did so, but the boy was dead to the world.

Penelope hurried forward and grasped Tam's hand, surprising just about everyone in the room.

Harris smiled at the family as he stretched while rising to his feet. "I think your father's familiar was a little upset he didn't get to be a part of the fight last night."

"BoKA!"

The Daxarian duke's attention fell to the chicken-duchess, and without pausing to think about it, he plucked her up. "Yes, yes, I'll take you along, too. I must say, Your Grace, we should see about getting you some feed. Your husband would think you're far too skinny. Though I suppose that might be for the better. Wouldn't want him turning you into dinn—OUCH!" The chicken had smartly jabbed her beak into Harris's hand. "Alright, alright! Sorry!"

The duke left the room, leaving behind Tam, Eli, the children, and Pina—who was slowly sauntering toward the door.

"Maybe Pina can convince Wixim to join us by being cute. She's done it with other ancient beasts," Tam speculated as they all moved out of the throne room.

"I'm doubtful of that," Eli contributed candidly.

Tam shrugged. "No harm in trying."

"He might eat her," she reasoned.

Tam guffawed. "Even if he doesn't switch sides, look at her. You really think anyone or anything could eat Pina?"

Tam watched as Eli's eyes drifted down to the familiar. Evidently understanding the conversation, she widened her pupils and craned her freckled nose up toward Eli. A soft purr sounded.

Momentarily stunned, Eli said nothing, then cleared her throat and snapped herself free from the trance. "Fair enough."

Smiling, Tam continued to exit the room. He wondered if they were in fact going to have to resume fighting with Wixim, or if somehow they could come to a solution that didn't involve having to continue battling well into the new day. He really wanted a nap, and he didn't doubt that every one of his family members—save for Kat and maybe his chicken mother—felt the same.

"HELLO!" Aradia hollered.

She listened to the way her shout echoed.

She made a noise of frustration then dropped her forehead to her hand.

Should she drink a vial of the water from the Goddess's Pool?

"Tamlin Ashowan… just what are you?" she muttered as she looked around the space and started to walk again.

In a way the dark solitude reminded her a little of the Grove of Sorrows her parents had allowed her to experience before coming to earth. Only she wasn't plagued by memories of her misdeeds.

Aradia halted abruptly and sat down.

A place of silence and darkness.

It could be restful depending on the occupant's state of mind.

Still.

Had her brother possessed a power like this? It would make sense in a way if he had, and she had simply never known about it. A place where he could hide… a place of darkness that perhaps he crafted all on his own.

"But Tamlin Ashowan was alive and well when my brother was alive in Troivack." Aradia's mind strained against the confines of what knowledge she had about the troubled Ashowan son.

Sighing, she closed her eyes and tried to concentrate on her senses.

What could she smell?

Nothing aside from the perfume and scented oils she used.

What could she feel? The ground and the clothes covering her. But the ground was cold and firm. It wasn't soft. It was like glass.

What could she hear? Nothing. Only her own heartbeat when she focused on it.

"Why hello, child. It has been quite some time."

Aradia's eyes snapped open.

She looked up into the weathered face of a peasant man with ethereal blue eyes and a familiar smile.

"Carriage driver!" Aradia's mouth opened in shock.

She had not seen him in a millennia.

Coming to her feet, Aradia pulled him into an embrace, tears dampening her eyes as she met the being she had longed to greet for many, many years.

She pulled away, cupped his face in her hands, disbelief still making her thoughts a jumble.

"How? Did the Ashowan boy finally kill me?" she asked, emotion seizing her throat.

She had more to do in the world… But to go home? Even for a little while?

Gods, she wanted to.

She wanted to go so badly.

She wanted to feel love again. She wanted to feel her parents' embrace. To hear the words of the Goddess soothe away the centuries of torture and pain she had endured because of her brother.

"He didn't kill you," Death answered softly, his gaze gentle. "Though your outer appearance will change if he keeps you in here long enough to starve, forcing you to regenerate."

"Where am I?" Aradia stepped back but continued to hold the warm wrinkled hands of her family friend.

Death smiled fondly. "You are in a space that exists within all matter."

Aradia's eyes widened, and she could feel the blood drain from her face. "What? You mean to tell me that a mere mortal has the power to command such a place? Wouldn't that mean he can manipulate the fabric of creation? That… that would practically make him a God!" she sputtered.

Death tilted his head, his expression remaining the same, unbothered by her speculation.

"All mortal power has limits, Aradia. Your parents made it so."

"Yes, but they also made witches with only four elements. A fire witch had a natural balance in existence with a water witch, and so on. Then suddenly, my parents changed the natural order of things with mutated witches!" she pointed out seriously.

Death said nothing.

"The world is a mess. I'm trying to fix it before traveling with you back to the Forest of the Afterlife along with my brother."

Death's wiry gray eyebrows rose. "Why do you think your parents never intervened in the feud between their children?"

Aradia stilled. She had forgotten how Death seldom liked to give straight answers.

"Because it is our duty to do our jobs to the best of our ability. I can still do better. They are giving me and the devil a chance. But he isn't improving, and he is making the world worse."

"He isn't doing better?" Death mused airily.

A line creased the space between Aradia's eyebrows.

She thought back to the boy she'd abducted. She thought about how innocent he was, and how well taken care of. Loved. Not feared. How she could tell he was happy with his father.

But if it was Tamlin Ashowan who was the devil…

He was known for aiding his mother in her underground work on behalf of the Daxarian crown.

That was a role her brother would certainly have taken on.

But Tamlin Ashowan was avoiding people and trying to keep this supposed family together. That wasn't like her brother at all.

Unless of course this was exactly the change Death was referencing.

"Am I supposed to simply give up? The witches are not living up to the tasks assigned by the Gods! They were almost completely erased off the face of Troivack! They—"

"There are many answers you are missing. But you will figure them out in time."

Aradia wanted to snap at Death. She wanted to tell him of all the pain she had endured while trying to fulfill her parents' tasks and meet their expectations, about how her brother and the world had only buried her in suffering over and over…

"Can you help me get out of this void?" she asked instead, barely masking her frustration.

Death inclined his head to her. "I can. But wait here a little first, and rest. You are tired, Aradia. You can return to the world and finish your purpose there, but time has chiseled sharp edges that cut you more than any other being."

Aradia opened her mouth to say she didn't have the luxury of time to wait, but time most likely moved differently here. And while she knew a great deal of things, she also knew Death had his own wisdom that would be foolish to ignore. Even if it was aggravating as hell at present.

With a long breath out that carried all her tension and stress, Aradia did as Death bade and sat back down on the ground. By the time she looked up again, Death was gone.

With nothing else to do but what he recommended, Aradia stretched herself out and stared up into the abyss.

Eventually, she felt her eyelids grow heavy, and the weight of her goals ebbed away as well.

In a way, this place where she knew she wasn't about to be stabbed, imprisoned, or tortured brought with it a peace and safety Aradia hadn't felt in years. So it wasn't all that surprising that she managed to fall into a deep, dreamless sleep.

The fate of the world would have to wait.

But not for long.

CHAPTER 52

A ROARING RESOLVE

Standing in a line on the bottom step leading up to the palace were Eli, Penelope, Luca, Tam holding his son's hand, Kat, Harris, Annika the chicken, and Kraken.

Below sat Wixim and Thomas Julian along with a handful of waterlogged witches all with chattering teeth.

Eli took a fortifying breath, stepped down, and slowly strode over to Wixim. The two stared at each other for a while before Eli lowered her chin and once again shifted into her beast form.

"*Hello again, little one*," Wixim greeted her with a growl.

"*Hello*," Kasha returned with a polite incline of her head.

"*I have come for the first witch and her companions*," Wixim rumbled.

Kasha shook her head. "*Nothing has changed, Wixim. We will not loose Aradia to wreak havoc, and her companions have turned Duchess Ashowan into a chicken. So we aren't going to be releasing Ansar and the chicken witch until that is fixed.*"

This new bit of information about Annika Ashowan made Wixim pause, his gleaming green eyes swiveling around Kasha to the black-and-white chicken that bobbed its head and clucked indignantly at him.

A stuttering choke sounded from Wixim that hinted at a laugh.

Kasha gave a loud huff out of her nose. She did not want the conversation dragging on. "*The Daxarian queen does not tire. Aradia's followers are exhausted. You cannot leave with all of them. You cannot protect all of them, either, should we resume fighting.*"

Wixim's long head wove forward, his lips curling to reveal his long fangs, when a throat clearing interrupted them.

Both Kasha and Wixim looked down to see that Kraken had somehow approached without either of them noticing.

He sat primly, gazing up at the dragon with an air of boredom.

"*I am Empurror Kraken,*" the fluffy feline announced.

Kasha was unable to mask her shock at hearing the black cat's voice.

His meows had always been chirps and squeaks; to hear his deep regal tones was a dramatic difference.

Kraken glanced up at her and then he, too, jolted to his feet in surprise.

"*Good Gods! It's like looking in a mirror!*"

Kasha was vaguely aware that the flat look she gave Kraken was identical to one Wixim gave the smaller familiar.

Recovering her senses quickly, Kasha responded, "*It is good to finally converse with you, Kraken.*"

Kraken sat back down, a quiet purr emanating from him.

"*You are the familiar to the house witch?*" Wixim called out.

The fluffy cat slowly blinked. "*That I am.*"

"*The one who was responsible for the death of the red dragon named Paiste?*" Wixim lifted his head and chest, expanding his presence.

Kraken watched, unbothered. "*Yes, I am.*"

Fury flashed through Wixim's eyes.

"*I protected my witch and a kingdom, as the Goddess would have expected. Someone as old as you should recognize how great my accomplishment is,*" Kraken declared flippantly.

Wixim's eyes narrowed, but he said nothing more on the matter.

Kasha's attention shifted back to the small group of shivering people. "*We can give you and these witches a head start, and we will not fight you or follow you for three days.*"

Wixim's gaze flicked back to her, the air around him starting to simmer. "*You will free Aradia, return the seer, and release the other companions first.*"

Kraken scoffed. "*We have the upper paw, you dumb lizard. Take what this magnificent creature offers you. I would not be as kind.*"

Wixim lowered his head until his nose almost touched Kraken's. "*I can eat you in a single bite, and while the Daxarian queen may be able to battle me, my flames will reach far.*"

Every muscle in Kasha's body tensed. It was starting to look like they wouldn't be able to get out of fighting.

Kraken yawned in the dragon's face, his breath making Wixim's nostrils flare. "*Your first witch will lose just about everyone left who follows her here. Your own life included. We offer you a mere chance of survival. Oh, and you and I both know the first witch will earn a hefty punishment from the Gods if a familiar is directly killed by anyone aligned with her.*"

Kasha's head snapped around. What was that about familiars not being allowed to be harmed?

She watched as Wixim twitched… almost as though he was hiding a flinch.

"*You forget, or you have scales for brains. I can freely roam the Forest of the Afterlife. I already know the divine laws.*" Kraken plucked up his paw and began loudly cleaning between his toe beans.

Kasha looked back and forth between Wixim and Kraken, at an utter loss.

Wixim's voice rumbled. "*The divine laws have already changed. Most witches are not even wielding pure elements—*"

"*Those are laws the Gods themselves have bent. Do you really think you have that kind of authority?*" Kraken asked wryly.

Wixim fell silent, and Kasha felt her mouth drop open.

She had heard that Kraken was fearsome and impressive, but really it had been hard to see or think of him as anything but a fluffy cat. Truthfully, she had secretly suspected that Duke Finlay Ashowan had merely used his familiar as a cute shield for his own machinations…

She was not too proud to admit that this assumption was completely wrong.

"I will take Ansar and anyone else that follows Aradia, and we will leave," Wixim declared.

"You will leave the chicken witch unless she agrees to return the Duchess Ashowan to her former state," Kraken persisted crisply.

Wixim shook out his wings with a disgruntled snap. *"Bring them."*

"Not until I have your promise." Kraken slowly rose then sauntered over to stand in front of Kasha, his fluffy tail swishing back and forth.

Wixim snarled. *"I can still burn this palace to the ground."*

"And the Daxarian queen can still cut your throat. Are you going to keep throwing a tantrum like a human toddler? I have yet to be given a proper meal since arriving here," Kraken retorted with a clear note of annoyance.

Wixim gnashed his teeth. *"Bring Ansar."*

"So that's a promise then?" Kraken asked with a satisfied twitch of his whiskers.

Wixim's forked tongue darted toward the fluffy empurror.

In a flash Kraken's paw shot out and swatted it.

Wixim reared back in alarm.

His furious glare bore down at Kraken, who was looking even more impatient with the conversation.

The dragon shook his head disapprovingly. *"Cats… All the same."*

"If I hadn't just clawed your tongue, I'd tell you to bite it. I am empurror of all. You will not forget it. Now make the promise. I'm tired of you," Kraken lectured gruffly.

Kasha was relatively certain Wixim was imagining Kraken roasting on a spit with a crackling fire turning him into a seared snack, but he still conceded, *"You have my word."*

Kraken leaned back to look up at Kasha. *"You need to shift back to tell the others."*

Kasha bristled a little. She had been in shock thanks to the ongoing stress.

Once she had returned to her human state, she turned and faced everyone who waited. "He will leave, but only if Ansar is released into his care and they can all go without a fight. We can pursue them later—and the chicken witch will stay unless she turns the duchess back."

Tam raised an eyebrow, then looked over at Harris, who nodded in understanding. The duke retreated up the palace steps to tell the guards. They had all been sweating profusely as they watched the giant dragon and Eli in her intimidating familiar form stand off in the courtyard.

For a few moments everyone waited, and Eli rejoined the group on the steps.

The sun had fully risen, and the witches Wixim had saved were gradually shivering less as the heat of the day continued to climb.

Penelope waved nervously at the man she referred to as Uncle Thomas. He gave a tight half smile back.

When Harris returned escorting Ansar, the Zinferan emperor followed behind in his wheelchair.

The monarch already looked exhausted, but his eyes still glinted with interest at the dragon in the courtyard.

Everyone watched as Ansar cast one final dark look at Tam, then proceeded over to Wixim.

When Harris returned to the step, Tam leaned forward. "I take it the chicken witch didn't agree to turn Mum back?"

Harris shook his head, and Annika clucked irritably on the ground.

While this took place, the other witches climbed onto Wixim's back, with Ansar seated at the front, and Thomas Julian at the back.

"This isn't over!" Ansar seethed at Tam.

"If you were smart, you wouldn't be saying that," Kat returned with a bellow, her golden eyes sparkling with violent whims.

Ansar didn't have a chance to retort before Wixim launched himself into the air—albeit at a much slower rate than he had the previous night due to the additional burdens he carried.

Everyone watched as his gilded scales flashed overhead, then disappeared in the direction of the mountains. Most likely he was taking everyone to the cave.

Eli leaned into Tam, exhaustion overtaking her as she dully noted that Kraken was already darting up the stairs.

Tam dropped a kiss atop her head before murmuring, "Let's all go find a place to sleep, hm?"

"That would be appreciated," Eli returned thickly, her eyelids heavy.

Tam wrapped an arm around Eli's shoulders as they all turned to make their way back up the stairs. Yet upon returning to the landing before the great doors, they found that the number of guards had increased from six to two dozen.

Everyone paused.

Something was odd.

Jiho Ryu was still present pushing the emperor's chair closer, but he looked pale and uneasy.

"Princess Elisara, welcome home," the emperor greeted her, his hands lightly clasped over his belly as he peered up at her, his eyes lingering on the red dress she donned.

Eli tensed, and she could feel Tam do the same.

"Your Excellency." She curtsied, and Tam bowed.

"Have you been told of my decree?" The emperor's eyes drifted over Tam appraisingly.

Eli's free hand briefly gripped into a fist. "The one about naming me the heir to the Zinferan empire? Yes, I have. However, as honored as I am that you would consider me, I must decline."

"Ah, you have not even had a good night's rest to consider this offer." The emperor waved his hand, and two lines of maids appeared from the flanks of the palace.

Eli drew backward. "I do not need to consider the offer, Your Excellency."

The emperor opened his mouth once again, but Tam spoke before he could. "Lady Elisara and I are going back to Daxaria. We need to attend to my mother and ensure she can be returned to her human form. The princess has been placed under my family's care by order of the Daxarian and Troivackian kings, and Daxaria is where she wishes to reside."

The emperor's expression sharpened. "With all due respect, Lord Tamlin, even if she rejects the offer of the throne, she needs to remain here in Zinfera. She must legally proceed with the paperwork. And if she wishes to leave the imperial family, she will also be required to forfeit her name of Taejo."

"Not if she's already married she doesn't," Harris announced breezily.

Every eye slowly turned to the Daxarian duke, who smiled pleasantly.

Eli's stomach roiled. Lying to Soo Hebin about being married would have been one thing. Lying to the emperor himself was another altogether. He would find out the truth in a matter of days.

"Oh? And are you suggesting that Princess Elisara has already wedded Lord Tamlin Ashowan under the authority of a magistrate?"

"Ship's captain, actually," Harris supplied seamlessly. "Besides, Your Excellency, these people have been through hell the past few months, and the divine threat of the first witch is no longer Zinfera's alone. We should go and alert Troivack and Daxaria and prepare for whatever attack is to come."

"I do not believe Daxaria and Troivack are facing the direct threat of the first witch and a dragon on their shores," the emperor pointed out icily.

"Yes, but that doesn't mean you can bar anyone from leaving. My niece also happens to be Tamlin Ashowan's familiar in her beast form," Harris pointed out.

The emperor did not yield. "I'm not barring anyone but Princess Elisara. She has her duty to her empire. Familiar or not."

"My duty to this empire?" Eli felt rage course through her veins in an instant, chasing away the shadows of sleep from her mind. "The empire that couldn't be bothered with me? I was abducted and sold. Most of your children were! And you think you can just pick and choose when you give a damn about our lives?" Eli released Tam and stalked toward the emperor, her ire steadily rising.

The emperor's expression hardened.

"No, Your Majesty. No efforts were made to recover me when I was abducted. Soo Hebin was not punished for harming thousands of people and leading the first witch to your shores. This is your own damn mess. You clean it up and keep me out of it, or so help me, Gods, I will drop your body in the middle of the Alcide Sea for the kraken to rip apart." Eli bore down over the emperor as the guards behind him shared nervous looks.

The emperor's brows lowered as he stared up at her. "Threatening me is a crime worthy of death."

"Oh, there will be death if you try me, Your Excellency. Just not mine. Now we are all going to get some sleep, and then we are leaving on the first boat out, returning to Daxaria."

"I will not let you—" the emperor began to shout, but Eli abruptly shifted back into her beast form, forcing Tam and Harris to launch themselves away from her to make room. Tam barely managed to wrap his arms around Luca to protect him from the move, and luckily Kat seized Penelope in time as well.

Kasha roared in the emperor's face, her fangs inches from his neck.

She could smell his fear, and she didn't care.

No one was ever going to imprison her against her will ever again.

"Couldn't have handled that better myself," Kraken purred from the sun spot he had flopped into off to the right.

Kasha didn't acknowledge his words, instead shifting back to her human form.

She looked over her shoulder at Tam, Luca, Kat, and Penelope and said, "Sorry about that."

Tam nodded and approached her carefully, gently touching her back before they proceeded into the palace. The maids had scattered upon Eli's initial transformation, and they cowered away as the couple passed. That was fine. Eli could guide them to where she remembered the guest chambers being.

Katarina Ashowan jovially called out behind her, "I've really been enjoying getting to know you better, Eli!"

Eli gave a subtle grumble.

She didn't want to talk or deal with anything until after she'd slept and eaten.

Though when she glanced up at Tam—who still looked dreadful following his concussion—she couldn't help but feel a spark of anticipation. They could once again sleep in a comfortable bed together, and whatever trials lay ahead, Tamlin and his eccentric family were going to be right at her side.

Hell, she was even happy to have the arsonist Lord Oscar Harris in her corner.

And with allies like that, what was there to worry about?